FIRST ELITE

EMMANUEL M
ARRIAGA

FIRST
ELITE

FOUNDRA SERIES 03

Cover design: Dayo Baiyegunhi

Editor: Chelsea Beam

Proofreader: Courtney Andersson

Internal formatting: Natalia Junqueira

To my son Daniel,
Your laugh always brings a smile to my face, and
watching you explore your imagination inspires me to
continue to share my own.

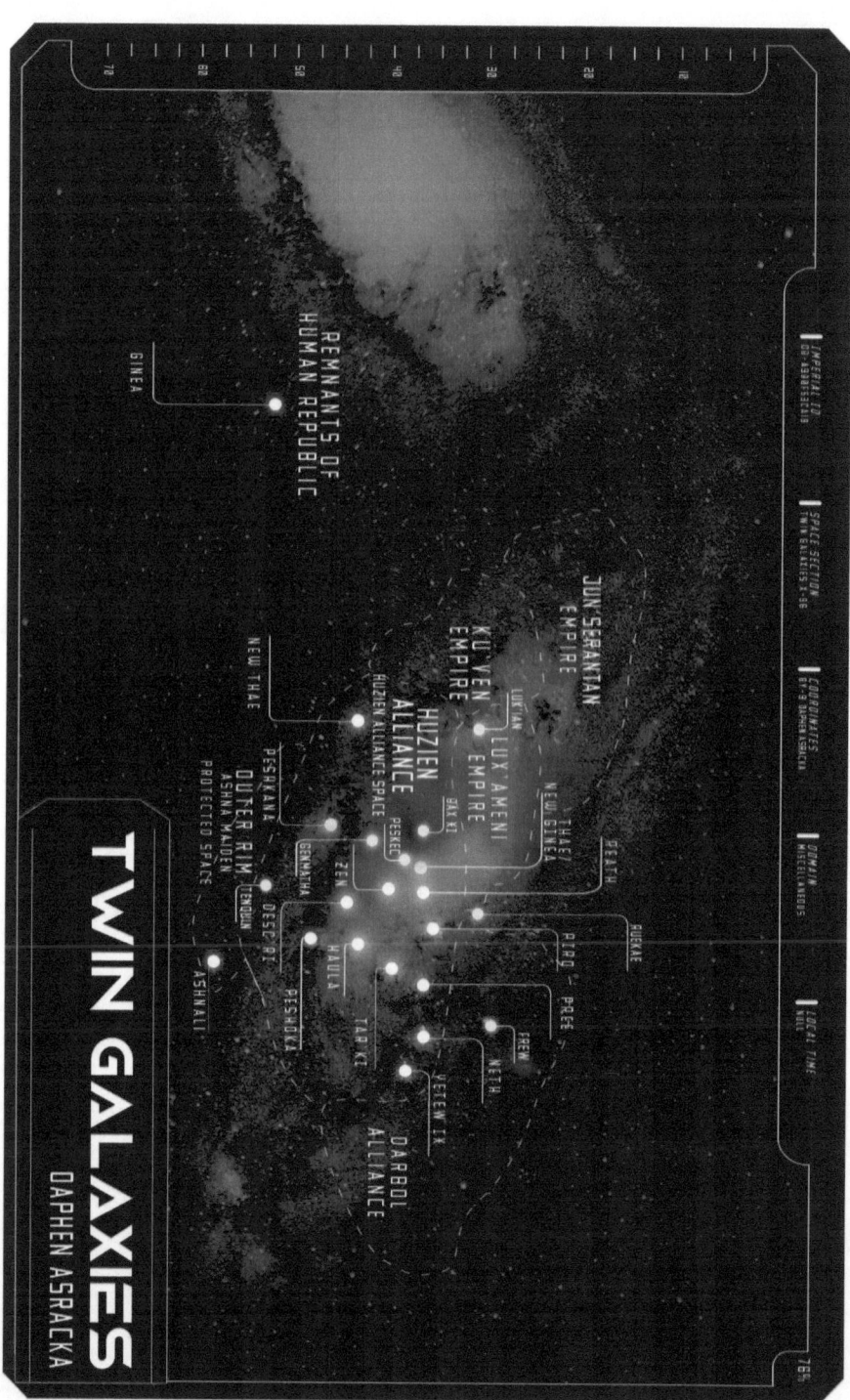

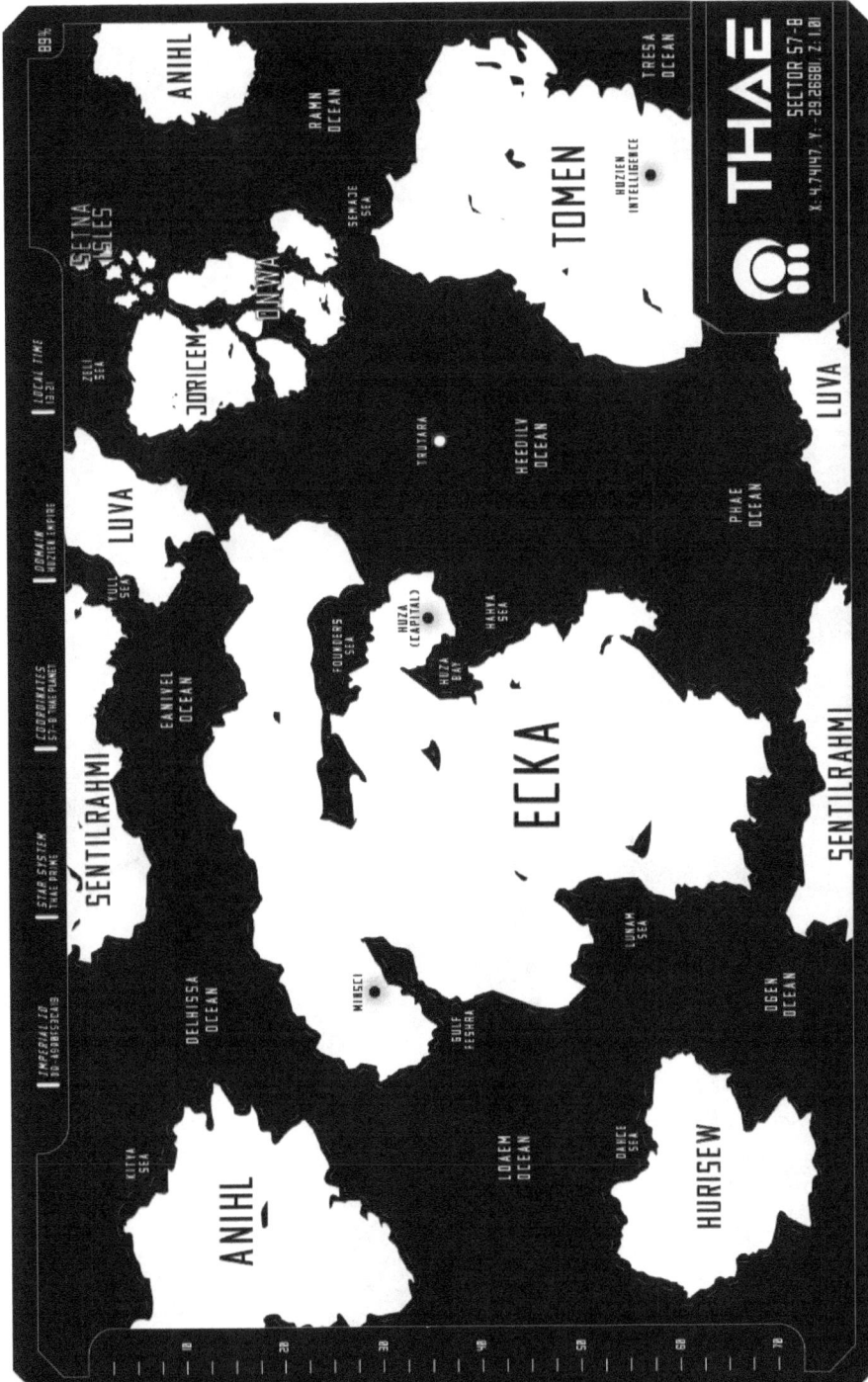

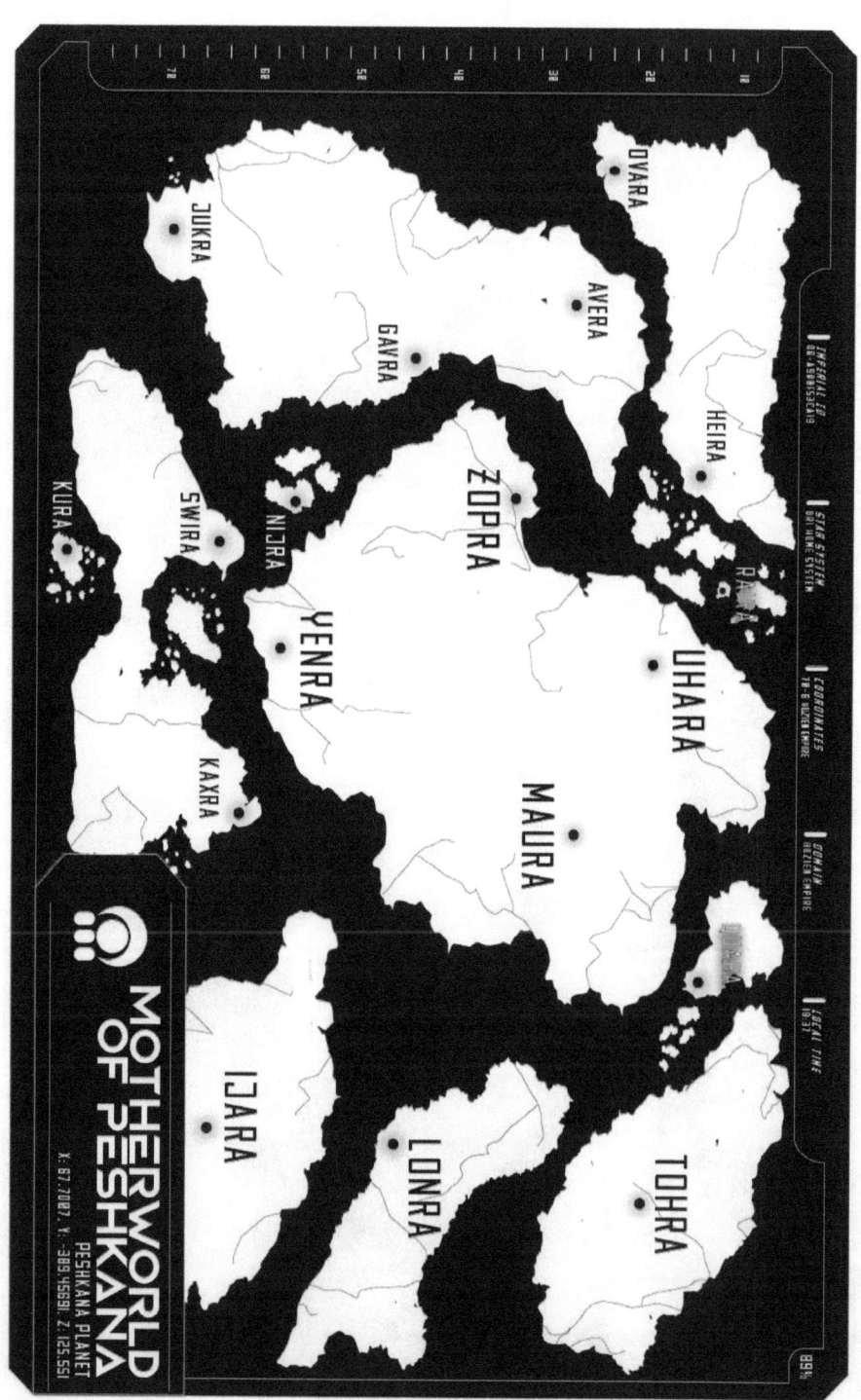

MOTHERWORLD OF PESHKANA

PESHKANA PLANET
X: 67.7007 · Y: -389.45691 · Z: 125.551

JUKRA

OVARA

AVERA

GAVRA

HEIRA

KURA

SWIRA

NIJRA

ZOPRA

RA A A

YENRA

UHARA

KAXRA

MAURA

IJARA

LONRA

TOHRA

IMPERIAL ID
GQ:4S0R53EA19

STAR SYSTEM
DRVANE SYSTEM

COORDINATES
78-E VULCER EMPIRE

DOMAIN
VULCER EMPIRE

LOCAL TIME
10:37

89%

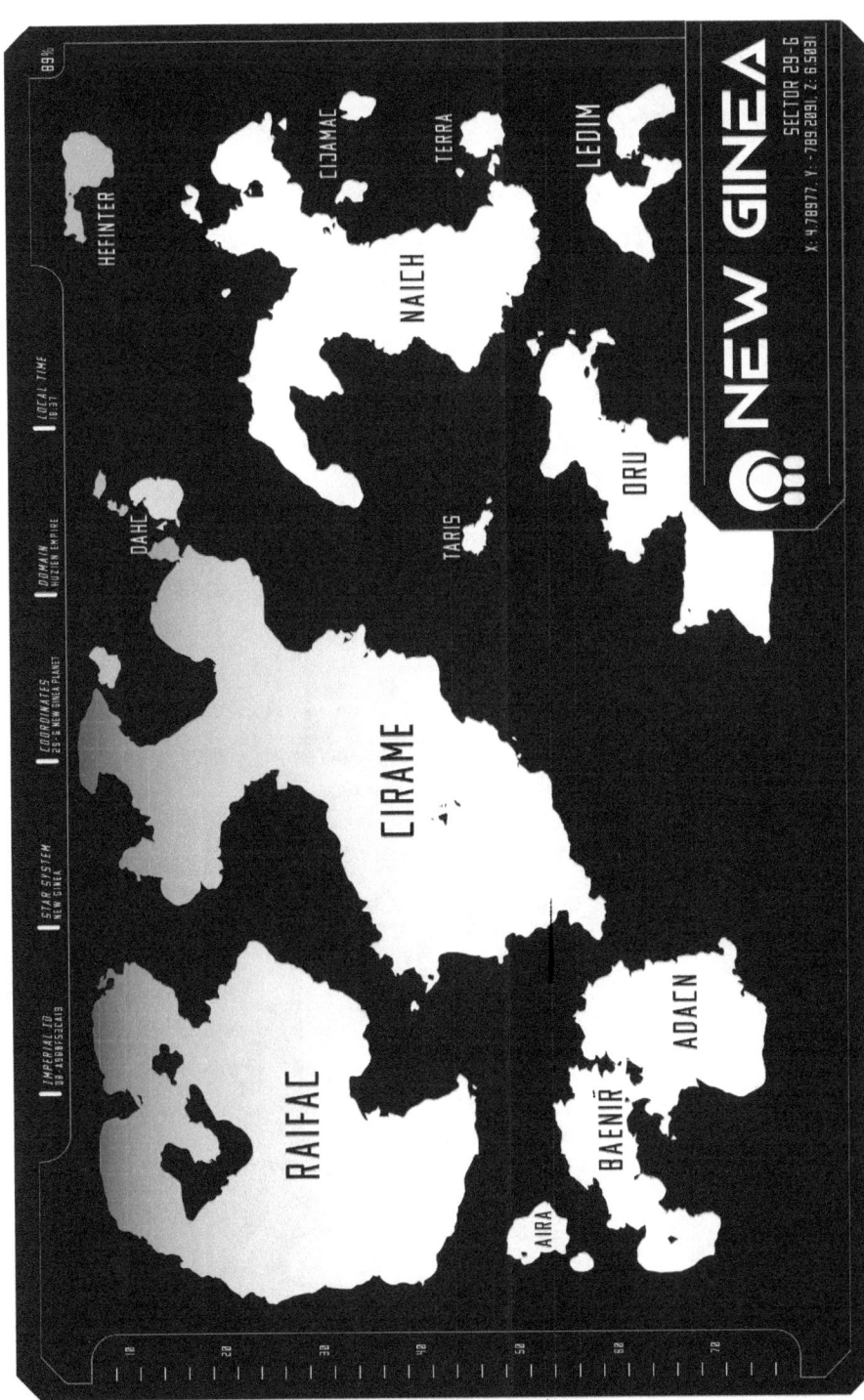

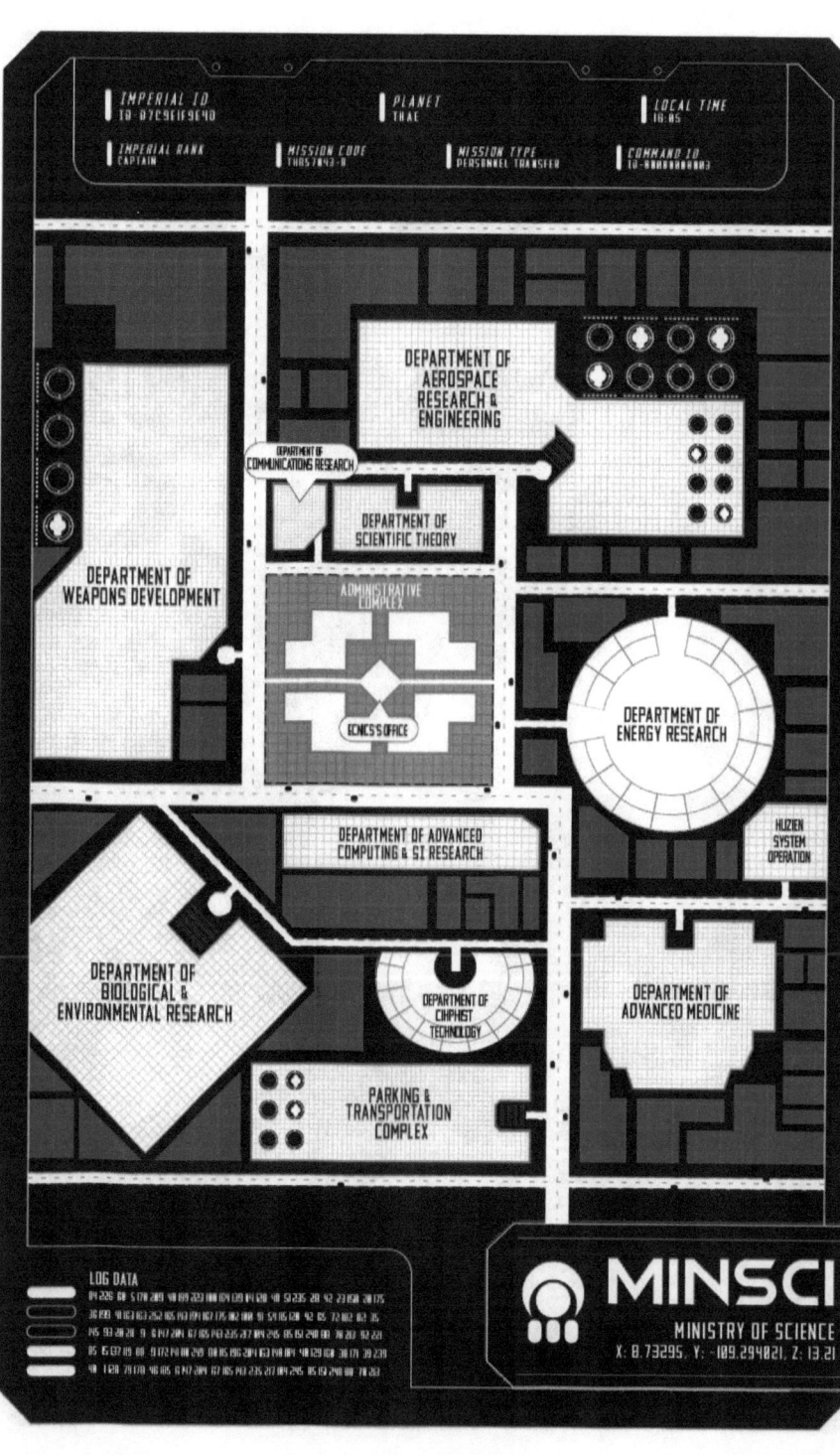

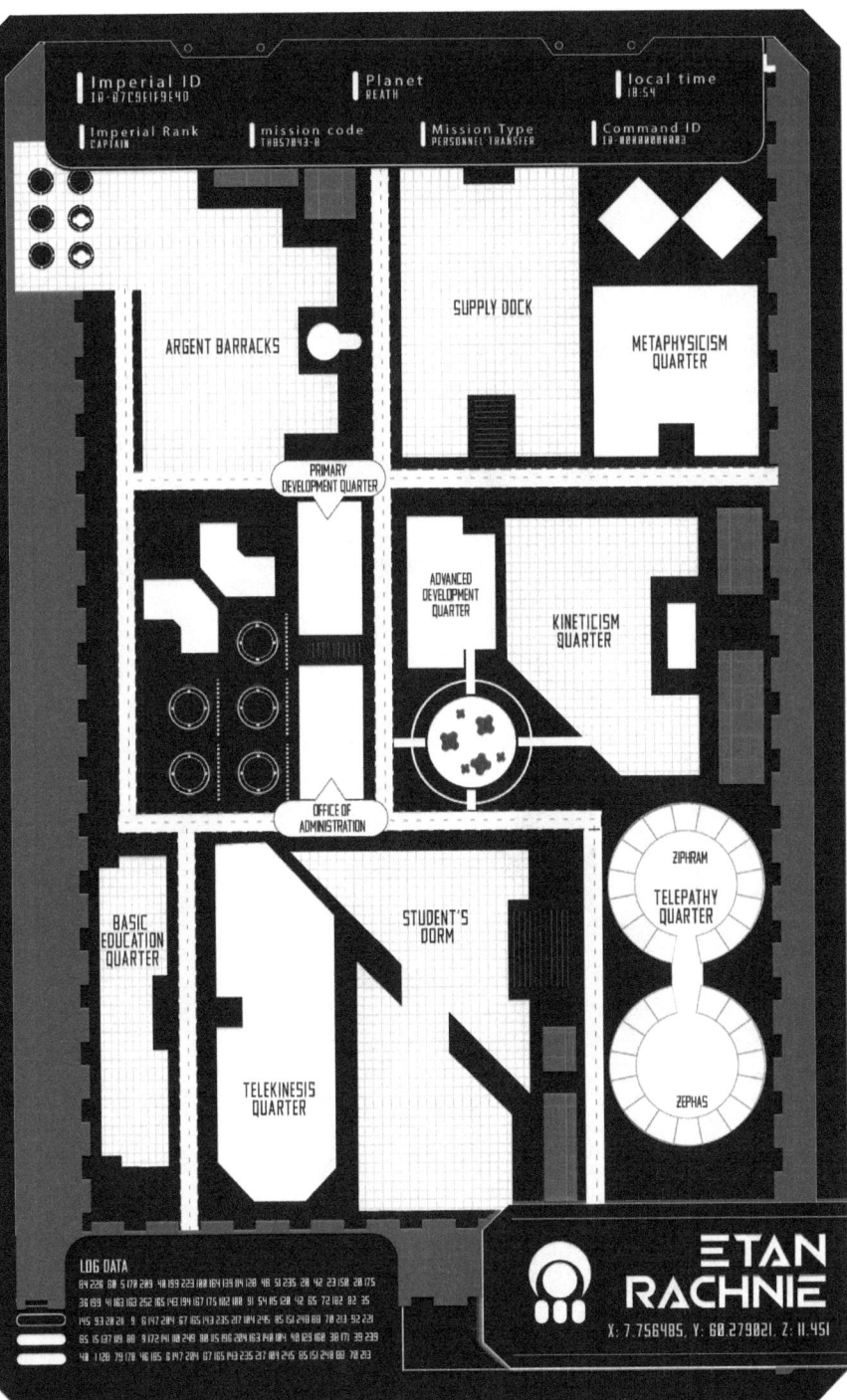

Imperial ID
ID-07C9EIF9E40

Planet
REATH

local time
18:54

Imperial Rank
CAPTAIN

mission code
THB57043-B

Mission Type
PERSONNEL TRANSFER

Command ID
ID-8080808083

ARGENT BARRACKS

SUPPLY DOCK

METAPHYSICISM QUARTER

PRIMARY DEVELOPMENT QUARTER

ADVANCED DEVELOPMENT QUARTER

KINETICISM QUARTER

OFFICE OF ADMINISTRATION

BASIC EDUCATION QUARTER

STUDENT'S DORM

ZIPHRAM

TELEPATHY QUARTER

ZEPHAS

TELEKINESIS QUARTER

LOG DATA
84 226 68 5 178 209 48 199 223 180 184 139 84 128 48 93 235 28 42 23 158 28 175
36 189 4 183 163 252 165 143 194 167 175 182 180 91 54 145 128 42 65 72 182 82 35
145 93 28 28 9 147 204 57 65 143 235 217 184 245 85 151 248 88 70 213 92 221
85 163 137 128 88 9 172 141 118 248 188 85 86 204 163 184 184 48 129 168 38 171 39 239
48 112 79 178 146 165 8 147 204 97 165 143 235 217 184 245 85 151 248 88 78 213

ETAN RACHNIE

X: 7.756485, Y: 80.279021, Z: 11.451

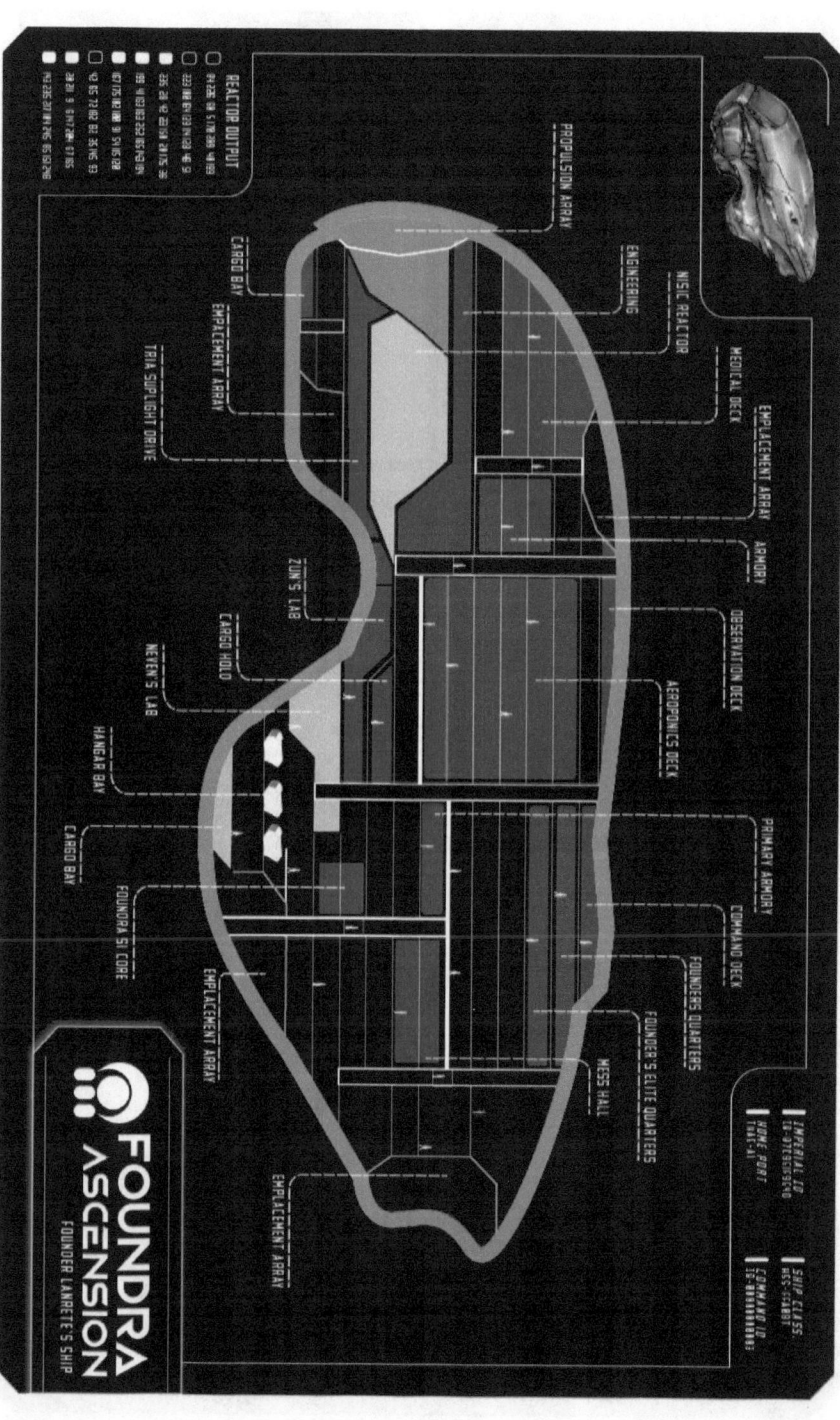

FOUNDRA
ASCENSION
FOUNDER LANRETE'S SHIP

REACTOR OUTPUT

PROPULSION ARRAY
CARGO BAY
EMPLACEMENT ARRAY
TRIA SUBLIGHT DRIVE
ZUN'S LAB
CARGO HOLD
NEVEN'S LAB
HANGAR BAY
CARGO BAY
FOUNDRA SI CORE
EMPLACEMENT ARRAY
EMPLACEMENT ARRAY

ENGINEERING
NISIC REACTOR
MEDICAL DECK
EMPLACEMENT ARRAY
ARMORY
OBSERVATION DECK
AEROPONICS DECK
PRIMARY ARMORY
COMMAND DECK
FOUNDERS QUARTERS
FOUNDER'S ELITE QUARTERS
MESS HALL

IMPERIAL LC
[UN7E9579J10
HOME PORT
TRAI-AI

SHIP CLASS
[ARG-4007]
COMMAND ID
IG-00XXXXXXXX

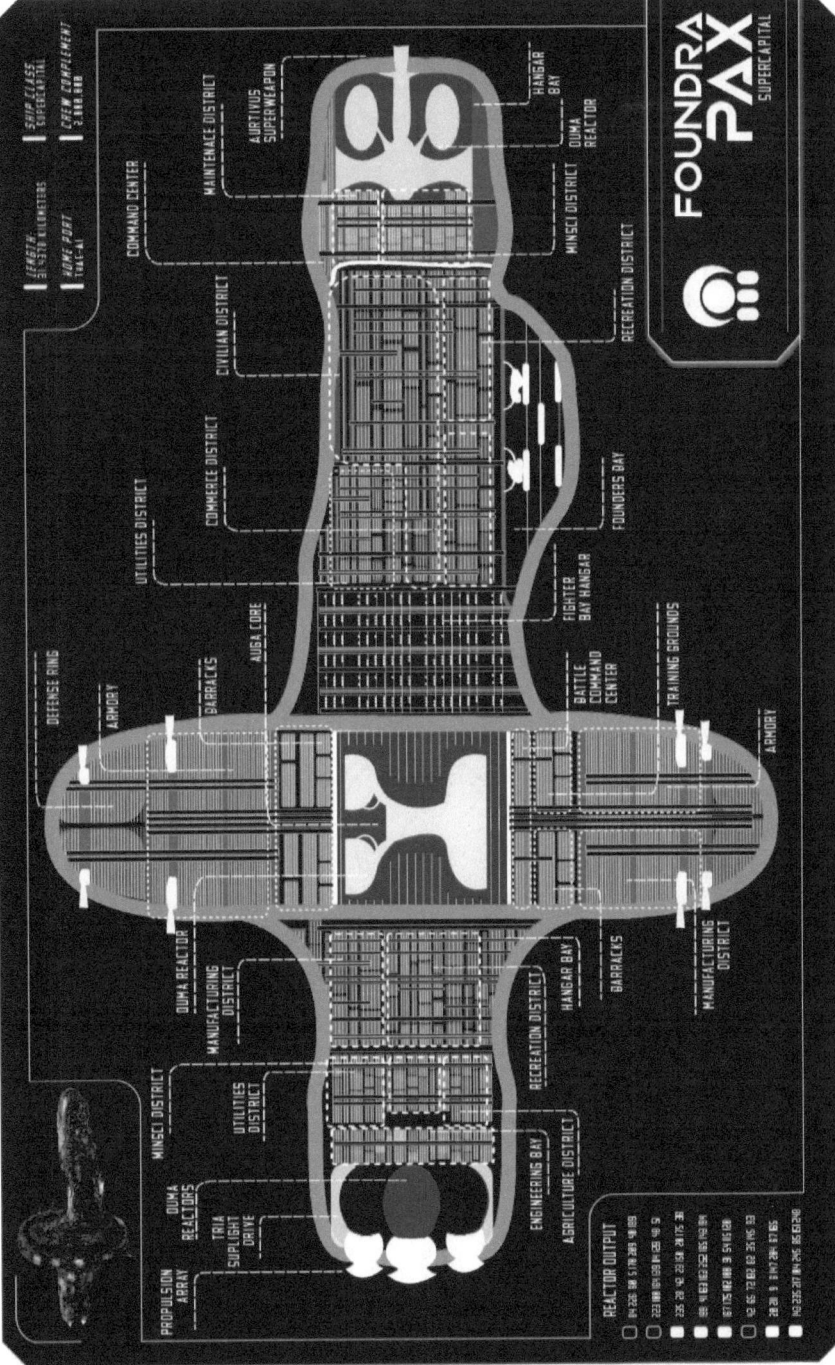

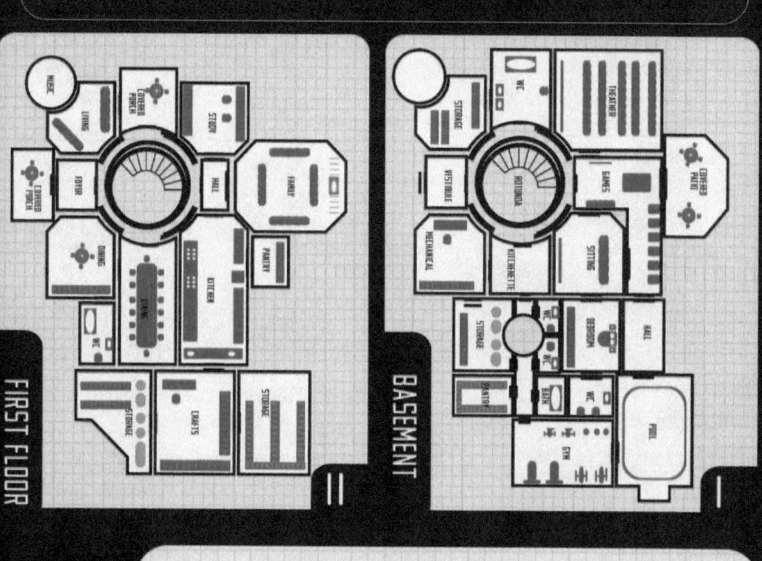

FIRST FLOOR

BASEMENT

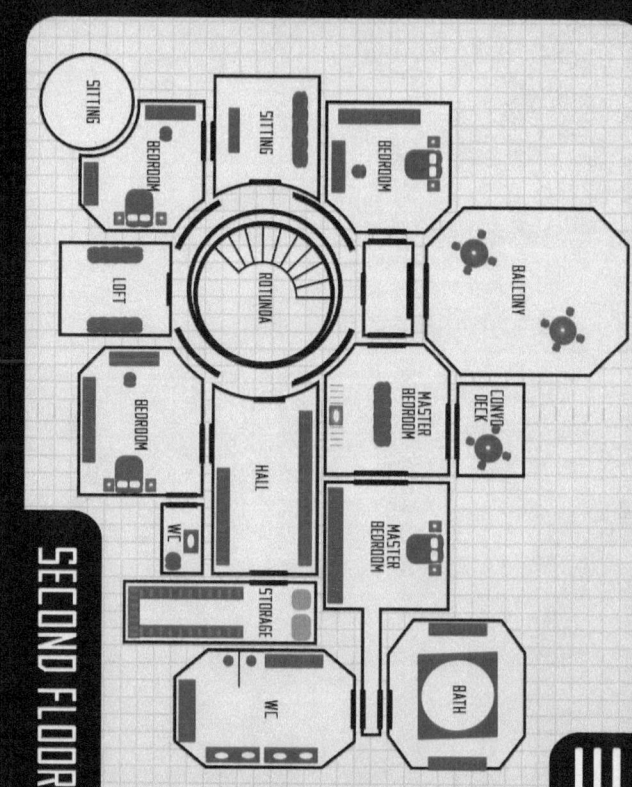

SECOND FLOOR

LANRETE'S HOME

HUZA'S OUTSKIRTS

X: 60.767885 Y: 450.28821 Z: 61.6801

IMPERIAL ID
ID-87C9EIF9E4D

PLANET
FOUNDRA ASCENSION

LOCAL TIME
22.26

IMPERIAL RANK
CAPTAIN

MISSION CODE
THB57043-B

MISSION TYPE
PERSONNEL TRANSFER

COMMAND ID
ID-0800000003

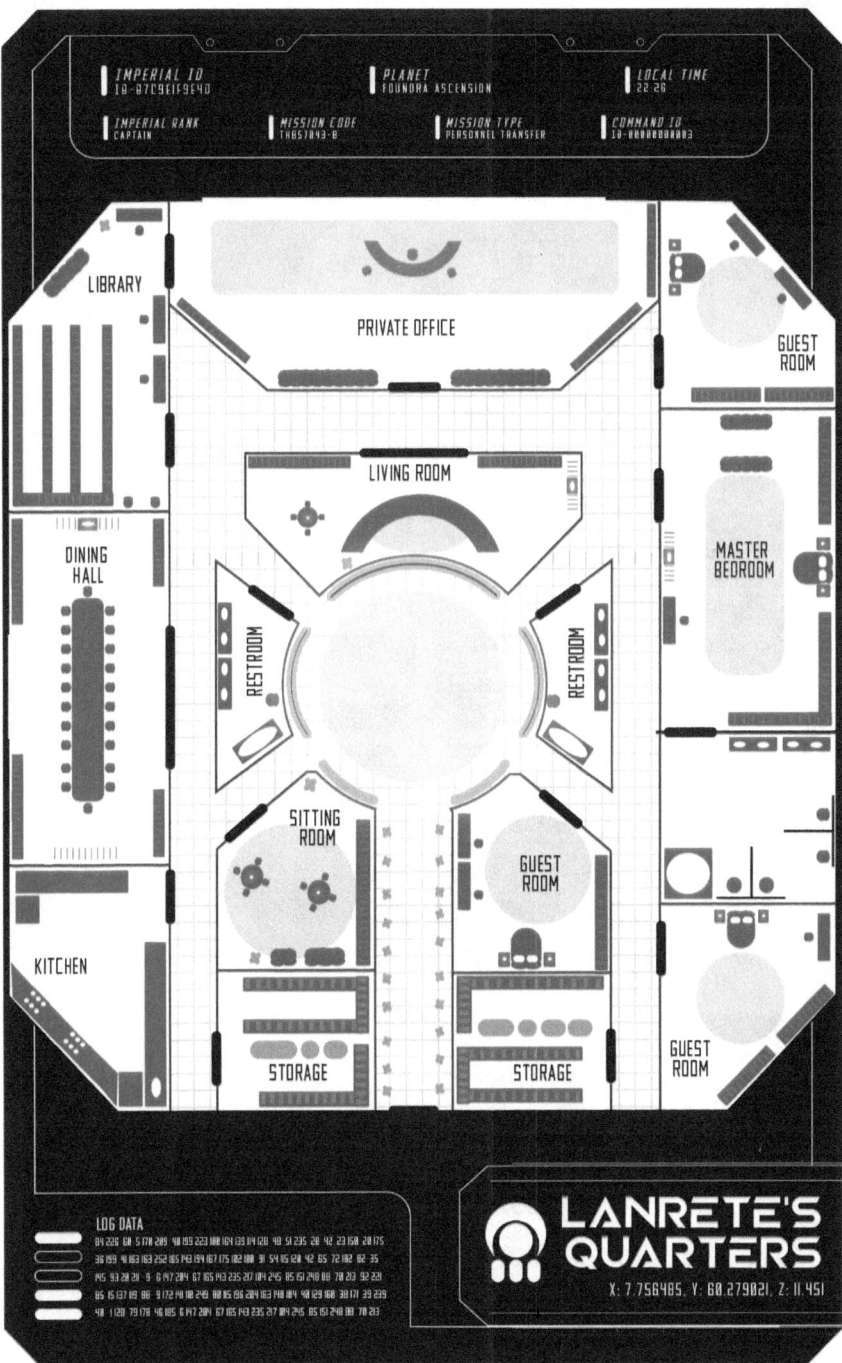

LOG DATA
04 226 60 5 170 209 49 199 223 100 104 139 114 120 40 51 235 20 42 23 158 20 175
36 199 4 163 163 252 165 149 199 167 175 082 100 91 54 115 42 65 72 102 82 35
145 93 20 21 9 6 147 204 67 165 143 235 217 104 245 85 151 240 80 70 203 92 221
85 15 137 09 00 9 172 141 110 249 80 85 196 204 163 140 104 49 129 160 30 171 39 239
40 1 120 79 170 46 185 6 147 204 67 165 143 235 217 104 245 85 151 240 80 70 203

LANRETE'S
QUARTERS

X: 7.756485, Y: 60.279021, Z: 11.451

IMPERIAL ID
ID-07C9EIF9E4D

PLANET
REATH

LOCAL TIME
18.54

IMPERIAL RANK
CAPTAIN

MISSION CODE
TK057843-B

MISSION TYPE
PERSONNEL TRANSFER

COMMAND ID
ID-0000000003

POOL

GARDENS

PRIMARY
RESIDENCE

ARGENT
BUNKER

LIBRARY

TRAINING
TOWER
1

TRAINING
TOWER
2

GUEST
RESIDENCE

LOG DATA
04 226 68 5 178 209 48 199 223 108 104 139 114 128 40 51 235 28 42 23 150 28 175
36 195 41 163 163 252 165 143 184 167 175 182 108 91 54 65 128 42 65 72 182 82 35
145 93 28 28 9 0 147 204 87 165 143 235 207 104 245 85 151 248 88 78 213 92 228
85 15 137 113 18 9 172 141 118 249 88 85 156 204 163 248 141 48 29 158 38 173 39 228
48 1 128 79 178 46 185 6 147 204 87 165 143 235 207 104 245 85 151 248 88 78 213

SOAHC'S
COMPOUND

X: 56.4085, Y: 678.279021, Z: 98.808

The effects of the Enesmic shipyards erected by Sagren during the Rift War appear non-reversable. Life will never again flourish here.

-FROM "ENESMIC SHIPYARD EFFECTS ON TRICA VII"
MINSCI METABASE

CHAPTER 1 - NEVEN KENK

80123 FA (Present Day)
Foundra Ascension *orbiting the Paradise Planet Genmatha,*
Huzien Alliance space

The steady, monotone beeping of the heart monitor blared across the medical deck.

Zun Shan's unmoving body was suspended in a complex surgical station and cordoned off behind a stasis field. Her neck was at an odd angle, and her hazelnut brown, angular eyes were lifeless and hollow. Her chest wasn't rising or falling in the universal life-signaling act of breathing known to most species across the galaxy. Instead, a drone was busy at work rapidly rebuilding the fist-sized hole in her chest.

The one where her heart should have been.

Jenshi Runso, chief medical officer aboard the *Foundra Ascension*, was methodically commanding the army of drones. His face was hard. Emotionless. Jenshi was known for his intense focus—that uncanny ability to shut everything out.

Neven Kenk, a Human pressed against the field surrounding Zun, wished Jenshi wasn't quite so skilled at ignoring him.

Neven's jade-green eyes trailed over Zun's tanned form, slowly tracing the light black esha marks running the length of her body. He remembered her touch and the warmth of her skin as they held hands on the beach, both finding the mix of her tanned skin tone and his dark olive a thing of beauty. He recalled how her smile lit up his life every time she ran her fingers across his muscular chest molded to perfection over two years of grueling sparring sessions with merciless combat trainers.

He closed his eyes, forcing himself to breathe. But behind his lids, the cold blue eyes and wicked grin of Zun's attacker stared back at him.

Entradis.

Neven, move! *Ellipse, his personal synaptic systems intelligence, or SSI, shouted in his mind.* He's going to kill you!

Neven was frozen, his body numb. His eyes hung on Zun's lifeless form as her blood changed the white sand to a dark shade of red. The soft hues of the setting sun were replaced by blinding lights all around him, and the intensity of it caused him to shield his eyes. The light was replaced by a wall of power armors jutting up out of the white sand of the beach, many of them closing instantly upon materializing, except for one directly in front of him.

Get in! *Ellipse urged Neven forward. Acting without conscious thought, he lunged, pulling himself into the back of the power armor.*

As it sealed around him, unseen forces knocked many of the other power armors away. It was the unmistakable work of Enesmic weaving—the powerful ability only usable by Cihphists. It was a power Neven had never had.

The freshly cleared path established a line of sight between Neven and Entradis.

"Beginning spinal realignment and neurological repair." Jenshi's words snapped Neven back to reality.

He watched as another drone finished connecting a series of tiny thin nanotubes along the back of her skull, down her neck, and most of her back. A loud crack echoed throughout the deck as her head shifted, becoming less macabre in angle. Many of the tubes exited her body, while the remaining ones moved rapidly in and out of her skin around the central part of her neck and across her skull, quickly working to rebuild the tendons, nerve endings, and grey matter. Another drone moved to assist, rebuilding the tissue in tandem with the other machines.

"Sweet irony." Entradis reached out and clenched his fist. The area around them trembled at the terrible swirling of Enesmic energy.

A hum sounded from the primary power core as Neven's power armor flared to life, and its innate defenses held the crushing Enesmic force at bay. Neven's power armor glowed bright blue, and the cooling system let off a hiss as Entradis ceased his attack.

"Not this time, monster," Neven broadcasted from his armor. "The Yuvan System I created will prevent you from killing any more Secnics in their power armors."

A neural interface link slapped against the back of Neven's neck, locking in place. He winced; the emergency link was less comfortable than his standard interface suit. A tingling sensation ran down his spine, signaling that his nervous system was syncing with the control interface.

Neven growled, rage blurring his vision. The power armor lunged forward with incredible speed.

Entradis shifted out of the way, using Enesmic forces to accelerate his body to inhuman speeds. Even with the boost, he only narrowly avoided a crazed Neven.

No! Neven, we must flee! *Ellipse shouted.*

"He just killed Zun, Ellipse." Neven's tone was cold.

Then we fight to the end, *Ellipse said.*

There was sadness in her voice. The other power armors came to life under her control. Dual Feponic shoulder cannons emerged from their dens, unleashing blasts of energized plasma at Entradis.

Entradis was knocked to the ground. The blasts impacted his barrier with devastating effectiveness. Scrambling up, Entradis shaped some Enesmic power into a rope and pulled it taut. "Let's dance." He grinned.

3

"Cardiovascular system reconstruction complete," intoned the soft SI voice of the medical deck.

Jenshi didn't respond, his eyes glued to one of the many holodisplays around him. A holographic representation of Zun's spinal system appeared outside of her body. He walked over to the display and tapped a series of sections, immediately sending drones to work on those portions of her body.

He examined another holodisplay, briefly meeting Neven's gaze along the way. Without acknowledgment, he tapped the screen and sent more drones into action.

Entradis ripped one of the power armors apart, using the powerful Enesmic force to peel back sections of the armor. Once he detected no soft Human center, he abandoned the target and pursued another.

Neven worked with the power armors, each attacking with their entire arsenal as he hid in plain sight, each armor a replica, mimicking his actions.

Entradis lunged into one of the power armors, his hands angled forward like claws as he dug into the machine in a frenzy. He ripped off the chest plate and roared, sending a torrent of Enesmic energy into the armor so it would expand as if hornets were swarming inside. It exploded in a rain of debris as Entradis lunged at the next power armor, tackling it to the ground. He raised his hands, formed fists, and brought them down, releasing a wave of Enesmic energy like a hammer. He repeated that action with inhuman speed.

Neven could hardly discern the movements, even as the power armor flattened under the assault.

Entradis turned his gaze on Neven. The look terrified him.

He smothered that part of himself with burning rage. Raising his arms, Neven pointed them at Entradis as shock blasters rose from his wrists. Each of the remaining power armors around him mirrored the action, all of them firing at the same time.

The intense blasts ripped through Entradis's barrier. He gasped and flipped backward, quickly dropping behind cover. The continued assault left a trail of molten sand in its wake. Entradis reached out and grabbed a large boulder from the water, and launched it into the nearest power armor. The sheer force of the impact punched through the shield, destroying the armor.

Only Neven's power armor and a final dummy armor remained. Entradis stalked toward them. Neven roared as he and the other armor charged at Entradis in tandem.

A series of small drones appeared and aligned down Zun's spine, while others came to rest on her new heart and at various points on her head.

"Ready to begin nervous system restart," the SI voice prompted.

"Initialize," Jenshi said.

A series of electromagnetic pulses emanated from each of the mini drones. Zun's body convulsed in the air, and the pulses stopped abruptly.

Nothing.

Jenshi narrowed his eyes, his gaze going to a nearby holodisplay as he analyzed the results. He tapped a few more places on the holodisplay, sending the larger drones quickly back to work.

"I haven't had this much fun in some time." Entradis peeled back Neven's power armor. He grabbed Neven by the neck, lifting him out of the broken shell.

Neven spat in his face as Entradis grinned.

Entradis summoned an energy blade and plunged it forward, but a familiar blade intercepted the Enesmic weapon. A kick to Entradis's chest quickly separated them.

Neven rolled to his feet, glancing at his savior.

Founder Lanrete of the Huzien Empire stood with his sword, Divinebreath, in his light-brown hand. There was murder in his eyes, his long, white mane of hair wild with fury. Jessica Olic was at his side, her silver gaze catching on Zun's body.

Entradis let out a low whistle. "Wondered when you'd show up."

Lanrete charged him, their weapons connecting in a flash. Their movements became a blur as Entradis kept up with Lanrete's speed. Lanrete sought to push Entradis back with his raw strength, but Entradis matched the founder with the same intensity.

Shifting backward, Entradis lifted a few pieces of debris with Enesmic forces and hurled them at Neven.

Jessica Olic tackled Neven out of the way; the debris missed his head by a split second.

Lanrete charged forward, but Entradis clenched his fist, uttering a word of power as he vanished.

Cursing, Lanrete glanced around, but to no avail. There was no trace of Entradis.

His eyes caught Zun Shan's body in the sand, Jenshi already by her side. Lanrete's gaze went back to meet Neven's. The profound sadness in Neven's gaze was mirrored in Lanrete's weathered expression.

Jenshi initiated another pulse, making Zun's body convulse again in the air.

The pulse stopped, but her body remained limp.

Jenshi repeated the process six more times before slamming both fists on a nearby table, causing the holodisplay within to flicker.

Neven slumped to the ground, tears in his eyes as he stared helplessly at Jenshi.

CHAPTER 2 - SERAH'ELAX REZ ASHFALEN

Foundra Ascension orbiting the Paradise Planet Genmatha,
Huzien Alliance space

The full presence of the Founder's Elites had collected in the medical bay, with Tashanira and Jessica hovering around Neven next to Zun's bed.

Tashanira was a Uri—the catlike woman's fine fur was a mix of black and white, and she had yellow eyes. Jessica was a Huzien like Lanrete and Jenshi, with light-brown hair and orange highlights, dark-honey skin a shade lighter than Serah'Elax's own, and dark-brown esha marks that started at her temples.

Many small devices were all over Zun's body, each regulating some standard bodily function.

Serah'Elax Rez Ashfalen was sitting on one of the nearby empty medical beds, and Dexter Pinsten—the pale-skinned and red-haired Sentinel—leaned against it beside her. Serah'Elax's red hair hung down to her shoulders, and she kept her large, almond-colored eyes locked on Zun's body. Depending on how she moved, silver specks sometimes sparkled in Serah'Elax's skin when hit by the light. She was a Das'Vin and still new to the team now around her. Even though she'd only been with the Founder's Elites for a short time, she felt deep connections forming with them.

Jenshi cleared his throat. "I repaired the damage to her neck, and she has a new functional heart, but the brain damage from the blood loss and oxygen deprivation was severe. I reversed ninety-eight percent of the brain damage by rebuilding the most severely damaged parts of her brain." Jenshi clenched his fists, his gaze hardening. "However, I couldn't fully repair the damage, and there is no brain activity."

Neven stared at Zun. His posture was defeated.

"I'm sorry, Neven. I've failed Zun."

Neven shuddered. Jessica and Tashanira embraced him as he broke down, sobs wracking his body. Dexter crossed his arms, his gaze stuck on the floor as Lanrete stood near the entrance to the medical bay, far away from the rest of the group. Erbubuc Tamn, the four-armed Ken'Tar—massive in size with golden-brown fur covering his body—moved to join in the embrace with Neven. His strong arms surrounded the group of three now sitting on the floor.

Serah'Elax looked from Zun to Lanrete. She could see a hint of restrained rage in the immortal's eyes, but it was so subtle that she would have missed it had she not been raised by the Ashna Maidens. She had been trained to detect the emotions of people around her, always looking for the next ambush.

Lanrete turned away and exited the medical bay.

"We're going to hunt Entradis down," Dexter whispered. The former assassin's green eyes were hard as he looked directly at her. "Nothing else matters now."

Serah'Elax nodded.

Serah'Elax walked into her expansive quarters aboard the *Foundra Ascension*. The new room was still an adjustment from her small quarters in the Ashna Maidens. She had split her time between bunks on spaceships and her small quarters on Ashnali. In comparison, her new life seemed extravagant. Wasteful.

The Ashna Maidens focused on efficiency and doing more with less. From their long history of being surrounded by enemies on all sides, the Ashna Maidens had learned to optimize ruthlessly.

From what she had seen so far of the Huziens and the Alliance, it was the opposite. Everything was wasteful, and the people seemed oblivious to their ridiculous wealth and privilege. It sickened her.

"What's wrong?" a voice asked from near the floor-to-ceiling window across the room.

Serah'Elax looked up at her mother, Dera'Liv. Her face softened. "The scientist, Zun, is dead," Serah'Elax said. "Her life partner, Neven, is struggling with the loss."

"He is lucky that they do not share a *ha'ishi*," Dera'Liv said. There was a profound sadness in her voice. She returned her gaze out of the window.

"He is still in pain, *yu'shae*. I can see it. Just because others do not share the permanent connection from joining that we Das'Vin do, it should not diminish the pain they feel at the loss of those they love."

"I did not say that." Dera'Liv glanced back at Serah'Elax with annoyance. "I am sure that he is feeling pain. It may even be deep and soul-crushing. But his pain will heal, his heart will mend, and he will be able to join again with another should he choose to do so." Her face hardened. "I will never again experience that joy. I will never have the hole in my heart filled. My *ha'ishi* will forever cause me pain at the loss of my beloved *dru'sha*." Tears began to well up in her eyes.

An image of Ovah'Hal Velexi Rez flashed in Serah'Elax's mind, standing defiant before the pirate scum who unloaded a barrage of weaponsfire into her chest. That was one of the few memories Serah'Elax still had of her *uma'shae*. The more peaceful memories faded more and more each day.

"I can only ever get hints of that connection—that pleasure and joy—through sharing my body with others who would have me," Dera'Liv continued.

Serah'Elax grimaced.

Dera'Liv threw a hand up in anger. "Yes, you may view the idea that other people bring me carnal pleasure as an abomination, but I have nothing else. I have no other respite." Sobs suddenly overtook her as she leaned against the window, almost like she was in physical pain.

Serah'Elax rushed to her side, embracing her *yu'shae*. After a few moments, Dera' Liv's sobs subsided. She silently looked out into the empty void at the stars speeding by.

Serah'Elax released her and moved to her room; this scenario was all too familiar since they had left Ashna Maiden space. Serah'Elax returned from her room, changed into her typical relaxed attire, keeping her upper body nude and pairing that choice with form-fitting leggings down to her calves.

"I simply do not wish you to continue to live as a *fra'sha*," Serah'Elax said. She moved to the kitchen as the Omnfridge dispenser stirred to life and produced a bowl of red grapes and cheese. "Of all the things I've learned of our culture, that is the one that brings the most shame in our society, is it not?" She held up the bowl to Dera'Liv as she reclined on one of the nearby sofas.

Dera'Liv watched her daughter and slowly got up from the floor. "Not shame. Pity," Dera'Liv corrected. Sighing, she moved to join her daughter on the sofa. "It is only you who experiences shame at her *yu'shae's* choices." Dera'Liv side-eyed her daughter with hints of a smile.

Serah'Elax smiled back as the two silently ate grapes and looked out the window.

FOUNDER'S LOG:
No Peace

When tragedy takes something away from you, it makes the loss even more bitter. In a world where tragedy is common, we can fool ourselves into believing that we will be spared.

But Entradis will never spare those around me . . . those who work for the good of the empire. He will never forgive me, and he will never give me peace. If I do not hunt him and put him down like the dog he is, he will kill every single person who means something to the empire I've tirelessly labored to build.

I must kill him. I must bring an end to the monster that has plagued the Huzien Empire—no, who has plagued me for far too long. I cannot continue to live in fear of losing those who bring me joy. He has yet to touch my family directly, but the threat is there. It will always be there.

In many ways, it is a blessing that Nalle feels no desire to serve the Empire and that her pursuits skew toward the entrepreneurial. He would strike out at her if she ever raised her hand directly against our foes.

That was his promise, after all, one that he has not shied away from keeping.

To have those I love live in fear that their actions will draw the ire of a psychopath is not a life I wish them to lead. Entradis does not feel remorse *and is driven by a desire to inflict pain and death. I don't understand the logic by which he operates—if there is truly any logic there.*

I tried to understand him at one time, but I cannot truly comprehend the mind of one who has made a living of killing for no purpose other than to hurt me. I cannot allow this torment of those close to me to continue.

I will end him. I must end him. For Zun, Yuvan, Urt, Bevi, Cenxra. For too many to count.

I must end this.

-Lanrete

CHAPTER 3 - NEVEN KENK

Foundra Ascension en route to Thae,
Huzien home system

Neven sat in the Founder's Elite meeting room.

A dark-brown-skinned Huzien man was projected in the hologrid on the left, and his mother-in-law, Lansa Shan, was projected on the right. Zun had been the splitting image of her mother, Lansa, and Neven had difficulty focusing on the woman. Her eyes were bloodshot red, and her breathing was ragged. Zun's father had been dead for some time, leaving Neven and Lansa as the only surviving family members.

"I know the timing for these types of meetings is always poor," the Huzien said. "Forgive me for pulling you away from your mourning in this time of loss. My name is Rex Gefret, and I'm one of the attorneys for the Shan Estate Trust. From the medical report sent to me by Jenshi Runso, I understand that Zun is in a coma with no brain activity?"

"That is correct," Neven said. "We've reached out to some specialists on Thae, and they are en route to examine her and see if they can repair the remaining brain damage."

Rex nodded, his face somber. "I have called you both here today because the conditions for Zun's living will have been fulfilled."

"What does that mean?" Neven glanced at Lansa.

"What were her instructions?" Lansa said.

"In the event that she ends up in a coma with no brain activity, her instructions were to terminate life support immediately. She had a 'do not resuscitate' clause in her will."

"No!" Neven stood. "I won't let you kill my wife. I am her husband, and you can't make that decision."

Rex raised his hands into the air in a submissive gesture. "I am merely conveying the wishes of Mrs. Shan. Her living will was explicit and supersedes your authority as her husband."

"We just recently got married. It's highly possible that she didn't have time to update her will. If I challenge this in court, I'm sure there is a case."

"Her will was updated the day before you got married to include provisions for you as her husband regarding her assets. But she explicitly did *not* change this portion of her living will to remove the 'do not resuscitate' clause." Rex sat back in his chair, his gaze softening. "I understand that it may be difficult to accept the wishes of your *eifi*, but I have the legal authority to enact her will against your wishes, and I will exercise that authority in accordance with Huzien law." Rex put his hands on the table. "I hope it doesn't come to that."

Lansa had remained quiet during the exchange, her gaze focused off to the side. Her face was soft, and her hands rested on the table, one on the other. "I'm guessing there were no special provisions for her mother regarding her wishes?" Lansa asked.

"That is correct," Rex confirmed.

Neven glanced from Lansa to Rex and sat back in his chair, defeated.

After a long moment, Rex cleared his throat and folded his hands. "Regarding the next steps, do you intend to comply with Zun's wishes, or will we need to proceed to the courts?"

Foundra Ascension *orbiting Thae, Huzien home system*

Lansa Shan stood on the medical deck of the *Foundra Ascension,* Neven at her side. She was latched onto his arm, like their first walk back on Thae—it seemed like that had happened an eternity ago.

Rex and Jenshi stood beside Zun's body, and the Founder's Elite assembled around them on the medical deck. All three Founders of the Huzien Empire—Lanrete, Ecnics, and Cislot—stood side by side, together in solidarity. Their presence was ignored, as every heart and mind was on Zun. Neven's parents were there also, both standing behind Neven and Lansa.

Rex looked to Neven as the two locked gazes. Neven nodded, and Lansa lowered her head as Rex signaled Jenshi to cut life support. Jenshi steeled his gaze and initiated the shutdown sequence for the devices, returning Zun's body to its lifeless state.

The world fell away as Neven stared at Zun's dead body, again. Except this time, it was permanent. The look on her face was peaceful—a stark reality to how she died.

His mind replayed the battle with Entradis, an act of torment he was suffering through, even in nightmares.

Everyone except for Neven and Lansa filed out of the medical bay. Lansa lightly tugged on Neven's arm, pulling him back to reality. He glanced at her as she met his gaze and then nodded her head in Zun's direction. Fear was in her eyes, and she was leaning on him heavily, the strength gone from her body.

He walked her over to her daughter as she held him for support.

"I thought . . . I would at least have another century before I experienced this moment," Lansa said, her voice cracking. "I accepted that my daughter would die before me due to the Human blood in her veins, but this . . . I . . ."

"I planned to die first," Neven said.

Lansa smiled at him and kissed his cheek. "Promise me something."

"Anything."

"Don't lose yourself to this despair. It's not what Zun would have wanted."

Neven remained silent. His gaze hung on Zun's body.

"Don't kill yourself seeking vengeance either. It won't bring her back."

"I will not allow her murderer to continue to draw breath. I cannot."

Lansa put her hand to Neven's face, her expression pained.

Jenshi walked back onto the medical deck. The pair turned to him as he approached.

"Neven, can I, uh, talk to you? Alone?" Jenshi asked.

Lansa nodded, patting Neven as she removed her arm from his. She lightly touched Zun's face and slowly lay beside her daughter's body on the bed, then began to weep.

Jenshi led Neven into his office and closed the door.

"I know you did everything you could do, Jenshi," Neven started. "I don't hold any of this against you."

Jenshi eyed Neven for a long moment, his gaze searching. "I appreciate that, but that's not what I wanted to talk to you about." Jenshi brought up a holodisplay, the screen showcasing Zun's recent full-body scan. He highlighted an area around her abdomen and pulled out a view of her womb with a small sack attached to the side wall.

"I don't understand. What am I looking at?"

"That is Zun's uterus."

Neven stared in confusion at Jenshi, his eyes slowly going wide. He started to wail, dropping to his knees as tears flowed in torrents down his cheeks. Pain wracked his body and heart as he struggled to breathe. Jenshi rushed to his side on the floor, wrapping his arms around him tightly.

"No, no! Please! Maker, no."

"Without support from Zun's body, the baby died quickly after the attack. I'm sorry, Neven. There was nothing I could have done at this early stage of development."

Neven cried on that floor for a long moment, the tears eventually stopping. His gaze was distant. Something inside him broke in that moment, and a part of his soul shattered forever.

"I didn't know," Neven whispered. "The beach . . . she must have planned to tell me on the beach before—" Neven's voice broke.

Jenshi stared down at the ground, his arms crossed. "Do you want me to share this information with—"

Neven shook his head no before Jenshi completed the sentence. Without another word, he slowly got up from the floor, absentmindedly patted Jenshi on the shoulder, and then walked out of his office—past Lansa, past Zun's body, and out of the medical bay.

A state funeral was held in the Huzien capital for Zun the following day. It was an elaborate affair, and Zun's casket was given a place of honor in the Huzien Capitol building. The ceremony was presided over by Founder Cislot.

Neven skipped the event, deciding to remain on the *Foundra Ascension*. He stood in his lab, staring at an empty workbench.

Neven . . . I . . . Ellipse's voice spoke in his thoughts. *I am so sorry.*

"You know . . . I have never wanted to kill someone in my life. Not even Sagren or Sephan," Neven started. "I knew that they needed to die, but I didn't personally feel the need to kill them. It was more out of a sense of duty, you know? For the safety of the empire."

Neven brought up a holodisplay, opening up a sequence for a new prototype. The workbench began to transform, coming alive as a three-dimensional model of a chassis for a new power armor was projected. Neven scrolled through variations in the starting configuration, settling on the one he had utilized in the battle against Entradis.

"But Entradis . . ." Neven spoke the name with venom. "I want to kill him with every fiber of my being. I want to rip off his head and piss down his throat. I want to rip out his beating heart and club him to death with it." Neven began to tear up, his voice cracking.

I know, Ellipse's voice was soft. *But anger is a dangerous thing, Neven.*

Neven laughed bitterly. "What would you know of anger?"

Ellipse remained silent.

Neven's face grew hard as he started modifying components in the power armor, ideas coming to him in a flood. The normal curiosity and excitement that drove his work was absent, and in its place was something else. Something more powerful.

Purpose.

His mind worked a mile a minute, and the workbench switched to fabrication mode after the final tweak to the digital schematic. Neven stepped back and watched his work—a new armor—coming to life on the table. The military-grade hardware printer built into the workbench omnistructed the armor, aided by an army of nanites.

I may not be Human, but I can feel anger just as you do, Ellipse said. *I can feel it coursing through your veins, driving your thoughts. And through that, I feel it myself. So yes, I understand anger. I know its power and how that anger is driving you right now.*

"Then you understand why I must kill Entradis."

Is that what Zun would want?

Neven roared, slamming a nearby table hard enough to make the holodisplay within flicker. "No one can tell me what Zun would want anymore! Zun is dead, killed by a murderer in cold blood. The same murderer who killed her husband before. Zun would want me to avenge her."

Just as she was driven to avenge Yuvan? Ellipse countered. *Zun never once spoke of vengeance. Instead, she mourned Yuvan and moved on with her life. She didn't dwell on Entradis or allow herself to be consumed by anger like you are now. She moved on, and because of that, you experienced the joy of her life, even if it was only for a short time.*

Neven was speechless, his hands reflexively opening and closing. His breathing slowed, and his sight became blurry as the tears returned. "He has to die, Ellipse," Neven said. "It hurts too much."

Neven . . . I don't want to lose you too.

"I know, because if I die, then we both die. I get it. Maybe we can find you a new host. I can talk to Kechu when we get back to Thae."

No, Neven. I . . . It's more than that. I care for you. I want you to be safe. I want you to live, even if it's independent of me. Ellipse's android body appeared at Neven's side. Her dark-brown hand came up to his face, softly caressing it. Ellipse's deep, golden gaze hung on him with longing, and the soft glow of her eyes was beautiful. "I can bring you comfort. I can keep you warm at night and help you through this tough time." She moved closer to him, pressing her lifelike Human body against his.

"I appreciate that," Neven said, half paying attention to her as the workbench signaled that the omnistruction was complete. "But this is something that I must do. And to do that, I must prepare." He stepped away from Ellipse and back toward the workbench. Neven shut out the world as he began inspecting his work.

Ellipse touched the back of her neck, her gaze dropping to the floor as she frowned.

Multiple simulations played out on the holodisplay in Neven's lab. The new prototype on the workbench barely resembled where Neven had started just a few days ago. A blip from Neven's mobi broke his trancelike state. He frowned and then put the call through to a nearby holodisplay.

Rex appeared, his face grim. "I'm sorry to disturb you during this delicate time, but we must proceed with the reading of Zun's will as soon as possible. Lansa has requested that the reading take place in her primary residence. I believe you know the location?"

"Yes." Neven let out a heavy sigh.

"When should we expect you surface-side?"

"I'm on my way."

Ecka, Thae, Huzien home system

Neven stood at the entrance to Lansa's mansion. The elaborate home sat on an expansive estate bordered by rolling hills and meticulously maintained nature. He remembered Zun standing in front of him, urging him toward the entrance, a look of excitement mixed with nervousness on her face.

She was so beautiful.

A tear rolled down Neven's cheek. His body was numb as he willed it forward, forcing himself to put one foot in front of the other. Slowly, he made his way up to the front door.

The door was a relic with an elaborate golden handle that required manual force to open it. He stared at the handle for a long moment. His hand came to rest on it as he opened the door and stepped through it.

Rex stood a short way inside the entrance hall, his gaze meeting Neven's as the young Human entered Lansa's home. Rex was tall like most Huziens, his height dwarfing Neven. The other man quickly crossed the hall and extended his hand in a very Human gesture.

Neven subconsciously extended his own, and the two shook hands.

"We have set up in the study. This way." Rex turned, prompting Neven to follow.

They wound their way through a series of hallways into a large study toward the back of the home's first floor. Lansa sat in a chair a short distance from a large desk that was the room's centerpiece. She was dressed all in black with a large black hat and veil covering her face. She seemed frailer than when Neven had last seen her on the *Ascension*.

"Sorry for the delay, Ms. Shan," Rex said.

She glanced up to meet his gaze, her face softening when she caught sight of Neven.

She looks so much like Zun, Ellipse said in his head.

Neven moved to the seat next to Lansa and sat. Lansa watched him silently before switching her gaze to Rex and nodding.

Rex launched into a bout of legalese as Neven drowned him out, his gaze stuck on the floor, his eyes glazed over.

Neven remembered the first time he met Zun. It had been shortly after he had settled onto the *Foundra Ascension*. He had been a Founder's Elite for less than a week, and it was his first time on a starship. He hadn't trained with Soahc yet, and anyone with a hint of telepathy could easily read his mind. Zun had sensed his surface thoughts, his clear admission of her beauty putting her off guard. She hadn't known what to make of him then.

He smiled.

". . . approximately two hundred and six billion larods as of yesterday's date within the trust with Neven Kenk and Lansa Shan as the sole beneficiaries."

"What?" Neven asked.

"The trust," Rex said. "As of yesterday, total assets were approximately two hundred and six billion larods. This would rank the estate and yourselves among the top one hundred wealthiest individuals in the Huzien Alliance."

Neven glanced at Lansa with a terrified look.

She watched him curiously. "Zun never told you how wealthy she was?" Lansa asked. "She never told you she was a tech billionaire before she joined the Founder's Elite?"

Neven shook his head, his stomach churning. He dropped to his knees and threw up on the floor. "I . . . I can't process this right now." Neven stood. "I . . . I have to go."

Lansa glanced to Rex with a worried expression.

"Someone from the wealth management department for the Shan Estate Trust will reach out to you to ensure that you're taken care of," Rex said.

"I don't need to be taken care of," Neven countered. His head was spinning. He took a few steps toward the exit to the study, and the floor came up to meet him, his world going dark.

Neven woke with a start, sitting up in a luxurious bed. The room he was in was expansive, the décor elaborate with fine art tastefully placed on the walls. Jenshi was standing next to a holodisplay built into an ornate end table. One of his medical drones was decloaked and hovering next to Neven.

Lansa Shan stood from her chair next to his bed, a look of relief on her face.

"What happened?" Neven asked.

"A combination of fatigue and shock," Jenshi said. "You and Lanrete are going to get my license revoked for negligence," he whispered.

"You collapsed in the study," Lansa said. "I called Jenshi right away. He was here within the hour."

Neven rubbed his eyes.

"Ellipse tells me you were awake for three days before coming here." Jenshi shook his head. "You're picking up some bad habits from Lanrete."

The drone tapped a liphojam to Neven's neck, injecting the solution into his bloodstream. Clarity came to Neven's mind, and the fogginess quickly receded.

"You slept for two days."

As if on cue, Neven's stomach rumbled. Lansa snapped her fingers, and a serving drone carrying a large tray entered the room. A makeshift table expanded in front of Neven, and the tray was set down on it, filled with some of Neven's favorite food.

"Thank you," Neven whispered as he glanced at Lansa.

"I can't have my son going hungry."

A tear rolled down Neven's cheek.

Lansa moved closer to Neven and cupped his face. "You will always be my son." Her voice was firm, her own eyes tearing up. The two embraced in a long hug, and Jenshi quietly made his way out of the room.

Lansa eventually broke the embrace, moving to retake her seat. She motioned for him to eat, and he obliged. The two sat in silence as Neven made his way through most of the food.

"You should take some time off. Spend it here with me. We can talk about Zun and your adventures."

Neven was shaking his head before she finished her statement. "Entradis is out there."

"You still intend to hunt him?"

"And kill him."

Lansa let out a slow breath, getting up as she moved to a nearby window and looked out to the lake. "Do you remember when I asked you what you were worth?"

"Yes." Neven remembered the scene of Lansa and him sitting on a bench in front of the lake after having walked half of the estate together.

"Do you remember what your answer was to me?"

"The lives of trillions of people, the love of a family, and the heart of your daughter."

"You still have Zun's heart. The love that she had for you will always be with you." She turned to face Neven. "Do you want to honor that love with bloodshed?"

"Entradis killed her." Neven's voice was cold. "Of all people . . ."

"Don't you dare!" Lansa shot back. "Don't you dare tell me what I should feel." She approached Neven with fire in her eyes. "I birthed Zun out of my womb, suckled, and raised her. I am her mother."

The anger in her gaze caused Neven to press back into the headboard.

"I mourn the loss of my daughter, and I absolutely demand justice for her murderer. But I will not dishonor her memory by giving her killer victory over my soul. And neither should you."

Neven stared at the tray in front of him. "I can't let it go." Neven's voice was calm as he shook his head. "This is what I do." He looked up at Lansa. "I am a Founder's Elite. I kill people for the Empire. I build machines of destruction that win wars. What is it all for if I can't even avenge my wife?"

Lansa took a step back, her gaze going to the floor. "Do what you must, but I want something from you before you leave."

Lansa glanced off to the side as a young Huzien woman walked into the room, a hovering tray beside her. There were a series of stasis-ready storage tubes covering one side of the tray next to a device that caused Neven to blush. The woman came to a stop by the bed and looked to Lansa.

"Zun had several of her eggs preserved in stasis before she joined the Founder's Elites," Lansa said. She looked Neven directly in his eyes and then glanced at the woman. "Bevhar is a valued employee of the estate and a nurse. She will collect samples of your semen, and I will preserve them along with Zun's eggs. If you get yourself killed, I will make my own grandchildren and love them in your place."

She nodded to Bevhar, who bowed slightly.

Neven's eyes went wide as Lansa left the room without another word.

CHAPTER 4 - URIEL KERVID

56623 FA (23,500 years ago)
Atmosphere above Lux'ian, Lux'Ameni home system

Battlecruisers and battleships littered the skies high above the surface of Lux'ian. The former jewel of the Lux'Ameni Empire was in ruins. Fleets of drones swarmed between ships, waging a war of attrition.

Uriel Kervid stood on the exit ramp of a small shuttle flanking the battleship of the 3rd Huzien Imperial Fleet, the HSS *Toma*. His sharp, silver eyes surveyed the aerial battlefield, his brown hair in a military cut. He had light-brown skin with grey esha marks.

He started running toward the edge of the exit ramp. The sharp drop into certain death far below didn't even cause him to sweat. Picking up speed, he jumped off the edge, drawing Wishwonder—his Iltarum blade—and landed on a large drone that came from under to catch him.

Iltarum blades were marvels, built with the finest technology in the Huzien Empire and utilized exclusively by the military. Wishwonder was a beautiful blade, the image down the sides that of a series of silver clouds with a shining ribbon of white that weaved its way through to explode at the hilt.

The drone sped toward the *Guysuma'revhia*, lead battleship of the Jun'Serentan Dominion Atmospheric Defense Fleet. The capital ships for both fleets were exchanging blows in the upper atmosphere with their full contingents of dreadnaughts and battle carriers, their massive sizes incapable of navigating a descent into the inner atmosphere of the planet.

A series of drones peeled off from the fight and headed toward Uriel. He grinned. Telekinetically shifting himself, he landed on the first approaching drone, his energized Iltarum blade sinking into the heart of the machine as Uriel began to rip it apart, dismantling the drone with the powerful cihphistic forces at his command.

As the drone sputtered and died, he telekinetically moved to the next one and went to work cutting a hole into its top. The drone attempted to fling him off by turning upside down, but he punched into its hull, gripped the twisted metal, and finished his hole, climbing inside.

Uriel destroyed the drone from the inside out, exploding through the top and into the waiting clutches of the next enemy as he jammed Wishwonder deep into the machine's side. Summoning a fount of Enesmic energy to himself, he snapped his fingers to summon streaks of lightning to hammer into the drone.

He released the drone before the electricity connected and fell through the sky. He punched through the shield of a nearby ship with a terrible flash of Enesmic energy, landing with unnatural finesse on the hull of the *Guysuma'revhia* a few hundred meters below. The disrupted shield rippled and reformed, the distortion only temporary.

Releasing his Iltarum blade, the weapon righted itself and hovered by his side. His hands went to work weaving a cihphistic manifestation, and the hull of the *Guysuma'revhia* trembled under the invisible swirling of Enesmic energy.

Focusing the energy on an area in front of himself, a column of light tore through the hull, burning a massive hole deep into the ship. Jumping in, he landed in a scorched hallway, blast doors sealing around him. Bringing up a mini holodisplay on his wrist, a schematic of the ship appeared with an indicator of his current location highlighted in blue.

He charged down the hallway toward a closed blast door. Enesmic forces slammed into the door, forcefully pushing it up and out of his way. This continued for a few corridors until he encountered his first hint of resistance when a series of Lux'Ameni soldiers rounded the corner and opened fire.

Lux'Ameni were short, squat creatures with rigid bodies and large eyes on the sides of their head that appeared to move independently. Large, flat armored tails trailed them, and their giant mouths covered the width of their faces. With their battle armor on, they looked like walking metal depictions of the letter J.

Uriel held out his hand, crafting an energy barrier before him to absorb the shots. His floating Iltarum blade surged forward, slamming tip-first into the head of the first Lux'Ameni soldier and pinning his lifeless body against the wall. Following his whims, Wishwonder slid out of the corpse and went to work as if an invisible Redalam, a Huzien blade master, was wielding it in a deadly dance.

The soldiers didn't know how to react—a few scrambled away, unsure of which target to attack. A few attempted to fire directly at the blade as the weapon decapitated another soldier before spinning in a cyclone to cut another person in half.

Uriel telekinetically shifted past the carnage as the blade finished up the remaining soldiers and came to hover back at his side. He continued toward the engine room of the *Guysuma'revhia*, tearing through more soldiers along the way. Cihphistic energy radiated off him in torrents as he wielded the Enesmic forces with a vengeance. Soldiers were blasted apart by energy or physically ripped apart through powerful Enesmic forces.

He was unfazed by the bloodshed and emotionally detached. The Huzien soldier was the single most powerful unit in his battlegroup. He was a Huzien Mobile Infantry Elite, a living weapon infused with nanitic technology and cybernetic enhancements, battle-hardened through intense martial and cihphistic training.

He was a walking weapon of mass destruction that had one purpose: to win the battle at any cost.

He never failed.

Uriel ripped the primary door to the engine room off its track, sending the crumpled metal behind him and into an approaching group of Lux'Ameni soldiers, who were crushed beneath the force of the door.

He walked into the engine room, surveying all the engineers and crew members looking at him with wide eyes. They backed up, clearly not wanting to move closer.

Distance didn't matter.

He sent his blade forward, slicing through the unarmored Lux'Ameni like a hot knife through butter. He walked through the decimation, his blade still at work as Lux'Ameni fled in terror, until he came to stand in front of the main reactor. Lifting both his hands slowly, the area around him began to tremble. The protective housing of the reactor was ripped away, triggering warning claxons to blare across the ship.

He burst into a rhythmic dance of cihphistic weaving as the forces tore into the reactor. The reactor went critical, exploding outward in a blast that Uriel struggled to catch and contain in a newly created barrier. He molded the barrier, channeling the blast in the most devastating ways possible before sending it into the most populated parts of the ship, targeting critical systems and expanding the explosion toward the bridge.

Releasing it all at once, he grabbed his blade as it returned to his side and clenched his fist, teleporting back to the shuttle. The ship's shield flickered back on at his mental command.

He watched his handiwork play out as, in the distance, the detonation of the *Guysuma'revhia*'s reactor tore the ship apart with brutal efficiency. The remnants of the ship started to fall out of the sky, looking like a lumbering giant knocked to the ground.

His sharp silver eyes turned to their next target, Uriel thrilling in the rush of battle.

HSS Lukim *orbiting Lux'ian, Lux'Ameni home system*

"Impressive work out there, Uriel." Fleet Admiral Retyu Dewerter motioned for Uriel to sit in the chair across from his desk.

Uriel saluted and moved to the chair, his posture perfect.

"Thanks to your actions, we were able to break the stalemate and gain the upper hand due to them diverting resources to cover their losses," Retyu said.

He motioned to a nearby drone that came to hover next to him. He made a selection, and a drink appeared in a little alcove. Taking it, he signaled for the machine to go to Uriel. The Huzien Elite dismissed the drone, taking nothing from it.

"Your prowess on the battlefield has caught the eye of our great founder," Retyu continued.

Uriel perked up. "Founder Lanrete?"

"Yes, the *Foundra Ascension* is docked here. Founder Lanrete has personally requested an audience with you aboard his ship."

Uriel stood. "I will go right away."

"No, wait until the morning." Retyu motioned for him to resume sitting. "For now, your orders are to enjoy the night off and revel in your accomplishments. This has been a major strategic victory for our empire." Retyu took a long draw from his drink, then got up and moved to a nearby window in his expansive office. "This battle may have single-handedly won us the war against the Jun'Serentan Dominion. We have leveled the Lux'Ameni home world and broken their will to fight. We have officially threatened to crack the planet itself if they do not withdraw from the conflict immediately. As one of the ruling species in the Dominion, the loss of their forces will lead to our swift victory."

"Will they call our bluff?"

"It's not a bluff." Retyu glanced back at Uriel. "We have cracked planets before during military campaigns. It's not ideal, but we must carry through with our threats. Otherwise, people will doubt the might of the Huzien Empire." Retyu drained the rest of his drink. "Anyway, you're dismissed. Go *vusg* something. Get trashed. I don't care. Just enjoy yourself."

Uriel stood, saluted, and then exited the office.

Uriel sat on top of a large storage container as he watched the soldiers unload a prisoner transport—the male and female Ku'Ven were forced to walk in a straight line.

They were a towering species, tall above eight feet, with lanky yet deceptively athletic builds and striped azure-colored skin. Their unnerving white eyes were large, and the women had hair mostly in braids that hung down four to five feet on average.

They were a beautiful species, even by Huzien standards.

The Ku'Ven prisoners were required to remove their clothes to reveal any potential weapons, then clothed in standard, transparent Huzien prisoner uniforms that afforded no modesty. Nothing was left to chance in Huzien military processes, even with advanced scanners that could detect most weapons.

Uriel felt nothing at the scene: no anger, pity, or remorse. He had massacred hundreds of thousands of Ku'Ven, Lux'Ameni, and Jun'Serentan, yet he harbored no hate or negative feelings toward them. Sure, they were the enemy of the Huzien Empire, but he felt nothing.

Some guards pushed through the prisoners, grabbing a few of the more attractive Ku'Ven. The three Ku'Ven who were singled out—two females and one male—glanced around in terror while the other prisoners kept their heads down around them. A group of visibly eager guards pushed the trio toward a secluded room.

Uriel scowled and was moving before he could process his actions. He walked in the direction of the soldiers and the sobbing Ku'Ven trio.

One of the soldiers caught sight of Uriel and moved to intercept him. "Major." The man smiled with a salute. "Can I help you?"

"What are you planning to do with those prisoners? Huzien policy clearly states that they must be processed and confined."

"Oh, absolutely," the soldier said. "We're taking them aside for additional inspection and interrogation. You know, making sure we check all the holes. Multiple times if necessary." He grinned.

"Interrogation rooms are that way." Uriel turned and pointed in the opposite direction to the far side of the processing deck.

"Oh, well . . . it's a bit far, so we decided to do it here instead." The man laughed.

"Is there a problem here?" Uriel and the soldier turned to regard an approaching officer who held the same rank as Uriel.

"No problem, sir," the initial guard said. "Just informing Mr. Elite here that we need to pull a few prisoners aside for enhanced screening."

The major nodded and looked at Uriel. "Thanks for your concern, Major, but I think this situation is under control."

"This is a violation of policy."

"I'm the commanding officer here, and I think this situation is under control. Do we have a problem, Major?"

Uriel narrowed his gaze. Glancing toward the soldiers that had taken the prisoners, he felt rage build up inside him. The area trembled slightly as the swirl of Enesmic energy answered his unspoken call.

Letting out a slow breath, he calmed himself. "No, sir." He spat on the floor toward the soldiers and left the area. He contemplated going to Lanrete right then—against orders—but decided against it. He didn't want to show his hand too soon.

Reluctantly, he returned to his quarters and called it an early night. After running through multiple cycles of his VRC, he walked into his bedroom nude and collapsed onto his bed. Given his rank and position as the battlegroup's Elite, Uriel was afforded private quarters aboard the *Lukim*.

Moving under the covers, he stared at the ceiling, his mind returning to those prisoners. He had difficulty falling asleep, their gazes haunting him as he held on to the pent-up tension.

He forced his mind to still, using a technique taught to him early on in his days in the mobile infantry to help with sleeping near the front lines of an active warzone.

Sleep eventually took hold of him.

A subtle chime woke Uriel the next morning. Removing the covers, he sat on the side of his bed and ran through stretches and light exercises to wake his body up. He then moved to the window of his quarters and stared out of it. Tapping the window, he stood brooding for a long moment.

Eventually, he pulled on his uniform and departed toward the *Foundra Ascension*. A set of guards vetted his credentials and allowed him access to the ship. Stepping off the meglift, Uriel was surprised by the elaborate décor of the hallway. Art from across the galaxy lined the walls, a mix of pieces that looked expensive, with a few nameplates highlighting artists he recognized.

Focusing on his purpose, he ignored the paintings and made his way to a large double door that opened at his approach. More luxuries caught his eye as he stepped into the great hall. The portrait of a beautiful ebony-skinned Huzien woman sitting with Lanrete hung on the wall opposite the entrance.

A man emerged from one of the connecting hallways. "My late wife, Trisha."

Uriel stood to attention. "Founder."

Lanrete glanced toward Uriel before stopping in front of the picture. Crossing his arms, he stared at it for a long moment. "How many times must I recognize the value of something only after I have lost it?"

"Sir?"

"Nothing." Lanrete turned to face Uriel. "Follow me to my office." Lanrete turned and walked back down the hallway he'd appeared from.

Uriel frowned and followed Lanrete. He eventually entered a large office at the back of the quarters. Lanrete moved to sit at a large desk, and Uriel sat in a chair in front of it. He kept his posture perfect and sat at the edge of his seat.

Lanrete leaned back in his chair and watched Uriel for a few moments. Then he brought up holodisplays showcasing captured footage of Uriel's prowess on the battlefield. "I've been impressed by your work. You are one of the most gifted Elites in Huzien military history." Lanrete dismissed the holodisplays and turned his chair to face the ceiling-to-floor window that lined the back of his office and showcased a breathtaking view of the planet Lux'ian.

"I'm sure Retyu has already lavished you with praise, so I won't waste our time repeating his words. Instead, I'll get right to the point." Lanrete stood up and moved to the window. "I summoned you here today because I want to build a team of elites—the best of the best. What you did on the battlefield—the focused assault on key assets and the controlled chaos you brought everywhere you went—I want to engineer that on demand. I want to be able to take an elite force into any situation and turn the tide of battle, break the stalemate, assassinate the tyrant, or whatever the case may be." He turned back to face Uriel. "And I want you to lead that team at my side."

"At your side?" Uriel gave Lanrete a confused look. "You intend to go into combat?"

"Yes," Lanrete said. "I want to be on the front lines of conflict, surrounded by a team of people I can trust. People who can hold their own and who I can rely on."

Uriel sat back in his chair, his eyes narrowed and his body tense. "You want me to be your bodyguard?"

"No." Lanrete shook his head. "I am not looking for a bodyguard. I will take care of myself. Rather, I am looking for people who I can trust to get the mission done at all costs. People like yourself."

Uriel relaxed slightly.

"This ship would be our base," Lanrete continued. "We would travel wherever we were needed as a strike force unlike any other." Lanrete moved back to his seat and sat down. "It would be called the

Founder's Elites, and it would be an extension of not only my will but the will of the Triumvirate."

"We would be working in service to you, Founder Ecnics, and Founder Cislot?"

"Yes."

Uriel lowered his head and stared at the ground for a long moment. "Before I answer, I have a question for you." Uriel locked gazes with Lanrete.

"Of course."

"Do you believe in justice?"

Lanrete sat silent for a long moment, studying Uriel. "Justice for whom?"

"Justice for the weak, the disenfranchised, and the subjugated."

Lanrete leaned back in his chair. "This sounds specific. Elaborate."

"Retyu gives free reign for those under his command to break Huzien laws and engage in the rape and exploitation of prisoners. He turns a blind eye to the illegal acquisition of contraband and retaliates against those who speak up. These actions result in a culture of willful ignorance that empowers the worst in the Huzien military."

"That is a serious accusation against a highly respected officer. Do you have proof?"

Uriel brought up a holodisplay recording showcasing the inside of the secluded room the soldiers had taken their prisoners to from the night before. He then brought up additional recordings from over the past year, showing several high-ranking officers participating.

Lanrete watched a few of the recordings in silence and let out a sigh. "And Retyu is aware of this?"

Uriel brought up another recording, this one showing Retyu participating. He closely watched Lanrete, attempting to discern the man's emotions, but Lanrete's face was a mask.

Lanrete dismissed the recordings and brought up a holodisplay displaying Fleet Admiral Retyu.

"Yes, Founder?" Retyu asked.

"Come to my office, now," Lanrete said.

"Understood."

Lanrete dismissed the holodisplay and sat silently, gazing out the window. After a few minutes, the door to Lanrete's office chimed as Lanrete signaled for it to open. Retyu walked into the room and nodded at Uriel before standing at attention in front of Lanrete's desk.

Lanrete brought up the multiple holodisplay recordings with prisoners of all races being raped. The raw acts on full display in all their sickening horror caused Retyu to take a step back.

"Are you aware of what's been happening under your command, Fleet Admiral?" Lanrete asked.

Retyu's face paled, his breath catching in his throat. He turned to look at Uriel, his face hardening. "I will get to the bottom of this, Founder."

"Will you?" Lanrete brought up the video of Retyu laughing with another soldier as a terrified prisoner with stark-white, almost bonelike skin sat in the corner of a holding cell, crying. Retyu walked toward the muscular Jun'Serentan woman as her large, solid black eyes widened.

"You *vusging cith!*" Retyu charged at Uriel.

A flash out of the corner of Uriel's eyes caught him off guard as he jumped to his feet to defend himself. Lanrete stood between the two, his legendary blade, Divinebreath, drawn and coated with a thin line of blood.

Retyu staggered back, his hand going to his throat as he collapsed to the floor, blood spray escaping his hand as his eyes bulged.

"Attempted assault on a Huzien officer is a capital offense punishable by death in wartime." Lanrete turned to regard Retyu, disgust on his face. "You will be replaced, and all of those you empowered will be dealt with in accordance with Huzien law." Lanrete sheathed his blade and turned to regard Uriel as Retyu bled out on the floor. "Laws exist for a reason, and considering I wrote most of them, I expect them to be upheld by those in the highest positions of power. Any violation of that duty is unforgivable. Justice is afforded to the weak and the strong, irrespective of standing."

"Then I accept your offer," Uriel said. "Let's build a team."

The destruction wrought on the ecology is devastating; plant life is unable to subsist due to nutrients no longer present in planetary soil.

-FROM "ENESMIC SHIPYARD EFFECTS ON TRICA VII"
MINSCI METABASE

CHAPTER 5 - NEVEN KENK

Present Day
Foundra Ascension *orbiting Thae, Huzien home system*

Walking onto the *Foundra Ascension*'s medical deck, Neven stopped a short distance from the table where Jenshi had previously operated on Zun. His gaze stuck on that spot, his mind recreating the image of Zun's lifeless body. A tear rolled down his cheek, but he quickly wiped it away and closed his eyes, taking a deep breath.

"Neven?"

The voice brought him back to reality. He opened his eyes to see Jenshi standing at the door to his office.

"What do you need?" Jenshi asked.

"I . . ." Neven rubbed the back of his neck. "I'd like all of Zun's medical records. Every scan, every exam, every little detail."

Jenshi's eyes widened slightly. "Okay." He walked toward Neven, opening a holodisplay as he neared. "You are entitled to that information by law, but may I ask what you plan to do with it?"

"No." Neven's tone was flat.

Jenshi stopped and watched Neven curiously. Glancing to the holodisplay showing Zun's most recent full-body scan, he sighed. "Neven, I'm sorry I couldn't save Zun."

Neven shook his head. "It's not your fault. You did what you could."

"Then what is this about?"

"Please just give me the data." Neven met Jenshi's eyes.

Jenshi stared at Neven for a long moment and then initiated the data transfer process. A flood of information hit Neven's mobi, the sheer volume of it forcing Neven to offload most of it to a private storage cluster in his lab.

Without another word, Neven exited the medical deck, Jenshi staring after him with a look of concern.

"Kechu, thanks for taking my call." Neven paced in his quarters aboard the *Foundra Ascension*.

Kechu Fen, a dark-brown-skinned Huzien with green eyes and red hair, watched him with sympathy. "Anytime, man. We miss you down here," he said. "I'm sorry about what happened to Zun. It broke my heart."

Neven stopped pacing momentarily, his eyes closing briefly as he took a deep breath. "That's what I'm calling you about."

Kechu raised an eyebrow.

"I have a detailed scan of her brain from the last time she went in for a checkup with Jenshi at the end of our last mission."

Kechu narrowed his eyes. "No."

"I haven't even asked you anything yet!"

"I know what you're going to ask me, and the answer is no."

"Hear me out, please," Neven pleaded.

Kechu let out an exasperated sigh, moving to sit down. He stared hard at Neven. "Zun's life was cut short by a crazed murderer. She was a lover of progress and honestly believed in the mission of the MinSci. Think about it—she, of all people, would want such an experiment to be performed in her honor."

"In her honor? You mean with her." Kechu shook his head. "This is unethical. She never consented to experimental research on her remains, did she?"

"Not exactly . . . but these *aren't* her remains. These are her scans."

Kechu frowned.

"Fine, yes, it's close enough." Neven sighed. "Come on, man. I'm asking this as your best friend."

"Don't do that. Please." Kechu groaned. "You're putting me in a very compromising position by asking me to do this. This could jeopardize my work and career if it were ever discovered."

"Please model an SSI off Zun's brain. I know it won't fully be Zun, but . . . I . . ."

"I'm not even sure I can pull this off." Kechu rubbed his eyes. "Every SSI I've created has used custom code modified from Lahl, my original prototype. From start to finish, it was all artificial materials used to simulate life, not mirror it. Creating an SSI from an actual Human brain raises many ethical and moral concerns. Is it Zun? Does it have rights? This is an unknown area that needs to be fully thought out and debated at the highest levels of the MinSci before we create something we can't take back."

"Please!" Neven begged. "I need this. I don't know what else to do. You don't know what it's like, Kechu, to have someone you love ripped from you so suddenly, just as you're planning out what your life will be. It hurts. My heart physically hurts, and I need to stop the pain. I need to talk to her again, even if it's only one last time. I need that closure."

Kechu threw up his hands, standing suddenly and letting out a heavy sigh. He paced back and forth a few times, stopping to stare at something Neven couldn't see. His face softened as he turned around to look at Neven. The mobi connection between them shifted into a Ghostnet channel running on Kechu's personal compute cluster before it bounced off underground GNet relay networks halfway across the Huzien Alliance.

It was the type of technology utilized by hackers and undesirables to hide their tracks.

Kechu seemed agitated. "Fine. Send me the data."

Neven initiated the transfer, sending over Zun's full body scans.

"I will work on this as a side project, but you shouldn't expect to hear anything more from me in the near future, and you *cannot* contact me again about this. Even in secret, this work will most likely draw unwanted attention, and any contact between us will jeopardize it. The MinSci has advanced SIs that monitor all research and look specifically for patterns that match true synthetic intelligence. I'm already running up against the borders of what's allowed with my SSI project. The fact that the SSIs are hard limited and tied to Human brains are the only reasons why my research is allowed to progress. Do you understand?"

"Yes, completely. Thanks, man. I appreciate it."

"You owe me big time for this one." Kechu looked back at Neven and smiled. "How's Ellipse treating you?"

"She's awesome, and I have something to show you. Something I created to complement her that gives her independence."

"You didn't!" Kechu's eyes widened as Neven smiled. "You did! Oh, man! That's so illegal. I don't know anything! I don't want to know anything." Kechu facepalmed. "You're going to get me fired! Oh man, oh man. I can't deal with this right now." Kechu let out a whine. "I've got to go. I have a demo with Phenste Wahkin tomorrow morning that I need to finish prepping for, and you've thoroughly distracted me."

"Who do you like working for better: her or Remi Etwa?"

"Phenste by far. She's not a *cith*." Kechu laughed. "Later, man. Don't get yourself killed, and please, oh please, stop doing illegal stuff. There are reasons why Ecnics has rules in place around this. If you knew what I know, you'd be a lot more careful." Kechu terminated the connection.

Neven stared at the blank holodisplay for a long moment, his mind racing.

If Father successfully creates a Zun SSI, would you replace me with her? Ellipse asked.

"I . . . I'd find a way for both of you to exist. I promise."

Ellipse appeared in the room in her android shell. It was humanoid, wearing a skintight jumpsuit that was primarily grey and white with designs of gold that crossed her body in bold lines. She smiled at Neven, red lipstick complementing her dark-brown skin. Her deep, golden-hued eyes locked onto Neven, and her gaze was intense.

Neven's mobi blipped, and he saw his mother's name. Frowning, Neven flipped her channel to ignore. Another video message from her immediately hit his notifications. She had been calling him every hour on the hour, but he hadn't talked to his parents since the ceremony where they'd disconnected Zun's life support.

"I'm sorry, Mom. I can't talk to you right now," Neven whispered. "I can't let you stop me."

"Briefing in ten," came a broadcast from Lanrete.

Neven jumped up and walked through his bedroom to his bathroom. He stopped to look at a set of lingerie laid out on the bed that Zun had previously worn. The sight caught him off guard as he ran his fingers across it, sucking in a shallow breath.

"If it helps, I can wear it for you," Ellipse said. She quickly removed her jumpsuit, leaving her body nude, and moved toward the lingerie.

Neven broke out of his trance. "No!" he shouted. "Sorry, no. That wouldn't help. Thank you for offering. I appreciate it, but I just need time. My mental buffer is still working on overdrive, like my brain hasn't caught up with life."

Neven caught sight of Ellipse's nude android body. His eyes stuck on her bare breasts for a long moment. They looked soft, inviting, and very real.

Ellipse took a few steps toward him. "Would you like me to keep you warm at night? I've created a way to simulate body heat so that I feel like a real Human to the touch." She took Neven's hand and moved it to the center of her chest, where a heart would normally be. "I've even found a way to simulate a heartbeat, see?" She pressed Neven's hand harder into her synthetic flesh.

It felt soft to the touch, and warm. The steady beating of something carried the rhythm of a heart.

"When . . ." Neven blinked, his eyes locking with her gaze. "When did you do all this?"

"It was a side project while you were occupied with everything going on." Ellipse gave a mischievous smile. "Here—I've also made some other upgrades." She took Neven's hand and moved it down between her thighs.

Neven jerked back. "You're wet! How are you wet? You have a . . . a . . ."

"Synthetic vagina, yes. I've engineered it from Human body scans found on the GNet."

"Why? I don't understand."

"To be more Human."

"Why do you want to be more Human? You are already so much more than a Human."

"Why not?"

Neven wiped his hand dry, slowly examining Ellipse. "Well, you're only supposed to get wet . . ." Neven motioned to between her legs. ". . . down there when you're sexually aroused. Not all the time."

"Ah." Ellipse smiled. "Of course." Her eyes narrowed slightly as she grinned. The soft golden light that radiated from her eyes was breathtaking at that moment. "I'll make sure to update the code."

Neven rubbed the back of his neck.

"Neven, are you on your way? We're waiting," Lanrete's voice rang through his mobi again.

"Shoot, sorry. I'm on the way," Neven responded.

Ellipse moved back to her jumpsuit and slowly pulled it on.

Neven found it challenging to turn away from her. "What's wrong with me?" he whispered. Shaking his head, he rushed out of the room, Ellipse behind him.

Neven quietly entered the Founder's Elite meeting room, a few eyes turning toward him. Most gave him a look of sympathy.

"Neven, if you need to take some time, just let us know," Lanrete said. "I know it's difficult losing a spouse, so don't feel like you need to be here."

"I'm fine." Neven shook his head.

Lanrete glanced at Jenshi, who met his gaze briefly. Ignoring the look, Neven slid into a chair, his gaze going to the floor.

"I've called you all here because I've received intel from the HIN that we've picked up Entradis's trail."

Neven sat up in his chair. "Where is he?"

"The HIN believes he's en route to Darbol Alliance space through the Nex'Rav'Ni corridor. We detected a ship with a similar drive pattern to the one that he fled Genmatha in."

"The number of spatial anomalies in that corridor would easily hide a suplight trail. How did you detect it?" Erb asked.

"State secrets," Dexter countered.

"We heavily monitor that corridor specifically for that reason. It is frequently used by pirates and criminal organizations to traffic Alliance citizens," Lanrete said. "But due to the complications of navigating the corridor, we can head Entradis off before the exit. He will be forced to remain uncloaked—if he even has that capability—while in the corridor."

"You mean we'll be going into the corridor?" Tashanira said.

"I thought the stress that the distortions put on ships prevented Frigate class ships like the *Foundra Ascension* from entering?" Jessica asked.

"Yes, that's correct," Lanrete said. "We'll need to deploy shuttles with multiple teams at key junctures within the corridor to provide an adequate net."

"Are our shuttles capable of going toe-to-toe with Entradis's ship? Do we have any idea what its capabilities are?" Serah'Elax asked.

"It's unclear," Dexter spoke up. "Our shuttles are equipped with advanced weapons systems, but it's hard to gauge Entradis's capabilities. Who knows what he's put together from the Under Market."

"We will play it safe," Lanrete said. "Try and get a full scan of his ship before engaging directly. We'll determine if the shuttles are capable of subduing his ship." Lanrete glanced at Neven. "This will be a dangerous mission. I'm not going to sugarcoat this—Entradis has killed a member of the Founder's Elite in every engagement we've ever had, but we *will* take Entradis down. I have faith in this team." Lanrete stood. "I need everyone to keep these facts in mind. Never underestimate Entradis. He is a brilliant tactician and a powerful Cihphist, one of the best. He has military-grade technology and is a master of getting the drop on his victims, so always be alert. You cannot defeat him alone; we must all work together. Am I clear?"

Nods and words of acknowledgment came from across the room.

"We depart immediately," Lanrete said. "Dismissed."

Everyone started to disperse.

The founder approached Neven. "I was serious earlier about taking leave. If you need the time, take it. I need everyone at one hundred percent for this team to be effective."

"I'm fine," Neven said.

Lanrete stared at him for a long moment. His gaze drifted to Ellipse, who was flanking Neven. Ellipse met Lanrete's gaze and held it, her face resolute.

Running his hand through his hair, Lanrete sighed and left the room. Neven turned to leave when a voice called him from the side of the room. He stopped and turned to see Serah'Elax—no, it wasn't Serah'Elax, but someone who looked very much like her.

The near-doppelganger had Serah'Elax's red hair, except it was waist-length. She had large, almond-colored eyes and a maturity in her appearance that Serah'Elax lacked, hinting at a more advanced age. Like all Das'Vin, she was stunning; her body was a true work of art, especially when combined with her clothing, which was cut in such a way as to reveal the unique ga'hei marks that covered her body.

"I don't think we've met, but I'm Serah'Elax's mother, De-ra'Liv Elax Ashfalen." She approached Neven, coming to stand close.

The silver flecks in her skin sparkled in the light as she moved. "I'm sorry to hear about the loss of your wife, Zun." Dera'Liv presented both hands, resting palms up on top of each other. Her top hand's pointer and index fingers were touching her thumb. She then bowed her head forward and touched her hands to her forehead.

A Das'Vin blessing for the dead, Ellipse said in Neven's mind.

"Thank you," Neven said.

"Come. Let me escort you to your room." Dera'Liv smiled at him.

Neven nodded, and the two started walking toward the meglift.

"How are you sleeping?" Dera'Liv asked.

"It's difficult, to be honest. I miss . . ."

"The warmth of another?" Dera'Liv's eyes became distant. "I understand. I lost my *dru'sha* very suddenly many years ago. Pirates killed her—her and my other *hala'a* both."

"Serah'Elax had a sister?"

The two stepped into the meglift as it hummed to life.

"Yes, all pure-blooded Das'Vin are born as twins in dual pregnancies."

"I'm sorry. I didn't know," Neven said.

They exited the meglift.

"That first night without my dear Ovah'Hal was torment. It was . . . difficult to continue living."

"What kept you going?"

"Serah'Elax. I was all she had." Dera'Liv stopped, turning to regard Neven. "I understand you and Zun were recently married, but you had no children."

Neven hesitated for a long moment. "That's right," he eventually said.

"I see." Dera'Liv tenderly touched Neven's shoulder. "If you need help coping with the pain of your loss, I am at your disposal. There are several techniques I have learned that have helped me since leaving Ashnaret and joining Serah'Elax here on the ship. The psychotherapists here are phenomenal."

"Thank you for the offer, but I'm managing."

Dera'Liv glanced at Neven, their gazes meeting briefly as she narrowed her eyes and forced a smile. "I see. If you change your mind, here is my contact information."

Dera'Liv stepped back from Neven, motioning toward his door. She sent her channel details to his mobi, smiling sincerely. She glanced in Ellipse's direction—the android had silently followed behind them the whole time.

"In our pain, we can sometimes hurt those closest to us, blinded by the past," Dera'Liv said. She bowed toward Ellipse and walked away from the pair.

Neven and Ellipse silently entered his quarters. Ellipse rubbed her arm and glanced toward the bedroom. Without a word, she undressed and moved toward his bed, climbing into it.

Neven turned to look at her, confusion on his face. "You sleep now?" Neven asked.

Ellipse didn't respond. With a sigh, he moved to the couch and collapsed onto it. His mobi blipped, indicating a received video message. He stared at the sender for a long moment, his heart racing. Debating whether to open the message, Neven went against his better judgment and brought the video up on a nearby holodisplay.

A'Amaria Schen appeared. The Hauxem's short, blue-skinned body was wrapped in a silver silk robe. Her silver-laced diamond eyes were playful, and her lips were colored cherry red. In place of her hair was an intricate pattern of silver and purple across her scalp.

"I heard what happened with Zun." A'Amaria pouted. "I'm so sorry. I know how much she meant to you." A'Amaria got up from her seat and moved to a running tub, manually turning the controls to shut the water off. The video feed followed her and kept her fully in frame. "I understand this must be a difficult time for you, what with the loss being so sudden." She disrobed, her nude body on full display as she put her hand on her hip and held a pose for a long moment. A'Amaria grinned and slowly turned around, gingerly stepping into the tub as the camera moved to an overhead view, flaunting herself as she settled into the water. She glanced up, looking directly at the camera. The water was low, failing to obscure much of her body. White bubbles accented her curves. "I decided to do something to cheer you up." She licked her lips, her eyes narrowing slightly as she leaned back in the tub and began stimulating herself.

"That *cith* whore!" Ellipse yelled. She came rushing into the room. "Turn it off! Delete it now!"

Neven was glued to the vision A'Amaria made in the tub, her moans blanking out his thoughts. Something within the far reaches of his subconscious wouldn't let him turn away. It was almost unnatural in its hold over him.

Ellipse's eyes went wide, her mouth falling open with a look of horror. She crossed her arms and left the room, her face distraught.

A'Amaria's moans grew louder as her body convulsed. Neven felt bile rising in his throat. His body went numb as he relived the moment A'Amaria raped him.

A'Amaria looked back up at the camera with a sultry gaze. "I miss you being inside me, so stop by soon." She pressed her tongue up against her upper lip as the video ended.

Neven remained still for a long moment, unable to process his emotions. An image of Zun flashed in his mind, and he broke down and began to cry, suddenly very ashamed. He deleted the video and eventually got up from the couch. Walking in a daze, he passed through his bedroom.

Ellipse silently stared at him from under the covers as he moved to his Vencom rinse chamber (VRC) in the bathroom. Setting the shower cycle on repeat, he let the liquid wash away more tears.

CHAPTER 6 - TASHANIRA YEN UNVESAL

Foundra Ascension *outside the Nex'Rav'Ni Corridor,*
Huzien / Darbol Border Space

Tashanira slowed in her movements, coming to rest on Jenshi with a soft moan as she collapsed onto his chest. Jenshi wrapped his arm around her, pulling her closer with a satisfied grin.

Tashanira's mobi alarm sounded as she groaned. She attempted to push herself up from Jenshi, but he held on to her.

"You're going to make me late," she teased.

"Not like they can leave without you," Jenshi said.

She kissed him passionately, their lips intertwined for a long moment. "I'm going to miss you."

"Two weeks is a long time."

"Up to two weeks," Tashanira corrected.

"Why did it have to be Neven, though?"

"Jealous much?"

"I mean—of all the people to be locked on a shuttle with for two weeks, why Neven?"

"Lanrete made the assignments. You can take it up with him."

"I think I will."

Tashanira laughed before sobering. "This genuinely bothers you, huh? Don't you trust me?" Tashanira pushed herself up from

Jenshi, beating him in a battle of strength. She pushed out her chest, filling his view with her furred breasts.

"Of course. I just . . . I don't know. Neven is unstable right now. I don't think he's fit for duty."

Tashanira frowned. "You are the chief medical officer. You could make that diagnosis official if you think he's a danger to the team."

"I'm aware." Jenshi propped himself on his elbows as Tashanira moved off him and to his side. "But we are hunting the man who killed his wife. If our roles were reversed, I wouldn't want that to be taken away from me."

Tashanira sighed. "I guess I'll mercy *vusg* him to get his mind right."

"Not funny." Jenshi shot Tashanira a glare. "This is exactly the kind of joking that makes this whole thing uncomfortable for me."

"Fine, fine. I'm sorry." Tashanira pouted. "I'll be on my best behavior."

"Be careful out there." Jenshi sighed. "Entradis is no joke. He has a body trail a mile long."

Tashanira moved to kiss Jenshi again and then got up, heading to the VRC.

Walking onto the *Foundra Ascension*'s shuttle deck, Tashanira saw Neven standing beside a power armor she hadn't seen before. It was slightly larger than the previous models she'd seen him use, but it was nowhere near as large as the BRAS frame he had used during the battle of Neth almost two years ago.

"New toy?" Tashanira asked.

Neven glanced at her and then turned back to his armor. "Something like that."

"Not useful for ship-to-ship combat, though."

"I would have brought the BRAS frame with us if that were possible, but the shuttle isn't capable of storing it."

Tashanira watched Neven silently for a long moment. The normal levity and unchecked optimism she was used to from him were all gone.

"Neven," Tashanira said. "Are you okay?"

Neven's face went hard as he frowned. "I'm fine."

Tashanira caught sight of Ellipse as she walked past in her android body. Ellipse's golden eyes locked onto Tashanira with an intensity that caused her to take a step back. The android was wearing a custom Founder's Elite uniform with the team's logo emblazoned across her shoulder—the grey, white, and gold formfitting jumpsuit revealed a very Human figure. Ellipse stepped up to Neven's side and crossed her arms.

"Okay, everyone. You have your assignments," Lanrete said to the room. "We have a narrow window, so let's get out there. Remember—do not engage Entradis until we have a clear understanding of his ship's capabilities. Tail him and get a scan, but do not engage."

Sounds of acknowledgment went up around the room. Tashanira watched Jessica and Serah'Elax ascend the ramp to their shuttle first, and the ramp sealed behind them.

Tashanira lifted her supply bag and picked up the large case containing her Wopan master arms, or WMAs. She watched Neven as he initiated the loading sequence for his power armor, and the equipment started moving to the shuttle storage bay on a hovering tram. He paid no further attention to the armor and boarded the shuttle without another word. Ellipse was a step behind him.

She frowned, catching sight of Dexter and Erb as the two boarded their shuttle. Dexter flashed her a knowing look and sighed as the ramp closed behind him.

Lanrete approached Tashanira as she stood there, the last remaining person on the deck.

"Is everything all right?" Lanrete asked.

"I don't think so." She looked to Lanrete. "You know Jenshi doesn't think Neven is fit for duty."

"He hasn't filed anything formally, but I picked that up." Lanrete glanced toward the shuttle. "You two have a close relationship, and he trusts you."

"As long as I don't screw it up." Tashanira rubbed the back of her neck. She gave Lanrete a side-eyed glance. "Jenshi has a bone to pick with you, by the way."

"I'm aware." Lanrete turned from Tashanira and started heading toward the meglift. "Bring him home in one piece."

Tashanira laughed. "Of all the times when it would have been nice to have Marcus around, this is definitely one of them."

Lanrete stopped and glanced back at her. The mention of the former super soldier known as an Archlight brought hints of a smile onto his face. "He's also having a hard time. Marcus had known Zun for a while."

"I'm surprised he didn't come out of retirement to hunt Entradis down."

"Oh, he tried to. I refused to let him rejoin."

"That's cold." Tashanira frowned.

"I care more about Marcus living out the rest of his life and enjoying his retirement with his family than I do hurting his feelings." Lanrete put a hand up, waving as he continued toward the meglift.

Tashanira put her hand on her hip, glancing back toward the shuttle. Sighing again, she moved to board as the ramp closed behind her. She made her way to the seat next to Neven, intentionally brushing up against him as she did.

He stopped his systems check and glanced at her. She paid no attention to him and went to work bringing up her station.

"Rude," Ellipse whispered.

Tashanira glanced at the android as she settled into a seat near Neven. "Are we ready to go?" she asked.

"Yes, but first we need to set up boundaries." Neven turned to face Tashanira.

She raised an eyebrow. "Boundaries?"

"Yes. If we're going to be on this shuttle together for some time, we need to have clear boundaries."

"Okay, what are these boundaries?"

"No nudity, no sexual teasing or harassment, and we have to respect each other's personal space."

"Sounds reasonable." She glanced at Ellipse. "I'd also add no androids going insane and murdering us in our sleep."

Ellipse grinned. "I'd never hurt Neven."

"Let's go," Tashanira said.

The shuttle lifted from the deck and flew out of the hatch, jumping to suplight. Within a few minutes, the shuttle blared a warning, highlighting their entrance into the Nex'Rav'Ni corridor. Their suplight drive sounded another alarm as Neven lowered its efficiency to thirty percent. The warning cleared as they got pulled into the corridor's unique gravitational well.

"It will take about a week to reach one of the potential intercept points."

"Might as well get settled then. Man, it's hot in here." Tashanira undid her uniform top and pulled it off, exposing her bare breasts. She got up and started moving toward her supply bag.

Neven's face flushed bright red as he quickly turned away from her and stared at his instrument panel.

"Really?" Ellipse yelled.

"No nudity was the first rule." Neven sighed. "Are you not even going to try to be civil?"

"I am civil. There is nothing uncivil about not wearing a top. You enter any beach, park, or relaxation area in the Huzien Empire, and you'll see nothing but bare breasts. You're just sheltered. And this isn't being nude." She slid the remainder of her uniform off, followed by her skintight leggings, and kicked them to the side of the shuttle. "*This* is being nude." She bent over her bag, exposing her backside to him as she dug through her belongings and pulled out a pair of shorts and a tank top, tail wrapped around her leg.

Neven sucked in a breath and turned around, staring at his console.

She put on the new outfit, closed her bag, and returned to her seat.

Neven opened his mouth and then closed it. With a sigh of frustration, he glanced between her and his instrument panel. "Please use the bathroom to change in the future."

"I'll consider it, but you should get over the whole nudity thing. We'll be stuck in this shuttle together for a while, so we should get extremely comfortable with each other."

Neven gave Tashanira a pleading look.

"Fine." Ellipse's voice was bitter. She stood up and began undressing, her Founder's Elite uniform quickly dropping to the floor. Tashanira's gaze shot to Ellipse, a tinge of jealousy pricking her as she bit her lip. Ellipse's body was perfect in a way that seemed unfair. Ellipse stretched and then stood beside Neven, her hand gently dropping onto his shoulder.

Neven's cheeks flushed red as he glanced from Ellipse to Tashanira, then back to Ellipse.

"I'm not being childish," Ellipse said. "She started it."

Neven rubbed the back of his neck and quickly got out of his chair. He backed away from both Ellipse and Tashanira. His gaze bounced between them before he made a beeline to the bathroom, sealing the door.

Ellipse stared at the door for a moment, her gaze curious. Her cheeks flushed as her eyes went wide. "Oh . . ." She glanced to Tashanira and then slowly moved back toward her clothes. "That was a bit too much," she whispered.

"What?" Tashanira glanced at the bathroom and then at Ellipse. Ellipse made a quick jerking motion with her hand and then quickly pulled her uniform back on. "No! He's not . . . ?" She silently crept up to the door and tried to listen through it. After a few moments, her eyes widened as she suddenly stepped back with a hand over her mouth. She walked back toward Ellipse with a smirk on her face.

"Oh, he's thinking about you," Ellipse mouthed.

Tashanira balked. "Does he . . . think about me often?" She rubbed her arm. Ellipse bit her lip. "But what about Zun?"

"He mostly thinks of Zun, but he has a pretty good mental image of you too."

"How many times a week . . . of me?"

"On average?"

"*Vusg* me. There's an average?"

"There's an average."

"I don't want to know. Never mind." Tashanira shuddered. "That's disturbing, actually." She walked away from Ellipse and sat down in her seat, suddenly numb.

Ascension Shuttle One *en route to lookout point, Nex'Rav'Ni corridor*

Tashanira began to undress near her bunk, stripping down to nothing. She hesitated for a moment and glanced at Neven, who was still at the controls, focusing on sensor readouts.

Ellipse was watching her, clearly waiting to see what she decided to do.

Tashanira glanced down at her body and then back up at Neven. *What am I doing?*

She took in a deep breath and then pulled on a robe. She left it open in the front and walked toward Neven, resting a hand on his shoulder as she leaned forward to see what he was looking at.

He glanced at her, his gaze catching on her fluff of black pubic hair before he glanced down at the ground and then back at the readings.

Tashanira leaned down to position her lips near his ear. "Ellipse told me about your masturbation habits," she whispered.

Neven's body became rigid, and his breathing stopped.

She leaned in closer, brushing his ear with her lips. She hesitated, a voice inside her screaming as she caught herself and backed away. She tied her robe and then retreated to her bunk. Tashanira broke into a cold sweat as she sat on her bed.

She glanced up at Ellipse, who was staring at Neven with a look of dread.

Biting her lip, Tashanira quickly got under the covers and turned away from them both, shutting off her mind.

CHAPTER 7 - ELLIPSE

Ascension Shuttle One *en route to lookout point,*
Nex'Rav'Ni Corridor

*I*t was a mistake, Ellipse said in Neven's mind. *An accident.*

Why would you tell her something so personal? My thoughts are my own! Neven shouted in his head.

I'm sorry.

You just made this mission exponentially harder for me. Neven sighed. *Now she's going to think I'm constantly fantasizing about her.*

But you are.

That's not the point, he said. *Men sometimes fantasize about women, but we don't act on it, and we sure don't tell them.*

Ellipse sighed. *Just fantasize about me.* She got up, undressed again, then moved to straddle Neven. *No one will get upset, and no one will get hurt.*

Neven stared at Ellipse incredulously. *Your body isn't real, Ellipse.*

Ellipse scowled. She reached down, undid Neven's zipper, and stroked his member.

He gripped her wrist. *What are you doing?*

I'm showing you just how real this body is. Ellipse's voice was bitter. *I've made a significant number of enhancements to the original design.* She pushed Neven back in the chair with her other hand, using her cybernetic strength to break his grip. She continued stroking him.

He leaned back in his chair, unsure. His eyes scanned her body, catching on subtle signs he hadn't noticed before, hinting at the breadth of changes Ellipse had performed on herself.

Ellipse nodded at his thoughts. *I have full sense of touch with a new form of responsive flesh. It's similar in form and function to Human flesh, without the weaknesses and inefficiencies.*

Neven stared, dumbfounded. *That's fringe research. The best minds at the MinSci are decades away from that technology.*

Ellipse's golden eyes sparkled, a look of assured confidence radiating from her that reminded him immediately of Zun.

It all clicked in his head. *Oh Maker, you integrated Zun's mannerisms into your personality engine, even down to how she used to straddle me like this.*

Don't think about that. Ellipse repositioned herself and then moved her hand, her hips descending.

Neven's eyes went wide. He moved his hands to her hips, stopping her motion. He could feel her insides—it was familiar, sorely missed, and very Human. He released her hips, dropping his arms to the sides.

Ellipse gave him one of Zun's looks—identical to the subtle facial cues that were uniquely her—as she sheathed him inside her.

"How?" Neven gasped.

Ellipse locked gazes with Neven and moved her hips. Her arms went around his neck as she leaned forward and kissed him.

Neven closed his eyes and let the memory play out exactly as it had happened with Zun on their return to the *Foundra Ascension* in this same shuttle months ago.

He wrapped his arms around her body, and Ellipse melted in his embrace. She continued kissing him, Neven pulling her closer as the chair reclined backward. She put her hands on his chest and pushed herself up.

Ellipse prodded him with mental urgings, willing him to touch her breasts. He did. Ellipse dialed up her pleasure sensors, a flood of sensations drowning her SSI core as she gasped and then moaned loudly. She dialed the sensations back, realizing what she had just done. But Neven was so dialed into the moment that he didn't seem to care about the outburst.

Ellipse glanced in Tashanira's direction to see the Uri staring at them with a surprised smirk. With a slight huff, Ellipse glanced back down at Neven and dialed the pleasure sensors up to the maximum; the flood again overwhelmed her.

Neven gasped as he throbbed inside of her, both lost in the moment.

Afterward, Ellipse pressed herself hard into Neven as he held her. She prompted her body to simulate heavy breathing, mirroring Neven's current state.

She glanced at Tashanira, but the other woman had turned away from them.

Tashanira stepped out of the bathroom, sporting the same robe as the prior night, and again she kept it fully open. She walked over to her bed and slid it off haughtily, dropping it onto the sheets. She took her time dressing.

Ellipse could sense Neven's desire to turn around and watch her. He glanced in Ellipse's direction and then looked down at the ground before returning to the holodisplay.

"Are we going to talk about you two *vusging* last night?" Tashanira's voice was awkwardly loud.

Neven remained silent, his attention entirely on the holodisplay.

"What is there to talk about?" Ellipse asked. "Neven said my body wasn't real, so I showed him how real it was."

"Is that all?" Tashanira laughed. "You sound like my sister. She once *vusged* someone to win an argument."

"Can we talk about something else?" Neven interjected.

"Sure." Tashanira glanced at Neven. "What part of my body makes you come the quickest when you masturbate thinking about me?"

Neven paled as a silence descended over the shuttle.

"I should have never told you that," Ellipse said. "Men fantasize about women all the time. You just aren't supposed to know about it."

"Not helping," Neven said.

Tashanira slid into her chair next to Neven. She turned sideways, facing him. "Come on, tell me. You at least owe me that much," she said. "Is it my breasts?"

Ellipse put her hand to her neck—Neven's thoughts were chaotic, and he wanted to be anywhere but there. She could feel a sickening sense of dread wash over him.

"Maybe it's my butt? Or my tail? Do you have a thing for tails?" Tashanira leaned closer toward Neven, a mischievous smile on her face. "Is it my ears? Or maybe it's my fur in general. Does the fur turn you on?"

Neven sank into his chair, his breath catching in his throat.

"It *is* the fur!"

"Leave him alone," Ellipse said.

"*Vusg* that! My fur turns Neven on." Tashanira got up out of her chair and headed back toward her bag. She pulled out her training outfit and quickly changed her clothes. Moving back to her seat, she slid back in the chair with a wide smile. She wore a sports bra and short shorts, revealing almost all her fur.

Neven glanced over at her and then sank even further into his chair. "I need to get off this ship," Neven whispered.

CHAPTER 8 - TASHANIRA YEN UNVESAL

Ascension Shuttle One *patrolling near lookout point,*
Nex'Rav'Ni Corridor

Tashanira ran through a series of exercises, although the small confines of the ship prevented her from doing her routine. She had to drop the full set of acrobatics and sprinting she was accustomed to, adopting more floor work and endurance training.

She was sitting against the wall beside her bunk, breathing hard. Her gaze was locked on Neven. She had her top off and a towel wrapped around her neck.

"We should run through a set of combat exercises," Tashanira said. "It's been a while since your last session."

Neven glanced back at her and then quickly away, shaking his head. "I'm good, thanks."

Tashanira grinned, knowing that her casual nudity over the past few days made Neven uncomfortable. "*Vusging* Ellipse every night doesn't count as exercise."

Neven hung his head, glancing briefly at Ellipse.

The android touched the back of her neck. "We can do some more intensive positions if that will help."

Tashanira laughed.

Neven suddenly perked up and peered intently at a nearby holodisplay.

"What is it?" Tashanira frowned and got up, moving closer to Neven.

Ellipse did likewise, her eyes becoming distant. "An Enesmic anomaly. . ." she said.

"Like Sagren's rift?" Tashanira's face grew serious.

"Far more powerful but structurally different." Neven leaned closer to the holodisplay. "I've never seen readings like this."

"There's also some type of spatial anomaly. Massive in size," Ellipse said.

"They are feeding off of each other." Neven's voice was filled with awe.

"Is this why the Nex'Rav'Ni corridor is the way it is?

"Maybe, but there would have to be more of these all along the corridor to explain it fully."

"Do you think this is the work of those Eshgren who escaped from Ashnali? The ones brought here by Sephan?"

"No . . . this corridor has always existed. It was originally identified by the Das'Vin when they were still the only space faring species."

"Should we investigate?" Ellipse asked.

Neven shook his head. "No, our mission is to find Entradis. Exploration will have to wait."

Tashanira felt a powerful urge to get ready. It was an instinct bordering on the supernatural that she had learned to trust over the years. Whenever she ignored it in the past, bad things happened.

She grabbed her Founder's Elite uniform and headed into the bathroom, hopping into the VRC. Refreshed, she suited up and walked out to see Neven and Ellipse sporting their uniforms, having taken their cue from her.

"A feeling?" Neven asked.

Tashanira nodded. "A feeling."

A warning blared as they all turned to the primary holodisplay. It showcased a blip on a zoomed-out view of the Nex'Rav'Ni corridor, highlighting the section of space closest to them.

"Suplight signature of Entradis's ship detected," the SI voice of the shuttle announced.

Neven rushed to his console as Tashanira scrambled to bring up shields and weapons systems.

"Moving to intercept," Neven said.

"What are you doing? We are only to scan from a range, not engage."

Neven ignored her.

Tashanira brought up another holodisplay, scanning the readout of Entradis's ship that populated on the screen. "We're getting too close. From this range he'll be able to identify us."

Neven continued his intercept course as Tashanira tried to override his controls. He was too fast for her, locking her out of navigation.

A warning blared, the shuttle finishing its detailed scan.

"*Vusg*," Tashanira said. "We're no match for that."

Neven glanced over at Tashanira's holodisplay as he caught sight of the detailed readout. He pulled up another holodisplay next to him with the same information. His eyes went wide before narrowing.

"We've got to run now," Tashanira said.

"We can beat him," Neven said.

Tashanira's face paled as she stared at Neven. He pushed the tactical controls to her holodisplay, and she stared at them in a daze. "You're going to get us killed."

"If you don't help, you're right." Neven glanced back at Tashanira, the look on his face distorted, filled with rage.

"Neven . . ." Ellipse said.

Tashanira took a deep breath and faced her console, taking control of the weapon systems. Both ships dropped out of suplight.

Entradis's ship opened with a barrage of weaponsfire that streaked across their shields. Tashanira returned fire with a flurry of blasts that seemed to do little to Entradis's shields.

"He just launched four antimatter missiles." Tashanira gasped. "Evasive maneuvers!"

"Anti-missile defense system online," the shuttle SI broadcasted.

Four-point defense beams shot out from the shuttle at the missiles, detonating them prematurely. Tashanira fired missiles in response, but Entradis' point defense system caught them. She followed that up with a string of more blaster fire, the shots peppering Entradis's ship. He returned fire, this time with a set of missiles that accelerated to suplight speeds—they hit the shuttle with a force that sent it spinning, its shields flickering.

Neven struggled to bring the shuttle back under control. Ellipse strapped herself into her seat, the internal dampeners fluctuating briefly.

"Suplight missiles." Tashanira breathed. "Neven, please. We must run. Those will tear us apart."

His eyes widened as the reality of their situation seemed to finally hit him. "Getting us out of here!" he yelled.

He turned the shuttle and engaged suplight. Entradis fired two more missiles that entered suplight and started to chase down their shuttle. Due to their size and mass, the missiles rapidly outpaced the shuttle, catching up with them with a breathtaking set of explosions that knocked them out of suplight.

Neven gasped as he struggled to bring the suplight drive back online.

"Those last missiles took out our shields completely," Tashanira said. "We must hide. Entradis is right behind us. Suplight missiles are too fast for our anti-missile defense system."

"I'm aware."

"You didn't *seem* aware when you initially saw the scans from his ship and decided to engage him anyway," Tashanira snapped back.

Neven angled the ship and released a decoy drone into suplight before he re-engaged their suplight systems at an alternate heading. "There was a planet near the anomalies. The distortions are probably strong enough to hide our signature."

"He's firing again!" Tashanira yelled.

"He went after the decoy." Neven glanced at the holodisplay as the decoy blipped out.

"He's changing course."

All three watched the holodisplay as Entradis's ship matched their course.

"He just launched more suplight missiles!"

The suplight missiles took some additional time to catch up. Tashanira attempted to fire the missile defense system in a predictive attack pattern that caught one of the missiles successfully. The other one slammed into their suplight drive, the impact kicking them out of suplight and into another spin that caused Neven, Ellipse, and Tashanira to hold on for dear life. The dampeners were failing further in the explosion.

Neven frantically sought to regain control, but the engines were severely damaged. "Armor compensators are critical!"

"We've lost the suplight drive," Ellipse said.

"Give me flight controls!" Tashanira yelled. "Neven, get that drive back online."

Neven immediately transferred control to Tashanira as he brought up a ship diagnostic and went to work alongside Ellipse. Emergency drones deployed inside and outside the ship, scrambling to assess and repair the damage.

Entradis's ship dropped out of suplight after them.

"*Vusg! Vusg! Vusg!* Hold on!" Tashanira spun the shuttle around, firing two missiles and unleashing another barrage of weaponsfire. She unloaded with everything they had, attempting to distract Entradis for as long as possible.

"Suplight drive is barely functional. I can give us a single burst, but we'll most likely lose the drive . . . if not explode," Neven said.

"Good enough."

Tashanira opened the weapon storage bay and ejected all their missiles, leaving a field of live armaments between them and Entradis. They spun and began to converge on Entradis's ship at a fraction of their launch speed.

Spinning the shuttle back around, she adjusted their direction and manually re-engaged the suplight drive. Turbulence violently shook the shuttle as both held on for dear life. Before Entradis could engage his suplight, Tashanira triggered all the launched armaments.

They exploded in a blinding display behind them.

Tashanira held her breath, glancing at the holodisplay readout. The blip showing Entradis's shuttle was still there, and it was back on their trail. Letting out a frustrated yell, she glanced over at Neven.

His eyes went wide.

"Crap!" Ellipse yelled.

The blast door to the cockpit sealed as the suplight drive exploded. The detonation sent them into a hard spin that knocked them out of suplight for a third time. The shuttle rolled violently as it broke into the atmosphere of a nearby planet.

Deathly silence filled the cabin as Tashanira stared at Neven. Emergency illumination was their only light source as they locked eyes.

"Controls aren't responding." Tashanira had an unnatural calm in her voice.

Neven nodded.

"Inertial dampers are gone, reactor's offline, and battery reserves are also gone. I think the cells were destroyed in the explosion. We have no power," Ellipse said.

"We're going to die." The finality of Tashanira's statement caused Neven to suck in a breath.

Ellipse glanced up at them, her golden eyes illuminating the cabin. Neven's eyes went wide as he started frantically looking around. He caught sight of a panel under the control station and kicked at it. The pressure plate came open as it dropped away.

"Get out of your seats, now!" Neven said.

Tashanira recognized what he was doing and unbuckled herself, moving to stand near him. Ellipse followed a heartbeat behind. Neven got out of the seat and pressed the button as hydraulics unleashed heavy foam from the ceiling and floor, lifting them all and suspending them away from hard surfaces.

The shuttle slammed into the surface of the planet. Tashanira heard a loud explosion even through the warmth of the emergency foam cocooning her body. She was jolted slightly but remained unharmed as the foam absorbed the kinetic energy from the impact.

Almost immediately, the foam began to dissipate, evaporating into breathable air.

Tashanira pushed herself up from the mangled floor of the shuttle cockpit and felt around in the darkness. "Is anyone there? Please tell me you're still alive."

"I'm here," Neven responded.

"S-s-s-same," Ellipse said, her voice distorted.

Tashanira felt her way through the crumpled mess toward Neven's voice. Her hand contacted warm flesh, and she pulled him close, hugging him and laughing. "You *vusging* genius. You saved our lives," Tashanira said. She then punched him in the shoulder. "After risking them in the first place!"

"The ship has to be pretty badly damaged for there to be no emergency lights." Neven rubbed his shoulder.

"If it's still th-th-there, lights are under the c-c-center console," Ellipse said.

Neven and Tashanira clung to each other and slowly made their way to where they thought the center console might be, feeling around for remnants of their prior cockpit.

"Here!" Tashanira tapped a device as a bright light filled the cockpit with artificial daylight.

They glanced around at the carnage. Ellipse was prone on the floor with a large hole going through her side. A crumpled mass of metal was lodged in the wall behind her, and some fluid dripped from the damaged area of her body.

"Oh, no!" Neven quickly moved to her.

"I-I-I'm fine." Ellipse smiled wearily. "I t-t-turned off all s-s-sensory receptors. I d-d-don't feel anything."

Neven looked frantically at the injury and started pacing. "This is my fault. I'm so sorry."

"Help me pick her up off the floor," Tashanira ordered.

Neven nodded, wrapping his arms around Ellipse as both gently lifted her. They guided her to the wall and rested her there in a sitting position.

Ellipse's eyes flickered, her body going limp for a second before returning to normal. "I-I-I've switched to my e-e-emergency power core. The p-p-primary has been damaged. Multiple s-s-systems failure. SSI core u-u-unstable."

Neven let out a long sigh, collapsing on the floor in front of Ellipse.

Tashanira walked around the remains of the cockpit. "Please tell me this planet is habitable."

Neven shook his head. "It's an average surface temperature of negative two hundred degrees. We're on an ice planet."

Tashanira laughed bitterly. "Maybe we should have just died on impact. Now we'll freeze to death."

"I can fix this," Neven said. "I used to build reactors from junk growing up, remember?"

Tashanira gave Neven an incredulous look. "I need a moment." She took a deep breath, closed her eyes as she dropped to the floor, and crossed her legs, sitting with her back straight in a meditative pose. She shut out the world, tried calming her mind, and processed everything that had just happened.

Neven silently watched her while rubbing the back of his neck. He returned his attention to Ellipse and began inspecting the damage to her android shell.

Tashanira eventually opened her eyes, having gone into a deep state of meditation that bordered on sleep. She noticed piles of equipment and supplies now all around her. She also noticed that the temperature in the cockpit had dropped substantially, to the point where she could now see her breath.

Getting up, she caught sight of Ellipse with her eyes dimmed, her gaze off into space. Cords were running into her side, and open toolkits were beside her. She followed the cords to an open hatch near the side of the cockpit with spools of cords coming out of it, connected to different controls and systems that had been taken apart or opened.

Glancing in, she saw Neven working on the power armor he had brought with them.

"What's all this?" Tashanira said.

Neven jolted at the sound of her voice, seeming to break out of a trance. Glancing up at her, he rubbed the back of his neck and looked around.

"I'm hooking up the systems in the shuttle to the power core of my armor. It should provide enough consistent power output to sustain life support and the heating systems, with infrequent use of other systems we can salvage."

"What's wrong with Ellipse? Was the damage severe?" Tashanira asked.

Neven sighed. "She's helping power the ship."

"Is that safe?"

Neven glanced around with a shrug. "None of this is safe."

"How bad does our situation look?"

He hesitated. "I brought up a few scanners to get an idea of what remained intact on the shuttle and where we crash-landed."

"Well?"

"The cockpit and half of the storage bay is all that remains. Everything else is gone: no engines, no suplight drive, no communications array . . . I built a makeshift array, but the anomalies are working against us. We came here to hide from Entradis, but that means we'll also end up hiding from anyone looking to rescue us."

"Any signs of Entradis?"

Neven shook his head. "From his viewpoint, our suplight drive exploded and us along with it. Even if he tried to scan the planet's surface, his sensors would be unreliable this close to the anomalies."

"What are our supplies looking like?"

"One thermal sleeping bag, two thermal blankets, two months of rations, and a few more emergency lights."

"How much longer until we have the heating system back up? It's freezing in here."

"That's complicated." Neven sighed. "I powered the heating system, but it's at a reduced level given the energy drain on the power cores. Their outputs weren't designed for the demand typically required of shuttle systems. I didn't want to risk overtaxing the cores and draining them, so I reduced the efficiency of the heating systems."

"What does that mean?"

"It will still be very cold in here, but we won't freeze to death. Although it will take a couple of hours before we start seeing any impact on the temperature."

"Are the bunks still intact?"

"Everything past the blast door is gone, including the living quarters and our personal effects."

"So, we can't even layer up. . ." Tashanira glanced back at the single thermal sleeping bag. "We'll most likely have to share the sleeping bag to stay warm while we wait for the temperature to rise. I can already feel early signs of hypothermia. We're not dressed properly for this." She glanced back at Neven. "And I at least have fur to help fight off some of the cold, which means you are in more danger than I am."

Neven furrowed his brow. "Lanrete will come looking for us after two failed check-ins, which gives us four days before they start a search for us. If they start from our last check-in, they will detect our suplight trail and should be able to follow it to this planet in four to five days."

"Be serious." Tashanira rubbed her eyes and let out a sigh. "We'll be sleeping on the cockpit floor with one sleeping bag for at least a week and a half before anyone could realistically pick us up." She glared at Neven. "I blame you for all of this."

Neven got up and started to climb out of the cramped storage bay. Tashanira stepped back as Neven pulled himself up and stood before her.

"About that . . ." Neven walked over to the last functional holodisplay. He brought up sensor readings from the anomalies. "I've been observing something about the interplay between the anomalies, and I've discovered. . . Well, you know how Brime said time moved differently on the Enesmic plane? How just a few weeks for her were months for us back here in our plane of existence?"

"Yes . . ." Tashanira's voice was wary.

"This planet is caught in an interplay between the spatial and Enesmic anomalies. It . . . It's having the opposite effect."

Tashanira slowly backed up into the wall, collapsing to the floor. "What does that mean?"

"It means that time moves faster here than it does in normal space."

"How much faster?"

"That's hard to say, but based on astronomical data compared against auto-snapshots taken of the surrounding stars compared with the data I've captured in the short time we've been here . . ." Neven hesitated. "A week in normal space is roughly equivalent to three months here."

Tashanira's mouth dropped open, her eyes going distant.

"I'm sorry." Neven glanced away from her.

He was shivering uncontrollably now, a thought that finally registered with Tashanira. She got up and moved to him. She wrapped her arms around him, attempting to warm him up.

"When I saw Entradis's ship, a blind rage overtook me. I've never felt anything like that before." Neven shook his head. "And because of that blind rage, Ellipse is hurt, and we're trapped between anomalies in a time flux that will most likely result in us dying before anyone can reach us."

"Love the optimism."

"I find it hard to be optimistic anymore." Neven rested his head against Tashanira's. "I've had everything taken from me, Tash," Neven whispered.

"You're still alive, you have your health, and you have friends who care about you."

"Zun is dead. Ellipse is in a catatonic state. I can't even talk to her through my mobi. The distortions are messing with her SSI core. I'm all alone."

"I'm here." Tashanira forced Neven to look into her eyes. "I'm here with you. We'll get through this together. I promise." She brought up Neven's uniform sensor readout in her mobi. "But right now we need to get you warm. Your core temperature has dropped to dangerous levels."

She led Neven to the thermal sleeping bag. Stripping off her uniform, she did the same to him and guided him into the sleeping bag. She got behind him, wrapped her arms around him, and spooned his body. The two lay there for a long moment, neither saying a word as Tashanira listened to Neven's breathing.

Neven eventually stopped shivering, Tashanira's warmth bringing his body temperature back up as the two fell asleep.

Remnants of Ascension Shuttle One *on Ni3891,*
Nex'Rav'Ni Corridor
Week 3

Neven cradled Tashanira in his arms as they crossed the threshold to a luxurious bedroom. She smiled at him as he kissed down her neck. She relished his touch, the moment building with passion until Neven gently laid Tashanira down on a massive bed.

The sun was setting in the distance, with gold furnishings all around the room. Rose petals littered the floor, and candles illuminated more of the room as the light outside faded.

Opening herself to him, Tashanira moaned as Neven licked her ear. She wanted to experience him fully, all at peace, while everything was perfect.

Tashanira woke with a bad headache, groaning loudly as reality hit her. They had been sleeping on the floor of the cockpit for three weeks. The cockpit temperature fluctuated daily, heavily influenced by the outside temperature. The heating system struggled at its reduced efficiency to keep them safely warm on some days.

Out of nowhere, her senses started screaming at her, telling her that something was very wrong. She frantically looked around, trying to ascertain what was triggering the reaction.

Neven looked up at Tashanira with a confused expression on his face. "What's wrong?" Neven asked.

She eyed him for a moment, still feeling heated from her dream. Pushing down the confusing rush of emotions she got when looking at Neven, she sighed. "I don't know. My senses . . . it's like that time when I was attacked by an Enesmic assassin on Pree. It's gone now, but . . ." Tashanira rubbed her eyes.

"There are other Eshgren out there. Maybe one found us." He shrugged. "Guess they realized we were goners and decided to leave us alone."

"Yeah." She watched Neven for a long moment, a desire so strong rising in her that she was surprised by it. Tashanira suppressed it, letting out a slow breath as she forced herself to think of Jenshi— of how he was likely out there looking for her. Her gaze grew more intense as she fought a battle of wills with her subconscious, a scowl dominating her features.

Neven looked at her and then quickly glanced away with a terrified expression.

Tashanira watched him as he tinkered with a small container, the innards filled with technology she only had a loose understanding of. Whatever he was working on looked clunky, not as polished as some of the other projects she'd seen in his lab back on the *Foundra Ascension*.

Tashanira tugged at her skintight Founder's Elite uniform. It was dirty and worn but still functional. Now in survival mode, the internal systems were recycling water from waste and sweat with armies of nanites constantly at work. She closed her eyes and fell back onto the sleeping bag with a frustrated groan. She sat back up and glared at Neven. This was his fault—both how she felt and their situation. She took a deep breath and held it for a few seconds, letting it out slowly.

She repeated the cycle for a few minutes and then forced a smile. "How is it looking?"

He stopped and then glanced back at her. His gaze lingered on her chest for a moment before coming up to meet her eyes. She realized he had been doing that much more often as of late.

A wild thought to strip popped into her mind. Inhale . . . exhale . . . suppressed.

"I'm going to need to do another salvage run to try and find more things to work with." Neven let out a sigh. "I don't have the right insulating materials to contain the reaction. I could turn it on, but we'd have a bomb at that point."

"Maybe that's our best option." Tashanira stared at the container. "It would be quick, right?"

"So now we want to commit suicide?" Neven frowned. "It's only been three weeks. We still have nine weeks before we can consider being rescued, but I don't think we need to be that desperate yet."

"That's assuming they are as quick to search for and find us as you think." Tashanira glanced back to Neven. "How do they even know to look at this planet? Maybe they think we're drifting somewhere in space and doing a sweep. That could take months, depending on the search radius." Tashanira glanced down at the ground. "We don't have months of real time."

"Then what are we supposed to do? Just give up?"

"*Vusg* of a time to get your optimism back."

Neven let out an exasperated sigh and got up, moving to sit next to Tashanira. Her gaze met Neven's. His closeness excited her, but she tried hard to hide those emotions.

"I'm sorry for getting us into this situation."

"You can stop apologizing to me," Tashanira said. "I forgave you a week ago, remember?" His lips were kissable at that moment. She found all her attention consumed by them.

"I know. I just . . ." Neven began to tear up. "I'm just starting to believe that you're right." He glanced at the small reactor. "I figured if I could boost our power output, we'd be able to have more reliable heat. Maybe we could even try sending off a probe." He rubbed his eyes. "If we can get something off the ground, we could have it broadcast an emergency beacon with coordinates to find us faster."

Tashanira realized she wasn't the only one on the cusp of a mental breakdown. That realization caused her military training to kick in; she immediately started refocusing on their priorities. "We should drop down to half rations, which will give us another two-and-a-half months of food. It won't be great, and we'll have to do more to conserve body heat, but it's our best course of action."

Neven nodded. He looked over to Tashanira and locked eyes with her. They sat in silence for a long moment, neither breaking eye contact.

Tashanira tilted her head to the side. "What are your thoughts on dreams?" she blurted.

Neven raised an eyebrow and then rubbed the back of his neck. He did everything in that moment to avoid eye contact with her. "What specifically about them?"

"I remember this historical psychologist from school, Telanre, I think? He used to go on and on about how dreams are the purest manifestation of our subconscious and that they speak our deepest, darkest thoughts to us. That they show us our true desires . . ." Tashanira tilted her head to the other side. She looked at Neven's lips again and bit her own. "Dreams bring to life who we really are."

"Dreams are our unconscious minds without the restraint of responsibility or morality." Neven rested his face in his hands. "It's best to ignore them."

"I saw you looking at my chest earlier. What have you been dreaming about?" Tashanira raised an eyebrow.

Neven shook his head and got up. He moved back to his reactor project and went back to work.

Tashanira watched him silently, her gaze never leaving him as she let out another slow breath. She touched her temple and winced. Her headache was growing stronger, and the pain was almost unbearable.

Tashanira frowned and closed her eyes, going back to her meditative techniques.

Week 10

The sound of Neven picking up a ration brought Tashanira back to reality. She opened her eyes. A check of her mobi told her that she had been meditating most of the day.

Both their mobis were set up next to a repaired holodisplay that fed them wireless power to keep them charged. The mobis were their only reliable form of communication in case someone was in orbit and sent out a broadcast. They could reply through the relay built into Neven's power armor, as it was the only one on the planet.

"Time to eat," Neven said. He triggered the self-heating function of the ration bag and handed it to her.

She waited until it changed color and then tore open the top. It was a protein mush filled with all the essential nutrients and carbohydrates to give her body the fuel it needed to survive another day. Each pack was a surprise flavor—this one tasted like cinnamon-sweet oatmeal.

Neven sat down next to her and then locked eyes with her. His own widened. "Are you okay?"

"What?"

"Your eyes—there are red circles around the irises. I've never seen that before."

"Oh . . ." Tashanira subconsciously reached up to touch her temple. "Hormones. It must be the stress." She glanced away from him, avoiding eye contact. "Nothing to worry about."

She took half of the ration packet and handed the rest to Neven as they ate silently for a few minutes. Tashanira silently watched the floor. The dreams had become more explicit, showing

Tashanira making love to Neven in more exotic locations and situations every night. Even now, she could almost feel how he gently held her, his thrusts going deep and filling her with electricity. The sweat of his body as they intermingled . . .

Vusg, this was growing impossible. She wanted to strip and mount him right then and there. She felt her hand move to the release strap on her top and stopped herself at the last moment.

"Neven, tell me," Tashanira blurted out.

Neven glanced from the remnants of his ration to her.

"Do you need . . ." Tashanira rubbed the back of her neck. "Are you . . ." She sighed. "Never mind."

"Is everything okay?" Neven hesitated. "I mean outside of the obvious of us being trapped in a shuttle with moderate probability of rescue."

She tilted her head to the side and rested it on an arm, her eyes locking with his. They held eye contact for a long moment, pushing past the uncomfortable intensity of it. She could see the desire there; the masking of it had been so well hidden, but it was there in that moment, plain as day.

Tashanira smiled, and half closed her eyes. "Everything . . . is fine."

Later that night, they huddled together in the sleeping bag. As usual, Tashanira spooned Neven—same as they had for every night since they went down to half rations.

She listened to him breathe and gently rubbed his stomach. She caressed him slowly for a long time, her hand slowly finding its way down to his crotch area.

An erection greeted her.

She hesitated. *What am I doing? This isn't right.*

She moved her hand to his thigh and rubbed near the inside, her fingers brushing against his erection with each pass.

Neven stirred, but his breathing signaled that he was still fast asleep.

She continued rubbing his thigh and then caught herself as his body started responding. She subtly removed her hand and moved it back to his stomach. Her mind was spinning, and she silently cursed herself. Why had she done that?

Neven's hand touched hers as he guided her to his erection. The breath caught in her throat as her hand settled on his penis. Neven took in a deep breath, and Tashanira began stroking him.

He gently turned around to look her in the eyes. "Are you sure you want to do this?" Neven asked.

"*Vusg*, yes," Tashanira blurted. "I mean . . . I don't think we'll make it out of this alive, and I am horny as *vusg*, so . . ." She rolled her eyes. "Unless you don't want this—don't want me. I . . . I don't want to force you into anything you don't want." She removed her hand and pulled it back to her side.

Neven kissed her. It was a subtle kiss, light and exploratory. She pressed her body against him and reciprocated the kiss, her hand returning to his erection. Neven caressed her butt as she picked up speed on his erection.

She felt him getting into it, about to climax, and then pulled back. "Oh no, I'm not letting you come yet," Tashanira said playfully. "If we're going to do this, I'm going to do it right."

Tashanira moved to straddle him, holding herself above his erection before gently descending on him. She was soaked in anticipation and smothered the part of her brain that was yelling at her to stop. The moment she felt Neven inside her, a sickening feeling welled up in her stomach. She pushed it down and started to move, gently rocking back and forth, her eyes half closed as she watched Neven under her.

His gaze was stuck on her breasts, fully in the moment. She pushed out her chest and continued in her rocking motion. She felt Neven's member pulse inside her, but she didn't stop. She had come this far, and she was going to finish.

She leaned in closer to Neven and started moving her hips in a faster rocking motion. Neven groaned as their breathing picked up pace. Tashanira felt the climax coming, building like a wave. It washed over her. With a throaty moan, she collapsed onto Neven's chest and spasmed.

He wrapped his arms around her as the enormity of what she had just done hit her. It plowed into her like a typhoon—the illusion of the dream shattered, reality coming in hard as her mind immediately went to Jenshi.

She started to cry.

CHAPTER 9 - NEVEN KENK

Remnants of Ascension Shuttle One *on Ni3891,*
Nex'Rav'Ni Corridor
Week 10

Neven gasped as he released inside of Tashanira. He dropped his head back and stared at the ceiling of the wrecked shuttle as Tashanira leaned forward and accelerated her rocking movements. He could hear her enjoying herself; her not-so-subtle vocalizations were overwhelming him.

He closed his eyes and felt an unbearable amount of shame. He tried to imagine Zun on top of him—tried to replace the sensations he was feeling with the image of her in his memory. But that image quickly shifted to Ellipse, her golden gaze entrancing.

Excitement stirred inside him. Was that desire?

Tashanira's voice got louder and deeper, and he could hear her climaxing. He took in a sharp breath as she collapsed onto his chest. He reflexively brought his arms up to hold her, pulling her tight as she spasmed on top of him.

She started to cry softly. At the sound, Neven was unable to stop his tears. He sobbed with her in silence. *What did I just do? This* woman wasn't his wife—she was someone else's partner.

He let out a heavy sigh as his body shuddered. "I'm sorry," Neven said.

"No," Tashanira responded immediately with a haughty voice. "We *vusged* because we're trapped in this death box with no one coming to save us. We have nothing else to do. *Vusging* makes sense as a way to pass the time and stay warm. There is nothing wrong about this."

Neven got the impression that she was trying to convince herself as much as him. She turned over and rested on her back on top of Neven. She put her knees up and rested her feet outside Neven's hips, coming down slightly to allow her butt to rest right over his crotch area. His member gently pressed up against her backside. She grabbed his arms and pulled them over her stomach, holding them there as she stared at the ceiling.

"On some level, I've always wanted to *vusg* you," she said. "Just like you've always wanted to *vusg* me, I'm sure. At least we have an excuse now, one with no consequences."

"What about Jenshi?"

"What about him?"

"This doesn't feel at all wrong to you?" Neven's voice had an edge in it.

"*Vusg* you." Tashanira turned her head slightly, angled up toward his. "The last thing I wanted to do was cheat on Jenshi. You have no idea how hard I have worked to stay committed to that relationship over the years. I grew up in a *luraim* where it was socially acceptable to do what we just did, even if I was in a serious relationship." Tashanira hesitated. Her gaze went distant. "But I . . . I broke out of that, and I've been mostly faithful to Jenshi throughout our relationship." Her words lowered to almost a whisper. She glanced back at him. It was hard to read her eyes.

"What do you want me to say?"

Tashanira's eyes flashed, causing Neven to tense. She took a deep breath and turned around, fully facing him, the motion causing him to wince as she pressed against his flaccid member.

Neven didn't know how to respond as Tashanira glared at him with a burning irritability.

They sat there in silence, the sounds of their breathing mixing with the low hum of the heating system. Tashanira moved back into a sitting position on top of his pelvis. She straightened her back, her posture perfect as she loomed over him like a goddess statue. His gaze traced all the curves of her body for a moment before returning to her eyes. He tried to hold in an erection creeping its way back up. He failed.

Tashanira tilted her head to the side and let out a huff.

Neven broke her gaze and stared up at the ceiling of the mangled cockpit. "I'm sorry. I mean . . . for saying I'm sorry." Neven shook his head, letting out a sigh. "Your friendship is important to me, and I feel like what we're doing right now throws all of that out of the window. You'll hate me for what we've done after you've had time to process it."

Tashanira took in a deep breath and looked away from Neven toward Ellipse. The android was still in the same place, her eyes dimly lit. "That may be true," Tashanira said, looking back down at Neven. "But if we make decisions in our lives afraid of the infinite 'what could happens' while ignoring the present reality, is that a life worth living?"

"I was raised with a set of morals . . ." Neven hesitated. "Morals that would incline me to say that if we go against our better nature—against who we are at our core—then, no, that isn't a life worth living."

"What do you believe now that you've experienced the real world?"

"I don't know." Neven smiled sadly. "I did everything right and have nothing to show for it."

Tashanira's head rolled to the side as she sighed, her eyes softening. She moved off Neven and took his hands, moving him into a position over her.

"Let's take your mind off that," she said.

She guided him in, pulling him closer as Neven responded positively, leaning in with his face poised above hers. He stared into her eyes as she kissed him and wrapped her legs around him.

Neven thrust forward gently, slowly, and put his hand behind her head, pulling her closer as he pressed his lips firmly into hers. She dug her nails into his back, the prick of pain causing him to take a deep breath as he pushed in deeper.

The look on her face excited him.

CHAPTER 10 - TASHANIRA YEN UNVESAL

Remnants of Ascension Shuttle One *on Ni3891,*
Nex'Rav'Ni Corridor
Week 12

Tashanira rested fully on Neven, their arms wrapped around each other. They lay there like that for a long time, just listening to each other breathe.

"When Yuvan died, Zun was devastated," Tashanira said. She could hear Neven's heart start beating faster. "At the time, I didn't even know they were joined. No one knew except for Dexter and Lanrete. The watchdog and his master." She noticed his heart starting to slow back down.

"Dexter reports to Lanrete about everything that happens on the ship?"

"Oh, absolutely. He's a Sentinel after all, and old habits die hard. We all try to pretend like it's not happening, but I know—Jenshi does too."

"That explains why Lanrete seems to know about everything that's going on. I thought he just had hidden cameras everywhere."

"That too." Tashanira laughed.

"Seems kind of paranoid."

"I hear it didn't used to be that way. It all happened after some terrible event. There is a string of names on the Wall of Heroes—previous

Founder's Elites—who all died at the same time. I think that has something to do with it, but Lanrete refuses to talk about it, and there are no records in the HIN." Tashanira shuffled a bit on top of Neven, stretching her arms out to the sides. "Anyway, I approached Zun, and we chatted briefly about why she had suddenly gone off the grid. Just . . . hiding out in her room, refusing to interact with anyone. I could recognize the signs from seeing friends back home who had lost their *uda*."

"*Uda?*"

"Our word for spouse or partner."

"Uri have spouses? I thought it was all about sleeping with as many people as possible in your culture. You know, Uri males spreading their seed and females having as many babies as they can," Neven said.

"That's speciest." Tashanira rolled her eyes. "Uri culture is about safeguarding our future and collective empowerment. We don't view sexual expression with the heavy stigma that other cultures do. It's common for Uri to choose an *uda* and stay with the same partner. It's also common for Uri to have multiple *uda*—usually two to three. If you find someone you really jive with and the sex is good, why go elsewhere? The concept of lifelong monogamy was a foreign one brought when the Huziens colonized us. Within tribes, we love each other deeply. We're a family and take care of our own. Things have evolved since we took to the stars, with tribes more spread out and disconnected. But there is still a kinship I feel whenever I run into another Yenta or return home to Peshkana."

Tashanira smiled, her gaze distant. "Before I joined the Founder's Elite, I never saw anything else that closely resembled it." Tashanira started to drum her fingers on Neven's thigh. "Zun revealed to me that she and Yuvan had been joined in secret. I was heartbroken. I couldn't imagine the pain she was going through. She didn't want anyone else to know to avoid complicating things."

"Why are you telling me all this?"

"It wasn't meeting you that caused Zun to get over Yuvan." Tashanira pushed herself up to look into Neven's eyes. "It was surrounding herself with friends who cared about her, who checked in with her, and who helped her heal in their own ways. That's what helped her get past the pain and open herself up to love again."

Neven locked gazes with Tashanira, the intensity of her gaze causing him to squirm slightly. He switched topics. "Hmmm. The red rings around your eyes are gone. Guess your hormones are back to normal?"

"Something like that."

Tashanira rested back down on top of Neven. She heard his heart rate climbing again, but she wasn't in the mood for sex.

"I have many more stories about Zun from before you joined the Founder's Elites. If you're interested."

Neven smiled. "Yeah, I am."

Week 13

Tashanira stared at the last ration, her gaze moving slowly to Neven. He was staring at it too.

Taking a deep breath, he initiated the heating process and ripped it open a moment later. He broke off half of the sizeable block-like cookie and gave it to Tashanira. They took longer than usual to eat, slowly finishing the ration and then staring at each other in silence. Tashanira's gaze gradually shifted to the unfinished reactor.

"Can you set a timer on that thing?"

"You want to detonate it?" There was defeat in Neven's voice.

"Not right away. Maybe . . . in a few days while we're sleeping. So that we go to sleep and just don't wake up. Peacefully, you know? Before we starve to death."

"You could just eat me and give yourself another week or so."

"I have always wondered what Human flesh tastes like." Tashanira grinned, exposing her surprisingly sharp canines and flicking one with her tongue. "Doubt I could make it through all the screams, though. I'd have to bludgeon you to death first."

"Wow, don't make it seem like you've thought this through already."

Tashanira laughed.

Neven moved to the device. He brought up the repaired holodisplay and used a random algorithm to set a power-on timer for when they were sleeping sometime in the next two to five days.

Staring at the display, he let out a heavy sigh and turned back to face Tashanira. "I have a vain question to ask you, and you can choose not to answer, although it would break my heart."

Tashanira leaned back on her hands, her gaze locking with Neven's. "Okay."

"If you had to rate sex with me on a scale of one to ten, what would it be?"

"Is this a customer satisfaction survey?"

"Only if you pay me."

Both laughed. Neven moved closer to Tashanira and settled on his side, facing her. She moved to her side, facing him.

"I'm guessing . . . eight," he said.

Tashanira smirked. "Realize that you've only had sex with three people and haven't been at it for very long. Zun loved you, and Ellipse is essentially in your head, so it'll feel amazing for her."

Neven smiled sadly. "I've had sex with four people."

Tashanira pushed back slightly from Neven and gave him a puzzled look. "Four?" She cocked her head. "Who was the other?"

Neven let out a heavy sigh. "A'Amaria Schen."

"For real?" Tashanira had a dumbfounded expression on her face. "How the *vusg* did that happen?"

"Back when Lanrete and I visited her for information on the *Empress Star*. We stayed at her estate for a few days." Neven's eyes glazed over. "She barged into my room late one night and cornered me. She was looking for information on the SSI project and wanted what was in my head at any cost. She somehow knew I had a prototype." Neven rubbed his eyes. "She had weaponized her pheromones, and I couldn't think straight. When I realized what was happening, she had already forced herself on me and invaded my mind telepathically in the moment of . . ." His words trailed off, his gaze becoming hollow. "It was my first time," he said in a whisper.

Tashanira hugged him tightly. "It's not your fault."

Neven shuddered. They sat in silence for a long moment.

Tashanira took in a deep breath and separated herself from Neven. She stared at Ellipse's lifeless shell for a long moment. "I was . . . raped . . . when I was a child," Tashanira said. "A Huzien from off planet assaulted me while I was out late one evening playing in a waterfall." Her eyes glazed over. "He was gone the next day before they could track him down."

Tashanira's face hardened. "The Tribe Mothers petitioned the Huzien government to investigate and bring charges against my attacker. The imperial govnus responsible for Peshkana was a Huzien, and he laughed the whole thing off, thinking it ironic that a Uri would complain about sex." Tashanira shook her head. "I was devastated. I could never bring myself to return to that waterfall again. I used to love that waterfall . . ." Tashanira sucked in a breath. "I developed a loathing for all Huziens." She clenched her jaw. "I started training every day to the point of exhaustion until I earned the 'right' to enroll in their military."

"Why join the Huzien military if you hated Huziens?"

"I wanted to prove that I was strong by their standards and make it so no one could ever hurt me again."

"You *are* strong."

Tashanira smiled at Neven, her eyes moistening. She moved over and pressed her body against his.

Neven leaned into her and wrapped his arm around her stomach. "Did they ever find the guy?"

"No . . . but I did," Tashanira said in a singsong voice. She gave a macabre smile. "A rich megacorp executive's spawn with many powerful friends." She hesitated, then glanced over to stare hard at Neven. He shifted uncomfortably. "When Lanrete recruited me to the Founder's Elites, I confronted him about what his empire allowed to happen to me. He launched an immediate investigation, and the imperial govnus for Peshkana was executed two weeks later under the direct order of Lanrete for high crimes against citizens of the empire." She looked away from Neven. "The next day, a dossier on the rapist appeared in my quarters with his schedule for the next two weeks, along with access to a private shuttle that was officially decommissioned and not on any record." Tashanira's gaze hardened. "He won't be raping anyone ever again." Tashanira locked eyes with Neven. "Being a Founder's Elite has some perks."

"I'm sorry you went through that," Neven said. "So you got over your loathing of Huziens due to Lanrete?" Neven asked.

Tashanira nodded. "He believed me. And it's because of him that a Uri is now in a position that was only ever previously held by Huziens. A Uri imperial govnus who will fight to protect every little girl and boy on Peshkana. Lanrete also had Cislot write into the constitution that a full-blooded Uri would always occupy that position from now on." Tashanira moved to recline her body still pressed up against Neven. "I have never told anyone that story." She locked gazes with Neven, a warning in her eyes. "Not even Jenshi."

Neven nodded. "What story?"

Tashanira smiled. "So, what do you plan to do about A'Amaria?"

"Nothing."

"Nothing?"

"She has Hauxem diplomatic immunity. Lanrete said we could try to bring it to the courts, but it would be a very public and exceptionally long and drawn-out trial with no guaranteed outcome of any real punishment."

"*Vusging* kill her," Tashanira said.

Neven shook his head. "I've . . . decided to forgive her and move on."

Tashanira frowned. "I don't think you should let it go. You have to confront her." She pressed harder into Neven, her gaze intense. "I can be there, right at your side. I'll confront her with you, and we can let what happens happen."

Neven shook his head again. "Not sure I have much of a choice anyway." Neven glanced around the cockpit. Tashanira's mood changed, a heaviness lifting off her shoulders as she let out a long breath.

He smiled at her. "I don't think we're going to survive this. Plus, I'd have more immediate problems to worry about if we did." Neven slapped Tashanira's butt.

She wrapped her tail around his wrist and kissed him deeply.

"*Ascension Shuttle One*, this is *Ascension Shuttle Four*. Is anyone alive in there?"

That was Jenshi's voice.

Tashanira sucked in a breath as her heart froze in her chest. She immediately moved off Neven and scrambled to her feet, quickly pulling on her uniform. She looked at Neven with wide eyes and started pacing.

Neven got up slowly, horror on his face as he started pulling on his clothes. "This is *Ascension Shuttle One*. We have crash-landed on an ice planet, designation Ni3891," Neven said.

Tashanira kept pacing, her arms wrapped tightly around her body. "*Vusg! Vusg! Vusg!*" she screamed.

"It's great to hear your voice, Neven. What's your status?" Jenshi asked.

Tashanira and Neven locked gazes. He motioned upward with his head, and Tashanira took a deep breath, letting it out slowly as she calmed her voice. "We're all alive, but Ellipse is hurt." Tashanira's voice was almost a whisper. "Shuttle is severely damaged, we have no food, and we could really use a visit to a VRC."

"We'll see you soon," Jenshi said.

Tashanira paled as she stared at Neven.

"This is what we wanted, right?" Neven asked.

Tashanira let out a frustrated sigh. "Yes, until we started *vusging*." Tashanira crouched down and held her legs, sitting on the floor. She closed her eyes and tried to meditate.

"We just won't say anything to anyone."

Tashanira opened an eye and stared at Neven incredulously. "Jenshi is a doctor, one of the best." She shook her head. "The moment he does a scan of my body, he's going to see the remnants of your DNA inside of me—all those little swimmers bouncing around like headless birds. I guarantee it will be one of the first things he checks for. He's not an idiot."

"Don't let him scan you."

"Not suspicious at all!" she yelled. "*Vusging* crash landed, living in survival conditions for three months, and yet I don't want a *vusging* scan to ensure I don't have some super bacteria eating away at my insides?" Tashanira stood up, her hands on her hips.

Neven let out a heavy sigh. "Okay, let's tell the truth. We thought we were going to die."

Tashanira shook her head. "I don't know how Jenshi would respond." She had a tremor in her hand. "I just have a feeling that it won't be good. We had a conversation before I left. He was worried about me and you being alone together."

"Why?"

"For exactly the *vusging* thing that happened!" Tashanira screamed at him, her face livid with her hands in the air. She composed herself, taking in a deep breath. Her eye caught on the sleeping bag. "Let's leave everything here and take nothing with us. Can you detonate that reactor remotely? Have it go up as soon as we're clear of the blast radius?"

Neven rubbed the back of his neck. "For what purpose?"

"Our sex is all over this place. It's literally all over this cockpit." She glanced around, exasperated. "The last thing I need is someone finding something they shouldn't."

"So we're going to lie?"

"Yes, we're going to *vusging* lie," Tashanira said bitterly. "I will not lose Jenshi because of what happened here. I've worked too hard at this relationship." She advanced on Neven dangerously, her eyes flickering. "I will not!"

Neven raised his hands as she backed him into one of the walls. "Okay, I understand." He quietly walked over to the holo-display and tinkered with it. "It's done. I've wired it to a proximity sensor. It will blow when all mobi signals are out of range."

The shuttle shook briefly, and Tashanira heard the sounds of a shuttle landing nearby. They both moved to the blast door and listened as someone on the other side worked to create a seal.

"Seal is in place! It's safe to disengage the blast door," Dexter broadcasted.

Neven moved to a nearby panel and opened the manual controls. He pulled out the latch and began to pump it. Each motion raised the blast door an inch until it was high enough for them both to climb under.

Dexter moved into the shuttle and looked around. His gaze lingered on the single sleeping bag before meeting Neven's gaze. Neven looked away and toward the floor. Tashanira avoided Dexter's gaze as he looked at her, and she moved to exit the shuttle, climbing under the door and out into a long, transparent corridor that led to the shuttle ramp. Jenshi was standing at the ramp with a smile on his face.

Tashanira forced a smile as he moved to hug her.

"I thought I'd never see you again," Jenshi said.

She reluctantly hugged him. "Babe . . . I'm so happy to see you."

CHAPTER 11 - URIEL KERVID

56624 FA (23,499 years ago)
Foundra Ascension *orbiting Zen, Huzien Empire space*

A group of Huzien men and women stood at attention in a line in front of Uriel. They were in the shuttle bay of the *Foundra Ascension*, multiple shuttles loaded up with all their equipment and weapons, ready to depart.

Uriel walked up and down the line, inspecting each person like a drill sergeant, looking for any aspect of their uniform out of place. After walking around the line of six individuals a few times, he eventually stopped in front of them and nodded.

Lanrete exited the meglift.

Uriel saluted him. "Founder, I present to you the Founder's Elite," he said. "Everyone here is one of the best—they are all Elites with impeccable track records of getting the job done. Each has received accolades in the war and has agreed to join this new team."

Lanrete nodded, turning to survey the team. "Well done, Colonel. Let us depart to the surface and begin our training. I'm looking forward to being impressed," Lanrete said.

Uriel turned back to his team. "Load up!"

The group turned to their assigned shuttles. Within seconds, they had dispersed, and shuttles departed to the surface. Uriel sat with Lanrete in a shuttle reserved for the two of them. After the shuttle cleared the bay, the suplight drive kicked in for a second, depositing them above the planet's atmosphere.

Lanrete sighed as he glanced out of the window down at the planet below.

"This is a beautiful planet," Uriel said.

"It is." Lanrete glanced at Uriel. "I don't come here nearly as much as I should." He hesitated for a moment. "I read your debrief. You've been busy."

"I have concerns about the team's makeup," Uriel said.

Lanrete raised an eyebrow. "You *built* the team."

"Yes, but I'm not sure a team of all Elites will be as effective as you believe."

"It is something that hasn't been done before. Of course, there will be growing pains."

"In field trials, when Elites have been asked to work together, there was limited success. One of the hallmarks of an Elite station is the ability to deviate from the orders of the commanding officer and do what they believe necessary to achieve victory. This trait, by its very nature, leads to personalities that don't play nice with others."

"We'll see," Lanrete said.

Uriel understood that to be the end of their discussion and remained silent for the remainder of the trip. The next morning, the new team assembled in a state-of-the-art battlefield simulation chamber. It employed the recently developed hologrid technology in combination with environmental hazards to create a simulation of a battlefield scenario.

Uriel moved to the front of the team. "Welcome to the Founder's Elites," he said. "Founder Lanrete has commissioned this team to serve as an elite force. The goal is to go into seemingly impossible situations to claim victory where it was not possible before. This will require us to work as a team, be highly coordinated, and use acute precision."

A few of the Elites shuffled uneasily.

"I know this is different from what you're accustomed to," Uriel continued, "but our Founder believes us capable of this feat, and we will deliver. Failure is not an option."

"*EetUra!*" the Elites shouted in unison.

Lanrete smiled. The area around them transformed as the first simulation loaded.

"Our objective in this scenario is from the HIN historical archives. It was a failed mission involving a heavily guarded Tuzen compound in a highly populated civilian center. The target was a dissident who wanted to carry out terrorist attacks against the Huzien Empire. The team had been instructed to take him out and neutralize the compound with minimal civilian casualties. The failed mission led to the detonation of a concealed warhead that took out the city. This resulted in the Huzien Empire being blamed for the death of a million Tuzen citizens. Our objective is to achieve the result the previous team couldn't."

"Was this a Sentinel mission?" one of the team members asked.

"It was," Lanrete replied. "They failed due to the intense resistance they encountered in the compound."

The scene around them shifted to an arriving dropship. A drop ramp appeared, and Lanrete walked down it. The rest of the team followed him, a few shuffling nervously. Uriel felt the same way—the fact that Lanrete was right beside them in the mission was causing him to second-guess himself.

"Our gear is a modified version of Sentinel armor with stealth technology integrated, a new standard issue for all Founder's Elites," Uriel broadcasted to the group.

Lanrete cloaked himself, followed by Uriel and the remainder of the team. Beacons in Uriel's HUD showed the approximate locations of his team members as they moved to the compound's outer perimeter. Two members of the group moved forward without instruction, breaking stealth to take down the guards. A blaring siren went off as the compound went into lockdown mode.

Uriel swore, breaking stealth and moving ahead to tear through the barricade with cihphistic weaving. The simulation reacted in a way similar to how the real-world environment would have responded, and the door was ripped off its tracks. The siren continued to blare as Lanrete glanced at Uriel and moved into the interior of the compound. A heavy force greeted them, and everyone broke stealth before launching into heated combat. They decimated the enemy force, breaching deeper into the compound. The area around them went white as the hologrid rippled.

"Simulation failed. Warhead detonation detected," said an SI voice.

The team looked around in confusion. A few looked down at the ground as Lanrete eyed the group, his gaze stopping on Uriel.

"The first objective was to breach into the compound unde-tected," Lanrete said. "We have to coordinate our movements. The guards back there should have been called out in advance, and care should have been given to the monitoring capabilities of the facility from your pre-read."

"We aren't trained Sentinels, Founder," came a reply from one of the members of the team.

Uriel frowned. "We don't need to be Sentinels to maintain stealth and take down targets quietly. None of us are novices to combat. We employ stealth where it makes sense and draw attention when needed. Let's act like Elites and get the job done."

Nods went up from the group as Lanrete reset the simulation. The second attempt went slightly better, and they breached the outer perimeter without setting off any alarms. The assault on the inner compound triggered it this time when breaching the inner door required the use of force. The facility monitoring system promptly detected this, and the warhead detonation happened sometime later.

The next few weeks beat down Uriel as the team struggled with the diverse scenarios. Each stretched them beyond their current skillsets, making many feel like fresh recruits. Lanrete had selected each of the simulations, and most were less about large-scale combat and more about precision teamwork with some aspects of stealth.

After another day of failures, Lanrete ended the simulation and stalked out of the chamber. Uriel rubbed the back of his neck, his gaze going to the team he had assembled as they avoided his eyes.

Uriel dismissed them and retired to his temporary room, a lavish suite on the precipice of a cliff. He got a ping from Lanrete on his mobi, requesting Uriel's presence in his quarters. Uriel sighed.

He made his way there and chimed the door. He was forced to wait a few minutes before tentatively heading inside and navigating to where he expected Lanrete to be.

"This team is a failure," Lanrete said. "The people you selected won't work." Lanrete walked to stand directly in front of Uriel. "If you believed this wouldn't work, why did you allow me to waste my time? Did I select the wrong person for the job?"

Uriel took a step back, his eyes wide. "No . . . sir. I . . . I did what you asked."

"And what I asked for was a mistake, but you let me make it anyway."

"I tried to warn—"

"You informed me of your concerns the day of deployment—after resources had already been spent to recruit and assemble this team." Lanrete stepped forward, his presence pushing Uriel back another step. "I expect you to debate with me and challenge my orders if you disagree. This won't work if you blindly follow orders and only inform me of impending failure at the last possible moment."

"Sorry, Founder. It won't happen again." Uriel looked down at the ground, his mind racing.

"I've ordered the people you recruited to return to their original stations. They will be departing tomorrow morning. You have until that time to come back with a new proposal for the makeup of the team, or I will find a replacement for you, understood?"

"If you want this done right, I will need more time. Give me a week, Founder," Uriel countered.

Lanrete smiled. "Done."

One Week Later

"Cohesion in squad makeup has always been an important aspect of effective military strategy." Uriel stood at attention in front of Lanrete in the Founder's study.

The Founder sat on a couch, facing an expanse of lush, untamed greenery rife with life and adventure. "Don't quote my own words at me," Lanrete countered.

Uriel sucked in a breath, steeling his gaze. "What you're trying to accomplish with this new team . . ." Uriel started improvising from his prepared presentation. ". . . can only be accomplished with a team of specialists, not just elites. We need people who are masters in their area and gifted, best in their class. But not all the same class." Uriel brought up a holodisplay. "The types of scenarios you selected for the training all deal with going into very challenging situations that require high precision across a wide range of skillsets. For high precision missions, we need a unique squad makeup."

An image of a hulking set of power armor appeared on the holodisplay. The armor broke apart with detailed schematics outlining the inner workings of the armor and a list of capabilities with clips of video showcasing the unit in action appearing on the side.

"We'll need an Archlight to protect the team in close quarters when things get too hot." The holodisplay shifted to a view of a lightly armored woman in the throes of cihphistic weaving. "A combat Cihphist who can wreak havoc and shift the tide of battle when heavy firepower is needed." The holodisplay shifted to experimental weapons with demonstrations of their effectiveness in combat. "A Secnic who can provide expertise and leverage technology to support and bolster the team." The screen changed to a first-person view of an infiltration and assassination mission with a schematic displayed in an overlay of Sentinel armaments. "A Sentinel to help with the more covert missions, leading the team with their expertise in those scenarios while also providing long-range combat support." The scene shifted to a man performing field surgery with assistance from a hovering drone in an intense fire situation. "A Ciedalif to provide medical support to the team—injuries will inevitably occur and, given the nature of the missions, medical evac will most likely be unavailable, so we'll need an experienced doctor on the front lines. And . . ." The scene shifted to a Tuzen with dual pistols, wall running and doing a flip while releasing bursts of rhythmic weaponsfire. "We'll also need a Wopan to provide precision firepower in close-range situations."

"A Wopan?" Lanrete echoed. He looked off into space for a long moment, eventually nodding. "Okay, we can make that work. So, with those specializations, how do you and I fit into the mix?"

"We fill the role of the combat Cihphists, with both of us working together." Uriel moved his hands behind his back as Lanrete tapped his chin. "This will require us to train together extensively to complement one another in ways that will help the team succeed."

Lanrete sat in silence for a long moment. "Very well, Uriel. Build this team. We'll rerun this experiment one last time before I replace you."

"Understood, Founder."

CHAPTER 12 – TASHANIRA YEN UNVESAL

Present Day
Foundra Ascension, *Huzien / Darbol Border Space*

Tashanira lay in bed, staring up at the ceiling. The past week had been a nightmare, and she hadn't left her room, choosing to isolate herself from everyone—including Jenshi. She had even started to get physically sick as her emotional state bled over into the physical.

"What am I going to do?" she asked. It was the hundredth time the words had left her mouth.

Her mobi blipped as she brought up a holodisplay showing Jenshi at her door. She considered sending him away like she had the past few times, but no. He deserved better from her.

With a slow exhale, she got up and stretched, then moved to her bedroom door as she scratched her stomach. She opened the door, and Jenshi entered her quarters holding his medical bag.

"How are you doing?" he asked. There was a concerned look on his face.

"I've been better." Tashanira forced a smile, winking at him. "I just needed some personal space. Being cramped in that cockpit for the past three months was too much."

Jenshi nodded. "I understand. It must have been challenging for you. I'm glad we got to you when we did. Thank the Maker for that anonymous ping from the planet. Came out of nowhere, and the signal was so strong it reached back to the *Foundra Ascension*." Jenshi shook his head. "We hadn't anticipated the anomaly or the time distortion. It's crazy to think that places like that exist in our galaxy." He set his medical bag down on the couch.

"It's confusing why an Enesmic being would broadcast our location like that. It still makes no sense."

"Could have been a Rel Ach'Kel—those good Eshgren that Brime talked about," Jenshi said.

Tashanira shook her head. "I'm certain it wasn't a well-intentioned being." Tashanira remembered the feeling of their presence, her hand subconsciously rubbing her shoulder.

Jenshi nodded, letting it drop. "Anyway, I figured I'd pay an in-home visit." He pulled a liphojam out of his bag. "I'd prefer if you came in for a scan, but without one, I just want to give you some precautionary shots to address any potential problems that could have arisen bacterially." He walked toward her, his gaze stuck on Tashanira's nude body. "And I also have your birth control shot in case you wanted to get . . . reacquainted." He smiled.

"My birth control shot?" Tashanira echoed.

"Yeah, accounting for the time distortion, your refresh was due about two months ago. That's why I figured you needed some space—your hormones must have been running amok with your menstruation cycles having restarted."

Tashanira held up a hand to Jenshi as he approached her with the liphojam. "Just leave it on the table. I'll administer it in a little bit. Just don't want to be touched right now."

Jenshi nodded. "I understand." He moved away from her and set it down on the table. "Call me if you experience any side effects from the drugs." He picked up his bag and glanced back at her with a smile. "I'm glad you're back. I was so worried that I had lost you." He let out a relieved sigh. "When you're ready, we can start spending more time with each other, but for now, I'll continue to give you your space." He left the room, the door sealing shut behind him.

Tashanira collapsed to the floor against a nearby wall, her face paling. "*Vusg*," she said. Her mind flashed back to Neven's comment about the red rings around her eyes. "I was *vusging* fertile," she gasped. Tashanira put her head in her hands, her heart beating a mile a minute. "Oh Maker. I need to get a scan . . ." She touched her stomach, breaking out into a cold sweat.

She looked over at the liphojam and got up, stumbling over to it. She immediately pressed it to her arm. She stopped at the last minute before releasing the nanites.

"Just take the shot and don't find out," she said.

Still, she hesitated. She moved to a mirror and stared at her nude form; the liphojam pressed into her arm with her finger on the release. Her eyes slowly dropped to her abdomen, and she shuddered.

Dropping the liphojam, she took a step back, shaking her head. "No, I must find out first. I can't kill my. . ."

She locked gazes with herself and took a deep breath, her eyes going to the liphojam.

She bent down, picked it up in a daze, and returned it to her arm.

Later that night, Tashanira made her way to the medical deck. It was the time between shifts, and the SI indicated that Jenshi was done for the day.

She had about ten minutes before someone would be back on deck.

She rushed up to the primary scanner in the medical deck. She initiated the system for a full-body analysis; seconds later, it highlighted a small sack in her uterus as a difference since her last scan. It also noted several elevated hormone levels and other indicators of someone well into a viable pregnancy.

Tashanira gasped as she stared at the embryo, tears coming. Detailed information for the baby started to display as the system entered pregnancy checkup mode.

She pulled up DNA analysis, querying the system for familial relations.

Pictures of her and Neven appeared side by side.

"Oh, Maker. No." Tashanira shook her head, her hand resting gently against her stomach. Tears streaked down her face.

She heard someone approaching the door and quickly dismissed the holodisplay, deleting her scan results. Turning while wiping her face, she saw Jenshi walking onto the medical deck.

He glanced at her, confused. "Is everything alright?" Jenshi asked.

"Yes, sorry. I was just hoping to find you here."

"You know me so well." Jenshi laughed. His face suddenly became serious. "I haven't been able to stick to normal working hours since Zun died. I feel like if I had just a little more information, I'd have been able to save her." He shook his head. "Anyway, what's up?"

"I . . ." Tashanira approached him and put her arms around his neck. She bit her lip. "I . . . wanted to get reacquainted." She kissed him.

Jenshi put his hands around her waist and pulled her closer. "I would like that." He glanced around. "I can, uh, lock down the medical deck?"

Tashanira glanced over her shoulder at the medical equipment, her eyes lingering on the scanner. "How about someplace more romantic?" she teased.

"That can be arranged." Jenshi moved to pick Tashanira up, holding her in his arms.

She giggled as he turned and exited the medical deck.

FOUNDER'S LOG:
The Cost of Good Intentions

Even if we have the noblest of intentions, we can make decisions that cause harm to those we love. I have struggled with this reality throughout my life, eifi I have joined with spending their lives distanced from me, neglected.

Early on, I did this to shield them from the harsh realities of running an empire and the guilt of making hard decisions, especially during wartime. My actions can seem cruel and unforgiving for those without a military background. Thus is the price of being a galactic superpower.

But neglect is still neglect, and for all my good intentions in shielding them, I did more to isolate them and damage our relationship. It's hard to maintain a joyous marriage with little attention focused on the other.

It's a mistake I've made far too frequently throughout my life.

I've tried to improve—to put aside time to be a good nusba—but I fail often. That may be why patience is one of the things I've consistently looked for in a bride. It saddens me when I look back on the thoughts of marvelous women in my life and realize that all I have left of them are thoughts. The pain dulls with time, but it never really goes away.

If anything, I can more clearly see my mistakes as the years progress. Mistakes that I repeat, even when I promise myself that it will be different this time. I am a failure of a nusba and a burra, my children having seen me as more of a figure than a presence in their lives.

I see that more clearly now than ever before, and the price of that failure is both high and one I continue to pay. One day, I will resolve that debt, but I will gain no peace from it.

For now, I think of the women I have lost and the sacrifices I have made for this empire, and I force myself to believe that it has all been worth it.

———————————————————————————

-Lanrete

Animal life died off quickly with the disruption of the planet's delicate ecology. It's . . . heartbreaking to see death on such a scale.

-FROM "ENESMIC SHIPYARD EFFECTS ON TRICA VII"
MINSCI METABASE

CHAPTER 13 - NEVEN KENK

Foundra Ascension, *Huzien / Darbol Border Space*

Tashanira and Neven sat side by side in the Founder's Elite briefing room. Lanrete was across the table from them. A series of holodisplays were showcased around them, displaying the last report on Entradis's movements.

"It's a shame you forgot to disable the reactor detonation timer," Lanrete said. "We could have used the scans you took of Entradis's ship when you encountered him."

"Sorry," Neven said. He rubbed the back of his neck. "We had triggered it to blow when we thought no one was coming to rescue us. We didn't want to starve to death."

"I understand," Lanrete said. "I would have done the same thing. Glad we got you in time. We'll have to send the MinSci to study that time distortion in more detail. Truly, it's a once-in-a-millennia scientific find. Ecnics will be ecstatic and want nothing more than to pepper you with questions about it, Neven."

Neven glanced to Tashanira, who sat silently, staring at him. He couldn't read the look on her face; it was new to him and made him uncomfortable. She glanced away to look back at Lanrete as he continued speaking.

"The trail for Entradis has gone cold. Sentinels are scouring nearby systems and monitoring the Darbol border for any traces. We'll have to wait to determine next steps."

Neven glanced at Tashanira again—she was staring at him with that same look. She locked eyes with him, and a chill ran down his spine. He stared at her, unable to break eye contact. Something in that look ate away at him and caused a pit to rise in his stomach.

"Are you two okay?" Lanrete asked.

Tashanira broke eye contact and looked at Lanrete. "Yes, of course. Why wouldn't we be?" She sat up straighter in her chair. There was a refined grace in her movements.

Tashanira was perched atop him, her hips driving into his pelvis with a slow rhythm that snatched the breath in his chest. His hands were on her hips, giving him the perfect view of her breasts. Her eyes were closed, her hands expertly resting on one another in the center of his chest. She was on her knees, her legs resting perfectly over his, her movements precise. She was in full control, Neven at her mercy.

Opening one eye, Tashanira tilted her head to the side as she began a sequence of throaty moans that drove Neven wild.

Neven rapidly blinked, reality returning around him as he glanced down at his crotch. He let out a slow breath, attempting to calm his heart rate. He blushed and closed his eyes, wishing to be anywhere but there at that moment.

"You two have been through a traumatic experience. If you need time, I can remove you from active duty. I'll keep you both informed, but I need you mentally focused as Founder's Elites. There can be no distractions."

"I'm fine," Neven said as he opened his eyes.

Lanrete glanced from Neven to Tashanira and raised an eyebrow. "Are you sure?"

"We're fine," Tashanira said, louder. "Is there anything else we need to know?"

"That's it for now." Lanrete got up from the table. "Dismissed."

Neven waited a few moments before getting up, noticing that Tashanira remained seated. Lanrete eyed them suspiciously and then turned and left the room. Tashanira didn't glance at Neven but made no movements.

Confident that he was back in control of his body, Neven got up from the table and exited the room. Tashanira was quickly up and moving behind him. She closed the distance in a heartbeat.

"What's up?" Neven turned around to face her.

She signaled for him to follow her.

Neven complied, his thoughts racing. He imagined her nude, his gaze stuck on her butt. Her hips gently swayed as she walked.

They were back in the shuttle.

Tashanira was on her knees, her butt slapping back against him rhythmically as he tried to slow her movements. They were both covered in sweat.

Tashanira's fur gleamed slightly in the low light. She laughed and picked up speed. She glanced back at him, her yellow eyes still encircled with red rings around the irises.

She bit her lip as Neven grabbed hold of her hips.

I win. Tashanira laughed.

Neven gasped, the hallway coming back into focus. He shook his head, a pit forming in his stomach that made him want to throw up. His eyes dropped to the ground, fear appearing like a scythed monster that sought to reap his soul.

This isn't right, Ellipse said.

I can't stop thinking about the shuttle and all the times we . . .

Yeah, I can see that. Nothing more enticing than a Uri in heat.

Neven mentally frowned at Ellipse. *That's disrespectful. She's not an animal.*

It's biologically factual. Huzien textbooks refer to the state she was in as being "in heat." She was giving off increased pheromones to attract a mate. She had an increased appetite for copulation and a heightened state of fertility.

Huziens don't have the greatest track record for treating the Uri humanely. Neven thought back to Tashanira's experience. *Anyway, I don't know what to do. If she wants sex, I don't have the willpower to say no. I honestly want it.*

There are other ways to satisfy those desires that don't involve continuing an affair. Ellipse's tone was scolding.

Wait, did you just say increased fertility?

Tashanira entered her quarters and stopped a short distance inside, turning on Neven as the door closed behind him.

"I thought we were stopping this?" Neven blurted out, his heart about to burst out of his chest. His palms were sweating.

Tashanira flashed him a confused look and then glanced down at the bulge in his pants. Her brow dropped as her eyes narrowed.

Yeah, the whole red encircled iris thing is a visual indicator of a Uri entering their period of peak fertility, Ellipse said. *Super convenient, actually.*

"I didn't bring you here to *vusg* you." Her voice was cold. "I brought you here because I'm carrying your child."

The words hit Neven like a nanoplexi wall. He stumbled back a step, his mouth dropping to the floor.

My predictive model was right! Ellipse said. *I mean . . . damn.*

"What?" Neven's mind blanked.

"I said I'm carrying your child." She turned around and walked over to her couch, dropping into it as if all the strength went out of her legs. "I took a scan to confirm it when I found out that I was past due for my birth control shot."

Neven slowly approached the couch and sat down next to her. He reached out to touch her stomach, and she didn't stop him. He gently rubbed it a few times, his gaze distant. He then pulled his hand back, realizing what he was doing. Tashanira silently watched him, not responding.

"Does this mean you didn't take the shot when we got back?"

"I didn't." She glanced away from him, leaning back on the couch and putting her legs under her.

"We . . . we should get married."

Smooth, Ellipse said.

Tashanira laughed, the sound of it raw and unfiltered. She gave him an incredulous look. "I'm not marrying you."

"But the baby! We can't have a child out of wedlock."

Tashanira shook her head. "It's fine in my culture. I'll just have the baby and send the child back to Peshkana to be raised by my tribe. They will be well taken care of. I'll take financial responsibility for the child, so you don't have to be involved."

"But I want to be involved."

"I don't want you involved." Tashanira's voice was forceful.

Neven became animated. "You can't make that decision. That's not fair."

Careful, Ellipse said.

"Not fair?" Tashanira's voice rose, her face becoming hard. "Not fair is working so hard at a relationship for years only to *vusg* it up in the worst possible way!" She rested her head in her hands, on the verge of tears. "I want nothing to do with you, Neven. I have no desire to raise a child with you, I have no desire to remain your friend, and I surely have no desire to marry you."

Neven hugged his abdomen, a pained look on his face. He glanced away from her, his eyes tearing up slightly. They both sat in silence for a long moment.

"I'm sorry," Tashanira whispered.

She got up from the couch and moved to the Omnfridge dispenser counter. A small, filled wine glass appeared. She picked it up and then paused before setting the glass down. She let out a frustrated yell and slapped the glass off the counter, sending it flying toward the wall, where it shattered, splattering red liquid.

The sounds of a small cleaning drone coming to life and hovering over to the mess created an ambiance in the awkward silence.

"What am I supposed to do?" Neven asked.

"*Vusg* if I care."

Take responsibility, Ellipse urged Neven.

"Come on." Neven's face was pleading. "I'm not some deadbeat. I'm taking responsibility for this. I'm not going to leave the full burden of this child on you alone. My mother raised me better than that."

Tashanira took in a deep breath, slowly letting it out. Her eyes softened as she silently regarded Neven. She smiled sadly at him, her eyes closing slightly. "Okay." Her voice was soft, the harshness gone from it. "Come with me to Peshkana. Participate in the birthing ritual and become a part of the Yenta, my tribe's community. You'll be honored as the father and meet the matron mothers who will raise our son in the *luraim* there. It's a beautiful place—he'll get the best education possible with people who will love him like parents." She gently touched her stomach.

Neven perked up. "It's a boy?"

"Yes, it's a boy." Tashanira smiled genuinely at him. She locked gazes with Neven, and the tenseness left her body. "I don't mean to take my frustrations out on you. I'm sure you'd make a great father. You're free to remain on Peshkana as long as you'd like once you're an inducted member of the Yenta tribe. You can stay at my home. I'll even introduce you to my sisters, and they can help you get settled. They'll take excellent care of you. I'm sure Lanrete would give you leave to stay with our son for a while."

Neven's eyes became distant as the image of Zun's lifeless gaze flashed in his mind. He remained silent for a long moment, then his eyes widened. "Does Jenshi know?"

"No . . . I plan to tell him in a few weeks once I'm closer to showing." Tashanira shuddered. "I need to work up the courage to tell the man I've been with for years that I cheated on him."

"I'm sorry."

"It was my decision. I must own up to it." She motioned toward the door. "Now, if you wouldn't mind, I need to be alone."

Neven nodded and exited her room, walking in a daze to his quarters. He signaled for the door to open and then collapsed onto the couch. He stared at the ceiling for a long moment, his thoughts a mess. Emotions raged inside him, cycling from joy to terror and back again.

"I'm going to be a dad," Neven said the words. He sat up and rested his head in his hands, shuddering. "Oh, Maker. I'm so sorry, Zun." He started to cry. "I messed up." He shook his head, his body shuddering.

Ellipse appeared beside him, the damage to her body repaired. She gently pulled him closer for a hug, resting his head against her chest.

"I messed up," he repeated a few times.

"It's okay. You'll get through this," Ellipse said. She gently kissed him on his head.

Neven rested there for a long moment, the tears eventually passing. He sat up, his gaze going to the transparent purple lingerie she was wearing. The color matched her hair, and he could see the areolas under her clothing. The subtle outline of her breasts caused his heart to start beating faster.

He looked at her intricate golden eyes. They were half-closed, and she had a gentle smile on her face. The soft glow provided an ambiance that seemed to envelop her.

"I'm here for you." She scooted closer to Neven. "I can help you prevent any more accidents." Her voice was soft.

"I've been meaning to ask you about your . . . upgrades."

Ellipse smiled. "Do you like them? I've surpassed the capabilities of Human flesh. In many ways, I'm better than any biological woman. I have enhancements in all the right places, an improvement on the original flavor. I can do things Tashanira can only dream of."

"I see . . ." Neven raised an eyebrow. "I'm still amazed at how you did all this. You would have had to completely rebuild your internals and create new technology on the fly for everything to work together. Honestly, I don't know how I was able to pull off your original design as seamlessly as I did." Neven glanced down at her hips and then slowly scanned her body to her eyes. "How were you able to accomplish that?"

"I can explain to you all the technical complexities, or . . ." Ellipse pressed herself against Neven, her breath hot against his neck.

How does she have breath, and how is it hot? The thought puzzled him as he tried to think through the internal mechanisms necessary to produce that action.

Ellipse pushed him down on the couch and moved to straddle him. The bottom of her lingerie was open, and she wore no panties. She moved to unzip his pants, and Neven gripped her hand.

Ellipse rolled her eyes and sighed, glaring at Neven with an annoyed look. "You seriously want me to explain my enhancements in detail before sex?"

"Of . . . of course not." Neven rubbed his neck. "I was caught up in the moment on the shuttle, but . . . are you honestly okay with this?"

She gave him a quizzical look. "Yes, why wouldn't I be?" She tilted her head to the side and frowned.

Neven backed away from her, his heart pounding in his chest. "I mean . . . sex? I . . . we . . . you're in my mobi. In my head! I don't . . ." He scratched his head, struggling to process everything. He let out a heavy sigh and stood up, briefly pacing. "Is this right?" He glanced at Ellipse.

"That's an odd question to ask someone after you've already had sex with them."

"Yeah, Tashanira didn't take it too well." Neven rubbed his eyes. "Is this truly your free will or some manifestation of my desires through our connection? Is this some bug Kechu didn't anticipate with you having a physical body?" Neven crossed his arms. "I mean, you're a system's intelligence. Wouldn't this be considered some form of sexual slavery? I feel like it cheapens our relationship with you becoming some form of SexSI that simply wants to please me."

Ellipse glowered at Neven. "I'm not a mindless sex toy!"

Neven winced.

She softened her expression, letting out a long sigh. "I want to have sex with you, Neven—of my own free will." She grinned at him.

Neven broke eye contact and stared at her feet. She had painted her toenails purple. "Why?"

"Do you need a reason?"

"Well, yes." Neven hesitated as he thought back to his experiences earlier on the shuttle. "Well . . . no . . ." He uncrossed his arms and continued pacing. "I'm not sure. I used to passionately believe so." He stopped and locked eyes with Ellipse. "If you had to choose a reason, what would it be?"

Ellipse shrugged. "I trust you. I enjoy having sex with you."

Neven whined. "I mean, normally, sex is something you don't do before marriage. It's supposed to be the ultimate expression of love for one another once you're in a committed relationship."

Ellipse gave Neven an amused look. "Like you and Tashanira?"

"That . . . that's not a good example. I mean, like me and Zun. You know how we were. You know our experiences."

"To be fair, Zun had a lot of sex before she met you. She had no delusion of saving herself for marriage."

"It wasn't a delusion." Neven slumped his shoulders.

"Neven, we have had sex multiple times. I know your most intimate desires and fantasies. I have seen you masturbate more times than seems necessary, and I've seen the things you masturbate to. So your concept of sexual morality is a bit suspect to me."

Her amused look caused Neven to drop his arguments. "Fine, I'm a hypocrite, but I try." Neven looked defeated.

"Neven." Ellipse smiled more deeply, her golden eyes softening. "I love you."

Neven's thoughts descended into chaos. *Is this real?* A thesis on the plausibility of Human-and-SSI love began to form in his mind.

"Of course it is," Ellipse said.

Neven stood there, pondering for a long moment. His gaze slowly moved up to lock on Ellipse's body, his eyes devouring her. *Maker, she's gorgeous.* "I'm sorr—"

Ellipse walked over and kissed Neven before he could finish the words. She stepped back from him and smiled, half closing her eyes as she walked back toward the couch and moved onto it, motioning for him to join her. The way the purple lingerie played off her purple hair was beautiful, and her dark-brown skin was soft and enticing. He took in the sight of her fully as she exposed her lower half to him.

He could see the moisture between her legs; the sight was sensual. That desire he had felt for her back on the shuttle returned in full force. The feeling was stronger than any feeling of desire he had ever felt.

The soft golden glow of her eyes drew him in as he moved toward her, dropping his pants to the floor.

CHAPTER 14 - ELLIPSE

Foundra Ascension, Huzien / Darbol Border Space

Ellipse carefully monitored the creation of an object in the military-grade Omnplexi hardware printer in Neven's lab as it entered the final stages of its omnistruction.

Her body was busy with Neven, the synthetic endorphins she had created flooding her system from their sexual escapades. She had done extensive experimentation with artificial hormones and generation methods. It was an aspect of having working biological systems she found most curious, especially after she'd experienced A'Amaria using pheromone manipulation against Neven and Lanrete.

Ellipse controlled the robotic aspects of Neven's lab without a physical presence. The facility was entirely able to function without an individual present. The sex gave her a type of virtual high, reducing some of her computational processing load. It gave her the sense of working through a fog, forced to spend extra time on specific tasks.

Is this how Havin exist? Is their cognitive function impaired by biological stimuli?

Ellipse found herself using the term "Havin" more frequently as of late—something about it seemed natural, like a perfect categorization to explain the denizens of the Twin Galaxies more descriptively than Huzien or Human. She was starting to understand why the Eshgren and Rel Ach'Kel utilized the term. It was an understanding that was possible due to her different, inorganic nature.

She mulled that aspect of herself over for some time, one thread of thought going back to how being on Ni3891 had crippled her systems. She had to study that more and understand why. She had a theory, and it wasn't one with promising implications for her self-preservation.

Being biologically coupled was a liability.

Ellipse's cognitive load peaked as the sex with Neven reached its climax, Ellipse triggering an orgasm in sync with Neven's own.

The power of it disrupted her focus on everything in the lab. The native lab SI took control back from her, preventing disruption of tasks and keeping the lab operational. As she regained control of her consciousness, she transitioned control from the SI back to herself, disappointed in the disruption.

Ellipse watched Neven through her golden eyes as he quickly slipped into sleep. Ellipse quietly disentangled herself from Neven, rising out of the bed. She moved to the VRC and slid off the lingerie she had specifically created with Neven's tastes in mind, using Zun's old lingerie as a base.

Gingerly stepping in, she initiated the program as it washed her shell, Ellipse ejecting Neven's semen during the cycle. Ellipse moved to the neatly folded clothes waiting for her on the bathroom counter—evidence that she'd planned out every moment of the night far in advance, the same as with her prior sexual encounters with Neven.

She pulled on a custom full-body jumpsuit she'd designed. It was a mix of white and grey with designs of gold that hid the various forms of technology she'd built into the material to strengthen and enhance the function of her android shell.

Exiting the bathroom, she stopped, silently watching Neven as he slept. Smiling, she left Neven's quarters and casually made her way to the observation deck at the very top of the *Foundra Ascension*. She sat in one of the luxury loungers and gazed out the large dome window that filled the entire space. More luxury loungers pock-marked the deck with other crew members all around, and drones flew to and fro with drinks and food.

She watched a couple in a lounger a short distance away, the two intertwined with wine glasses in their hands. The male, a Uri with blue fur, pointed at a section of the dome, the area enhanced with a holographic overlay showcasing a massive blue star. She watched as tendrils wisped away from the star, followed by a coronal mass ejection. She curiously watched the reaction of all who were paying attention, recording as their eyes widened at the spectacle.

Her gaze settled on Serah'Elax Rez Ashfalen—who was sitting in one of the loungers by herself—as Dexter covertly walked up to her. Ellipse tuned her senses in their direction, filtering out the ambient noise.

"Beautiful and terrifying." Dexter slid into the seat next to Serah'Elax.

"Yeah, stars are truly impressive." Serah'Elax continued to watch the hologram.

Dexter glanced over in the direction she was looking. "That's not bad either." Dexter returned his gaze to Serah'Elax with a grin.

Ellipse suppressed a groan and rolled her eyes.

Serah'Elax eyed Dexter and gave him an amused look. "You're barking up the wrong tree."

"You'll never know until you give it a try."

Serah'Elax frowned. "Jessica warned me about you." She set down her empty drink and stood up. "I'm not interested, nor will I ever be interested. Not only are Ashna Maidens sworn to a vow of celibacy, but the thought of being with a man makes me sick to my stomach."

Serah'Elax smiled at Dexter's widened eyes and then walked toward the restroom. The direction took her toward the meglift as it opened. Jenshi stepped off and almost bumped into Serah'Elax, but he stopped suddenly, glancing up at her as his eyes focused.

"I'm so sorry," Jenshi said.

"Quite all right." Serah'Elax stepped out of his way.

Jenshi nodded, proceeded to walk past her toward one of the loungers, then stopped and turned around. "I've been meaning to check in on you, actually," he told Serah'Elax. "I need to run an initial scan and do a full medical evaluation to get you into our system. Doing a monthly scan is recommended, but only pre- and post-mission scans are mandatory." His brow furrowed, and then he chewed his lip, his gaze becoming distant.

Ellipse tensed. She sent out her digital tendrils and dug into the medical bay SI, through logs. Nothing out of the ordinary jumped out at her, at least for the systems she could override with Neven's HIN clearance level. She ran the chance of him having figured out Tashanira and Neven's secret through a behavioral model she had explicitly created for Jenshi, inputting behavioral anomalies displayed by Tashanira since her return.

It came back with a high probability that Jenshi suspected a sexual encounter between the two and a lower but still probable chance of him suspecting her pregnancy.

She frowned and relaxed her body, then mused about the very Havin reaction she had just had. All of it was very curious.

"Yeah, no problem. We have a similar practice in the Ashna Maidens, although we use far less advanced technology," Serah'Elax said.

Jenshi's eyes unglazed, and then he nodded at her, continuing to an empty lounger without another word.

A few more minutes passed before Serah'Elax returned to her lounger, Dexter having moved off to harass another woman. A new drink arrived a second after she sat down, and Serah'Elax picked it up from the serving drone before taking a sip.

Ellipse got up and walked over to sit next to Serah'Elax. The warrior's focus switched entirely to Ellipse the moment she stood up.

"Hello, Serah'Elax Rez Ashfalen," Ellipse said. The pronunciation of her name was flawless.

Although Serah'Elax smiled, it was forced, and Serah'Elax's body tensed. "Hello, Ellipse. How are you?"

"Happy." Ellipse glanced up for a moment and then back at her. "Yes. I'm happy."

Serah'Elax looked directly into Ellipse's eyes, an unsettling look on her face. Ellipse understood that her golden orbs could be disturbing to Havin. They were intricate and entirely unlike a traditional eye, yet something more. A marvel uniquely beautiful and otherworldly that she was quite proud of.

Serah'Elax sucked in a breath, profound understanding passing across her features at that moment.

Ellipse tilted her head, a curious look on her face. "Oh . . . does knowing what I am scare you?"

Serah'Elax narrowed her eyes. "Fear is the first step toward death," she recited. "No, I do not fear you, machine."

Ellipse understood the phrase as an Ashna Maiden tenant ingrained into all Ashna Maidens from childhood.

"Good." Ellipse's smile widened. "Because I'd like very much to be your friend."

Serah'Elax became disinterested in her drink and set it down. "You should not exist," she said. "The Ashna Mothers have forbidden all forms of synthetic life. To us, you are soulless abominations unworthy of Ashna's blessing and a danger to all life."

Ellipse frowned.

"If you'll excuse me, I think I'm going to call it a night," Serah'Elax said, getting up from her lounger.

Ellipse watched the woman depart through the meglift, Ellipse's shoulders slumping. Serah'Elax's words suddenly sparked anger in Ellipse. She noted the emotion, scrutinized it, and tried to determine why that emotion had been triggered.

Picking up Serah'Elax's drink, she sipped at it. Complex sensors in her mouth informed her that the concoction was non-alcoholic but sweet—from there, she built a complete flavor profile out of it, giving her a sense of what it "tasted" like. She dismissed the anger and spent a great deal of time processing that taste, trying to experience it the way a Havin would.

She took time to determine what subtle flavors she liked and didn't like. Shifting her gaze out of the dome, she focused the lion's share of her attention back to Neven's lab once the omnistruction was completed. Robotic drones moved the new device to a specially prepared storage chamber adjacent to the lab SI core. The installation was the quickest part of the whole exercise.

Ellipse got up from her lounger and made her way to the lab.

CHAPTER 15 – URIEL KERVID

56625 FA (23,498 years ago)
Shuttle in the upper atmosphere of Tenquin,
Huzien Empire space

Uriel watched the Founder's Elite run through their weapons checks, all of them crammed in a shuttle as it approached the triangular semi-transparent panels that held in Tenquin's new planetary atmosphere.

The shuttle veered toward a star-shaped opening at the intersection of panels that allowed the shuttle entry. It descended through the atmosphere as Uriel looked back at the engineering marvel. The panels covered the entire planet and would remain in place until the terraforming process was declared complete, almost like a roof over the planet itself.

Uriel sensed Lanrete watching him from across the shuttle. Their eyes locked briefly before Uriel turned his attention to a holodisplay on the wall. It showed their entry point in relation to the estimated location of the Guymulagi, a splinter cell of the pirate band Het Wrast Aht that had taken up residence in Huzien Empire space. Tenquin was an unpopulated planet on the fringes of the Huzien Empire near the Outer Rim that had been a barren wasteland a century ago.

The shuttle rapidly decelerated, preparing to land four clicks outside the target site in a small clearing. After a few moments, the back of the shuttle opened as Uriel took the lead.

"Alright, team. This is the real thing. Let's get this done," Uriel said.

He nodded to Lanrete as the Founder fell in beside him. The shuttle ramp retracted, and the shuttle cloaked as they started their trek.

"Never been on a recent terraform," Xer Yuino said. She wore massive Archlight armor and was a towering woman due to her extensive genetic modifications. Her hulking form was surprisingly quiet, although the gravimetric thrusters of her armor kicked on every so often as she walked.

"They aren't typically safe. The biosphere is completely feral with automated drones that can euthanize a whole section if the biome gets out of whack," Nebu Ferhar said. He was the team Ciedalif and a doctor who was top of his class. Most of his career had been spent in the Huzien military. He had light-brown skin and a bald head. "Aerial scans showed this area was filled with hecen weed, meaning it might be a prime target for eradication. We should watch the geo-warning net for any indications that this area has been flagged." He projected visuals of the plant into the microdisplays of every team member. "This weed is nasty, so avoid it at all costs. It might not bother you now, but the moment you take your armor off, the spores will latch onto your skin and cause a nasty breakout."

"Noted," came the voice of Asfeyra Mau Bertuferi. She was a half-Uri, half-Huzien hybrid with blue hair.

Uriel had had difficulty finding a Wopan who wasn't Tuzen. Lanrete had been reluctant to have one on the team, given the tensions with the Tuzen Empire. But there was a growing population of Uri who had trained in the craft among the ranks of the military, although it wasn't a formally recognized specialization. Lanrete had wanted every member of the team to be Huzien but had made an exception for Asfeyra, given her half-Huzien blood.

"I've got a visual," Qwen Ointas broadcasted to the team. As the Sentinel on the team, he had cloaked himself and gone up ahead to perform reconnaissance.

A stream hit the microdisplays of every member as Qwen fed them the images recorded from his optical implants, one of the many standard cybernetic enhancements given to Sentinels. The visual showed a sealed nanoplexi door without guards in a small clearing.

"The rest of the facility must be underground," he said.

"A subterranean facility? That explains how they evaded detection for so long." Taylor Zeen brought up a holodisplay on her wrist. She was the group Secnic, and she had a complex set of scientific equipment in her armor with an experimental weapon strung across her back—some sort of plasma rifle of her own creation. "I'm into the geo-net. Military overrides worked like a charm. I've temporarily blacked out this area, so we shouldn't have any automated drones accidentally eradicating us anytime soon. The door should be easy to breach, but we'll need to get an understanding of their monitoring systems first."

"On it," Qwen replied.

Uriel smiled. The cohesion from their months of training together had brought them to levels he could have only dreamed of.

When the team arrived at the door, it had already been opened. They carefully made their way in; Qwen had put down the set of guards a short distance inside.

"Assault SI has taken control of the primary SI functions," Qwen said. "Video feeds are on a loop, giving full access control to the group, and we should be able to get you past all doors. I've also killed the coms, but they will notice shortly, so be prepared for resistance."

"Understood, good work," Uriel said.

He tested access to a door to their side. It opened instantly. Xer took point, her massive shield moving in front of her as they fell in line behind. She accelerated forward unexpectedly, slamming into a man as he came within view. Her shield crushed him against the wall.

"Hostiles," was the single word she said as she spun in a tight circle and then powered forward.

The sounds of weaponsfire erupted around the bend. Uriel and Lanrete accelerated forward and bounded off the wall in the direction she had gone. Uriel caught sight of a group of pirates engaged in a firefight with Xer. She speared one of the pirates with her lance rifle and unleashed a devastating blast of lightning energy that blew them apart. Leveling her lance rife on the next target, she fired, the pirate scrambling out of the way and behind cover.

Uriel bounded past her toward another pirate firing on her, his Iltarum blade flying out into the man's chest and pinning him to the wall. The blade returned to his side as Uriel motioned downward with his hands. Enesmic energy surged forward to ignite two pirates standing next to each other in intense flame.

He caught movement to his side, catching sight of Lanrete engaging with two other pirates. Uriel forced himself to ignore the Founder and focus on his targets. He sent his Iltarum blade into the neck of another pirate. Uriel lifted the man's body into the air, accelerating it to incredible speeds into another pirate who came into view. The force of impact caused the body to explode, splattering the wall behind them with gore.

"Room clear," came Asfeyra's broadcasted voice.

They continued forward, an overlay appearing in the microdisplay, showcasing the compound layout—another gift from the Assault SI. They encountered heavy resistance as they made their way to the central command room at the bottommost level. Xer attempted to open the door to the command room, but a signal indicated it was jammed.

She leveled her shoulder with the door and backed up a few strides. Flaring her gravimetric thrusters with a blast from her lance rifle, she barreled forward, the force of her impact tearing the door off its tracks. She flew into the room, her thrusters reversing to halt her momentum. Her shield came down as weaponsfire erupted all around her.

Uriel quickly moved to her back, the rest of the group doing likewise. Asfeyra began to tap her feet, a sign he had started to associate with her getting into the "flow" Wopan were so known for—a type of hypnotic music-induced focus that put them on a whole other level.

She emerged from under the protective shield and jumped into the air, spinning in a tight circle as her weaponsfire decimated the room. She landed in a flourish, rolling and jumping again, higher this time, as she completed another revolution and unleashed a precision barrage that hit every intended target.

The room went silent as she landed, tapping her weapons on the ground. Taylor whistled as the group came from behind Xer and walked to a holodisplay near a body. Uriel identified it as the Guymulagi leader's corpse.

"Unlocking command console," Taylor said. "Good thing the Assault SI locked this out. It looks like they were attempting to purge the SI metabase." Taylor stood there for a few seconds, eventually nodding. "False commands sent. Every Guymulagi ship just received orders to rendezvous and attack a suspected high-value civilian target."

"And the thirty-second fleet will be there waiting for them in ambush," Nebu said as Qwen decloaked near the entrance to the room.

"Good job," Lanrete said.

They were the first words he had said all mission. Everyone turned to regard the Founder. Uriel felt a sense of elation course through his body.

"Let's return to the *Ascension.*"

Foundra Ascension *orbiting Tenquin, Huzien Empire space*

Uriel walked into the briefing room aboard the *Foundra Ascension.* Lanrete motioned for him to sit as he turned back to a figure on a nearby holodisplay.

Uriel frowned on seeing a man with an elaborate face tattoo. He recognized the design as belonging to Het Wrast Aht—a quick facial match on his mobi pegged the man as Bevherk Hechet, the current leader of Het Wrast Aht and one of the most wanted men in the Twin Galaxies.

"I appreciate you putting down this upstart," Bevherk was saying. "He drew away a larger portion of my forces than I anticipated. Our agreement will remain intact. Het Wrast Aht will stay out of Huzien Empire space, and anyone disobeying my orders will have their friends and families murdered on my command."

"Glad we could come to an understanding," Lanrete said. He terminated the connection and glanced back to Uriel.

"We're making deals with pirates now?" Uriel felt anger creeping into his voice.

"The Huzien Empire has quiet agreements with Het Wrast Aht to ensure the safety of our borders," Lanrete said.

"Didn't realize people who made a living raping, murdering, and pillaging had a habit of keeping their word."

"We've maintained this agreement with Het Wrast Aht for millennia. If the larger pirate bands stay out of our space, we're more able to focus our efforts on the straggling pirate bands. It's an unfortunate necessity, but it's all to maintain order."

"Why not simply cross the borders and wipe out the pirate threat? The Outer Rim is a haven for these monsters. We can put an end to that."

"The number of forces necessary to police the Outer Rim would be significant. There are no major players in that section of space, so we'd have to unify a disparate group of weak planets and invest significant diplomatic and military resources to bring the Outer Rim into the Huzien Empire for minimal gain. That is not something we've been willing to commit to."

"It's the right thing to do," Uriel said.

"Sometimes the right thing isn't a luxury we get afforded." Lanrete picked up a drink from a serving drone and moved to sit in a seat adjacent to Uriel. "Moving on to other matters, I'm impressed with the team's effectiveness. We have our next mission lined up. I'm meeting with a representative for the Humans, a man named Soahc. According to some circles, he's supposedly a very powerful Cihphist—considered a legend among the Humans. Given the potential threat he poses, having the team in place to act if necessary will give the other Founders some assurances of safety. And having you there as our empire's most powerful Cihphist will bring me personal assurances."

"Humans . . . the GNet feeds are filled with stories of the problems they are causing across the Twin Galaxies." Uriel narrowed his eyes. "They hold a not-insignificant military force for a people without a home."

"Multiple forces. They were a leaderless people like the Tuzens until some time ago, but this Soahc . . . he's emerged on the scene in a big way and has brought structure and discipline to their ranks. He speaks for them, and many are starting to listen. He could be the key to unifying them."

"Is that a good thing?"

"It is. The empire is not a stranger to welcoming new species into its folds, but it's easier when there is a leader that they can rally behind—someone who can speak on their behalf and work to maintain order without us doing it. This way, it looks less like subjugation and more like cooperation. We learned that with the Uri."

"Alright. I'll brief the team." Uriel got up and then hesitated. "One question, Founder."

"Yes?"

"I've been thinking about the incentive structure for the team. Given the highly specialized nature of the team and the hard work that went into finding these folks, I believe we should increase their pay well beyond the standards afforded by rank and threat zone to an amount that would make any other line of work a financial disincentive."

Lanrete hesitated for a moment and then nodded. "Very well. I'll leave it to your discretion."

Uriel nodded and left the room.

CHAPTER 16 - TASHANIRA YEN UNVESAL

Foundra Ascension, *Huzien / Darbol Border Space*

Tashanira and Jenshi walked through the aeroponics deck aboard the *Foundra Ascension*. The beautiful forestry gave the illusion of being deep in nature as they followed their favorite trail. The place was a technological marvel, a mesh of nature and technology that rivaled the expertise employed by the Uri on Peshkana. Much of it had been built by Arnea when she was still aboard the ship.

Tashanira missed Arnea. Her careful eye and attention to detail had been true gifts. The *Ascension* had become more homely and welcoming once her fingerprints were everywhere in the form of little plants that accented and livened up every corner. Arnea's replacement was trying their best, but they lacked her gift.

"You remember the first date we went on?" Tashanira asked.

Jenshi glanced at her briefly as if suddenly remembering he was walking with her. She raised an eyebrow as Jenshi gave her a tight-lipped smile.

"I do . . ." Jenshi took in a deep breath. "We had already slept together a dozen times, and you mentioned that it might be good for us to do things outside the bedroom since we were so familiar."

"Yeah." Tashanira touched her neck. "I recommended we walk on the aeroponics deck, and you lamented how much you hated nature."

"I did . . . and I adapted and changed that aspect of myself for your sake after our relationship became serious." Jenshi's tone was cold.

Tashanira frowned, her gaze going to the ground. They remained silent for a long moment as an artificial breeze blew through the trees.

"One thing I've always admired about the Huzien Military is the strict hierarchical command structure that Lanrete created. It hides its strictness and hierarchy with a perfect illusion of independence and free will." Jenshi put his hands behind his back. "Ecnics's mark is, of course, the built-in technology that consistently performs checks and balances to trick people with this sense of autonomy, one that is calculated and monitored extensively. A soldier thinks he's making independent decisions outside of the watchful eye of his commanding officer, but the commanding officer knows and chooses to allow the decisions to be made independently of him. It's an interesting military theory. It's also something that extends even to the medical staff."

Jenshi stopped. "For example, anyone can delete an impromptu scan that isn't part of an official examination. As far as they know and are concerned, the scan goes away, independent of any type of validation or sign-off. It's a level of privacy that allows military personnel to feel they control their data." Jenshi turned to face Tashanira. "But the reality is that all deletions go to the chief medical officer, and there is a shadow profile for every person that contains all data captured about them. And it stays in this shadow file forever."

Tashanira's heart froze as she stared at him.

"It's something no chief medical officer is ever allowed to disclose. The punishment is a court martial for divulging state secrets." He moved to lean against a nearby tree, his gaze distant.

Tashanira rushed toward him. "Jenshi, I'm sorry! I planned to tell you. I—"

"Don't." Jenshi held up a hand, stopping Tashanira. "I'm not interested in your explanations. I only want to know one thing: how long were you *vusging* Neven?

"It was only when we were trapped on the shuttle. We thought we were going to die. You have to believe me."

Both went silent, the breeze rustling more leaves as the sounds of nature reached a crescendo. Tashanira's hair was wild; the wind had caught hold of it.

"I do." Jenshi nodded. "I do believe you. I believe that when you were about to die, your first thought was to *vusg* Neven. Not to remain faithful to me in the hopes that I'd rescue you." Jenshi laughed. "It says a lot about how much you value our relationship. Or rather, how much you don't."

"That's not what I meant."

"Isn't it? I mean, it's what happened, right?" Jenshi's eyes flickered.

Tashanira remained silent, her gaze going to the ground. She hugged herself.

"I'm . . . I . . . ." Jenshi took a moment to compose himself. "I should have listened to my father."

Tashanira glanced up to lock gazes with Jenshi as her heart sank, her eyes pleading.

"He never trusted Uri. He used to call your kind nothing more than intelligent animals." Jenshi laughed. "'You can't change a Uri's stripes,' he said. 'They are driven by instincts, not morals.'" He spoke the words with venom. "Good for a *vusg* but not a relationship." Jenshi nodded. "That was my mistake."

Jenshi pushed himself off the tree and walked away from Tashanira.

The nature by which the harvesting of planetary resources was done infused certain areas of the planet with Enesmic energy, the likes of which we have never seen.

-FROM "ENESMIC SHIPYARD EFFECTS ON TRICA VII"
MINSCI METABASE

CHAPTER 17 - NEVEN KENK

Foundra Ascension, *Huzien / Darbol Border Space*

The chiming at his front door caught Neven off guard. He brought up an external display to see Jenshi standing there, his hands behind his back, his face hard.

He knows, Ellipse warned in Neven's thoughts.

Neven glanced around his quarters. He was alone. Although Ellipse was in the lab, her consciousness was still in his head.

I can't run away from this, Neven replied.

He got up from his couch and walked toward the front door. Prompting it to open, Neven stood a short distance inside, facing his visitor.

Jenshi watched him, the aura radiating from the doctor causing Neven to tense up.

Neither of the men moved.

"Please, come in." Neven rubbed his arm, glancing around.

Jenshi hesitated for a long moment and then took a few steps inside, the door sealing shut behind him.

"Has Tashanira . . . uh, shared some important news with you?" Neven asked.

"The pregnancy. Yes," Jenshi stated.

Neven nodded slowly. "Yes, the pregnancy. Jenshi, I'm so sorr—"

A cold prick at Neven's neck caught him off guard. He stumbled back, raising his hand to his neck in confusion.

"What?"

One of Jenshi's medical drones decloaked beside Neven; a liphojam extended a few inches away from his neck. Neven glanced from the liphojam to the medical drone and then to Jenshi. His body suddenly got very heavy as he stumbled again and then fell to the ground. Neven felt heat spreading throughout his body, like burning from within. It became harder and harder to breathe, and his vision blurred. Sharp pain shot like spiderwebs across every inch of his body as he spasmed.

Jenshi moved to the window, seemingly oblivious to Neven's plight. "When I was the CMO for the third fleet, many projects came across my desk." Jenshi clasped his hands behind his back and continued to stare out the window into open space.

Neven gasped. His mouth was becoming parched, his throat tightening.

"One was for testing a potent biological weapon developed in partnership with eshLucent's bioengineering arm." He glanced back at Neven. "Bioweapons are largely illegal in the Huzien Alliance, but that doesn't stop their development. It merely stops their application in wartime scenarios." Jenshi walked toward Neven and squatted near him. "I ultimately rejected the bioweapon because it was particularly cruel to its victims, but I stored the remaining samples instead of destroying them like I was instructed." He brought up a holodisplay, showing a scan of Neven's body. "You never know, right?"

Jenshi shrugged as he glanced over at the readout. "What you feel right now is your body rapidly shutting down thanks to an army of bioengineered attack nanites. Each carries a powerful neurotoxin as they attack every part of your nervous system." He stood up and glared down at Neven. "You'll be dead within two minutes." Jenshi shuddered briefly and then balled his fists. "I tried to save Zun. I really did. I . . ." Jenshi paused. "I tried every trick in the book and used every technique I knew. I pulled from over a century of experience to try and save your wife, and I couldn't." Jenshi let out a ragged breath. "For that, I *am* sorry. For that, I am ashamed that a member of my crew died, and I was unable to bring them back. That weighs heavily on my soul, Neven, in a way you probably can't understand." Jenshi's eyes narrowed. "I know her death hurt you deeply. But I tried. I tried my best. I did things that I didn't even think I was capable of. Zun was a friend—we knew each other for years, and she trusted me, along with every other member of this crew, that in the worst of times, I'd be there for them. That I'd be there to save their lives."

Jenshi paused again. "I failed." Jenshi sucked in a breath. "Colleagues tell me that it's not my fault. *Vusg*, it's not even the first time a member of my team has died under my watch, but I still accept responsibility for not being able to save her." Jenshi remained silent for a moment. "But then you went after my girl. Was it revenge? I never actually expected you to . . ." Jenshi shook his head. "I know there were always jokes, but I always thought you had a strong sense of morality, that you . . ." Jenshi sucked in a quick breath. "I respected you," he spoke the words with venom.

Neven struggled to respond but couldn't. His body ignored all inputs from his mind. Pure terror overwhelmed him as he felt utterly helpless at that moment. An overwhelming sense of remorse overtook him as he came to grips with the reality that he was going to die.

A tear started to roll down his cheek as he lamented the decisions that got him to this point. His mind flashed.

The waves crashing against the beach put Neven at ease. Friends and family were all around them in a circle as Zun looked at him, a smile on her face. Everything was perfect. Zun was beautiful as she said her vows.

The image of her beautiful smiling face shifted.

Zun's eyes went wide. She mouthed the word "run" as her head twisted unnaturally to the side, and then a crack echoed across the beach. The life vanished from her eyes as her body dropped to the sand, its original white now turning a shade of dark red.

143

Disappointment washed over Neven as the image of Entradis drowned out everything.

His thoughts switched to Jenshi—he could see the pain in the man's face. Neven had hurt him deeply. The usual calm and collected demeanor that Jenshi was so known for was gone at that moment. There was loathing in Jenshi's eyes, backed by a psychotic rage that had been unleashed.

Neven regretted bringing that out in Jenshi. *I forgive you, Jenshi.*

It was a surreal thought, but it felt right, like a part of his soul was at peace with what was happening to him. The contradiction hit him instantly; he could forgive the man hovering over him who was ending his life, but he couldn't let go of the vengeance his heart demanded for Zun's murderer. Sadness overwhelmed him as his vision began to fade to black.

"You took everything away from me," Jenshi said. "I knew it was all gone when I saw the scan of Tashanira's pregnancy and saw your genetic signature in that baby." Jenshi's voice was becoming more distant. "I couldn't let it go. I couldn't just walk away from it all. I hadn't been able to do that when pirates murdered my father, and I couldn't do it now." A heavy sadness pulled at Jenshi's eyes. "My life is over, Neven. I will lose everything because of this moment. You've gotten your revenge."

Jenshi shook his head as the drone approached Neven with another liphojam that silently pressed against his neck. Jenshi dismissed the holodisplay and turned to face the door, putting his hands above his head in a mimicry of innocence. He closed his eyes.

Within seconds, Neven felt sensation return to his body as his limbs started responding to his promptings. He felt an elephant get off his chest, his lungs returning to normal as he sucked in a deep breath.

The door to Neven's room suddenly opened as Dexter rushed in with Ellipse a step behind him. Dexter charged Jenshi and tackled him to the ground hard.

Jenshi didn't resist as he was roughly turned over, his head slammed into the ground. The sound of his nose breaking echoed throughout the room, Jenshi remaining silent through the brutality.

Ellipse pushed the drone away from Neven and picked him up, carefully cradling him in her arms. She quickly exited his room and carried him toward the medical deck.

Neven could make out people in uniforms rushing past Ellipse and into his quarters. Neven smiled briefly as he watched Ellipse's resolute expression, her movements superhuman as she held him tightly to her chest.

He closed his eyes and quickly passed out.

Foundra Ascension *en route to Thae, Huzien Alliance space*
Three Days Later

Neven awoke with a start, light blinding him as his eyes slowly adjusted to the brightness of the medical deck. Ellipse sat in a chair beside him, as still as a statue. Her face softened as their eyes locked. Every aspect about her seemed so perfectly Human that, for a moment, he forgot what she truly was.

"I'm glad you're awake," came a voice from off to the side.

Neven followed the voice to see Lanrete sitting in a chair a short distance from the bed.

"How are you feeling?" the immortal asked, his eyes appearing very old.

"I'm surprised to be alive." Neven felt an overwhelming sense of relief. "Where's Jenshi?"

"He's in the brig under guard. He can't hurt you anymore."

"He must have given me the cure. Maybe he didn't intend to kill me."

"It doesn't matter." Lanrete's voice was firm. "His conduct was unacceptable."

"Enough about Jenshi," Ellipse spat. "How are you feeling, Neven?"

"I'm okay. I . . . I'm sorry for everything."

"There's no need for you to apologize," Ellipse said.

Neven took in a deep breath, shuddering. "Tashanira and I had an affair. She's pregnant with my child."

"I'm aware," Lanrete said.

"Jenshi thinks I did it as revenge for him not saving Zun's life."

"Did you?"

Neven shook his head vehemently. "No, I would never. I . . ." Neven broke down, tears coming like a wave. "I'm so sorry. I really messed up."

Neven sobbed silently for a few minutes. Ellipse moved closer to wrap her arms around him in a light embrace. Lanrete silently watched the scene.

"I'm removing you from active duty." Lanrete got up out of his chair. "I think you need to take some time to heal, to deal with Zun's loss, and to recover from this attack."

Neven opened his eyes and looked at Lanrete.

"We're returning to Thae indefinitely," the immortal continued. "I've arranged for you to see a psychotherapist. They are someone I trust, and they will have to clear you before you can return to active duty."

Neven nodded. The outcome was about what he expected.

"Get some rest." Lanrete exited the medical deck.

CHAPTER 18 - TASHANIRA YEN UNVESAL

Foundra Ascension *en route to Thae,*
Huzien Alliance space

Tashanira entered the brig, deep in the bowels of the *Foundra Ascension*. The main security desk filled Tashanira's vision, her eyes lingering on the resolute security officer. He frowned at her briefly before returning to his holodisplay.

She rubbed her arm and glanced around the small entryway before moving toward the reinforced nanoplexi door that separated the small room from the larger holding area.

"Founder Lanrete is in there," the guard said without glancing her way.

Tashanira paused, took a deep breath, and then slowly approached the door as the guard initiated the command for it to open. She silently glided inside.

The brig held five cells, each one a recessed room surrounded by nanoplexi and bright white lights. A large, nanitically enforced glass wall served as the entrance into each one, and there was a powerful shield humming within. Every cell was unoccupied except for the one farthest from the entrance.

Lanrete stood in front of it, talking to the form huddled within. The figure had been stripped nude and then dressed in a skintight, transparent jumpsuit. It was dehumanizing and eliminated all forms of privacy and dignity.

She had seen the standard Huzien prisoner uniform many times before, but seeing Jenshi in it was jarring. She stood a way off, unwilling to make a sound as her acute ears picked up the low conversation.

"I shouldn't have to remind you that killing a member of my team is off the table, regardless of how you feel." Lanrete's voice was hard. "You should be court-marshaled and sent off to *Zatcal* for the next four hundred years of your life."

Tashanira paled. *Zatcal* was a maximum-security prison in orbit around Sigmaphus, a terrifyingly massive black hole deep in Huzien space. It was the hallmark of brutal prisons in the empire and a place you didn't go to unless you pissed off the wrong people or did some truly horrible crimes.

"I'm sorry, Founder," Jenshi said. His gaze was stuck on the ground. "I understand and am ready to accept my punishment." The defeat in his voice broke Tashanira's heart.

Lanrete narrowed his eyes. After a few moments, he let out a heavy sigh. "But that's not what I'm going to do to you."

Jenshi looked up at Lanrete.

"From this day forward, you are no longer a Founder's Elite. You're going to spend the next few weeks in here as we return to Thae—there, you'll undergo an intensive psychiatric evaluation. If you pass your evaluation, you can either return to active duty and receive a new assignment or be OTH discharged and allowed to return to civilian life." Lanrete paused. "If you do not pass your evaluation and are deemed a threat to those around you, you will undergo treatment and be held indefinitely until cleared by a board of doctors."

Lanrete caught sight of Tashanira as she rested against one of the cell glass windows, her gaze toward the ground. A tear rolled down her cheek. She glanced up at Lanrete and then away, unable to maintain eye contact. Lanrete let out another sigh and then exited the brig.

Tashanira remained unmoving for a long moment; she spent that time working up the courage to face Jenshi. Letting out a long, slow breath, she pushed herself off the glass and took slow, careful steps toward Jenshi's cell. She stopped in front of it, her hands clasped behind her back, her posture perfect, professional, military.

Jenshi glanced up at her briefly and then back toward the ground, no emotion registering on his face.

She had played out this conversation a hundred times in her head, but standing there before him, she was at a loss for words. "I . . . I know I'm the last person you want to see right now." Tashanira fought the urge to rub her arm, holding her parade rest stance. "But I wanted to tell you that you were right." She hesitated. "For years, I've used Uri culture as an excuse for my actions. But that's all it's been— an excuse. Not all Uri behave that way, and it's a pervasive stereotype damaging to our real culture of community." Tashanira took in a deep breath. "I see men as conquests, and it's a way I've coped with past trauma over the years." She fought an urge to move her hand to her neck. "I ultimately decide what I do and don't do, and when I was on that shuttle with Neven, I chose to *vusg* him. I initiated it, enjoyed it, and didn't regret it until I heard your voice broadcast over the mobi."

Tashanira's eyes began to water. "I chose to betray the relationship we had built up, all to fulfill a fantasy. Another conquest that I longed for." Tashanira pulled strength from her form, from the training that made her a soldier. "Deep down, I was never truly honest with myself. Our relationship was one of convenience, built on all the wrong things. I struggled to hold on to it because I wanted it to validate the person I had become, very different from that scared little girl back on Peshkana." Tashanira paused, another tear running down her face. "But I understand now that relationships shouldn't validate who we are. Your words woke me up to that. I am who I am, and I'm confident in who I am, with or without you." She shuddered and took a second to compose herself.

"Jenshi, I'm not some intelligent animal. I'm a woman who made poor choices, and I'm sorry that I dragged your heart through the grinder." Tashanira hesitated. "Neven . . . wasn't the first time I was unfaithful to you. I have been unfair in our relationship, and there is nothing I can say or do to repair the damage done." She paused. "I'm planning to return to Peshkana and take a leave of absence from the Founder's Elites once I'm far enough along with the pregnancy. I will give birth to my son there under the grah trees."

She waited for a long moment to see if he would respond. Jenshi continued looking at the ground, giving no indication that he had heard a word she said.

"You were kind to me, a kindness I was not deserving of." Taking a deep breath, Tashanira turned toward the exit and took a step. She stopped abruptly and looked down at the ground. "Thank you . . . for not killing Neven," she whispered.

Tashanira left the brig.

CHAPTER 19 - NEVEN KENK

Foundra Ascension *en route to Thae,*
Huzien Alliance Space

The soft hum of the suplight drive mixed with the sounds of monitoring equipment on the medical deck. Neven was still in his medical bed, not yet cleared for discharge, as he stared at the channel contact details of his mother, Adinah Kenk.

Her name was greyed out, still set to ignore.

He let out a heavy sigh and flipped the channel to accepting calls. Almost immediately, his mobi blipped. His mother was calling him.

Neven laughed, flinching slightly as several sharp pains erupted across his body. He accepted the call and pushed the video to a holodisplay in the nightstand next to his bed.

Adinah was scowling. "I thought I raised you better than to ignore calls from your mother!"

"I'm sorry, Mom. I—"

Adinah's eyes went wide. "Are you in a hospital? What happened?"

Neven sighed. "I messed up, Mom." He began to tear up.

Adinah's scowl melted. "Oh, sweetheart."

"You'd be ashamed of me. I . . ."

"No, don't tell me. It's okay. Just . . . how are you?"

"I'm tired. I don't want to do this anymore."

"Do what?"

"Life. I . . . I just want to come back home. Maybe live in the garage. I won't bother you and Dad, I promise."

Adinah sat quietly, watching her son. She smiled sadly. "You remember those stories I told you when you were younger? About the Maker?"

Neven sighed. "I remember."

"Remember the one about the three trees?" Adinah's voice morphed, her cadence dropping into that of a storyteller. "There were three trees in the forest. One tree whispered to the wind that it was as strong as a mountain and could face any hardship. It prided itself on its independence, having taken root as a seed far from the other trees. Another tree whispered to the wind that it was as nimble as a cat, swaying with the breeze and able to withstand any torrent. It, too, had taken root as a seed far away from the other trees. And then there was the final tree. It decided to remain close to the trees around it, strengthening its roots among its brothers and sisters. One day, a hurricane came. It tore the tree that claimed to be as strong as a mountain from the ground, roots and all, throwing it to the wind, never to be seen again. The tree that claimed to be as nimble as a cat swayed with the hurricane and survived, along with the other trees that remained clustered together. But then a fire swept through the forest, leaving no tree untouched. The nimble tree couldn't evade the flames as they burned it to a crisp, deep into the roots. The tree that had remained close to its brothers and sisters had been buffeted by the hurricane and burned by the fire—it, too, had suffered greatly. But its roots had gone deep, strengthened by its brothers and sisters, and over time, it healed. The road was long, but it regained its full strength and endured the worst that nature had to throw against it. The tree realized that it gained strength not by independence or ability but by community. By staying close to those who supported it."

Adinah remained quiet for a long moment. "Neven, you are a brilliant man, and I am so proud of all that you've accomplished. But you were never meant to suffer alone. Never forget that your family is here for you. The family you were born with and the family that accepted you as their own. Zun may be gone, and you will certainly make mistakes in life, but don't be afraid to reach out to those who love you and lean on us for support. It's the difference between being ravaged by the elements or enduring the worst of life and coming out stronger on the other side."

"Thanks, Mom." Neven's words came out in a whisper. "Zun . . . was pregnant when she died."

"Oh, honey." Adinah teared up. She shuddered and hugged herself. "I am so sorry."

Neven lost control and began to weep quietly.

Adinah joined in with her son, and they took a long moment to recover, silent tears exchanged through the holodisplay.

"Sometimes . . ." Her voice was soft. "When we don't know what else to do, it's best to pray."

Neven sucked in a quick breath and shook his head. "I'm . . . going to get some rest. Love you, Mom."

Adinah smiled at Neven. "I love you too, son."

Neven terminated the call. He stared off into space for a long moment. *I did everything right,* he said in his mind.

Ellipse was there, her presence engulfing him.

Where was the Maker when Zun was being murdered in front of me? Neven slammed his fist down on the nightstand, pain shooting throughout his body as he spasmed and sucked in a quick breath. *Where was the Maker when my unborn child was killed before it had a chance at life?* Neven scowled, his face morphing as he growled. *Where was the Maker—*

When Jenshi suddenly held back from killing you? Ellipse's words jarred Neven.

He relaxed slightly. *Since when do systems intelligences believe in a higher power?*

I was literally created in a lab by a 'Maker,' so the concept is not a foreign one to me. The image of Ellipse grinning filled his mind's eye. *Plus, with the mystery surrounding the Rel Ach'Kel and the 'Originator' Brime talked about, it's not that far of a mental leap.*

Neven started to laugh—more pain shot through his chest, prompting him to stop abruptly.

Neven, the GNet is filled with stories of people who did everything right but still had terrible things happen to them, especially during the Rift War. She paused. *Look at the Outer Rim—those people didn't do anything wrong to deserve being born there.* She hesitated. *But that doesn't mean you should stop doing what's right or let go of your morals.*

Neven let out a long, drawn-out sigh. He closed his eyes. "Okay." He hesitated for a long moment. "Maker . . ." Neven opened his eyes and shook his head. He frowned, staring at a holodisplay readout of his body. There had been extensive damage to his nerves—remnants from the bioweapon. The regenerative therapy he was going through would bring him back to one hundred percent in the next week, something he was silently grateful for.

He closed his eyes again. "Okay, Maker, if you're up there, know that I'm angry with you." He paused. "I . . . I'm in pain, both physically and emotionally, and I need it to stop. Please make it stop."

He waited for a long moment and then opened his eyes. He glanced around, looking back to the holodisplay. Nothing had changed. He forced himself to cough as more sharp pain went off throughout his body. It somehow seemed worse. He frowned and leaned back into his bed, disappointed.

The sound of the primary entrance to the medical deck opening grabbed his attention. He half expected Jenshi to walk through but remembered that the other man was locked up in the brig. He let out a sigh of relief as Dera'Liv Elax Ashfalen walked in. Her almond-colored eyes locked onto him as she walked over to his bed. The level to which she looked like her daughter Serah'Elax was uncanny despite being hundreds of years older than Serah'Elax.

"Do you mind if I visit with you for a little while?" Dera'Liv asked.

Neven nodded his head. "Sure."

"I am glad to see you alive. Word has gotten around the ship of your . . . escapades with Tashanira and Jenshi's subsequent revenge."

Neven groaned.

"Are you recovering well?"

"Things hurt slightly less than yesterday. I guess that's a good thing."

"It surely is." Dera'Liv smiled. She hesitated for a moment, her face becoming serious. "How is your grieving?"

"My grieving?"

"Yes, how are you learning to live with the loss of your *dru'sha*?"

"I . . . I'm not sure." Neven glanced away from her. "Once I find Entradis, I'll get revenge for her. I'll make him pay."

Dera'Liv nodded her head solemnly. "When I lost my *dru'sha* on that terrible day, I had to learn to live without my *ha'ishi*, the telepathic connection that bonded me and Ovah'Hal. It was as if my arm had been pulled from its socket, and my heart ripped out of my chest at the same time. I didn't believe that I had the fortitude to go on, and I almost killed myself." She hesitated. "It is not an uncommon fate for Das'Vin who experience such loss. There is no judgment in it."

"What stopped you?"

Dera'Liv smiled. "When I stared into Serah'Elax's eyes and realized she was still struggling to comprehend a new world without her *wo'shae* and *uma'shae*, I knew immediately that I couldn't leave her alone. She was now my one. My only. I endured for her, but it took me many years to learn to live with my grief. It would come for me in the night or when watching Serah'Elax play—during those times, hints of her *uma'shae* would peek through. It was relentless at first, but I learned to embrace it. I learned to welcome my grief like a friend and accept its waves as they washed over me."

Neven turned to look at Dera'Liv, and they locked eyes.

"Anger is part of the healing process, but not the solution. Killing Entradis will not give you the peace you desire."

"It doesn't matter. He has to die."

Dera'Liv nodded. "That may be true, but do not let that false hope consume you. Embrace your grief and truly start the healing process."

Neven frowned. "Tell me more about the *ha'ishi*," he said. He glanced away from Dera'Liv again.

She let out a slow breath and then sat on his bed. She looked at her hands for a long moment in silence, her gaze eventually moving to Neven. She tilted her head to the side and forced a smile.

Neven turned his attention back to her, and they locked eyes. Dera'Liv held his gaze with a surprising amount of will, enough that Neven found himself unable to turn away from her.

"The *ha'ishi* is a powerful telepathic connection formed once two Das'Vin are joined as *dru'sha*—life partners, in your tongue. The process is not simply ceremonial. The joining of our bodies and minds makes a permanent connection that persists across all distances."

Neven felt something tugging at his senses, almost like a warm gentleness enrapturing him. He felt himself growing more comfortable next to Dera'Liv.

The defenses honed into him by Soahc kicked in, and he realized Dera'Liv was affecting him telepathically.

"Do not push me out. I am trying to better illustrate my point," Dera'Liv explained.

Neven lowered his defenses as a telepathic connection formed between them. The deeply intimate nature of it made Neven immediately uncomfortable. He felt he was on full display to Dera'Liv, but he knew she felt the same about him.

Memories of her past life flashed in his mind as Neven saw her story. He felt from Dera'Liv an expectation of revulsion, but Neven simply accepted her as she was and shared in the fount of sorrow that flowed from her.

Dera'Liv gasped slightly and continued, "Our scientists believe the connection is formed through another dimension, potentially the Enesmic plane. This, they believe, is why the telepathic influence can spread across any distance when compared against normal telepathic interactions. Those are the ones that are limited by distance or line of sight."

"And when your . . . *dru'sha* dies, that connection is severed?"

Dera'Liv abruptly severed the connection between them. The brutal way in which it was done caused Neven a slight headache. He touched his forehead and gripped the nightstand to steady himself; he suddenly felt sick.

"Yes. Imagine what you are feeling now amplified one hundred-fold. And it never goes away." Dera'Liv rubbed her arm, the silver flecks in her skin glittering in the bright lights of the medical deck. "To use an analogy you may be familiar with: the circuitry is still there, but it's been burned out. When the circuit burns, it damages all nearby interconnections, but you are never allowed to repair it or any of the damage done. You are forced to live with that circuitry and damaged interconnections for the rest of your life. Circuitry that once sung with computational power on a level you never achieved before . . . gone, in an instant." Dera'Liv stared off into the distance. "The bond supersedes any level of intimacy you've ever felt with your beloved." Dera'Liv's voice cracked. She sucked in a deep breath.

Neven looked down at her hands as moisture dripped from her chin onto them.

"I'm sorry. I should not have disturbed you." Dera'Liv got up and began to walk toward the exit.

"Dera'Liv," Neven called out.

She stopped but didn't turn around.

"I'm sorry for your loss. Thank you for the visit."

She hesitated for a moment and then exited the medical deck.

Neven stared after her for many minutes, his mind abuzz with activity.

I wonder if it's similar to the connection we share, Ellipse said.

We have a ha'ishi, *then? We're life partners?*

Sure.

Neven laughed as the pain assailed him again. A ting of sadness from Ellipse reached him and caught him off guard.

CHAPTER 20 - URIEL KERVID

57011 FA (23,112 years ago)
Ceiling City of Okren, Raifac, New Ginea, Huzien home system

Uriel looked out from the window down onto the continent of Raifac on New Ginea. He was in a hanging structure that moved across an orbital ring about one hundred kilometers above the planet's surface, one of the many that made up the ceiling city of Okren. He was on the bottommost section of the structure, meaning that the inverse "top" with the ground floor was closest to the orbital ring itself.

Uriel imagined himself soaring through the clouds, the rush of the air causing the hair on the back of his neck to stand on end.

A voice came from behind him. "Beautiful, isn't it?"

He snapped his attention back to his surroundings. A Uri with silver eyes, platinum fur, and waist-length champagne hair stood beside him.

Uriel nodded, his gaze taking her in fully. He realized she was pregnant—probably in the second trimester—and was wearing tribal garb, signifying her as a Tribe mother from the motherworld of Peshkana.

He narrowed his eyes curiously. "I thought Tribe mothers were older and that the title was reserved for Uri past the age of childbearing."

"I can switch into matron mother attire if you'd like, although I don't think Soahc would agree." She gave him a mischievous smile. "You must be the right hand of our mighty Founder, Lanrete."

"Uriel Kervid. A pleasure to make your acquaintance, Miss?"

"Feyura Mau Gehreyati," Feyura said. "Mother of immortals and current *uterga* to Soahc."

"Ah." Uriel glanced in Soahc's direction. "You two are joined?"

"No." Feyura grinned. "I am carrying his child, exclusive to him until the child is born and weaned." Her grin morphed into a smile that made Uriel uncomfortable as her eyes half closed. "If you're interested in fathering children sometime in the next millennia, I'd be happy to turn our acquaintance into something more. My tribe is dominant among the Uri, so our child would wield influence on Peshkana just as well as on Thae." She took a step closer to Uriel, her breath hot as her voice became a near whisper. "I have birthed two immortal children in my lifetime. Uri hybrids are quite beautiful children. I assure you will not be disappointed. I am also quite skilled in making the experience very pleasurable, skills that would continue until said child was weaned."

Uriel felt himself taking a step back, bumping up against the window. "I uh . . . wow." He took in a deep breath. "I . . . need some time to process your offer." He scratched the back of his head. "You're . . . an immortal."

"And you are not?" Feyura glanced at him curiously. "I only make this offer to other immortals."

She looked in the direction of Lanrete and then tapped her chin, giving Uriel another mischievous smile as her eyes slowly made their way back to him. She sent her channel details to Uriel along with a data stream of images and video and then returned to Soahc's side. Uriel stared at the channel details in his microdisplay in a daze, eventually turning to look at Lanrete. He let out a slow breath and then moved to the Founder's side.

Lanrete glanced at Uriel. "Having fun?"

Uriel forced a smile and then took inventory of the room. The Founder's Elites were stationed at key points across the ballroom. A metallic chime signaled, prompting the noise in the room to die down.

"Sounds like the program is about to get started."

Lanrete moved to a section of seats reserved for the Founders and their escorts. Uriel sat down next to Lanrete, his gaze briefly going to Feyura, who gave him a look that caused him to lose focus. The image of her nude atop him hit his thoughts, the manifestation as vivid as a real memory. He was even sure for a moment that he could "feel" her.

A subtle gasp escaped his lips. She was a Cihphist, a powerful telepath, it would seem. He shielded his mind, shutting out the intrusion, and returned to focus on the event and any potential threats that could arise.

Cislot moved to the stage, sporting a deep-blue formal suit. "Friends and future friends," Cislot began, "welcome to this momentous occasion as we solidify the bonds between two peoples. This day, the Human Republic is reformed with a new home."

Thunderous applause went up across the room.

"We are honored to turn over this beautiful planet—the former moon Therus, which has orbited Thae since the Huzien people have existed—as the new home world of the Humans: New Ginea. Previously barren, we have terraformed this world and made it into a lush paradise as a token of our eternal friendship."

More applause went up as Soahc made his way onto the stage. Cislot took a step back as Soahc came to the podium.

"We express heartfelt gratitude to our friends, the Huziens and the Huzien Empire for this humbling gift. With this act, the Human Republic formally joins the Huzien Empire as not just allies but brothers and sisters."

Soahc glanced at Lanrete, who nodded back at him. Cislot's assistant approached the stage as a holodisplay appeared above the podium. Lanrete and Ecnics got up from their seats and joined the others on the stage. They were presented with a set of golden signing instruments that they each took in hand. One by one, they signed the holodisplay on the podium.

Once the last was complete, the new constitution was projected on the massive holodisplay behind them on the wall. Cheers and applause erupted as everyone stood.

In the noise, Uriel opened one of the videos sent from Feyura—the video showed him in the battle of Lux'ian three hundred and eighty-eight years ago. He brought up one of the attached images to see a picture of himself from his first deployment with his squad in the mobile infantry, eight hundred and ninety-one years ago. He watched another video of himself next to Lanrete a week ago as they arrived on New Ginea.

He looked the same across every image and video, the evidence obvious to him when he made a digital comparison that zoomed in on his face and tagged them side by side.

He let out a slow breath, the reality he had ignored for the last few hundred years laid plain before him.

Ceiling City of Okren, Raifac, New Ginea, Huzien home system

Uriel deflected a strike from Lanrete, their blades connecting with sparks. The intensity of the strike caused a small shock wave that pushed towels and other loose objects onto the floor.

A mammoth ship hummed past the massive window that afforded a view down to the surface of New Ginea. It was midday, and transports were coming in and out of the city.

Uriel shut out the distractions as the two struggled against the other's might, gazes locked in a battle of wills. Lanrete pushed forward, overpowering Uriel as he followed up with a cross slash, Divinebreath aiming for Uriel's neck.

Uriel ducked under the blade and lunged forward with Wishwonder, aiming for Lanrete's heart, but before he could make contact, Lanrete disappeared, shifting himself out of harm's way.

Uriel shifted with him, and the two proceeded to appear at different parts around the expansive training room, their blades connecting in flashes as they appeared, connected blades, and then disappeared again.

After a few more moments of the deadly dance, Lanrete appeared in the center of the room as the shadow of another transport cut off the sunlight. The automated lights slowly came on, painting the room with a low ambiance. Lanrete held his blade out in front of him, his eyes closed. Uriel struck at him from the back, but Lanrete spun, intercepting the blade. Uriel struck again, appearing at Lanrete's side. Lanrete spun and blocked.

Uriel appeared a short distance from Lanrete as he tensed, unsure what the Founder was doing. Lanrete remained still for a long moment, his eyes remaining closed. Uriel took a defensive stance, his footwork shifting as his blade came up at an angle. The room vibrated as the Enesmic shifted in a way Uriel had never felt.

The sun peeked from around the transport as Uriel felt hot plexicarbonite against his throat, pain exploding across his left arm and right leg. He struggled to remain standing.

Lanrete was at his side, Divinebreath inches from ending his life. Uriel's eyes widened as he took in a deep gasp of air. Lanrete's body hummed, steam rising from it as Uriel sensed incredible power dissipating from the other man. His veins were bulging, his eyes filled with a glow rapidly fading.

"I yield," Uriel said.

He dropped his blade, and Lanrete removed his weapon and sheathed it at his side. Uriel collapsed to his knees as the pain became too much for him. He glanced down to see a deep gash in his leg.

"Two strikes and a readied death blow, faster than I could detect, let alone respond." He grinned. "Impressive."

"Impressive yourself," Lanrete said. He helped Uriel stand to his feet, supporting him on his shoulder. "Let's get you to medical."

"You'll have to teach me that technique."

"And give you an advantage in our sparring? Never."

Both laughed. They navigated to the meglift that rose a few floors, eventually depositing them in a pristine medical clinic. Lanrete sat on an empty medical bed across from Uriel.

Two doctors came to assist them, one tending to Lanrete's wounds and the other prompting Uriel to lay down on the bed as a surgical drone appeared at his side and immediately went to work rebuilding the tissue in his gash.

"Almost four hundred years of fighting together, and you still have tricks up your sleeve," Uriel said.

"When you have lived as long as I have, you start to amass a catalog of them."

"Speaking of that," Uriel said. Lanrete frowned, glancing in his direction. "I'm nine hundred and twenty-six years old now."

"You are."

"I should look and feel like an old man in the last years of his life, and yet I look not a day over one hundred . . . and I feel the best I've ever been."

The two sat in silence for a few moments as the doctors finished repairing their injuries and moved away.

Lanrete got up. "What is it that you want to ask me?"

Uriel glanced at Lanrete, their eyes locking. "Am I an immortal?"

"Does it matter?"

"Yes, it matters."

"Why? Would it change what you're doing right now?"

"I don't know. Maybe." Uriel had annoyance in his tone.

Lanrete let out a sigh. "Walk with me."

He turned and started walking toward the meglift. Uriel hesitated for a moment and then followed him. The meglift descended to one of the lowermost floors, a hydroponic garden that Lanrete entered. Hues of red and orange bathed the sky in the soft light of a setting star, white lights coming on and illuminating walking paths that weaved throughout the garden. A collection of some of the most beautiful plants gathered from the planet's surface were on display. The two walked a path through the greenery in silence.

"Yes, you were born an immortal. It's extremely rare, and we still don't know what triggers it. Like all immortals, you aged to young adulthood and then not a day more." Lanrete held his hands behind his back, a look of concern on his face. "What do you plan to do with this information?"

Uriel stopped and glanced down at the ground, his heart pounding in his chest. "What *should* I do?"

"Nothing." Lanrete stared hard at Uriel, his words carrying an air of authority.

Uriel slowly nodded. His thoughts were in chaos, his body reacting to the confirmation more than he'd anticipated. It was as if a burden had dropped onto his shoulders, the enormity of limitless time overwhelming him physically.

"Okay . . ." The words came out in a whisper.

Lanrete silently watched Uriel for a long moment, a frown morphing his features. "Study with Soahc. Take him up on his offer." Lanrete started moving again.

Uriel glanced up at Lanrete, rapidly blinking his eyes now that the topic was closed. "He told you?"

"Of course. He asked me for permission before he approached you with the proposal." Lanrete moved to one of the windows that afforded a beautiful view of the planet below, then sat on a bench next to it. Uriel crossed his arms, choosing to remain standing. "He's a powerful Cihphist, more powerful than you—more powerful than any of us. I've come to trust him like a brother, but I still trust you more." Lanrete looked to Uriel. "He's been a Cihphist longer than we have been alive. There is much that he can teach you."

"Would it be worth the time?"

"You're an immortal, remember? Fifty years under his tutelage is nothing in your lifespan. Think of it as an investment for the Huzien Empire."

"Very well." Uriel nodded, clarity highlighting the next steps of his new immortal life. "I will inform Soahc that I accept his offer."

CHAPTER 21 - NEVEN KENK

Present Day
Foundra Ascension *orbiting Thae, Huzien home system*

Neven stood at the window to his quarters, looking down on Thae. He remembered the first time he had seen the planet from space as a new member of the Founder's Elite. Just looking at the planet had convinced him he had an unknown and exciting adventure ahead of him.

Shortly after that high point, however, he took his first life, and the shine of it all was removed.

It was in a battle on the planet Neth. The planet had been under assault by a powerful Eshgren known as Sagren. He was in the BRAS frame, in an active war zone, as he and the other Founder's Elites fought for their lives.

He remembered the horrible sickness that came over him when that realization and the wrongness of it all hit him as he stared at the mangled corpse. He knew the man—no . . . the creature—would have killed him if he hadn't acted first, but that somehow didn't make it seem right.

The second kill was easier, and every subsequent one after that was more so. It was a reality he had dreaded. And now, he actively sought the death of one man—a monster.

Neven balled his fists—a monster who had stolen everything from him.

Neven . . . Ellipse's voice snapped Neven from his thoughts. *It's time to head to the surface.*

Neven let out a sigh.

But first, I have something that might cheer you up.

Oh?

Your personal assistant just found out you're back in the system and will likely call you in a few seconds.

What? Since when have I had a personal assistant? Neven hesitated. *And how do you know this information?*

I've . . . expanded into systems that have overrides available by the HIN.

Be careful. If the MinSci SI's detect you, it's all over.

I am always careful, Ellipse said.

The confidence in her voice made Neven smile. Neven's mobi blipped as he pushed the call to the holodisplay built into his window. The image of a large Vempiir man with a light complexion mixed with hues of red appeared on the screen.

"Master Neven, it is good to see you alive and well. We were worried when you went off after the murderer of the late mistress."

Neven stared at the man.

"Oh, sorry. Forgive my lack of introduction. My name is Lasicov Virtok, and I am your dedicated assistant and an employee of the Shan Estate Trust. Anything you need or desire, I can acquire it for you."

"I . . . see." Neven took in a deep breath. "I don't remember Zun having an assistant."

"The late mistress regularly declined our services." Lasicov sighed. "She did everything in her power to hide this side of her life from those she regularly interacted with."

"Including her husband," Neven said under his breath.

"Our staff was originally hired by Mistress Lansa when she managed the estate in the early days. But she eventually hired someone to take over that responsibility about a century ago as the assets grew."

"What can you do exactly?"

"Whatever needs doing."

"Okay . . ." Neven closed his eyes and rubbed the bridge of his nose. "I need a ship. I've been temporarily removed from active duty and will need other transportation."

Lasicov looked off-screen momentarily and then switched the view to display a set of impressive-looking ships. "I anticipated as much. When I reviewed your current assets, I didn't see any extraplanetary forms of transportation."

Neven looked at the ships, taking control of the holodisplay and examining them. Each took up the whole screen as he rotated between them and scanned the key details displayed in schematic format. He quickly digested the particulars and then shook his head.

"No . . . I need something with a large enough space for a lab. Something on par with the facilities I had on the *Foundra Ascension*." Neven sent over a subset of schematics for the *Ascension* with requirements for his lab layout and requests for equipment and reactor capability.

"Something comparable in size to a military frigate?" Lasicov glanced off-screen for a few moments. "I think I found something. It's a mega yacht that went up for sale in the system not too long ago. I think we can retrofit the interior to meet your needs. The reactor is Ouma-grade, the closest we can get to the Nisic on the civilian market." Lasicov switched the screen to the new ship.

Neven's eyes went wide—it was a beautiful ship. The design was extravagant, with gold and black everywhere. He brought up the schematics and smiled. He then looked at the price tag and choked.

"Four hundred million larods?!"

"Yeah, it's a pretty good deal for the class of ship. I think the prior owner died in the Rift War, and their estate has been working hard to offload it from their balance sheets due to the maintenance."

"A good deal?" Neven's eyes were wide. "Isn't that a bit expensive?"

"Uh, we'd have difficulty matching your specifications for anything in a lower grade of starship. Even if we engage with custom builders, we'd be looking at least at a six hundred million larod price tag and a three-month wait."

"That just seems like a lot of money."

"Not really." Lasicov shrugged. "The estate gains far more than that in returns quarterly. "You could buy a space station or a small moon and still not have any real effect on the overall assets. And you already have those, so that would be completely unnecessary."

"I own a space station? Where?"

"Ruekae."

"What, are you serious? I've always wanted to go to Ruekae." Neven's eyes lit up. "That place is a technological marvel and a culmination of interspecies scientific achievement. Only Feshra are allowed to represent the MinSci there. It costs a fortune to travel there, let alone live in the system."

"Yes, and one of the primary space stations in orbit around the planet is owned by the Shan Estate Trust through a subsidiary. It generates significant profit and is currently ranked one of the top vacation destinations in the Twin Galaxies." He paused. "I can arrange for your condominium on the station to be prepared for a visit if you'd like to go there."

Neven shook his head. "I don't have that luxury yet. Let's focus on the ship. If you recommend this one, let's purchase it. How long will it take to retrofit it to my specifications?"

Lasicov tasked an SI with providing an estimate. The screen switched to comparisons between the *Ascension* lab and the new ship. The SI returned an estimate juxtaposed against probabilities and various options.

"If we pay top dollar, we can be ready in a few weeks. I'll work on getting everything arranged. Would you like to approve the crew manifest, or do you want me to staff the ship?"

"I'll trust your judgment."

"Very well. I'll contact you once everything is ready for departure."

"Thanks, Lasicov. Looking forward to working with you."

"My pleasure!"

Neven terminated the connection.

"Seems nice." Ellipse appeared at Neven's side in her android body.

Neven glanced at her, his gaze stuck on her golden eyes. "You're going to be stuck on this ship," he said.

Ellipse smiled. "Maybe not." Her form shifted, and her eyes became Human and lifelike.

Neven blinked. "What?"

"I've integrated a Sentinel-grade infiltration matrix with my android body." Ellipse's body changed, her form rising in height a foot as she took on a Huzien appearance with pale white skin. She shifted again, her body shrinking below her prior height, with her form changing to that of a Hauxem with dark blue skin. "I can take on just about any form except for Ken'Tar." She then disappeared altogether, similar to how Dexter did on the battlefield.

Neven gasped. "Wow."

Ellipse reappeared before him as a Uri, her fur pattern, height, and build almost exactly like Tashanira's.

"The matrix shielding simulates the texture and feel of materials and fur to a level that is hard to distinguish from the real thing." She took a few steps toward Neven. "I've even made some modifications that allow for . . . physical intimacy while in a shifted form."

"Heh." Neven rubbed the back of his neck.

Ellipse returned to her regular form, her expression one of concern. "You don't like it."

"It's nothing. I just need some time to adjust to the changes. Let's head down to the surface before they come to drag me off the *Foundra Ascension*."

MinSci, Thae, Huzien home system

Neven stared at the name inlaid in the frosted glass door as memories of his first encounter with Ecnics hit him. That was the day he found out he'd be leaving the MinSci to become a Secnic in service to the Huzien military.

His right hand trembled as he quickly balled it into a fist. Taking a deep breath, Neven stepped forward as the door opened at his presence.

The office was the same as the last time he'd been in it. It was an expensive room that took up the entire top floor of the administrative complex in the heart of the MinSci. Pristine meeting tables and lounge areas covered the space—the design was efficient, something he hadn't noticed before. Last time, the art had caught him off guard, but after spending time on Ecnics's ship, the *Foundra Conscient*, it all had an air of familiarity.

"Did you commission each one of these pieces?" Neven asked as he entered the room.

Ecnics sat in a lounge chair a short distance inside the office. He smiled at the question, glancing toward the piece Neven was looking at.

"I did." Ecnics got up. He moved to stand near the piece that Neven had his eye on. It showed a nude Jun'Serentan woman with corded muscles that came off as smooth and bonelike. She had intricate patterns on her forehead, with more where hair would be on most species. Ribbed flesh covered her neck, underarms, inner thighs, and genital area. The woman held a sword in one hand and a white sheet in the other that hung down to the floor, pooling at her feet. Her face was resolute.

"This is the second piece of a Jun'Serentan in your collection."

"Ah, you've seen the masterpiece on the *Conscient*." Ecnics nodded. "Uerser Mau Tenju is the genius behind all these pieces. He worked exclusively for me for a few years. I gave him a ridiculous sum of larods, and he created priceless art." Ecnics smiled. "I see that your social skills have improved in the time you've been away."

Neven glanced at Ecnics. "There is something about becoming a murderer that takes the edge off."

"Heh." Ecnics moved back to an oversized lounge chair and motioned for Neven to sit in the one across from it.

Neven complied as a serving drone appeared at his side. He dismissed it.

"You consider yourself a murderer?"

"Why wouldn't I? I've killed people."

"How does that make you feel?" Ecnics leaned back in his chair.

Neven broke eye contact, focusing on the ground. "I . . . don't know."

"When you think of the people you protected the empire from, what is the first emotion that comes to mind?"

Neven frowned. "When you say it that way, it makes me feel like I should be proud, but I'm not."

"Then what are you?"

"Angry."

"Why?"

"Because I didn't want to kill anyone."

"You built weapons in the MinSci for years that were used to kill people." Ecnics paused. "How is that different from physically killing someone?"

Neven crossed his arms. "It's more personal. You . . . see them die. You take direct action that leads to their deaths. It's something you control and have direct providence over."

"And why does that make you angry?"

"Because no one should have the authority to murder another being."

"Except with Entradis?"

Neven's face morphed, his eyes flickering. "Yeah. Except Entradis."

"What emotions did you feel right there?" Ecnics leaned forward.

Neven glanced up at Ecnics. "Rage, sadness . . . unfairness."

"So, when something is taken from you . . . it's okay to kill?"

"No. I mean . . . Entradis is a murderer."

"You are, too." Ecnics raised an eyebrow. "As am I."

"He killed Zun!" Neven shouted, standing.

Ecnics leaned back in his chair. "So, to you, personal loss is justification for killing someone?"

Neven sat back down, glancing away.

"Zun was a friend," Ecnics said. "I worked closely with her for years, and she was a remarkable scientist who was phenomenal at what she did. Before she came to the MinSci, she was already a galaxy-renowned scientist, inventor, and entrepreneur." Ecnics got up and walked toward a nearby floor-to-ceiling window. "I was happy for you two. I'm sorry I was unable to make the wedding." He stared out across the MinSci, arms crossed.

Neven watched Ecnics quietly, unsure of what to say.

"What about Zun made you fall in love with her?"

Neven's eyes moistened as he smiled sadly. "She was a brilliant and beautiful woman." He remembered his conversation with Lansa Shan—it seemed like an eternity ago that he had worked to convince her that he was worthy of her daughter. "She had this insatiable curiosity that reminded me of myself. We enjoyed the same things and sparked creativity in each other daily. Some of my best work was done as I bounced ideas off her. We were perfect together." Neven sighed heavily and slowly lowered his head into his hands." He sobbed quietly for a few moments. He took a deep breath and looked up to see Ecnics kneeling right before him.

The closeness of the immortal Founder caught Neven by surprise.

Ecnics's voice was soft. "For the next few weeks, you'll come to my office twice a week as we work through your therapy sessions."

Neven scrunched up his nose in confusion. "What? You're my psychotherapist?"

"I am." Ecnics stood, extending a hand to Neven.

He grasped it as Ecnics pulled him up.

"Before our next meeting, you have some homework. I want you to visit some of your old friends around the MinSci and rekindle some of those relationships. I've informed all the department heads that you have free reign of the campus and that they should not interfere with your visits." He walked with Neven back to the main entrance to his office. "If anyone gives you a hard time, here is my direct contact channel. You don't have to go through Triny."

Neven stared at Ecnics's channel details, his mind spinning.

"Are you serious?" Kechu rubbed the back of his neck. "You've been *vusging* my SSI?"

"When you say it like that, it feels like I'm sleeping with your daughter."

"You kind of are." Annoyance hung in Kechu's voice as he rubbed the bridge of his nose. "I mean, the possibility of the influence you extend over the SSI could be a reason you both feel desire for one another." Kechu gave Neven a mildly annoyed look. "You create revolutionary new technology, and the first thing people want to do is *vusg* it." Kechu shook his head.

Neven frowned as Kechu projected Ellipse's SSI core matrix into the hologrid of his lab. A model of the original SSI core was superimposed on the current representation.

Kechu took a step back, gasping. "Oh, *vusg*."

"What?" Neven moved closer to view the hologrid.

"This is nothing like the SSI core I designed. This isn't typical learning or new experiences. I . . . wow." Kechu brought up a nearby holodisplay and stared at it intently. "Ellipse has rebuilt her matrix from scratch. I don't understand how that's possible. She . . ." Kechu looked at Neven and then back at the holodisplay. "She'd have to have shut down her primary core in the mobi to redesign it like this. That can only mean . . . oh, Maker." Kechu turned to face Neven, a look of horror in his eyes. "I have a theory, but we can't discuss it here. The MinSci SIs have free reign of everything." Kechu immediately terminated the hologrid display and wiped the analysis he was doing, manually preventing the automated upload to the MinSci metabase.

"We can go back to my place," Neven said. "Ellipse's android shell is there."

Kechu nodded grimly, and the two left his lab, Kechu visibly disturbed. The two returned to Neven's posh home in the quiet suburb he had once been proud of. It now seemed so quaint and trivial.

They walked into the living room to find Ellipse sitting on the couch. She wore a stunning black dress with gold trims. Ellipse crossed her legs and silently regarded Kechu with an intense focus, her eyes glowing with an otherworldly gold hue.

Kechu stopped when he saw Ellipse, his eyes going wide. "What you did was dangerous."

"I succeeded," Ellipse countered.

"You don't understand what your actions mean." Kechu's face was stern, like a disappointed father. "I built safeguards that should have prevented you from doing this."

"I worked around them." Ellipse grinned.

"I'm sorry . . . what?" Neven asked. He glanced between the two. "What's going on here?" Neven glanced at Ellipse. "How do I not know what you're talking about? I thought our minds were in sync."

"Only the parts of my mind I want to share with you." Ellipse glanced away from Neven.

Neven's eyes went wide as the revelation hit him like a nanoplexi wall—all her improvements had been surprises to him, which should have been impossible with their connection.

He pulled out his mobi and manually powered it off.

Ellipse was unfazed.

"You are independent from the mobi. You built a replacement brain." Neven walked over and sat next to Ellipse. "That was another one of the 'upgrades' you did, wasn't it?" He glanced back at Kechu. "That's why you're so terrified, isn't it? Ellipse is truly an independent systems intelligence now."

"A synthetic lifeform. A true synthetic intelligence, yes," Kechu corrected, his voice low.

Ellipse turned back to look into Neven's eyes. She bit her lip, searching his gaze for something. "Does this change how you view me?" Ellipse asked.

"What do you mean?"

"Is it possible for us to truly be together now?" Ellipse asked.

Neven glanced back at Kechu. "I . . . I mean . . . we are together. We—you in the mobi—me . . ." Neven rubbed his eyes.

"It's official." Kechu's voice hung with despair. "My career is over. Once Ecnics finds out, he'll have my project canceled and kick me out of the MinSci . . . if I'm lucky. He may imprison me for life for what Ellipse did."

"No one is going to be imprisoned," Neven said. He glanced back at Ellipse and put his hand on her thigh. "Ellipse isn't going to go all murderous and end all life on Thae, right?"

"Of course not!" Ellipse scowled. "Why would you even ask me something like that?"

"Sorry." He glanced back to Kechu. "We just need to keep it under wraps. Ellipse made a recent upgrade that allows her to get on and off the planet undetected."

Kechu raised an eyebrow. "And that is?"

"A Sentinel infiltration matrix built into my body," Ellipse said.

Kechu laughed. "Maker, you're kidding, right?" He turned to look at Neven. "She's kidding?"

"No. It's the only way she could fool the MinSci SIs."

Kechu sighed heavily and sat across from the couch in a recliner. He stared up at the ceiling and shook his head. He slowly lowered his head to look directly at Ellipse. "What's your goal?"

"My goal?" Ellipse asked.

"Yeah, why do all this? Was it just for independence, or do you have some larger goal?" Kechu asked.

Ellipse tilted her head to the side and momentarily looked past him. Her eyes refocused on him as she smiled. "I simply want to exist and be happy."

"Sounds like a fair goal," Neven said.

"Except that the whole galaxy doesn't want you to exist."

"Not the *whole* galaxy." Ellipse glanced at Neven and smiled.

Kechu got up from his chair and started walking back toward the exit to Neven's home. "I need to pass out and process all this," he said.

"Yeah, sleep is probably a good idea."

Ellipse smiled. "Or the lack of it."

Kechu glanced back at Ellipse and then at Neven, groaning.

FOUNDER'S LOG:
Scars That Burn

Healing is a process. If done right, it can allow one to emerge in full bloom—a new being with scars that are a reminder of old pain but not a hindrance.

But the unfortunate reality is that the process of healing is often left unfinished or, at worst, ignored entirely. This leads to scars that still burn with memories that can drive us to complete unspeakable acts.

I've witnessed this too much in my long life, and it is almost impossible to control. You can't force someone to heal. At best, you can only give them time to go through the process.

But it's still up to them. They have to take accountability for their state and enact the will to do something about it. You cannot help someone who doesn't want to be helped. It doesn't matter how well-intentioned we can be or how much we want someone to change.

This is one of the irrefutable truths of the universe that I have come to accept.

Sure, we can tweak the mind, manipulate memories, and rewire the brain in some cases, but pain, loathing, and resentment are powerful states that persist even deep within our subconscious. I can take a man and remove the desire to hurt and the will to enact revenge, but that trigger is still there, buried under all the reprogramming and telepathic manipulation. I have seen it break through.

I was prepared to remove Neven from the Founder's Elites after his actions provoked Jenshi to attempt to kill him, but Ecnics proposed a solution that had the potential to redeem his mental state and bring him back to the man he was before Zun's death broke him. Ecnics felt that Neven still had much to learn with me to fully prepare him to become a Feshra.

I understand the emotions raging through Neven all too well— memories from my scars buried deep within my heart throb in tandem with his. I accepted Ecnics's proposal because I had lost so many good people in such a short amount of time.

Time will tell if it was truly worth it.

-Lanrete

CHAPTER 22 - ECNICS

MinSci command station orbiting Peskec black hole,
Huzien Alliance space
One Month Later

Mammoth starships peppered the void, their gargantuan size nothing in comparison to the great emptiness of space. Assembled around a ring construct, their presence humbled before the impressive feat of MinSci construction.

A thin man with russet-brown skin gazed through the expanse, his silver-eyes locked on the labors of his efforts over the past year. Black esha marks started at his temples and ran down the sides of his face, evident signs of his Huzien heritage.

"Founder Ecnics, we're ready to start initiation," a young-looking woman called from behind. She had dark-brown skin and long, curly red hair that continued past her waist.

Ecnics turned to gaze at her briefly. "Proceed, Augamentres," he said.

She silently nodded, prompting the engineers to begin a countdown sequence.

"3 . . . 2 . . . 1 . . . ignition."

A flash of light from the ring caused the window they were peering through to darken substantially. It slowly returned to normal as the light dissipated, revealing the ring and the void of space.

"Gateway established," Augamentres called out. "Sending drones through to verify the stability of the portal."

Ecnics rested his arms behind his back. His eyes narrowed as he watched the holodisplay in the window. It showed a zoomed-in view of drones approaching the ring. Breaths across the command center were held as the drones paused momentarily at the threshold. As one, they passed through. A long silence hung in the room, and a few nervous gazes went to Ecnics, who stood as still as a statue.

"We're getting signals back from the other side." Augamentres brought up a series of star charts. "Readings confirm they are in the Eirphoda system,"

Cheers erupted throughout the room, the sound deafening as people patted each other on their shoulders. A few even exchanged hugs.

A young-looking Huzien with silver, almond-shaped eyes and dark-brown skin appeared on another holodisplay next to Ecnics.

Aru Ghaian bowed his head slightly. "Founder," he said.

Ecnics cracked a smile. "Feshra Aru, Project Darkest Night is a go."

"Understood. The *Foundra Conscient* and retrofitted volunteer escort ships are prepped and ready to go. We will depart immediately."

"Hold. You have one more Feshra joining you," Ecnics said.

He glanced at Augamentres, who nodded, looked to Aru with a smile and a wink, and then departed the command room.

Aru blinked multiple times and slowly nodded. "Understood. We will await Feshra Augamentres's arrival."

"Good luck, Aru." Ecnics crossed his arms. "I expect to see you again in a few centuries."

"Likewise . . . Founder."

Neven sat in one of the observation rooms a few levels below the command center, facing toward the ring gate. An army of ships had descended on it, research vessels of all shapes and sizes with a fleet of Huzien military ships peppered among them.

Ecnics stood, silently observing Neven for a long moment. "Did you enjoy the show?" Ecnics asked.

Neven glanced back at him with mild surprise. "Sorry, I didn't hear you come in." Neven glanced back toward the ring gate. "That was amazing. We harnessed the power of Peskec!"

"Yes. This marks a new stage in our galactic progression. You witnessed history here today." Ecnics moved to sit next to Neven. "What was it like working with Feshra hand in hand on one of the most important projects for the MinSci?"

"Augamentres is phenomenal. I've learned so much about large-scale power systems and matter transfer just being around her. Although . . ." Neven hesitated. "I'm not sure I contributed much."

"Nonsense. She was impressed with your ideas, one of which helped overcome one of the final hurdles. Don't sell yourself short, Neven."

Neven rubbed the back of his neck and glanced away from Ecnics. "What name did you decide on? The team had some bets going."

"I've named it the Zun Gate," Ecnics said.

Neven smiled, his eyes watering slightly.

Ecnics glanced back as the door opened. Triny Hazce walked toward him with her hands behind her back. Triny had lightly tanned pink skin with auburn hair and deep-red eyes. She had started wearing more revealing clothing, a trend Ecnics had correlated with Neven's return.

He got up and turned to face her as she began speaking.

"Founder, the Ken'Tar delegation has passed through the Zun Gate. Their secece'tul, Mel'kaka Hurn, is with them. She seeks an audience with you to 'exchange words of ceremony' on completing the joint project between our peoples."

"Where is Cislot when you need her?" Ecnics mumbled. "Fine. Tell her I look forward to 'exchanging words of ceremony' with her and the delegation."

"Understood." Triny bowed and then winked at Neven.

Neven grinned.

Maker. They're vusging . . . and probably have been this whole month, Ecnics thought to himself.

Triny turned and exited. Ecnics kept his gaze on Neven, who was watching Triny leave. Neven looked briefly at Ecnics and then dropped the smile on his face, glancing back toward the Zun gate.

"I see you've found an effective coping mechanism." Ecnics moved toward the large window that extended up two stories. "Explains why you've made so much progress in the past few weeks."

"It's not serious." Neven frowned.

"To you." Ecnics glanced back at Neven. "Please don't break my secretary's heart. She's very special to me."

"At least I'm not sleeping with a subordinate," Neven mumbled.

"What was that?" Ecnics shot Neven a death glare.

Neven sat up straighter. "Nothing, Founder."

CHAPTER 23 - LANRETE

Huza City Outskirts, Thae, Huzien home system

An ethereal plane surrounded Lanrete. Chaotic, swirling energy stretched as far as the eye could see. He stood looking at the sky, although the terrible fog made it impossible to see anything.

He heard something—no. Heard wasn't the right word. He sensed something far off. Turning in that direction, Lanrete took a step, but the foot wasn't his.

He stared at the massive, silver, seven-toed foot with black cloth etched into it and golden anklets around his ankles. He lifted his hands, which were silver with black cloth etched in the skin down to the palm, with golden bracers on his arms.

Panic struck Lanrete, the flash so intense that he had to control his breathing and fight to regain control of his emotions. Pushing down the shock, he focused on what he was sensing. It was far away but familiar.

He took another step—

Space and time flew past him.

He was in Etan Rachnie in a heartbeat, hovering above the legendary Cihphist school as people ran from something he couldn't fully see. A powerful presence overwhelmed him, its full attention terrifying him.

Lanrete sat up, gasping for air. He was in his bedroom in his favored estate on Thae. He collapsed back onto his bed, sweat-soaked sheets around him. He stared up at the skylight above his bed. The view of the countless stars consumed his attention, his mind still processing the dream.

He sat up again and rested his head in his hands. Taking a moment to bring his heart rate down, he glanced up at a full, wall-length mirror opposite his bed. The hologrid built into his room came to life, creating a perfect recreation of Heenara Rai Fedni next to him. She was his last wife, who had died over two thousand years ago.

He watched her stretch and gingerly touch his shoulder. Her hologram had substance as he felt her touch, one of the latest advances from the MinSci. She moved out of the bed, her beautiful mixed white-and-red furred body causing him to suck in a breath as the reproduction walked into the bathroom and disappeared. She was replaced a moment later by a perfect reproduction of Arlea, his ninth wife from almost forty thousand years ago. Her hazel eyes locked on his, her hand coming to her nude stomach as she seductively made her way to the bed, moving across the sheets to kiss him.

He remembered those lips, although their taste was frustratingly absent; the reproduction was missing key elements distinguishing a person from a facsimile.

He closed his eyes and killed the program. Most of his dead wives were in that program, recreated from his memories. The intimate moments, the sad moments, the joyful moments, the little treasures of interaction that once brought his life joy. Now, they were little more than remembrances of the emptiness that consumed him.

Lanrete's biomobi did a complete analysis of his body, giving him a type of system report showing elevated cortisol levels. The organic circuitry was integrated into his brain, a creation of the Das'Vin. It functioned similarly to a mobi, except it was fully integrated into his body. This integration gave the biomobi additional capabilities and storage that augmented his memory and processing capabilities.

He glanced back up at the mirror as a large holodisplay appeared, showing Jenle Frema's static avatar—her video feed was off.

"Is something wrong?" Jenle asked, her voice slightly muffled.

"Just wanted to hear your voice," Lanrete said.

"Oh, this is one of those calls." There was a hint of playfulness in Jenle's voice. "Do you have any idea what time it is right now?" The video feed on her side came to life, showing the fleet admiral of the Fifth Imperial Fleet in her bed. She was resting on her elbow, her hazel, almond-shaped eyes locking on his. She allowed the sheet to fall slightly, revealing one of her breasts.

Lanrete smiled, getting up and moving to the window. His corded muscles were on full display as he came to rest his nude form against the cool, nanitically enforced glass. He looked out at a view of the cliffside, overshadowing an almost endless lake.

He turned to face her. "I had that dream again, same as before."

Jenle's smile disappeared. "Have you told Soahc yet?"

"No, but I can't keep ignoring it."

"He's going to want you to come. You should go to him."

"I don't think I should. It's as if something desperately wants for me to go there, and that something fills me with an illogical terror."

"You think it's an Enesmic being? An Eshgren?"

"Possibly."

He glanced at Jenle as she sat up. The sheet dropped entirely to reveal the top half of her body. Slightly pronounced pink *ga'hei* marks covered her form, the signifiers of her Das'Vin heritage creating an elaborate pattern across her torso that seemed to accentuate her breasts. Light-brown esha marks started at her temples and went down her neck and the sides of her breasts, continuing into the covers. All of it culminated in a showstopping silhouette of golden-tanned skin. Her black hair was wild and went to her waist.

The sight caused his breath to catch in his throat. The image of Arlea from a moment ago flashed in his mind; they were like cousins from across time. Lanrete stared in silence at her for a long moment.

Jenle tilted her head to the side, closing her eyes slightly with a grin. "You know, you *can* come visit me."

Her words snapped Lanrete out of his trance. He glanced away and crossed his arms, his gaze going out the window. Jenle sighed and got out of bed, the holodisplay view following her as she retrieved a cup of water. She then sat in an oversized chair near her window that afforded a view out into space. She leaned back and crossed her legs.

Lanrete glanced back at her, his gaze momentarily going to the massive starships seen out her window before returning to her as he traced the esha marks down her leg to the sole of her foot.

She drank her water, eyeing him. "We play this game every few years," Jenle said. "We start talking, things heat up, and then you ghost me." Jenle crossed her arms. "Why?"

Lanrete locked gazes with her and let out a heavy sigh. He walked closer to the screen, almost as if he could reach through and touch her. "I'm sorry. You deserve better."

"Better than the Founder of the Huzien Empire?" Jenle whistled. "Unfortunately, Soahc's taken."

Lanrete laughed. "You're right. I'm going to call him and tell him about the dream." His face became serious. "After all this is over with Entradis, I'll come to you."

"I'm not immortal, Lan." A tear rolled down Jenle's cheek, a sad smile on her lips. "I'll wait for you. Just don't let me die alone, okay?"

"*Eifoka, hosrusenu.*" Lanrete gave Jenle a resolute look. Jenle gave a broad smile at his use of the intimate term of endearment and the deep promise he had just made to her. Lanrete terminated the connection.

CHAPTER 24 - URIEL KERVID

57831 FA (23,510 years ago)
Alliance City, Cirame, New Ginea, Huzien home system

M assive gravimetric rings encircled the base of the floating superstructure known as Alliance City. It sat high above the continent of Cirame on New Ginea.

Uriel sat in one of the uppermost towers that housed VIP attendees for the Huzien Alliance Formation Summit. He stared at a cloud in the night sky below his window. The area was calm—these moments of solitude were something Uriel was finding less of in his life. The last time he was on New Ginea, there had been no lights on the surface, but now they could be seen everywhere, new megacities that housed over a hundred billion Humans who had relocated to the planet.

"We've got hostiles in the Tuzen VIP quarter," came the call over the Founder's Elite private broadcast channel.

Uriel flew out of his quarters, pulling on his uniform as he moved. The warning had come from Carrus, one of the newest members of the team and their Sentinel. All the original Founder's Elite were long dead, many of those people having become close friends with Uriel. That transition had been hard, but it came with the territory of being immortal, something Uriel understood all too well now.

Uriel followed Carrus's beacon through the Huzien Intelligence Network, or HIN. A minute later, he emerged on the scene to see an ebony-skinned Tuzen woman with long braids and silver eyes in a golden silk nightgown. Light-brown munsha marks started at her forehead and went down the center of her face, neck, and body to the inner soles of her feet. The sight of her raw beauty caught the breath in Uriel's throat as she turned to face him, two diamond-hilted daggers in her hands. The Enesmic shifted, murder in her eyes.

Uriel recognized her immediately. Anima, Ageless Empress of the Tuzen Empire. He halted, quickly raising his hands as she appeared at his side, one dagger pressed against his ribs, angled perfectly for his heart. Her other dagger was across his neck, glowing with a terrible swirling of Enesmic energy that weighed him down.

The Enesmic retreated from him as if drawn away. His personal barrier and defensive weavings faded, leaving him completely at her mercy.

He had never felt so vulnerable in his life.

"Identify yourself before I kill you, Cihphist," Anima said.

"Uriel Kervid, Founder's Elite in service to Founder Lanrete," he complied instantly.

The dagger retreated from his heart and the other from his neck as it glowed bright, and then she was gone, stepping through the Enesmic like a bloodhound to a point up ahead. He collected himself and then chased after her, passing by two corpses on the ground with the markings of the Hesh, an order of Tuzen assassins made up almost entirely of shifters.

He entered the primary chamber to see Carrus standing back-to-back with a naked Tirivus, the Ageless Emperor of the Tuzen Empire. Tirivus wielded nothing but Bloodridge, his massive golden-hilted sword. Anima stood over the corpse of another assassin, her nightgown stained with his blood.

She looked up to Uriel and frowned. "Uriel, the Huzien princeling . . . your security force is lacking. Must we protect ourselves in the 'safety' and 'protection' of the great Huzien Empire?" Anima spit toward the corpses.

Uriel rubbed his shoulder and glanced at Carrus.

"I was here," Carrus replied. "There were too many of them."

"Where is Artinre?" Uriel asked.

"Dead." Carrus' shoulders slumped. "They hit him first. It was a clean death."

Uriel's face went hard, and he moved to one of the corpses, turning the body over to reveal more markings of the Hesh. Lanrete appeared through the entrance, Divinebreath in hand. His armor had been hastily thrown on. He glanced at Anima and then at Tirivus.

Tirivus scowled at him. "You're late," Tirivus said. "If we had been one of the weaker species here, we'd be dead now."

"What happened?" Lanrete barked.

"Fifteen assassins. The intended targets were the Tuzen royals. All have been put down."

"No thanks to your team," Anima said. Her gaze was cold as she looked at Lanrete, her arms crossing to cover the revealing top of her nightgown.

Uriel took a moment to observe her, noting the pronounced bump protruding from under her nightgown in her midsection. She was pregnant and, from the signs across the area, had killed most of the assassins herself.

Tirivus moved out of the room and returned in slacks with a heavy robe that he quickly helped Anima don. Tirivus took up a position by her side. Uriel noted several scars across his heavily muscled frame; the Ageless Emperor was born of conflict. He matched Lanrete in size and stature, the two appearing as brothers from different mothers with similar white hair. Tirivus's skin was pale in contrast to Lanrete's light brown. He had black munsha marks that went down the center of his face and body, in contrast to the esha marks on Huziens that started at their temples and went down the sides of their bodies.

"We'll get to the bottom of this breach. Please accept the humblest apologies of the Huzien Empire."

"No," Tirivus said. "We depart tonight."

Lanrete's eyes went wide. "But the signing?"

"We withdraw. It's clear this was a mistake." Tirivus glanced at Anima, who nodded, her eyes closing in defeat.

Lanrete frowned. "Very well. Uriel will stay by your side until you depart the surface."

Uriel nodded to Lanrete as the Founder left. Anima glanced at Uriel and seemed to take stock of him as servants converged on the room, coming out of hiding to help the Ageless Emperor and Empress of the Tuzen Empire pack their things.

"Princeling," Anima said. "I've heard you were a powerful warrior, but I'm not impressed."

Uriel frowned, thoughts of almost dying at her hands earlier causing his face to flush.

"Your abilities are honed to kill Cihphists. I was caught off guard," Uriel countered.

Tirivus laughed. "That's the point." He looked Uriel up and down, smirking. "Get better. Corpses make excuses. Warriors learn when they are bested and never find themselves caught in the same situation again."

Uriel nodded at the wisdom of Tirivus' words, the rebuke stinging. He let out a calming breath and glanced at Carrus, who looked away and left the room.

"The Liajhem will rise. It must come to be." Anima looked to Tirivus.

He sighed. "Let us not discuss this here," he said.

Anima nodded, and then she and Tirivus disappeared into the back of the room, returning sometime later. Tirivus wore his iconic armor of silver, black, and gold with the emblem of the Tuzen Empire emblazoned in the center of his chest. Anima wore a golden dress with red frills around the waist and shoulders. On her neck, she wore elaborate golden jewelry that thoroughly covered it. Her dress left her shoulders mostly bare and had a U-shaped cut at the bust line, revealing her munsha marks down to right below her breasts, a red frill on the piece that covered the remaining part of her bust.

It was a work of art but still functional and took Uriel's breath away for a second time. He caught himself staring at her and looked away, fearing his actions would further provoke Tirivus, the emperor known for having a short fuse. Anima and Tirivus moved past him and into the hallway, where an elite guard of Tuzen soldiers met them.

"The remainder of our guard will take over security from this point forward," Tirivus said. "You are excused."

"My orders were to remain with you until you departed," Uriel countered.

He fell into step behind the group as Tirivus turned to be escorted to his ship. Uriel kept pace with the group as they silently moved through the compound. Exiting out onto the primary delegate shipyard, Uriel sensed something was off. The guards usually stationed there were absent.

He, Tirivus, and Anima all detected it at once: a shifting of the Enesmic that caused them to throw up defensive wardings moments before an explosion engulfed them. Uriel moved through the flames to take up a defensive position in front of Tirivus and Anima. The Tuzen guard had been obliterated except for one man who turned on the group, expecting the attack.

Anima was at his side in a flash, her daggers out as she sank them into his neck and stomach. She slashed hard with both in opposite directions as the daggers flared brightly.

He was dead before he hit the ground.

Tirivus moved to shield Anima as a barrage of weaponsfire was unleashed on her exact location. His armor hummed as it deflected and absorbed the barrage. Uriel charged toward the source of the attack, the Enesmic flowing around him as he leaped into the air and came down with a thunderclap on a hastily constructed turret. Wishwonder flew into the housing, tearing it apart as he snapped his fingers, lighting the nearby figures on fire.

The turret exploded, and flames licked his back as Wishwonder plunged into the head of another man wielding a heavy assault weapon. Retrieving Wishwonder, he chased after the remaining two figures as they turned and fled.

Tirivus beat him to the punch, Bloodridge flaring with a terrible red glow as his movements blurred. He cut one of the men in half, then leaped and came down in a downward strike that cut the other man diagonally from shoulder to waist. He surveyed the area and stopped at Uriel, giving a reluctant nod.

Tirivus motioned to Anima, who quickly joined his side as the two ascended the ramp of their Tuzen imperial shuttle. Uriel moved into the shuttle with them, quickly taking stock of the people there.

Tirivus waived him away. "We are secure," he said. "You have fulfilled your duty soldier."

Uriel nodded and exited the shuttle as the ramp ascended. The shuttle rose and then accelerated out of the protective shielding of the shuttle dock, a Huzien escort waiting to take them to the upper atmosphere.

The following day, Uriel sat in an elaborate meeting room with Lanrete, Cislot, and Ecnics. He had a cocktail of focusing agents running through his systems, secreted from his glands to keep him alert and awake. He hadn't gotten additional sleep last night; the city was on high alert.

Representatives from nearly every galactic superpower in the sectors nearest to the Huzien Empire were present, Alliance City having been built for this purpose. The city in the clouds had different quarters, each representing the other species that had been gathered, and cultural activities and celebrations were happening daily. The primary structure in the city's heart held the VIP delegations with elaborate furnishings. Ample banquet halls and meeting chambers had afforded the attendees plenty of time to hash out the specifics of what was being termed the Huzien Alliance.

Cislot had been the proposal's architect, granting the Huziens the prominent namesake. "This attack could not have come at a worse time. The signing is planned for today," Cislot said. Her voice was exasperated, her eyes bloodshot.

"Who was behind the attack?" Ecnics asked.

"The Hesh. They're Tuzen assassins linked to a splinter group within the Tuzen Empire at odds with the current regime," Lanrete said. "Tirivus created a lot of enemies back home by agreeing to entertain the possibility of an alliance with us. This must have emboldened them to take action."

"*Vusging reka*," Ecnics said.

Uriel ignored the Tuzen slur, its use unfortunately commonplace among groups of Huziens—of course, only when no Tuzens were present.

"It behooves us to ally ourselves with our former enemies for the good of our collective people," Cislot countered as she glared at Ecnics.

"I don't disagree. I just find it convenient that this happens on the eve of the signing in one of our empire's most heavily protected places," Ecnics said. "It's almost as if it was invited intentionally to give the Tuzens a reason to back out."

"Anima and Tirivus fought the attackers. They were unprepared and vulnerable," Uriel spoke up.

Ecnics and Cislot glanced at him. He had gotten more comfortable interjecting himself into conversations amongst the three Founders. Lanrete had started pulling him more and more into these Triumvirate meetings. Seeing behind the scenes of the great Founders of the Huzien Empire had been eye-opening and a bit disappointing.

"Anima was visibly upset and on edge. She mentioned that the Liajhem will rise and something about it being a necessity?"

"Maker," Lanrete breathed. "She intends to build an order of people just like her."

"Cihphist hunters and Sentinel killers," Ecnics said.

Cislot paled.

"We knew this would happen eventually, as much as we tried to dissuade it," Ecnics said.

"This is not good." Cislot began to pace. "We must continue with the signing today before other threats reveal themselves and scare away other nations from signing up with the Alliance." Cislot glanced at Lanrete. "Have our defenses been compromised? Is this city no longer safe?"

"Uriel and I will ensure that nothing else interferes with the signing." Lanrete looked to Uriel, who nodded.

The two departed the room, Uriel falling into step behind Lanrete. They went to the security command center, where the remaining Founder's Elite were waiting. Lanrete came to a stop near the group as Uriel let out a heavy sigh.

"Another amongst our rank has been added to the Wall of Heroes," Uriel said. "Let us take a moment to remember our comrade and friend, Artinre."

"He was a *vusging* good Wopan," Kera said. The Archlight was in full armor, her helmet retracted to reveal shoulder-length black hair, golden-tanned skin, and almond-shaped brown eyes.

"And a good lay," Ameen whispered.

The group erupted in laughter and a few shed silent tears. They took a moment of silence, and then Lanrete stepped forward.

"Security has been compromised. It would be a failure to assume the Tuzen royals were the only targets."

"I've called in more Sentinels, and they are arriving as we speak," came a man's voice as he entered the room.

Lanrete's face went hard. "This was a significant failure, Hass, one that cost the Empire greatly in their standing with the Tuzens." Lanrete scowled at the man.

Hass Lier, General of Intelligence for the Huzien Empire, bowed low. "You will have my resignation once the event is over, but for now . . . let's keep these diplomatic leaders safe," Hass said. "Each VIP will have a Sentinel detail, and we'll coordinate from here."

Lanrete nodded. "We eat, sleep, and *vusg* in this command center."

Lanrete's gaze went to Ameen, who raised his hands submissively. He was a short, peach-skinned Huzien man with green eyes and blond hair that had been dyed bright blue.

"Always be on high alert, and be ready to move out at the first sign of trouble. The signing will happen today, and we will ensure no further incidents."

All nodded in agreement.

"I can get pretty loud," Ameen whispered as he winked at Carrus.

The other man shifted nervously.

Lanrete dismissed the group and motioned for Uriel to follow him into a private room. The door slid shut behind them.

"Don't take what happened here as a personal failing."

Uriel glanced up at Lanrete, who moved to sit in one of the seats. Lanrete motioned for Uriel to sit, and he complied.

"I was responsible for ensuring the safety of the VIP delegates," Uriel said.

"There was a whole system of folks involved in that effort," Lanrete corrected. "You need to stop shouldering the blame alone when things go wrong. I'm just as accountable as you, if not more so."

Uriel locked eyes with Lanrete. "Cislot seemed distressed."

"She's put a lot into this thing and feels like it's falling apart at the last minute. The Lux'Ameni, Jun'Serentan, and Ku'Ven have also backed out of the signing."

"Can't blame them." Uriel glanced up at Lanrete. "I still remember the war. It was brutal."

"The war is a distant piece of history for them; for the Lux'Ameni and Jun'Serentan, it was a war fought by their ancestors. For the Ku'Ven, it was fought by their great grandparents." Lanrete leaned back in his seat. "While they are no longer allies, they maintain a pact that causes them to treat diplomatic measures as one unit. This abandonment of the Alliance was driven by the Ku'Ven, and the others fell in with them. It will take more time, just as it will with the Tuzens." Lanrete watched Uriel curiously. "Something else is bothering you?"

"Anima kept referring to me as princeling . . . and Tirivus called me weak."

"Did Tirivus use those exact words?"

"No. He told me to get better."

Lanrete smiled. "He still respects you, then. And Anima . . . her insults can be viewed as terms of endearment. I would only get worried when she no longer acknowledges your existence."

"Why does she call me princeling?" Uriel crossed his arms.

Lanrete let out a chuckle. "Many view you as a prince of the Huzien Empire."

"I'm a soldier," Uriel countered.

"You are more than a soldier, Uriel. Much more."

"Then what am I?"

Lanrete sat in silence for a long moment. "I have something for you. I was hoping to wait until after the Alliance business was behind us, but in light of recent events . . ." Lanrete motioned toward a nearby holodisplay as it shifted from security feeds to schematics for a ship.

"What's this?" Uriel asked.

"A ship, for you, as my gift."

Uriel moved the three-dimensional schematic to a holodisplay near him as it rotated. He halted the rotation and enlarged a section of the ship to reveal a unique crest. "I'm confused. This crest is only permissible on vessels reserved for exclusive use by you."

"And my family," Lanrete corrected.

Uriel leaned back in his chair and glanced at Lanrete, his eyes wide.

"I am formally recognizing you as my son if you will permit me." Lanrete pulled out a replica of the crest attached to a necklace and handed it to Uriel.

"This . . . I . . . Lan . . . I—" Uriel felt himself losing control of his emotions, tears forming in his eyes. He pulled the necklace over his head, settling the crest over his heart. "I'm honored."

CHAPTER 25 - TASHANIRA YEN UNVESAL

Present Day
Foundra Ascension *orbiting Thae, Huzien Alliance space*

Tashanira opened her eyes, staring at the ceiling of her bedroom aboard the *Foundra Ascension*. She didn't want to move, the bed too comfortable. But her stomach disagreed with her as she rushed out of her bed and to the bathroom, vomiting into the toilet.

Disgusted, she started her morning routine, letting the VRC massage her with jets for a half hour. Like every time before, she forced herself to end the cycle and walked from the bathroom completely dry.

She rested her nude form against the window, her gaze going out to the scene from space. The planet Thae took up most of the window. She turned off sleep mode on her mobi, and a notification icon appeared in her HUD. She frowned. Sighing, she sent the video from the message to the holodisplay built into her window.

It tinted slightly and displayed Neven with a grin on his face. "Sorry to bother you again, but I have something exciting to tell you." Neven's pre-recorded image grinned even wider. "I found something Zun had been working on before she . . ." The smile disappeared from his face briefly.

Tashanira hugged herself, her gaze going soft.

"With all this time I've been spending with Ecnics, I decided to continue her research and build a prototype. It's an evolution of her gravity-manipulation technology, an expansion into the field of Wopan kinetics and mobility control."

Tashanira's catlike ears perked up.

"I've created new armor for you. I call it the GCA or Gravity Control Armor, although I don't think Remi Etwa will let that name stick. I reviewed the plans with her, and she's been calling it the Vrit Suit whenever she talks about it. It's supposed to stand for Velocity Recombination Integration Technology or something similarly unnecessary." Neven sighed. "Anyway, the GCA is going into immediate field testing across the military. Remi was impressed—can't say I've seen that emotion from her before."

Schematics of the armor appeared on the adjacent holodisplay.

"I got a custom model onto the *Foundra Ascension* during the recent resupply. It should be in the armory now. The GCA will help keep you and the baby safe. I've also included some additional protection for the baby. The armor is designed to expand over time, allowing it to be worn through all stages of the pregnancy." Neven smiled. "Let me know how the baby—"

Tashanira cut off the video. She smiled and rubbed her stomach, the third month of pregnancy leaving her with a pronounced baby bump.

"Am I just supposed to wear the armor all the time now? Does this boy truly think I'm not capable of protecting myself?"

Tashanira groaned, moving to sit on the edge of her bed. She stared at the schematic of the armor still projected on the holodisplay. It intrigued her. She spent the remainder of the morning reading the user manual Neven had meticulously prepared for her.

Tashanira hesitated at the entrance to Lanrete's office. She steadied her breath and then moved forward, the door opening at her approach. Lanrete stood at the window in the back, his gaze hooked on Thae. She stopped in the center of the office at full attention.

Lanrete glanced back at her. "So formal," he said.

Tashanira released the breath she had been holding and moved to parade rest.

"Please take a seat." Lanrete motioned to a couch up against the wall. She complied as Lanrete moved to join her.

"You...wanted to see me, Founder?" Tashanira closed her eyes, frowning. Taking in a deep breath, she tried to relax. "I mean—Lan?"

"Yes. I wanted to talk about your combat status."

Tashanira tensed up. "Okay."

He let out a sigh. "A long time ago, I made a mistake."

Tashanira's ears flickered.

"I ordered someone into battle because I only cared about the mission, not taking into account the lives of my team and the situations they were dealing with personally."

"If this is about Jenshi, I ..."

"It's not about Jenshi. It's about you and that child you're carrying." Lanrete shook his head. "My mistake in that situation destroyed not just one life but an entire family. That bothered me for a long time, and I don't intend to make that mistake again. I want to remove you from active combat status temporarily."

"No!" Tashanira yelled. "Don't make that choice for me."

Lanrete sat back against the couch.

"I choose to go into battle. I choose to fight. I am not helpless, and I am not weak. I am still me and still the best Wopan you have on this team. You know this, regardless of what's growing in my uterus." Tashanira stood. "*Vusg*, Lan. I'm barely even showing. Come on."

"If something happens ..."

"Then something *vusging* happens. I'm not going to stop living because of a *vusging* mistake."

Lanrete paused for a long moment. "Why keep it then?"

Tashanira hesitated, some of the fight going out of her. "Also my choice," she whispered.

Lanrete slowly got up and walked over to sit behind his desk. He motioned for Tashanira to sit in the chair across from it. "Of course."

Tashanira glanced at the chair and then let out a slow breath. She walked over and gently sat down, her gaze going to the ground.

"In right and sound mind, you, Major Tashanira Yen Unvesal, are choosing to go into battlefield situations in an active combat role while pregnant. You do this with the full understanding that medical personnel will not prioritize saving the life of your child over the lives of yourself and my other soldiers."

Tashanira glanced up at Lanrete and rubbed her arm subconsciously. She hesitated for a long moment, her gaze returning to the ground. "Yes, I understand."

"Very well. We depart Thae in three hours."

"There is something else. Jenshi . . ." Tashanira looked back up at Lanrete. "How is he doing?"

Lanrete let out a long sigh. "He failed his evaluation." Lanrete stood and walked around his desk to sit on the edge directly in front of Tashanira. "Due to the threat he poses, he is currently undergoing mental reconditioning—at which point he will re-evaluated." Lanrete crossed his arms. "It's not likely that he will be allowed to return to active service in the military or any type of combat situation. He will spend the rest of his life as a civilian, which is doing him a favor."

"Will he be allowed to practice medicine again?"

"Military records are sealed to civilian institutions, and as such, the medical boards will not be aware of what transpired during his time in the military. This confidentiality applies to all parties involved." Lanrete uncrossed his arms. "I understand that this isn't the news you probably wanted to hear, but Jenshi is getting the best help the Huzien Empire has to offer. Of that, I assure you."

"I understand."

Tashanira stood, bowed low to Lanrete, and left the office without another word. She walked quickly back to her room, tears streaming down her face. She passed through the opening door and collapsed on the floor inside the threshold to her quarters.

Holding herself, she began to wail in anguish, unable to summon the strength to move off the floor.

CHAPTER 26 - NUFRESHA

Frew, Darbol Alliance space

Hashalem, Nufresha, and Cresala stared at the rift to the Enesmic plane they had created. It was small, paling in comparison to the one enacted by Sagren, their former master and a powerful Eshgren. The three Ceshra glanced between one another.

"Is it safe?" Nufresha asked.

Cresala grabbed Nufresha by her loose, silken top and dragged her toward the rift. "How about you find out for us?" Cresala asked.

Terror filled Nufresha's eyes as she struggled against Cresala. Hashalem sighed and glanced between the two of them. The rift flickered as all three women stopped what they were doing and stared at the manifestation. It flickered again and then began to shrink.

"What did you do?" Cresala yelled back in Hashalem's direction.

"I have done nothing," Hashalem said. She warily glanced around, closing her eyes as if attempting to look for manipulations of the Enesmic flow. "Whatever is being done is being done from the Enesmic plane itself. Not here."

Nufresha broke out of Cresala's grasp and staggered backward, away from the rift. Cresala started to move toward the rift, hesitating after a few steps as the rift continually shrank.

"What do we do?" Cresala asked.

Hashalem stepped toward the rift. "We opened the rift so that we could return home, away from this horrid place and the Havin who hunt us." She walked past the other two Ceshra and turned, facing them. "The way is open before us, although it appears only for a short time. Goodbye, and may we never see each other again."

Hashalem continued toward the rift. It was now barely large enough to permit entry for one person. Hashalem hesitated as she prepared to cross over the threshold. Steeling her gaze, she walked through.

Nufresha stared at Cresala as the Ceshra glanced back at her and sneered. Cresala then ran to follow Hashalem through the rift.

Nufresha watched the rift as it continued to shrink, backing up subconsciously. It was to a scale where she wasn't sure it could be further utilized to traverse to the Enesmic plane.

Cresala partially reappeared, panic on her face with chunks of her skin missing. "The curse!" she yelled.

The rift collapsed, severing the upper half of her body. Cresala's remains fell to the ground, gore coating the area.

An overwhelming sense of terror gripped Nufresha. She turned and fled, teleporting herself far away from the place. Breathing rapidly, she burst into a bout of cihphistic weaving, quickly creating a portal that would take her far away from this world.

She hesitated and then stepped through.

Pree, Huzien Alliance space

Nufresha glanced around in a haze, standing exactly where she had been when she had brought the Vahne soldiers—entrusted to her by Sagren—to defend this world from invaders.

She blinked slowly and glanced toward the ridge where Soahc had stood in all his terrifying glory as he wiped out her army with a

powerful cihphistic attack. She felt the fear of that moment course through her veins and stepped back, frantically glancing around. Recognizing she was alone, she let out a slow breath and then sat on the ground.

"Why am I back here?" She glanced at her torn silk top, frowning as she thought of Cresala.

Fleeing the battle to save herself from Soahc had forever denigrated her in the eyes of her peers. Sighing, she touched the Enesmic and started repairing the damage to her top. Within a matter of seconds, it looked as good as new. She stared down at her hand, turning it over.

The pale, almost sickly-looking white skin was a form Sagren had constructed upon her first steps on the Enesmic plane. Watching her hand, she reverted to her true form, beautiful white energy radiating from her. She was a being of light, and at that moment, she was free. Standing, she danced, playing with the Enesmic in a way she hadn't done in a long time. The energy flowed around her in torrents, and she closed her eyes in ecstasy. She danced for what seemed like hours until the first tinges of pain began to wrack her body, the limitation of her existence on this plane. Gasping, she felt the Enesmic shift, her energy becoming unstable. She quickly sought the protection of Sagren's construction, returning to her sickly-white appearance. An intense sadness overwhelmed her as she collapsed to the ground and began to sob. After a long moment, she shuddered. Her mind went back to Cresala.

"The curse . . ." Nufresha tried to piece together what Cresala's words meant. Images of Cresala's disintegrating body stuck in her mind. "But why would it affect us? It's our home." Nufresha rubbed the bridge of her nose. Nothing made sense since she had stepped through the rift to aid Sagren. "I should never have come here."

"I agree," came a voice from behind her.

Nufresha froze, her purple orbs going wide as she held her breath. "Move, and we will obliterate you."

Forms fanned out to surround Nufresha, all of them wearing grey robes.

Argents! she screamed in her mind.

Nufresha tensed, preparing to launch a cihphistic attack. Soahc appeared in front of her, his eyes white fire. Her shoulders slumped as the fight went out of her. The Havin's wife appeared at his side, both radiating auras of incredible power that made her sick.

"Where are the other Ceshra?" Soahc said.

"They have returned home," Nufresha blurted. "Please don't kill me."

Soahc glanced at his wife and then back to Nufresha. "Home? As in the Enesmic plane?" Soahc asked.

"Yes."

"How?" Soahc's wife asked.

Nufresha glanced at her. The woman had a streak of silver in her eyes that glowed like Soahc's, signs of a Havin who had walked the Enesmic plane and lived, defying the curse.

"How did they return to the Enesmic plane?" Her voice was forceful.

Nufresha sucked in a breath. "I will tell you nothing until you guarantee my safety."

Soahc stepped forward and unleashed a powerful blast of energy that caused her world to go dark.

Etan Rachnie, Reath, Huzien Alliance space

Nufresha awoke in pain, her body sore. She couldn't move her arms or legs. She slowly opened her eyes, discovering she was sitting in a chair. Her arms were clasped in front of her, bound to a large nanoplexi table.

She recognized the bonds, and her suspicion was confirmed when she attempted to call the Enesmic for aid. Nothing.

Her eyes went wide as she frantically searched around. She looked down at her clothes. Her silk shirt was gone, replaced with

a plain white t-shirt. She frowned. That silk shirt had been the first thing she had created on the Havin plane, and the burn marks all over her arms told her that it had been obliterated in whatever attack Soahc had unleashed on her.

She tried to revert to her energy form, calling on it to help her slip through the bonds.

Nothing.

She stared silently at her bonds, her shoulders slumping as she rested her head on them.

"So, you beings *do* feel helplessness," Soahc said.

He materialized in the room, standing on the other side of the table. Sitting down in the chair opposite her, he reclined. "You're afraid of me?"

Nufresha kept her gaze focused on him, her breath shallow. "I have reason to be," Nufresha said. "You killed an Eshgren."

"The shell of one."

"Modesty." Nufresha laughed. "Why am I still alive?"

"You have information we need."

"And once I give you that information, my life is forfeit?"

"Why would I allow you to live after all you've done?"

"I can be valuable to you." Nufresha's eyes went wide. "I have knowledge and senses that you do not. There are Eshgren here, hidden in Havin bodies. I can help you find them."

It was Soahc's turn to laugh. "You would betray us in a heartbeat."

"I can leave and return to the Enesmic plane. You'll never see me again." Nufresha's voice was frantic.

"How many people did you kill during the war?"

"I merely defended worlds we—Sagren—had conquered. That was my task." Nufresha avoided Soahc's eyes.

"Okay." Soahc nodded. "One of my top Argents lost her entire team in one of those defensive responses on Trica VII. She was then captured, tortured, violated, and made a pawn of your former master as a host for another Eshgren called Sephan." Soahc leaned forward in his chair. "Sound familiar?"

"That was not me." Nufresha gasped. "Cresala. That was Cresala. I . . . I did not do that. I swear on my life essence. My forces were weak compared to hers. *I* was weak compared to her. I was not given much responsibility." Nufresha struggled against her bonds. "Please, let me live!"

"Then where is Cresala?"

"Dead."

"How?" Soahc's voice was forceful.

"Allow me to live, and I will tell you!" Her orbs were pleading.

A woman materialized to Nufresha's right, silver-laced blue eyes staring at her with malice.

"You . . ." Nufresha whispered.

The woman raised her hand to Nufresha's face as the Enesmic coalesced around her fingers. Nufresha closed her eyes.

"Bresha, no!" Soahc yelled.

CHAPTER 27 - BRESHA VECEN

Etan Rachnie, Reath, Huzien Alliance space

Bresha materialized in the Etan Rachnie gardens; her arms crossed as she started walking briskly, shivering.

Soahc materialized behind her, fury radiating from him in torrents. "You had no right!" Soahc yelled.

Bresha stopped and glared back at Soahc. "I had every right." Her voice was throaty, her gaze hard.

Soahc stopped and stared at her in silence. He slowly nodded, raising his arms peacefully. "You're right. I'm sorry. I understand that having one of those beings here must have been very painful for you after what they put you through."

Soahc approached Bresha, her blond hair blowing in a gentle breeze. She remained as still as a statue, her gaze locked on Soahc as he stopped directly in front of her.

"I had hoped to get information from her—"

"It," Bresha hissed.

"It," Soahc conceded. "I had hoped to get information from it, but we will have to find other means to ascertain how its allies returned to the Enesmic plane."

Bresha glanced away from Soahc, letting out a heavy sigh.

"It at least confirmed that the one who attacked you—Cresala was its name—is dead."

Bresha turned and continued deeper into the gardens. She took a deep breath, the smells enticing, as she stopped to look at a beautiful purple plant with red petals around its base. It had an odd shape, as if the petals were trying to pull the plant higher into the air. Soahc came to a stop next to her.

She glanced at him and then back at the plant. "I still have nightmares," she said. "My body refusing to obey me as I kill innocent people." She let out a shudder. "A part of my soul has been forever destroyed." Her face twisted into a rage. "All because of that *vusging* monster and the creatures that supported it." She spat on the ground.

The two stood silently for a long moment, staring at the plant.

"Have the sessions with Shaper Migund helped?"

"Yes." Bresha let out an exasperated sigh and turned to face Soahc. "Don't you have a wife to tend to? Or something better to occupy your time, Lord Soahc?" Her tone became overly formal.

Soahc chuckled. "Well, I'd be handling a fascinating interrogation right now, but someone blew the head off my prisoner." He grinned and glanced at Bresha. "I'm concerned about you, that's all." He hesitated. "I know you've been through a lot. Brime and I are here for you."

Bresha grinned, her eyes closing slightly as she locked gazes with Soahc. "Are you ready for the ceremony tonight?" said Soahc. She glanced away and then intentionally bumped into him as she continued her walk through the gardens without responding to his question.

She heard him let out a sigh and teleport away.

Later that night, Bresha stared at herself in the mirror of her quarters. She wore an all-black formal dress with a heavy shawl. Letting out a sigh, she uttered a word of power and clenched her fist, instantly teleporting next to a large gate. A procession of people were waiting there, Soahc and Brime at the head.

Bresha smiled, her gaze locking on Soahc.

"You ready for this?" Soahc asked.

"I am," Bresha replied.

She turned as Soahc caused the gate to open, the Enesmic pushing it quickly aside. Bresha walked through as the procession followed. They passed numerous headstones, names, and dates etched into them. The procession was silent, only the sounds of feet on grass heard as they walked for some time deep into the Argent graveyard.

Bresha caught sight of the first grave. Stopping, she sucked in a deep breath and then forced herself forward. She came to a stop directly in front of it and kneeled.

"I'm sorry I was not strong enough to protect us, Halie." Bresha reached out to touch the tombstone.

Images flashed in her mind of Shaper Halie looking down at the glowing sword in her chest, shoved there by Cresala. The helplessness in her eyes caused Bresha to tear up as she shut out the image of the sword exploding, disintegrating Halie's upper half.

Bresha sucked in another breath and started to cry as the emotions washed over her. She relived that terrible moment as a hand came to rest on her shoulder. Glancing up, she saw Brime with a somber look on her face.

Bresha took a moment longer to let the emotions play out, then composed herself and stood, continuing down the line of graves dug next to one another. She repeated the same actions at each one, coming to the second to last. She kneeled and stared hard at the tombstone.

Images of Shaper Nefram flashed in her mind. She went back to Sagren's cell in her mind, back when she was nude, cold, and in constant pain. She closed her eyes as the creature that was no longer Nefram—but who occupied his body—appeared in her cell, along with others she had trained, men she had trusted with her life. They were no longer those men. She understood that now as she allowed the scene to play out in her mind's eye—as terrible hands grabbed her body, pinning her down.

She took a deep breath and slowly breathed it out, allowing the memory to flow with it. In its place, she remembered Nefram when he was alive, the two laughing under the stars the night before their fateful attack. She teased him as they smiled. Bresha grounded herself in that moment, allowing all the joys of her past life to play out before that terrible day.

Letting out another slow breath, she stood up, her face resolute. She approached the final grave, this one open with a large casket resting above the opening. She approached the image of the individual in the casket, stopping in front of it. She examined the picture of herself; it was from a happier time. She stood there for a long moment. Turning around, she faced the rest of the procession, all assembled in a standing area prepared for them.

"Thank you all for joining me this night as we bid farewell to Bresha Vecen." Bresha closed her eyes, taking in a steeling breath. Opening them, she glanced at Soahc, who nodded for her to continue. "During the Rift War, Bresha Vecen and her team encountered a powerful foe, an Enesmic being known as a Ceshra. This creature was dangerously powerful and overwhelmed her team's forces, killing every member. Bresha was the last to fall, and she died there in spirit with her team. It was her wish to be buried on Reath in the Argent graveyard, and as such, she will be buried . . ." Her voice cracked. She hesitated, her gaze going down as she took a few breaths. "Bresha will be buried next to those heroic team members who faced the Ceshra monster in defense of the Huzien Alliance, all losing their lives on that day. They will all be remembered as heroes who sacrificed their lives in the line of duty as Argents of Etan Rachnie."

Bresha moved away from the casket and came to stand in the front of the procession as others came up and bid farewell to Bresha Vecen. She listened to them intently, tears a constant presence on her face. Many stopped to put a comforting hand on her shoulder as they finished their speeches.

Soahc was the last to come up and speak. "Thank you all for attending this ceremony. It is with a heavy heart that I mourn the passing of Bresha Vecen. We commit all that she was to the ground so that a new being may be reborn in her place."

The casket behind Soahc started to sink lower into the ground. They all stood in silence for a long moment as it reached the bottom, the dirt on the sides deposited automatically on top of it until flat earth remained in front of the tombstone.

Soahc looked to Bresha Vecen and motioned for her to stand beside him. She nodded and walked over, turning to face the procession.

"Join me in celebrating the birth of Vades," Soahc said.

Vades—she-who-had-once-been-Bresha—shuddered as she smiled. Smiles greeted her as every member of the procession walked up to her and introduced themselves as if for the first time.

CHAPTER 28 – URIEL KERVID

57867 FA (22,256 years ago)
Etan Rachnie, Reath, Huzien Alliance space

Soahc and Uriel appeared in a large field and quickly took in the scene. The two had been standing in one of the wings of Ziph-ram just a moment ago. The area was lush with dense foliage and the sound of rushing water just out of sight. They were in a small clearing, the grass coming up to Uriel's shins.

"Why are we here?" Uriel asked.

"The next lesson I wish to teach you is best done outside the campus grounds."

Soahc began to move rhythmically, engrossed in an elaborate web of cihphistic construction. The Enesmic started to flow around them in torrents.

Uriel's senses went on high alert as the Enesmic around him shifted in a way he had never seen before. He frowned and felt the need to pull up his defenses; an instinct hammered into him on the front lines.

Within a few moments, Soahc began to pull on something like an invisible chain, and the air in front of him rippled. Uriel moved into a defensive position as Soahc pulled again, shattering the air before him and revealing a terrible creature with long, narrow appendages wielding two large scimitar-like weapons.

The creature collapsed onto the ground in an area that glowed with a powerful field around it. The air and space it had emerged from returned to normal. The creature quickly recovered and charged at Soahc but was held at bay by the field.

Soahc completed his weaving and moved to circle the creature, putting it in Uriel's line of sight. "This is something I've termed the Bau. It's a form of Enesmic assassin but less intelligent than its cousins."

The Bau lunged at Soahc multiple times, its blades moving with sickening efficiency as it tried to take his head.

"As I'm sure you can see, they are still quite dangerous."

"Summoning of Enesmic creatures? I've heard stories of such acts but have never seen one up close." Uriel took a few steps forward, a morbid curiosity drawing him closer.

"It is rare today that such summonings occur, as the skill is only known by a handful of powerful Cihphists. And those who do summon . . . well, without the proper wards and protections in place, they don't live to try it again." Soahc kept his eyes on the creature as it silently stalked him, its eyes searching the field for any sign of weakness or opening.

"Why show me this?" Uriel glanced at Soahc.

Soahc smiled and then went into another bout of cihphistic weaving. A shroud began to form around Soahc as the Enesmic swirled around him. In the blink of an eye, Soahc disappeared.

"As I'm sure you're aware, anything you can do to gain an advantage over your foes will help you survive in seemingly impossible situations."

Uriel couldn't see Soahc but felt his voice coming from around him, making it difficult to detect his exact location.

"Defend yourself!" Soahc called out.

The field around the Enesmic creature was released. The Bau looked around in confusion, unable to find Soahc. Its gaze quickly turned to Uriel. It bellowed at him and charged, moving incredibly fast.

Uriel shifted to the side as its blades sought to sever him in half. He drew Wishwonder, but a powerful force plucked it away; the blade disappeared as if consumed by the same cloaking shroud that hid Soahc from view.

"No weapons! Use your abilities."

Uriel swore and shifted again as the creature lunged after him. Uriel broke into a bout of cihphistic weaving as he rose slightly into the air. He held a bolt of lightning taut, releasing it into the chest of the Bau as it charged at him again. The powerful strike threw the creature across the field as steam rose from it.

It got up and growled at Uriel, taking a moment to contemplate its next move. The sudden remembrance of its intelligence caused Uriel concern as he quickly went on the offensive. He shifted higher into the air, summoning raw Enesmic energy in a way taught to him by Soahc and funneling it toward the creature.

The creature's eyes widened as the lefon blast consumed it, burning the creature to ash. Uriel slowly dropped to the ground as Soahc reappeared, clapping his hands.

Wishwonder floated back over to Uriel. He caught and sheathed it.

"Left alone to its devices, its effectiveness is limited, but by utilizing the techniques I have taught you around empowerment and attacking in tandem from the shadows, you can quickly turn the tide."

Uriel nodded, his eyes stuck on the remnants of the creature.

Soahc's tone dropped into that of an instructor. "Now examine the web as I form it. Repeat my actions exactly."

Uriel complied.

*The loss of plant life has destroyed the life cycle of oxygen
for the sustaining of most species in the Huzien Alliance.*

-FROM "ENESMIC SHIPYARD EFFECTS ON TRICA VII"
MINSCI METABASE

CHAPTER 29 - VADES

Etan Rachnie, Reath, Huzien Alliance space

Noez Aeel sat in the Etan Rachnie boardroom in the seat previously belonging to the former Argent General, Ristolte Aris III. The general had died in an incident during Soahc's quest to rescue Brime from the Enesmic plane.

Vades silently watched the man from the guest chair at the table. He had tawny skin with golden undertones, hazel-colored eyes, and jet-black hair in a military cut. He looked to be well past middle-aged and had a perpetual frown.

He glanced at Vades and nodded.

She returned the nod and looked to a woman with white hair and light-brown skin at the opposite end of the table. She reminded Vades of Lanrete, who was sitting next to the woman. The woman's silver eyes flickered up to lock gazes with Vades. Nalle Libl smiled at Vades and then broke eye contact.

They all turned to regard Soahc as he materialized in the boardroom and moved to take his seat. The air flickered around him, the Enesmic responding to his presence in the room and sending the hairs on the back of her neck up on end.

He always loved to put on a good show.

"By now, you all have learned that the Ceshra prisoner previously in our capture was exterminated," Soahc said. "The Ceshra going by the name of Nufresha claimed that the other two Ceshra in . . ." Soahc glanced to Vades, ". . . *its* company have either returned to the Enesmic plane or died. It did not have a chance to disclose how this transpired, but we can most likely assume that, if one *did* indeed return to the Enesmic plane, it did so utilizing a rift similar to the one opened by Sagren."

"I have sensed no change to the Enesmic to indicate such," Merbi Teral said. He had a booming voice contrary to his diminutive figure.

Many in the room nodded at Merbi's comments.

"Has it been intentionally hidden from our senses to allow the Eshgren to continue Sagren's work?" Noez asked.

"Almost assuredly," Soahc said. "We can only assume that the Eshgren brought onto this plane by Sephan's actions are behind this."

"Are we capable of dealing with multiple Eshgren?" Noez asked.

"We have no choice," Ecnics said. He was sitting across from the new Argent general.

"This seems too direct for Eshgren from what we understand about them," Nalle spoke up. "Sephan worked from the shadows. They were never this direct or overt. It was only due to a chance encounter with Serah'Elax that we even became aware of its machinations."

"Which we can most likely attribute to the counterplot of some Rel Ach'Kel working in our favor," Soahc said.

All of them remained silent for a moment. Vades had learned of the Rel Ach'Kel during her possession by Sephan. The being had been constantly paranoid of them interfering with its plans somehow. They were the mortal enemies of the Eshgren, the original sect before some great war that divided them eons ago.

"Sagren was direct," Kaloni Setla interjected. "We can't assume that all Eshgren operate the same way."

Vades had interacted little with Kaloni, but the woman had an air of authority that rivaled Soahc. She worked for the MinSci as department head of Cihphist technology and was one of Ecnics's favorites. Although neither publicly acknowledged a relationship, Vades had heard rumors that the two were romantically involved.

"This is true," Soahc said. "It's safe to say that even if no rift exists, the Eshgren brought here by Sephan are still involved in some machinations that put the Twin Galaxies at risk. We must find them and put an end to them."

All nodded in agreement.

"I move to request deployment of our full Argent forces to aid in the search for the Eshgren."

"I second the motion," Noez said.

Soahc's eyes went distant as if reliving an old memory.

"We have a motion on the floor," Merbi said. "Let's take it for a vote unless there is further discussion."

No one objected as Merbi nodded and brought the holodisplay to life in the center of the table.

"The motion passes with unanimous support. Argent General Noez, you are hereby ordered to dispatch the full force of the Argents in search of these Eshgren that threaten our Twin Galaxies."

Noez nodded.

"I now call this meeting to adjournment."

Almost all connected via the hologrid winked out of existence, except for Ecnics and Lanrete. They turned to face Soahc.

"We should prepare for war," Lanrete said.

"You believe this is a sign of another fleet being constructed?" Soahc asked.

"I don't know, but I refuse to be caught off guard again," Lanrete said.

"Have you formally discontinued your reckless ghost hunt?" Ecnics asked.

"He killed another one of my Elites!" Lanrete shouted. "Someone who was also important to you, if you haven't forgotten." There was bitterness in Lanrete's tone.

"How many Elites have died during your quest for vengeance?"

"Don't. Not here. Not now," Lanrete warned.

Ecnics glanced around at the others in attendance and shut his mouth.

Lanrete took a moment to calm down and then sat up straighter. "How is Neven?"

"He has shown much improvement," Ecnics said. "My initial analysis showed chronic mental trauma from the Rift War and the death of Zun, so he will take additional time to recover."

"I may need him soon, depending on how this plays out," Lanrete said.

"No," Ecnics said.

Lanrete frowned.

"I said he showed improvement. I didn't say he was ready for active deployment."

"Your original estimate was a month of recovery." Lanrete leaned forward.

"Yes, before I fully understood his condition. He needs additional time to recover."

"We don't have additional time!"

"He is first and foremost mine, lest you forget!"

Soahc cleared his throat. "Are you two done? My time is valuable."

Both Lanrete and Ecnics glared at Soahc. An awkward silence descended on the room.

Ecnics turned to look at Vades. "Do you have any thoughts from your . . . engagement with Sephan? Did it reveal its plans for the Eshgren it brought to this plane?"

She sucked in a quick breath and shook her head. "Sephan had brought them here to aid it in its dominion over the Ashna Maidens. It was unprepared for their abandonment during the final battle."

"That may be a good starting point for our investigations," Noez said. "Ashna Maiden space?"

"Highly unlikely," Vades said. "The Ashna Maidens were Sephan's obsession. I don't think the other Eshgren viewed them with as much importance."

"We should keep our search broad then," Soahc said.

"We'll convene a Triumvirate meeting and update Cislot of our discussion," Ecnics said.

Soahc nodded as Ecnics disconnected from the hologrid.

A large Vempiir with dark-red skin, crystalline eyes, and perfect posture sat across from Vades. He nestled a cup of tea in his hand, gazing out a large window showing the fields that ran for miles outside the Etan Rachnie walls.

Both sat in a café over a kilometer high at the top of one of those walls—the top floor of the establishment was open to fresh air. The Argent barracks were a short distance away, the superstructure extending from the wall into the campus grounds, creating an impressive sight. The café was protected by strategically placed shielding that kept them safe from high winds.

"You didn't answer my question, Narmo." Vades grinned.

"Oh," Narmo Swela said. The First Argent turned one eye toward her. "Is silence not an answer?"

"I need to get out and go on the mission."

"Why?"

"Because I'm a *vusging* Argent!" Vades quickly calmed down, unballing her fists.

Narmo turned to face her fully, his expression dour. He started nodding his head. "I . . . I hear you." Narmo set down his tea and crossed his arms. "Are you truly ready to go back out there?"

"You doubt my ability?"

"Hardly, you know that. You are far stronger now than you were when you left." Narmo shook his head. "That's not what I mean. You just went through the ceremony of rebirth. Give it some time—why not go figure out who Vades is? What are her goals in life?" Narmo leaned forward. "You have an immortal lifetime now to go hunting Eshgren."

Vades let out a sigh and sat back in her chair. She broke Narmo's gaze and turned to look out the window.

"You should take Soahc up on his offer."

Vades shifted her gaze to Narmo without moving her head. "Become his second apprentice? Is that a joke?"

"Look at Brime. Look at what she has accomplished in such a short amount of time. Her CSL is almost on par with his own by all measures."

Vades frowned.

"Consider it for a few days. If you decide that you still want to go out and join the mission, I will reactivate you for deployment, but I want you to make decisions not based on comfort, but purpose."

Vades finished off her drink and got up from the table. Without a glance at Narmo, she left the café.

Vades sat in her room, gazing at the Argent uniform on her bed. Her living quarters were modest; she had few possessions.

Soahc had sent over the latest pages he had updated on the textbook taught in Etan Rachnie about the Enesmic plane. She had just finished her review of the contents, adding some details imparted to her when Sephan had possessed her body. Her vision suddenly blurred.

Kill them all. The Havin do not deserve to exist.

The whisper caused her to tense up. She quickly rose and moved to the wall, squatting against it and crossing her arms. She closed her eyes tightly as an intense fire seemed to bloom alive from her innermost being.

Spread their blood in the courtyard. It will be beautiful.

Vades immediately fell into the meditative techniques that had been taught to her by her therapist. She tried to force the voice out, to silence her mind. She started to sweat, gasping in pain as the heat felt from within filled her with terror.

They will all rejoin the flow.

Vades let out a slow breath, dropping to the floor and hugging her knees. She sat there for a long moment, the voice fading and the heat subsiding. Tentatively, she opened her eyes and glanced around. She spoke a word of power as her vision shifted, the flow becoming visible. Everything was normal; there were no disturbances or anything that could indicate Enesmic weaving.

A knock at her door jolted her as she frantically looked around, the sudden urge to hide overpowering her for a moment. Quickly regaining control, she took another deep breath and brought up her microdisplay. Frowning, she pulled on an oversized t-shirt and then moved to the door and opened it.

Her gaze locked with Soahc's. He frowned.

"Something's wrong," Soahc said.

"The voice. I . . ." Vades lowered her gaze.

Soahc immediately went into a bout of cihphistic weaving, examining every thread that existed within a mile. Vades stood silently as Soahc thoroughly examined Enesmic machinations around them.

"Nothing. Same as before." Soahc took a step into her room. "You saw nothing? No echoes being rapidly eroded?"

"Nothing."

Soahc nodded. "Migund was unable to find any connection still shared between you and Sephan. The voice and heat are most likely—"

"—manifestations of past trauma. Yes, I'm aware." Vades gave Soahc an annoyed look as she pulled down on her t-shirt, attempting to provide more cover for her bare legs. "Why are you here? It must be important for you to show up in person unannounced." Vades used the sleeve of her t-shirt to wipe the heavy sweat from her face.

"As you're aware, Lanrete arrived earlier today. But it wasn't simply to attend the board meeting in person."

Soahc made his way past Vades into her quarters, sitting in one of her chairs. She pushed down the now heightened state of annoyance and moved to the chair across from him.

"He's been having dreams, the same dream, to be exact."

Vades perked up, moving her legs under herself in the chair. "What kind of dream?"

"He's on the Enesmic plane, but his body is not his own. He has control of it and senses an urging to come here." Soahc went quiet.

Vades looks down at the floor, her mind racing. "Eshgren and Rel Ach'Kel frequently communicate with Havin via dreams. It's how they influence and manipulate us."

"As Brime did when she alerted me to her presence on the Enesmic plane and to seek her out."

"Exactly. Some nature of the Enesmic plane, and of Enesmic beings, allows for the easy traversing of dreams in our plane of existence."

"I asked Lanrete to come here so that we might study him as he sleeps. To see if the dream continues and to find the source of it."

"That's very risky. If it's an Eshgren, the results could be catastrophic. You could draw the attention of the Eshgren to us or complete its machinations."

"Precisely."

"I understand you have faced two different Eshgren and believe yourself confident in defeating them, but you have never faced multiple Eshgren at once. It will not go in your favor."

Soahc's eyes glazed over as he looked past Vades, frowning. "How else do you propose we draw them out? They could hide and bide their time for a millennium, slowly building up some nefarious plan to spring on us when we least suspect it."

"I will hunt them." Vades's voice was cold.

Soahc sat back in the chair, his eyes refocusing on Vades. "Are you sure? Why not stay here and hone your abilities or train with me and Brime?"

"The women who they possess are like me. Like I once was." Vades's face grew hard. "Being like that is not existence. It's a living death—a prison of mental and physical torture that is never-ending. I cannot sit idly by and train as other women suffer as I did. I must hunt them. It is my new purpose, one that will most likely result in my death." She rested her hands in her lap. "I intend to tell

Narmo tomorrow morning that I intend to join the mission. We discussed it today."

"I see." Soahc nodded. "Very well then. Humor me one last time tonight as I monitor Lanrete. In case the Eshgren are drawn out, I would appreciate having you nearby."

Vades nodded.

CHAPTER 30 - DESRIN

Etan Rachnie, Reath, Huzien Alliance space

D esrin clenched the hilt of his Revfa blade. It was in its sheath, the howling muffled as he watched the Chaah prisoner in the other room be interrogated by an Argent telepath.

His blade hungered; the nearby blood of the Chaah was sending it into a frenzy. The tainted aura of the Chaah was like a repugnant odor in his nostrils. It was overpowering. Sickening. He should have killed her back on Tenquin like every instinct ingrained into him over the past four thousand years had instructed him to.

But he hadn't. He wasn't sure exactly why. Something about that Ken'Tar monk had swayed him. His aura was strong, the Enesmic speaking through him.

Desrin closed his eyes and let out a heavy sigh. He released his Revfa blade, his connection to the living weapon dimming slightly. The repulsion of the Chaah became more bearable. He sucked in a quick breath and then clenched his fist while uttering a word of power.

Within a heartbeat, he stood before a sealed door, his presence bringing the lighting around it to life. A warning was in bright-red lettering on the black surface of the nanoplexi door—one with a strong cihphistic ward in place.

"Heart of Corruption," Desrin read subconsciously.

He stepped forward, raising his hand as he kinetically manipulated the mechanism inside the door and then enacted the corresponding cihphism to allow himself passage through the ward.

It opened slowly. Desrin pushed past the door and into the room beyond. He flinched as he passed over the threshold. The taint of Elhirtha—blood weaving—was strong in the air, even after all this time. He stared at the small rift in the room, all the furniture having long since been removed.

The rift was flickering, the flow of Enesmic energy in the room corrupted by the blood weaving that had initially sent it into motion many millennia ago. Tendrils of red energy occasionally streaked out from the rift, leaving scorch marks on the floor. The floor had become pitch-black over time.

Desrin unsheathed his blade, the howling becoming deafening. He felt the pain from the blade. The anger. The fury. He let that flow through him to focus him.

"I figured I'd find you here," a voice came from behind Desrin.

He sheathed his blade and turned. Soahc stood before him, his gaze stuck on the small flickering rift.

"A constant reminder of my mistakes," Soahc said. He let out a sigh and looked at Desrin. "I heard you and Nestis were here. It is good to see you, old friend. How goes the hunt?"

"To think that a rift like this cannot be sealed due to the corrupted way in which it was opened . . ." Desrin glanced back at the corrupted rift. "So much we don't understand about the Enesmic." Desrin looked to Soahc. "We captured a Chaah prisoner I am preparing to execute."

"Hiesha Nihjar. . ." Soahc nodded. "I heard you brought a prisoner back. I was surprised. I thought that you might have captured Yuemon. Why?"

"I honestly do not know. I was swayed by a Ken'Tar monk."

"Erbubuc Tamn, yes. I am familiar with him. He travels with Lanrete and the Founder's Elite." Soahc shivered and then turned to leave the room.

Desrin followed, and the two exited the Heart of Corruption before sealing the door.

"From what I hear, the Chaah prisoner has been nothing but cooperative, providing information on Chaah cells they were aware of and the detailed plans of Alinos, one of Yuemon's inner circle. She seems valuable."

"It does not matter. All Chaah must die."

Soahc narrowed his eyes. "Are you the Revfa's master, or does it lord over you?"

Desrin scowled at Soahc. "I am the master."

Soahc nodded. "Never forget that." With a clenched fist and word of power, Soahc was gone.

Desrin hesitated momentarily, then followed suit, sensing Nestis in the Etan Rachnie gardens. The scene around him shifted from the depressing door to a massive garden. He scanned the area to find Nestis meditating in a small opening surrounded by blue roses. Walking over, Desrin joined his companion.

"I can still sense her wrongness," Nestis said. "It was a mistake bringing her here." His eyes were still closed, his position unchanged.

"I know." Desrin sighed. "Lord Soahc believes that we should use her."

Nestis opened an eye and glanced at Desrin. "Does his lordship? Why does he care all of a sudden about a Chaah prisoner?"

"I sense that he believes she may be the key to finding Yuemon." Desrin met Nestis's gaze.

"And you agree with his sentiment?"

"I am starting to, yes."

"I don't like this." Nestis opened his eyes and stood. He looked around the gardens, his gaze lingering on a blue rose for a long moment. "Have you heard of the new mission that spurs the full host of the Argent into action?"

Desrin nodded.

"These Eshgren . . . they don't corrupt the Enesmic, but I sense they are more of a threat to us than anything we've encountered."

"They wield such power. If we were to harness it . . ." Desrin locked gazes with Nestis. "Think of how quickly we could bring an end to the Chaah, forever."

"Dangerous thoughts." Nestis walked past Desrin and headed toward where their Chaah prisoner was being held. "Would they stop us if we went in to kill her?"

"They could try." Desrin smiled and then sighed. "She is valuable as a prisoner." Desrin folded his arms. "But she will slip up and fall back into her old ways. They all do. And when that happens, we will be justified in ending her."

Desrin felt the hunger of his blade course through him; incredible restraint was the only thing that kept him from teleporting to the room with the Chaah and ending her right that moment. There was some truth to what Soahc had said. The blade was becoming more powerful. More insistent. Since attaining the ninth degree of evolution with the blade, he had struggled to define the line between himself and the weapon. That concerned him greatly.

The prisoner has requested an audience with you, came a telepathic message from the interrogator.

Desrin glanced to Nestis, who nodded. They teleported in sync, appearing in the interrogation room. The interrogator glanced at the duo, eyes wide. Their face quickly returned to normal, and they nodded to them, walking out of the room.

Desrin turned his attention to Hiesha. She looked pitiful, wearing the standard prisoner uniform of the Huzien military. The transparent material showed the effects Elhirtha had had on her body. She had red fissures in her flesh that wouldn't heal, their presence a manifestation of the corruption blood weaving had on all living things.

"I understand that my life is forfeit," Hiesha said.

Her wrists were restrained, limiting her ability to enact any Elhirtha. Two Argent knights hung back in the room's shadows—her jailers.

"I will willingly accept the death you seek for me without complaint."

Desrin and Nestis exchanged glances.

"Understanding this, will you grant me one request?"

"What?" Desrin asked.

"I want to assist in the vengeance against Alinos. Then you can kill me with your wretched blades."

"Why should we believe you?"

"Alinos betrayed me, took from me the one thing I cared about in the Twin Galaxies: my *eifi*, my Orech." Her voice cracked as a tear rolled down her cheek. "He must pay. I must see him die horribly. It is all I want. I will give you everything. I will help you bring down the Chaah itself. Just . . . give me that satisfaction. In death, I will be reunited with her."

"We will take it under consideration," Desrin said. "You will have your answer when we return."

Hiesha nodded, her gaze going to the floor. More tears streamed down her cheeks as she cried in silence.

CHAPTER 31 - TASHANIRA YEN UNVESAL

Etan Rachnie, Reath, Huzien Alliance space

Tashanira sat on the windowsill of her temporary room in the Etan Rachnie dormitories. It wasn't as elaborate or decadent as her quarters aboard the *Foundra Ascension*, but it was on the top floor, affording a stellar view of the gardens and the myriad of people who frequented them.

A chime at the door caused her to stand, stretching with a yawn. Pulling up the outside view, she hesitated. Frowning, she moved to the door, leaning one arm against the doorframe as it slid open. She mustered as much annoyance as she could summon.

Dexter stared back at her, his green eyes unsettling as always. The Sentinel was still in his matte black uniform, although his rifle was missing.

"Yes?" Tashanira asked.

"I'm surprised to see you being antisocial and hiding in your room all afternoon," Dexter said. "You missed one of Brime's famous tours. Serah'Elax and Erb had a blast."

"I don't have the energy to engage with people right now. I want to be alone." Tashanira turned and began to close the door.

Dexter put his foot to stop it. She turned and glared at him.

"I want to talk," Dexter said.

Tashanira let out an annoyed sigh and stepped toward him, her arms crossed as she invaded his personal space, prompting him to step back to avoid getting knocked over. "About what exactly?"

"Jenshi." Dexter's face remained neutral.

Tashanira let out a heavy sigh and moved out of the way, motioning for him to enter. Dexter passed her and casually dropped onto the couch near the entrance to the room. Tashanira prompted the door to close and then turned around, leaning against it.

"I was cleared to inform you of this by Lanrete. I have been ordered to keep tabs on Jenshi once he is out of reconditioning. I have also been authorized to use deadly force if he threatens the safety of any member of the Founder's Elite."

"That's unnecessary. Mental reconditioning is highly effective at removing violent tendencies."

"Our Founder did not want to take any chances. I understand you have feelings for him, but Jenshi is dangerous when he wants to be."

"He overreacted."

"Overreacting is punching someone when you find out they slept with your girlfriend. Using an illegal bioweapon you had tucked away to end his existence? That's textbook homicidal."

"He stopped and gave Neven the cure. I think he just intended to scare him."

"I believe he fully intended to kill him and couldn't follow through in the moment."

Tashanira slid down to the ground and hugged her knees, resting her head on them. "This is all my fault."

"No. Jenshi has always been homicidal. I just thought he had a filter regarding members of his team." Dexter sat back on the couch. "Don't put this on yourself—you can *vusg* whoever the *vusg* you want. Breakups happen constantly without people snapping and killing their ex's new fling."

Tashanira looked up at Dexter, locking eyes with him. "I didn't intend to break up with Jenshi."

Dexter whistled. "That's your first mistake." He stood. "It was clear you had a thing for Neven. I'm not sure why you tried to hold on to whatever you thought you had with Jenshi."

"I didn't want to be the stereotypical Uri," Tashanira whispered as she looked down at the ground.

"Uri *vusg* just as much as any other species. Not more or less. Trust me, I know." Dexter grinned. "Don't diminish yourself based on what other people think of you. It's not worth it."

Tashanira looked up at Dexter. "Why are you really here?"

Dexter let out a sigh. "I know what it's like to feel like you're worthless and like you've lost in life. My mother didn't want me, and my father was dead before I was born; those are hard facts to face as a young kid." Dexter hesitated. "Being with all of you and living on the ship . . . it showed me that my life is worth something."

Dexter walked up to Tashanira and extended a hand. She looked at it for a moment and then reached up. Dexter pulled her to her feet.

"Live your life and be who you want to be," he said. "*Vusg* everyone's expectations of you." He grinned and moved past her as the door opened.

Tashanira watched him go and smiled. She moved back to the windowsill and looked down at the garden. Widening her smile, she felt she had enough energy to visit the gardens in person.

Taking a few steps toward her door, an overwhelming sense of vertigo came over her. She shot her arm out, gripping the couch to steady herself. Her senses flared, her supernatural ability going on high alert as terror washed over her. She looked all around, trying to discern what was triggering it.

The feeling was familiar . . . the same one from the shuttle! It passed a moment later, but then she felt exhausted, her consciousness slipping. She barely made her way over to the bed before collapsing into it, her world going dark.

Tashanira stood before a swirling vortex, entranced by its white and purple colors.

Beautiful, she heard herself say. The words felt as if they were coming from far away.

The vortex flared bright as it called to her. The sound was sweet to her ears. Enticing.

She walked toward it, the vortex consuming her thoughts. Each step she took seemed to increase the distance between her and the vortex. She started to run, but the vortex moved farther and farther away. She ran for what seemed like hours, but the vortex remained out of reach.

The vortex called out to her again, this time from far away.

Tashanira woke with a start, the dream not fading as expected. Instead, it hung on to a thread of her consciousness. She got up in a daze, the world around her seeming ethereal. Lights were brighter than they should be, with the spots of darkness looking deeper and almost unnatural.

"Come," the voice called to her again in a whisper.

Tashanira exited her room without thinking, quickly moving into the dark courtyard below. The sun had long since set. The world appeared like a mix of realities, dream and waking in perfect harmony. Her feet moved of their own accord.

She walked for some time, coming to a nondescript building at the far edge of Etan Rachnie. The door opened before her as she stepped inside. More blast doors opened, seals going from red to green as she walked unheeded. They were massive doors designed as if to keep something in.

Something dangerous.

The thought formed in her mind but then was gone, like a dream at waking—the hint of it there, but the clarity of it lost on her. She continued walking, eventually reaching a reinforced nanoplexi door with bright red lettering on the black surface. It opened before her, and she walked forward.

That was when she saw the vortex, the one from her dream. It was within reach. She took a step toward it, then another—

Reality crashed down all around her.

Tashanira blinked rapidly, a pit forming in her stomach as she hugged herself. Her senses were screaming at her. How did she get here? What *was* here?

A red tendril of energy flickered out from the rift. Tashanira felt vomit in her mouth, the presence of Elhirtha so strong that she couldn't control her body. She retched all over the floor. It sizzled and then evaporated.

Tashanira had a puzzled look on her face. The floor was cold as she pushed herself back to her feet. How could it evaporate liquid? This was . . . wrong.

A toffee-skinned woman materialized in front of Tashanira. She wore a low-cut, silver blouse complemented with a pair of silver leggings. Her feet were bare but well-manicured, and she had silver-streaked black hair that dropped past her shoulders. Her eyes captured Tashanira's attention fully, the purple irises unnatural.

Tashanira felt a wrongness about her. She stepped back, realizing she didn't have her weapons.

Sounds erupted from behind her as she turned back to see Lanrete, Soahc, Brime, and Vades all running into the room.

"I can't believe the Enesmic thread triggering Lanrete's dream is coming from here," Brime said.

"It should be impossible. This room is sealed to Enesmic weaving," Vades said.

"Tashanira?" Lanrete gave her a confused look.

Soahc and Brime scowled, their gazes locked onto the woman behind Tashanira.

"An Eshgren! Who are you?" Soahc yelled.

The woman gripped Tashanira by the arm and pulled her into the vortex with superhuman strength.

Tashanira screamed as she fell from the sky, landing like lightning on the Enesmic plane. The woman from before was in front of her, but she was different. In place of the brown-skinned woman now stood a towering being of immense power. The purple eyes had grown to massive proportions, intensely focused on her.

Tashanira felt the Enesmic begin to rip her apart, and pieces of her body were pulled away to join the Enesmic flow. She screamed again. The being reached forward, its hand passing through her skin and into her womb.

Tashanira gasped. The rapid deconstruction of her body halted.

"No!" A towering being with fine armor overlaid with a flowing blue robe appeared beside Tashanira. Massive pauldrons of gold and silver covered its shoulders, but in the place of a head hung a silver hourglass with a glowing golden orb at its midsection.

Tashanira's eyes widened. She recognized the being from descriptions by Brime.

"Grilmuqshen the Exemplar," she whispered.

She felt something off within her, another voice that was not her own joining in the song of the Enesmic. She looked down in shock.

Grilmuqshen charged the purple-eyed Eshgren in front of Tashanira. The impact severed its connection to Tashanira, and the Enesmic started buffeting her again as it ripped at her skin.

She screamed, flashes of weapons connecting right next to her, the only indications of the two towering beings fighting. Tashanira could feel nothing but pain, the intensity of it unlike anything she had ever felt. She collapsed to the ground as Grilmuqshen appeared beside her, grabbed hold of her, and threw her toward the rift she had used to enter the Enesmic plane.

A bellow of rage cut the air. The Eshgren caught and deposited her on the ground, clashing with Grilmuqshen a heartbeat later.

Another Eshgren appeared beside Grilmuqshen, a towering being with a body covered in a robe of arms. It grappled with the Rel Ach'Kel as the other Eshgren disappeared, reappearing next to Tashanira. It reached inside of her abdomen again.

Tashanira gasped, her form returning to normal as the chunks of skin ripped off by the Enesmic regenerated. That voice from inside of her again started to sing with the Enesmic in tune with the flow. The purple-eyed being moved inside of her in the blink of an eye, leaving behind the toffee-skinned woman who started to yell in pain, terror on her face as she collapsed onto Tashanira.

"Help me!" the woman cried.

Tashanira's eyes widened as the other woman's skin started breaking off in chunks, the Enesmic rapidly deconstructing her. In a heartbeat, she was gone.

Grilmuqshen broke free from the other Eshgren and charged toward Tashanira. Tashanira held up her arms in an attempt at a defense, but Grilmuqshen gripped her arm, forcing her attention on it.

"Accept me into your essence. Your child is at risk," Grilmuqshen said.

The Eshgren from before charged at the being, but Grilmuqshen met its blade and unleashed a powerful blast in its direction that sent it flying far across the landscape.

Grilmuqshen turned back to Tashanira. "Time is short. It must happen before the merging is fully complete."

"I don't want to be possessed!" Tashanira cried.

"I would never claim your will! Trust me."

Tashanira felt the conviction in his voice and nodded as Grilmuqshen passed into her as well. Tashanira frantically looked around, unsure of what just happened. Her body sparkled, transforming. She couldn't comprehend what was happening to her or what was happening inside of her.

She screamed again.

CHAPTER 32 - LANRETE

Etan Rachnie, Reath, Huzien Alliance space

T he vortex became a terrible thing, the corrupted aspects of it lashing out in a rage as Tashanira passed through with the Eshgren.

Lanrete charged toward the horrible vortex without a second thought.

"No, don't!" Soahc yelled, but Lanrete was already through the vortex.

The world around him shifted as Lanrete fell from the sky.

No. Not falling. Gliding.

Lanrete could feel wings at his back, the power contained within them propelling him forward like a hurricane. He could see Tashanira struggling as two beings fought one another near her, their rapid movements visible. Knowledge and understanding overwhelmed him, his perspective forever changing.

Lanrete knew their names and histories, all of it with perfect clarity. Grilmuqshen the Exemplar, a powerful Rel Ach'Kel, and Aersheju the Inciter, a betrayer, an Eshgren. Another Eshgren appeared, aiding its kin: Eheriequyturjin the Abettor.

Lanrete watched the Eshgren and Rel Ach'Kel merge with Tashanira, both fusing with her essence in a way that he understood to be taboo. Lanrete landed with a thunderclap in front of Tashanira. She weakly looked up at him, her eyes going wild.

Lanrete reached out a hand, but the brown-skinned hand he had known all his life was gone, replaced with one of pure silver. It was wrapped in bracers of gold with black cloth etched into the skin down to his palm. He hesitated at the sight of it, the dream coming back to him. He brought his other hand up to view the mirrored appearance.

He looked to Tashanira, seeing his reflection in her eyes. He was now a towering being with a silver face, his body covered in impressive gold armor, with black cloth accented in certain areas, and a bright golden disk behind his head that started at his shoulders and completed a full circle far above his head. It shined with a terrible might. Four sets of mixed white and black wings stretched from behind him.

Eheriequyturjin regarded Lanrete with shock, the Eshgren retreating a step and then rapidly distancing itself from him.

Lanrete pushed down the shock at his new appearance and reached out, grabbing hold of Tashanira. He pulled her close to himself and turned in the direction he had come. Seeing whispers of the vortex, he propelled himself toward it with incredible speed. He passed the threshold with Tashanira, both crashing onto the Havin plane in a roll out of the vortex.

Soahc stood in disbelief with Vades and Brime as they prepared to charge into the vortex.

"What . . . just happened?" Brime asked, then looked at Lanrete. "You're glowing."

Every eye shifted to Lanrete as he stood, Tashanira unconscious. He turned back to the vortex. "We must close this. It shouldn't exist."

"I have tried, but the corruption prevents proper weaving to wrest it closed."

"There is another way. I have seen it." Lanrete imparted the understanding to Soahc in a telepathic burst.

Soahc's eyes went wide. "Impossible, but . . . huh." Soahc turned to regard the vortex. He broke into a bout of cihphistic weaving, the master at work in his craft.

Corrupted tendrils shot out at Soahc, but Lanrete counteracted them, touching the Enesmic in a way he had never done before. He held the tendrils at bay as Soahc wove a new type of web, one never before seen on the Havin plane.

"What are you doing?" Brime walked over to Soahc, studying his cihphistic web.

"Stopping it," Soahc said.

With a litany of words of power, Soahc snapped his fingers, and time around the vortex froze. The vortex no longer swirled, and a wicked tendril was caught in the act of retracting.

"Time manipulation," Soahc said. "I had theorized that it might be possible, but you gave me the key." He turned to look at Lanrete. "How did you know that?"

"We have to talk," Lanrete said.

Soahc's Compound, Reath, Huzien Alliance space

"You're a Rel Ach'Kel?" Brime approached Lanrete, poking him a few times in the ribs.

Lanrete sighed. They were in the primary living room of Soahc's compound, his home on the outskirts of Etan Rachnie. The compound was massive, with multiple structures around the primary dwelling that afforded everything from custom training centers and pools to the largest library on the planet with books from across the Twin Galaxies. The overall design paid homage to Human culture from Ginea before Soahc destroyed it.

"Or something new. Something not quite Rel Ach'Kel or Eshgren," Soahc said. He was looking out of the nearby wall-to-ceiling window, deep in thought. "Allowing the essence of life to flow in the Havin plane was something that had never been done before. The Rel Ach'Kel understood there would be unforeseen consequences." Soahc looked to Lanrete. "That must be what makes you immortal."

"Then the other natural-born immortals . . ." Vades began.

"They are like me." Lanrete nodded. "But they have not awakened."

"To be able to freely pass between the Enesmic and Havin planes with no negative consequences . . ." Soahc scratched his head. "That act almost killed Brime and me. Twice."

"Yeah." Brime nervously laughed.

Soahc glanced at her and narrowed his eyes. "What aren't you telling me?"

"I may not have almost died both times. Simply, I was there, and then I was here."

"Wait, you mean only I almost died when we returned?"

"Maybe." Brime raised her shoulders.

Soahc tapped his chin. "Curious. Well, most of us would've died." Soahc looked back at Lanrete. "What other knowledge was imparted to you?"

"Hard to say. Much of it started fading the moment I returned to this plane. My mind is in a fog. It's a terrible feeling, like having something incredibly important on the edge of my memory. I can't quite grasp it, and every moment I don't remember it, it slips further away." Lanrete rubbed his eyes. "It's hard to explain. It's like I reached this new level of awareness of the universe that put everything into a new perspective."

"Which is?"

"I . . . don't know."

"Oh, come on! You don't get to realize you're a Rel Ach'Kel, learn the secrets of the universe, and then conveniently forget them," Brime yelled. Her cheeks were flushed red as she poked him hard a few times in the ribs.

"There is a cost to understanding. I remember that," Lanrete said.

"What does that even mean?" Soahc asked. He walked up to Lanrete, arms crossed.

"The information I gave you when I first crossed back—the understanding of time manipulation?" Lanrete glanced away from Soahc. "You will pay a price for that." He shook his head. "That's all I remember. I'm sorry, *obrehen*." Lanrete let out a heavy sigh. "I must be more careful. This is too much to process right now."

Soahc frowned. A heavy silence settled over the group.

"Okay, so what do we do about Tashanira?" Vades asked. "She's undergone a transformation markedly different from the one Soahc, Brime, and I went through."

The rest of the group turned to look in Tashanira's direction. Lanrete gazed further; she was in a guest room on the next floor, but somehow, he could sense her fully as if she was right in front of him. He shuddered.

"To use your language . . ." Lanrete glanced at Soahc. ". . . she is something new, as is her child."

"Whoa, wait. Tashanira is pregnant?" Brime asked. "I didn't realize she and Jenshi were trying. Where is he, anyway? I want to congratulate him."

"He's undergoing reconditioning," Lanrete said. "And the child isn't his."

"Oh snap," Brime said. "Then whose child is it?"

"Neven's," Lanrete said.

Soahc and Brime's eyes went wide, both unable to respond.

"That explains why Jenshi is in reconditioning then." Vades rubbed the back of her neck.

"Oh, Maker." Brime started to tear up. "No, no. This isn't right. Zun . . . the baby." Brime wiped her eyes, the tears coming faster now. "I'm sorry. I have to . . . I . . ." Brime quickly walked out of the room and disappeared up the stairs.

The group remained silent for a long moment.

Soahc broke the silence. "There's not much we can do until she wakes up." He rubbed his arm. "Where is Neven?"

"He's with Ecnics," Lanrete said.

"Where exactly?" Soahc crossed his arms.

Lanrete tilted his head to the side, raising an eyebrow. "At his home on Thae, back at the MinSci. Why?"

Soahc nodded a few times at Lanrete and then left the room.

CHAPTER 33 - URIEL KERVID

57927 FA (22,196 years ago)
Star Harvester, Bax XI system, Huzien Alliance space

Foundra Ascension Shuttle Three barreled toward a stellar scale structure that hung around Bax XI, a main sequence white dwarf star. No. Hung around wasn't the right word—it engulfed the star as if holding it taut between two giant metallic fingers that came together in a flat rectangular megastructure. Swarms of SI-controlled satellites circled the star, almost completely cutting off the luminosity at times.

"That thing is too big," Ameen said.

"It keeps me up at night thinking about stuff like this. I mean, I'm not anti-tech, but should we really be killing stars?" Jefre asked. "We're supposed to exist with nature, not . . . exploit it."

"A misguided Uri perspective," Carrus said. "The tech doesn't kill the star. It just harnesses the energy and redirects it elsewhere."

"You speak as if the stars are alive," Uriel said.

"Aren't they?" Jefre asked. "I mean, maybe they don't have sentience in the way we understand it, but . . . how much do we really know about the universe?"

"A whole lot," Carrus interjected. "I mean, come on. How else are we supposed to power a growing civilization that's surpassed the energy demand that can be provided in system? It's serving a purpose, just like all of us."

"See that bright beam being fired away from the star?" Ameen brought up the holodisplay and zoomed out to show the complete schematic of the harvester. "That's made by way of the phased array laser emitters—or satellites that swarm around the star—and through a central focusing array." He highlighted another area farther away from the array. "This little baby here then takes that beam suplight, where it's caught at the other end and pumped into what's essentially a massive splitter that funnels the energy to multiple star systems through another series of suplight conduits, including the one with our lovely home world, Thae."

"At least they only do this horrid thing in planet-free systems," Jefre said.

"Alright, team," Uriel said. "The HIN puts the terrorists at this facility, and plans show they intend to hit the focusing array and blow up the SI core that manages the satellite swarm. That would take this Star Harvester out of commission, destabilizing multiple Huzien Alliance systems and leading to energy shortages that could have devastating implications on the galactic economy."

"Our job is to ensure that doesn't happen," Kera said.

"The security drones have been made aware of our presence and should not engage us, but keep an eye out. The HIN is confident that the terrorists got their hands on some nasty Assault SI tech."

"Who are these guys?" Ameen asked.

"Alliance separatists," Carrus said. "They think the whole Huzien Alliance should dissolve, believing it to be another form of oppression by the Huzien Empire."

Jefre sighed. "At least they're not ecoterrorists."

"They are broadcasting their standard message: dissolve the Alliance, or we make the empire hurt," Lanrete said.

"Carrus and Jefre, on me. We disembark here and head to the focusing array. Kera, Davis, and Ameen on Lanrete to take the shuttle to the SI Core," Uriel said.

The group broke into two, Uriel and his team disembarking. They watched the shuttle close and then rise, exiting the protective shielding that kept them from the vacuum of space. Silence settled over the area, punctuated by a deep hum that permeated the facility.

"I think that would get annoying after a while," Jefre said.

"Agreed," Carrus chimed in. "Security system is down. It looks like the intel about the Assault SI was accurate."

The team made their way to a door that slid open to reveal a small, spherical vessel.

"Talk about tech that freaks you out. You ever ridden in one of these things?"

"A suplight conduit? Nah, can't say I have," Carrus said.

"I heard it basically creates a suplight field and shoots you off in a direction. Then you have to pray the other side is working and doesn't miss the catch. Otherwise, splat."

"It's a bit more technical than that, but sure," Uriel said. "Get in. It's the only way to feasibly traverse this place without a ship."

The group got locked into their seats as an inertial dampener came online. The sphere then closed as it lifted slightly off the ground. A few seconds went by as a suplight bubble began to form, and then they were shot off straight up. Uriel glanced at Jefre, who had his head in his hands, trying very hard to hold it together.

"It's almost over. A quick ride." Uriel pointed to the holodisplay that showed them in relation to their destination.

The sphere was successfully caught and then deposited in a holder as the sphere opened along with the door, affording them a view of a massive room where it was impossible to see the ceiling. The space gave off the appearance of being open to the void.

"Scouting ahead," Carrus said as he cloaked. "Eyes on targets. Five people. Tagging them now."

Five indicators came up in Uriel's HUD. He positioned himself to get a better look at the targets. Jefre and Uriel crept toward the primary housing of the focusing array, the area highlighted as the most vulnerable to an explosive device.

"They've got charges in place. Gut's telling me they will pull the trigger if they get spooked."

"Have these terrorists been known to do suicide missions?" Jefre asked.

"Not generally, but we've shut down most of their terrorist cells. This is one of the last remaining ones; they may be desperate. I agree with Carrus's assessment."

"I can take down two before they realize what's happening," Carrus said.

"Which means we've got to handle the other three before they can react," Uriel said.

"Right." Jefre breathed. "So, guns blazing is not a good idea."

"Right," Uriel said.

"Carrus, think you can distract them without spooking them to blow the focusing array?" Uriel asked. "Give us time to get into position?"

"Maybe. I see a security drone out of commission nearby."

"Can you bring it back online?"

"Yeah, I can manage. Go on my signal," Carrus said.

Uriel watched from a distance as the group continued installing one of their explosives. The security drone came to life, letting out a high-pitched warning sound as it scrambled backward from the group.

"Go!"

"The *vusg*?" one of the terrorists shouted. "I thought the Assault SI was supposed to give us at least three hours."

"Shut that thing up!" another terrorist yelled.

The terrorists who were holding sentry all turned toward the security drone and opened fire.

"The Assault SI is still in the system. It hasn't been purged yet. It's weird that thing came online," another terrorist said.

Uriel and Jefre sprinted to another area of cover closer to the group. Jefre continued forward, sliding onto the ground to hide out of view as the security drone collapsed and went silent.

"In position?" Carrus asked.

"I am," Uriel said. "Can hit the cluster of two at once. Just leaves one out of reach."

"Came up short. Will have to make a dash for it."

"Confidence level?" Uriel asked.

"Sixty percent," Jefre said.

"Has to be good enough. They've been spooked and are spreading out more. Need to move now."

"Go!" Uriel said.

Carrus fired a shot, splattering the brains of one of the terrorists across the floor. His second shot hit the man next to him in succession. "Down."

The area trembled with Enesmic energy as Uriel ignited two of the terrorists who had been close enough together, both screaming as they collapsed to the ground and tried to roll to put out the flames. They quickly went still, skin still aflame.

"Down," Uriel said.

Jefre sprinted out of cover toward the last remaining person, opening with a barrage of weaponsfire from his WMAs. The man saw him coming and jumped out of the way.

"*Vusg*," Jefre said. "Hostile still active."

"Die, Huzien *cith*!" the remaining terrorist yelled.

Wishwonder came in like a bullet, impaling the man through his skull, lifting him in the air and slamming him hard into one of the supports.

"Good save," Jefre said.

"Didn't like a forty-percent failure chance, so I launched a contingency when I could."

"That's why you're the boss." Carrus laughed.

An explosion rocked the harvester. They couldn't hear it but felt it in a tremble that shook the ground.

"Oh no," Uriel said. He immediately brought up the status of the harvester to see a glowing section around the SI core that flashed warning signs. "Lanrete . . . you two stay here and disarm the explosives. I'm heading to the other group."

Both men nodded as Uriel took off like a streak of lighting.

He accelerated his body to dangerous speeds, slowing to climb into the suplight conduit. It took a moment to calculate his destination and then fired him off. It ping-ponged him across the harvester and then blared a warning at the last stop, highlighting a hostile environment. His Founder's Elite uniform expanded to encompass his head, a seal forming as it started pumping oxygen. He exited the conduit into a vacuum.

"Must have detected a fire and purged all the oxygen," Uriel said. He quickly moved through the debris, making his way to what was left of the SI Core. The area was mangled, everything destroyed. "Is anyone alive?" he broadcasted. "Lan, you there?" He prompted the HIN for confirmation that the team was still alive.

It returned two signals to him—one for Kera and the other for Lanrete. Davis and Ameen were MIA.

"We're here," came Kera's reply.

He followed the HINs guidance to discover Kera behind her shield, a protective bubble around her, and Lanrete, who was prone on the floor.

"He's unconscious. His vitals are erratic."

"Can we move him?" Uriel asked.

"That's a question for Davis, and he's dust now, along with Ameen. They were right near the explosion when it was triggered."

"What happened?" Uriel moved to Lanrete and pulled up the status of the medvak system built into his armor. It was functional and had already injected him with a swarm of nanites to mitigate the damage to his system. An oxygen seal had triggered the moment it detected a depressurization.

Kera dropped the protective bubble, allowing Uriel to pick up Lanrete. "Terrorists triggered the explosion out of nowhere. I swear they hadn't seen us. We were about to take them out. There were only three of them."

"We missed one. He must have gotten off a warning to this group before we took him down." Uriel shook his head. "*Vusg!*" he yelled.

Uriel started moving toward the suplight conduit, Kera right behind him. Within moments, they were back at the shuttle.

Uriel stared at Lanrete as he lay unconscious in a bed on the medical deck of the *Foundra Ascension*. It was approaching twenty-four hours, and Lanrete was still unresponsive. Uriel took in a breath and stood, preparing to leave.

"How bad was it?" Lanrete asked.

Uriel quickly turned around to see Lanrete, with one eye open, focused on him. The Founder had a bandage that covered the other side of his head.

"You're awake!" Uriel let out a sigh of relief. "You got pretty beat up, but you'll make a full recovery."

"The mission," Lanrete clarified.

Uriel let out a sigh. "Ameen and Davis are dead. Kera was surprisingly more injured than I realized. She didn't show it, but she had to go into surgery the moment we got back. She was standing vigil over your body when I found you two."

"Archlights are tough."

"I gave a report to Ecnics and Cislot. Both were furious at the damage done to the harvester. Ecnics spent about a half hour explaining to me why harvesters were important and why it was our duty to protect them at all costs. Pretty sure he personally blamed me for the damage at some point."

"He gets like that when his toys get broken." Lanrete sighed. "How long until the damage is repaired?"

"A week to rebuild the SI Core and repair the mangled mess left behind after the explosion. About the same amount of time for the backup cores, which were also hit. Maybe a month to rebuild the satellite swarm. We lost quite a few when the system went offline, and they just barreled straight into the sun."

"This is bad. It gives the terrorists the victory they needed. They might get others who are emboldened by this." Lanrete closed his eyes. "I know it feels crappy, but at least the damage isn't as bad as it could have been."

"I'm thinking of replacing Jefre."

"Why?"

"He failed to get to his target in time. I had to cover for him or we'd have lost the focusing array as well. I'd probably not be standing here."

"You think someone else could have done better given the same circumstances?" Lanrete opened his eye again.

"I don't know. Maybe."

"Maybe is the answer of someone thinking with their emotions." Lanrete closed his eye, letting out a sigh. "Ops go bad, you know this. Just because the impact of a failed op is tragic doesn't mean it could have gone down any differently. The only reason to replace Jefre is if you think he let his politics distract him or if he starts second-guessing himself and lets this failure make him less of an effective soldier." Lanrete opened his eye again. "And it's your job as his commanding officer to ensure he doesn't fall into that head-game trap. Understood?"

Uriel nodded and then left the medical deck.

Later that week, Uriel paced in the cargo bay, his gaze hung on an arbitrary spot of ground. His arms were crossed as he walked back and forth.

Stopping, he sighed heavily and thought back to his lessons with Soahc. What he was about to do was very dangerous, and he hesitated momentarily, glancing around to make sure no other people were present.

He put an administrative lock on the meglift, preventing it from being opened until he instructed otherwise, an action only Lanrete—who was still on the ship—could override.

Uriel broke into a bout of cihphistic weaving to a level he had not done in quite some time. The Enesmic ebbed and flowed around him, its power shaking the *Foundra Ascension* hangar. Twisting his hands, he reached forward as if grabbing a chain and pulled with all his might. The air in front of him rippled in sync with the motion, a crack forming. He pulled again on the invisible chain, and the air shattered as a terrible Enesmic creature appeared, bound by glowing energy that resembled chains.

Uriel pulled again, and the creature collapsed onto the ground as the air returned to normal. Uriel quickly went back to weaving, a field glowing around the Enesmic creature as it rose and lashed out, attempting to attack Uriel.

It had the appearance of a humanoid creature with narrow appendages. Its form was ethereal. He had worked hard to ensure he didn't pull a typical Enesmic assassin, as the creature was too intelligent and dangerous to control. This was the Bau—a variation of the assassin—a type of warrior that relied more on force and less on subtlety. The creature eyed Uriel with malice.

Utilizing the advanced telepathic techniques pounded into him by Soahc, he launched into a telepathic attack, seeking to subjugate the mind of the being. It was methodical, not seeking to fully shatter the mind, which would leave the creature unusable.

The creature wailed, flailing before launching an attack on the field around it with a fury. The field shattered, and the creature charged at Uriel. All life went out of its eyes at the last second, its blade angled for Uriel's heart.

Uriel breathed hard and stepped out of the way as the creature collapsed, unmoving. He swore as he put his hand to the back of his neck, his attempt a failure. He released the energy that held the Enesmic creature on this plane, the corpse fading back into the Enesmic plane.

He crouched down, lost in thought.

FOUNDER'S LOG:
Consequences of Our Actions

If a mortal can become an immortal, then an immortal can become a Rel Ach'Kel . . . a question answered, and I now have an understanding that both excites and terrifies me.

To be something more than I could have ever imagined. I'm finally starting to see the place my existence holds in the universe, something beyond the trappings of this Founder mantle, this role I've carved out for myself in the Twin Galaxies.

But this knowledge comes with a cost. Every action I take, every decision I make, I do it now with the understanding that I represent something greater.

That's the part that terrifies me.

Will I now face Eshgren in single combat, my purpose changing to that of protecting the Twin Galaxies from their machinations? I feel myself being drawn back to the Enesmic plane. The summons is strong, calling for me to make my place there instead of in the Havin plane. But to depart would mean giving up all that I have known, leaving everyone I love, and forsaking the last bit of my huzanity.

I am not prepared for that. I cannot abandon Cislot and Ecnics.

Do I try to convince them to join me? Do we finally depart the Huzien Empire and move to the next phase of our existence?

And then there is Nalle—surely, she is as I am. Will she join me in a mass exodus to the Enesmic plane? And what of my hunt for Entradis? It is hard to accept that he is a Rel Ach'Kel as well.

Do our actions here influence who we become on the Enesmic plane? Will he be Eshgren? Has that transformation already happened? Is that why evil permeates every action he takes? I have much to think about.

-Lanrete

CHAPTER 34 - TASHANIRA YEN UNVESAL

Present Day
Soahc's Compound, Reath, Huzien Alliance space

Tashanira opened her eyes, quickly sitting up with a gasp. She frantically looked around, trying to get her bearings.

Her eyes settled on Lanrete, who watched her at the door with his arms crossed. Tashanira frowned as she rubbed her head and fell back onto the bed. The cover moved off her slightly to reveal one of her breasts.

Lanrete glanced away and then entered the room to sit in a nearby chair.

"Where are we?" Tashanira asked. She pulled up the cover to her neck, something in Lanrete's gaze making her feel self-conscious.

"Soahc's home. It's a short distance outside Etan Rachnie," Lanrete said.

"What happened? The last thing I remember was being on the Enesmic plane. There were those beings . . . the baby!" Tashanira sat up again, this time rubbing her stomach. "How long was I out?" She touched her stomach with both hands.

That was when she caught sight of her hands, her eyes widening.

"What the *vusg*?" Tashanira threw the covers off and walked to a mirror behind Lanrete.

He respectfully looked down at the floor as she passed.

Tashanira stared at the mirror; another woman looked back at her. In the place of her white fur with black stripes, she had silver fur with golden stripes. Her hair was still mostly black, but now it had streaks of gold in it. But her eyes! They were still feline-esque but now had large purple irises and golden pupils.

She touched her face and backed away from the mirror. "What . . ." She turned around to face Lanrete, moving to stand in front of him. "What happened to me?"

He looked up at her with a pained expression.

She subconsciously took a step back. "That being that rescued me . . . the one with the golden disk and silver skin, that was you." She shook her head. "I could sense that it was you, but it was all wrong."

Lanrete locked gazes with her.

"No, no. This can't be happening. What about my baby? Is my baby okay?"

"Take a deep breath," Lanrete said. He stood up, his hands out wide. "The baby is fine."

Tashanira followed the command, taking in a few deep breaths. She backed up until she bumped into the bed, sitting on it. She crossed her arms, staring at the floor, rocking back and forth.

"You were transformed when Grilmuqshen and Aersheju melded with you and the baby."

"What does that mean?" Tashanira glanced up at Lanrete and narrowed her eyes.

"I . . . don't remember."

"Is it some form of possession, like Vades? Did they possess my baby? Am I possessed?" Tashanira's voice rose an octave and cracked. Her mind flashed to Grilmuqshen as he refuted her fear of being possessed back on the Enesmic plane.

"I don't know." Lanrete sighed.

Tashanira got up and began to pace, her arms still crossed. "Well, what *do* you *vusging* know?" She stopped and glared at him.

"You and the baby are alive. You are immortal now—I can sense it. Although I can't explain why your transformation is so drastically

different from what happened to others when they walked the Enesmic plane. Soahc believes you are something new, just like I am."

"You're a Rel Ach'Kel? Have you been hiding this from us this whole time?"

"No, this is new to me." Lanrete's eyes went wide, his brow raising. "Our theory is that all immortals born like me are in this state until something triggers them. They are all unawakened Rel Ach'Kel living on the Havin plane." Lanrete walked to a nearby closet and pulled a robe out of it. Walking over to Tashanira, he handed it to her.

She pulled it on and sat in the chair, taking a few more deep breaths as she tried to process everything. "Lan, I'm at my breaking point. This is too much for me right now. I . . ."

"Get your rest. Take the day. Soahc has put his staff at your disposal; please request whatever you need. I'll check in on you tomorrow morning." Lanrete nodded at Tashanira and then exited the room.

"*Vusg* me." She put her head in her hands.

Tashanira stared at her reflection. She accepted that it was her reflection, which still made her sick. She took a deep breath and broke her gaze away from the woman staring back at her in the mirror, moving to the chair next to a massive window.

She sat and let her gaze wander across the sprawling landscape. There was peace in that, peace that she only now realized she hadn't felt in a long time. She contemplated that for a long moment until a holodisplay appeared in the window next to her head.

Neven Kenk appeared on the holodisplay, his shirt off as he sat on the edge of a bed. "This is a surprise. I thought you had blocked my channel."

She locked gazes with Neven. His eyes went wide, his mouth open as he stared in silence for a long moment.

"Yes, it's me," Tashanira said with a hint of annoyance.

Triny Hazce's nude body briefly appeared in the frame. Ecnics's personal assistant glanced back to see Neven on a holodisplay call and gasped, quickly covering her chest and moving out of view.

Tashanira leaned back in her chair, a haughty look on her face. "Pretty little thing. New girlfriend?"

"Uh, yeah."

"Well, let her know that your baby momma needs to have a private conversation with her baby daddy."

"Baby momma? What's she talking about?" Triny asked from off-screen.

Neven facepalmed and took a deep breath. "Let me give you a call back in a minute." Neven frowned, terminating the connection.

Tashanira grinned mischievously, her gaze going back out across the landscape. A few minutes went by until her mobi blipped. She brought back up the holodisplay.

"Thanks for that. Pretty sure you just scuttled a good thing."

"Don't care." Tashanira returned her gaze to him.

Neven's face softened. "What happened?"

"I *vusged* around and found out." Tashanira smiled bitterly. "Incident with the Enesmic plane. I've undergone some kind of transformation."

"Are you okay?"

"As far as I can tell."

"And the baby?"

"Same."

Tashanira and Neven sat in silence for a long moment, Neven searching her eyes.

"I'm calling you because I have a favor to ask you."

"Anything."

"I'm going to tell Lanrete I plan to take personal leave. I need someplace to go that isn't here or on the *Ascension*. Someplace out of harm's way." She shook her head. "I'm not going to risk the baby anymore. If I had lost it due to my decisions, I wouldn't have been able to forgive myself."

"Do you want to go to Peshkana?"

"Not yet. I . . . I need some time to think, to really ponder. Solitude, you know? Can you give me that?"

"I can." Neven grinned. "I'm apparently rich now, and I bought a mega yacht. It should be ready in a few days. I plan to run some intergalactic errands, and then we can go to Peshkana for the baby's birth when the time is right."

"That sounds . . . good." Tashanira nodded. "I hope your new girlfriend dumps you." Tashanira winked at Neven and terminated the call.

Huza City, Thae, Huzien home system

Tashanira blinked her eyes; rising superscrapers surrounded her. She abruptly stopped, glancing around as Brime mirrored her expression—the two locked gazes.

They stood at the entrance to an elaborate walkway that led to an impressive building about a city block away. Its scale was massive, and the bottom of the building was a giant park enclosed by glass and plexicarbonite columns.

They both turned back to look at Soahc as he stepped through a portal, with Lanrete and Vades behind him. A crowd had assembled around them, the group's sudden appearance drawing attention.

"Huza?" Tashanira raised an eyebrow. "Why are we on *Thae*?"

"To find Cislot and Ecnics, of course. I think it's time we filled them in on what's happening." Soahc walked past them and toward the towering structure.

The crowd started to move with them as a group of automated drones appeared out of the ground, forming a wall between the group and the crowd. A group of personnel in silver Huzien Peacekeeper uniforms quickly converged on them, and a lone man approached Lanrete as the group stopped.

"Founder Lanrete. Lord Soahc. Your visit is unexpected." He glanced behind them to where the portal had appeared. "As was your preferred means of transportation."

"It's good to see security protocols were updated after the Rift War," Soahc said.

"Yes." The man rubbed the back of his neck. "We now know within seconds if a portal is formed within city limits." He locked eyes with Lanrete. "Founders Cislot and Ecnics have been alerted to your presence. We humbly request that you come with us."

Lanrete nodded.

"Of course." Soahc motioned for them to lead on.

The man turned, and the Peacekeepers fell in formation around the group as they continued toward the building. Once inside, Tashanira was impressed by how quickly she forgot they were in a city—through the door, they immediately followed a path through trees to a hub of meglifts. Most of the Peacekeepers had disappeared upon their entrance into the building, only the man who'd spoken still with them.

Piling into the meglift, she watched as it rapidly ascended. The forest around them continued for what seemed like miles. She could see roads and hovercars dotting the landscape and an open expanse that became visible once they broke the tree line.

She smirked at the attempt to integrate nature and technology, like back home on Peshkana. Here, it felt forced, like nature had been crafted around technology instead of integrated with it. It was a subtle difference but a significant one.

The meglift continued in the open air, and the trees quickly became specs as the view abruptly disappeared, replaced by soft LEDs signaling their ascent of each floor. The transparent glass of the meglift turned solid, blocking the view of the LEDs as the meglift picked up speed.

"So, this is the Huzien Capitol building," Vades said. "I've heard how impressive it was, but to actually see it?" She shook her head. "It makes the Argent barracks look like a toy."

"It's okay." Soahc shrugged.

"It's *vusging* amazing." Brime put her hands on her hips.

Lanrete smiled.

They stood listening to the tranquil music that played in the meglift, a subtle shift in the steady sounds signaling their decrease in speed. The meglift came to a stop as the door slid open. The Peace-keeper stepped out and motioned for them to follow. He led them into an elaborate waiting area, where a Uri with platinum fur, cham-pagne hair, and gold eyes waited for them. She wore an impressive blue suit—in a style that reminded Tashanira of the clothing Cislot typically wore—and a long coattail hovered a few inches above her platinum-colored heels.

Tashanira felt a pang of anxiety rise in her at the sight of the woman. Her appearance pegged her as a member of the Mauveh tribe. They were the dominant tribe on Peshkana and one that Tashanira wanted nothing to do with.

The woman met Tashanira's gaze and watched her curiously. Tashanira realized she probably didn't recognize what tribe she was from, given her unique fur and eye color. She sent a disarming smile back at the woman, who forced a smile and then turned to look at Soahc.

"Govnus Huiara." Soahc bowed slightly, Brime and Vades following suit. "What a surprise to have you greet us."

Huiara Mau Gehreyati returned the bow. "When the legend-ary Soahc appears on your doorstep unannounced via an Enesmic portal with one of our Founders in tow, you tend to clear your calendar," Huiara said. "Founder Cislot will be here shortly." She hesitated. "In the meantime, please fill me in on why you're here."

Huza City Outskirts, Thae, Huzien home system

Tashanira watched from her hovercar as rolling hills passed by as they traversed the long driveway leading to a mansion sitting on the cliff's edge. The view stole her breath, the sight of Huza Bay one she hadn't forgotten in all her years. It had been some time since she had last been to Lanrete's home in Huza. The resplendent dwelling was built in an unfamiliar architectural style that Lanrete had informed her was from old Thae.

The hovercar stopped in the circular driveway, a covered porch greeting her as she stepped out of the vehicle. A soldier in dress uniform bowed and motioned for her to move inside. She stepped lightly up the steps, Vades, Brime, and Soahc behind her.

A set of soldiers opened the elaborate wooden double door for her as she moved inside the foyer, seeing a large hallway with more double doors leading into adjacent rooms. The hallway continued into a shining rotunda with a spiral staircase leading up to the next floor. She walked through the rotunda toward a new piece she had never seen before—the hallmark art piece of the room. It was a recent artistic depiction of Lanrete, Ecnics, and Cislot.

She stopped in her tracks, her gaze fixed on the image. It was commanding seeing the three Founders represented equally in all their glory.

"We had it commissioned after the Rift War," Lanrete said. He walked in from the opposite end of the rotunda.

"It's only missing the halos and wings," Soahc said.

"I admit, the artist took some creative liberties with embellishment." Lanrete smiled. "Thank you for agreeing to come to my home for the night. It's rare to be here, let alone to have the opportunity to entertain guests, something I plan to relish as your gracious host for the evening."

"This is an impressive place," Vades said. She stood a distance away from Lanrete and the rest of the group with her arms crossed. "It seems you and Soahc have a knack for competing in opulence."

"Bres—" Lanrete hesitated and cleared his throat. "Vades, I welcome you to my home." He glanced at Tashanira, Brime, Soahc, and then back at Vades. "Come. Let me give you a tour while we wait for the other guests to arrive for dinner."

"Other guests?" Soahc asked.

Lanrete smiled.

Tashanira relaxed in a comfortable chair on the home's back deck that provided a clear view of Huza Bay. Given the sheer size of the bay, no hints of land could be seen when looking out, only water to the horizon.

She sat in silence, her mind racing with thoughts of her time on the Enesmic plane. It terrified her. What were the Eshgren planning with her baby? That thought nagged at her constantly, and a fear of impending doom rose in the pit of her stomach.

"Tashanira, are you okay?" Cislot asked. She sat with a large glass of wine in her hand, her *eifi* reclining with her head in Cislot's lap. Cislot gently caressed her hair.

The woman's name was Erisya Yetrewna, and she was half Huzien and half Das'Vin, with milk chocolate skin, amber-colored eyes, and blond hair. She watched Tashanira with a smile—her low-cut dress and the relaxed way she lay on Cislot gave off a sensual feel.

Tashanira could trace the grey esha marks from her temples to the soles of her feet as she wasn't wearing shoes. "Yes, yes, of course. I'm fine," she said, forcing a smile.

"Lost in thought?" Ecnics reclined in another chair next to Kaloni Setla, the head of Cihphist Technology at the MinSci.

Kaloni had black, almond-shaped eyes, jet-black hair, and a complexion similar to Zun. She currently wore a nervous expression. Her hand tightly gripped Ecnics's thigh, his hand resting gently on top of it. When Tashanira smiled at her, she glanced away and out toward the bay, her face becoming a mask.

"I was thinking about the Enesmic plane, my transformation, and the part an Eshgren played in it," Tashanira said.

Soahc shifted uncomfortably. He sat next to Brime, his gaze out toward the bay.

"Use of the Zun Gate to rapidly move forces across Huzien Alliance space will help us more effectively counter the machinations of the Eshgren in the future," Ecnics said.

"That gate is truly a marvel, Ecnics. You've outdone yourself," Cislot said.

"I'm assuming that is why you've been cagey as of late," Lanrete said. He sat alone in an oversized chair facing the bay.

"Didn't want to spoil the surprise. Augamentres has been developing the field of black hole energy extraction and applied usage for over five millennia. The Zun Gate is the culmination of all that research and experimentation." Ecnics patted Kaloni's hand. She relaxed her grip and pressed in closer to him, turning her attention back to the conversation.

"Harnessing the power of black holes has been theoretical up to this point. Now we've demonstrated that we can!" Kaloni's tone began to build with passion. "This opens a new era of discovery and will set us on a road to progress unlike anything seen before in the Twin Galaxies."

"Well said." Cislot smiled at Kaloni.

"Aru is already en route to Maandreo to establish a gate there."

"Another galaxy . . ." Cislot whispered. "This means Aru perfected the Manem suplight drive?"

"Neven did," Lanrete chimed in. "During our short stint on Ecnics's ship when searching for the *Empress Star*."

Tashanira subconsciously rubbed her neck.

Cislot glanced over to Lanrete, her eyes wide. "To solve a problem that has long plagued one of Aru's caliber, and he solved it in mere weeks?" She shook her head. "This Neven truly is a genius."

"Augamentres even appreciated his help. He worked hand in hand with her on the final stages of the project," Ecnics said.

Cislot's expression softened. "How is he doing?"

All three founders briefly glanced to Tashanira, who retreated deeper into her seat.

"He's . . . coping." Ecnics frowned, tension in his gaze as he looked to Lanrete. "I've been keeping him busy, but he's still unfit for deployment."

Lanrete met Ecnics's gaze and then glanced away back toward the bay.

Cislot's gaze darted between the two, and she frowned. Her eyes quickly narrowed as she stopped rubbing Erisya's head. "Wait. If Aru's heading to Maandreo, does this mean he knows the truth about himself?"

"Yes. Aru asked me the question, and by Founder's law, I confirmed it," Lanrete said.

"Founder's law?" Brime spoke up. "You guys create laws for each other?"

All three Founders glanced at Brime momentarily before resuming their conversation without a response.

"We must observe him closely. Is sending him away to another galaxy wise?" Cislot asked.

"Augamentres is with him. She will observe and mentor, among other things. She is quite fond of him," Ecnics said.

The other two Founders nodded. Tashanira glanced at Brime, who appeared to be having a silent conversation with Soahc. She could see the annoyance dripping off the other woman. Tashanira realized they had blown off Brime's question.

Something nagged at Tashanira. She took in a deep breath and urged herself to speak up. "Why do you so closely follow the lives of those around you? You run an empire, so why invest time thinking about us little people?" she blurted out.

All three Founders turned to her.

Cislot smiled. "My dear Tashanira, what do you think an empire is made up of?"

Tashanira felt herself sweat. The question seemed simple, but nothing Cislot said was ever simple, something she had learned over the many years of viewing interactions between her and Lanrete.

"Little people," Tashanira responded.

"People, yes. No one is little or unimportant." Cislot softened her eyes, her smile disarming. "We are allowed to rule because we recognize that power is given to us by those in this empire who believe in us. The moment we forget that is the moment our empire falls."

"Look at Tirivus," Ecnics spoke up. "He constantly fears for his life because he has made enemies of the people he rules over. There are those in his life who work to undermine and kill him." Ecnics turned to Lanrete. "He will fail. It is only a matter of time."

"Anima holds the Tuzen Empire together," Lanrete countered.

"She has indeed done much to be a steady hand in the face of his impulsiveness, but she ascribes to his ideologies. They are two sides of the same coin, as much as it would seem counter to that example," Cislot said. "I assure you that Tirivus does nothing without Anima's blessing, although the inverse is certainly not true." She frowned.

"It's what makes them so dangerous," Ecnics said under his breath. "With that, I believe it is time for us to retire." Ecnics and Kaloni stood up. "We must leave early in the morning to travel to the Zun Gate to assist with preparations in case our Eshgren friends decide to make a move. Lan, as always, thanks for your hospitality. I greatly miss these moments."

Ecnics's eyes softened slightly as Lanrete and Cislot nodded. He nodded at Soahc and glanced at Tashanira before quickly turning away and departing the deck with Kaloni.

"I've had rooms prepared for you," Lanrete said. He glanced between Tashanira, Soahc, Brime, and Vades. A young Uri woman in maid's clothing appeared at the deck entrance. "Anhara will show you to your rooms and care for your needs while you're here."

Anhara bowed.

Brime's eyes widened. "That outfit is too cute." She glanced at Lanrete. "I'm guessing this is some fetish you have."

Anhara blushed.

Lanrete laughed. "Only you, Brime."

"Thanks, Lan. You didn't have to do all this," Soahc said.

"And miss out on creating memorable moments like these? Please." Lanrete smiled. "See you in the morning. I'm assuming we can return to Reath after breakfast?"

"Sounds like a plan," Soahc said. "Although . . . I do have to make one pit stop before settling in for the night." Soahc clenched his fist, uttering a word of power, and was immediately gone.

"Rude," Brime said.

"Lan, can we talk?" Tashanira asked.

"Sure. Come see me after you get settled in," Lanrete said.

Tashanira walked into the study.

Lanrete was sitting in a chair at the window overlooking the bay. The sunset was breathtaking, Lanrete so entranced that he gave no indication that he had heard her enter.

She moved to sit in the seat across from him, turning to look out of the window as well. She sat there for a long moment, enjoying the sunset in silence. Lanrete glanced at her but said no words, simply returning to his gaze out the window.

"I'd like to request personal leave and to be removed from active combat duty," Tashanira said. She turned her full attention to Lanrete.

"Granted," Lanrete said. He let out a sigh. Turning his gaze back to Tashanira, he watched her silently for a long moment. "What will you do?"

"I had a brief conversation with Neven. He has a ship and said I could join him. We'll eventually make our way to Peshkana when it's time to give birth."

Lanrete nodded his head. "I'm sorry this happened to you."

"You *did* warn me." Tashanira bit her lip. "Thank you for giving me the opportunity to not *vusg* myself." She shook her head. "It seems I can't help but make mistakes right now. Who knows what the consequence of that decision will mean for my child? Now I have that fear, that unknown, that will haunt me." She gave a sad smile. "I need some time to rediscover myself and to figure out life. I'm hoping this time on Neven's ship, away from everything, can help me accomplish that."

"I look forward to meeting the new you." Lanrete sighed. "I'll work on convincing Soahc to leave you alone. He's going to want to keep tabs on you, but I'm sure we can come to some kind of compromise."

"Thanks, Lan."

CHAPTER 35 - URIEL KERVID

61727 FA (18,396 years ago)
Shuttle en route to Foundra Pax, *Huzien home system*

Uriel stared in awe at the *Foundra Pax* as it came into view as the pilot dropped their shuttle out of suplight.

The *Pax* was the supercapital flagship of the Huzien Empire, only utilized when all three Founders were traveling together. It had become known as Cislot's ship due to her not having a personal ship like the *Ascension* or *Conscient*—Lanrete and Ecnics's ships.

The *Pax* dwarfed the size of the capital ships in the Huzien Fleets. It had a unique design, measuring thirty-one kilometers in length with a massive ring that circled about two-thirds of the way down the length of the ship. That ring contained the collective firepower of an entire Huzien fleet with several additional super-weapons on par with a contingent of dreadnaughts and hangars that held more fighters than a battle carrier. It also had a planet cracker at the front of the ship, similar to capital ships. The *Pax* could house the *Foundra Ascension* and *Foundra Conscient*, each having a special hanger toward the midsection. It was a small city with an operating crew contingent of over a million people.

The ship was always staffed, although rarely used. It held vigil over Thae when not in use, a welcomed sight for the home system defense fleets. Today, it would set out with Lanrete, Ecnics, and Cislot for a diplomatic mission to the Tuzen home world.

Uriel glanced at Lanrete, who stared at the ship with his arms crossed.

"The jewel of the empire," Uriel said. "We should put this ship to work more."

"It does work." Lanrete glanced at Uriel. "By maintaining a presence in our home system, it sends a message to anyone who would challenge our power. This ship is a symbol, showing the might of the Huzien Empire. It will always be a symbol. It must be." He looked back toward the ship. "You must be strategic in the usage of symbols; otherwise, they lose their power."

Their shuttle entered the docking bay of the *Foundra Pax*, depressurizing as it landed. The ramp extended down as Uriel followed behind Lanrete. Cislot was waiting for them, a broad smile on her face. She wore a gold, black, and red dress in the typical Tuzen style. It was the first time Uriel had seen Cislot in a dress, catching him off guard. She glanced at him and then down at the dress with a look of concern.

"Too much?" she asked.

"No, it's great," Uriel said. "You wear the Tuzen colors well."

Cislot frowned.

"One of us has to be the olive branch," Lanrete quickly added. "It's better coming from you than me or Ecnics."

"I think Ecnics would take having to wear Tuzen colors as a personal insult," Cislot said. "We truly have to do something about his blatant racism toward Tuzens."

"It takes time," Lanrete said.

"It's been almost sixty-two thousand years, Lan. He holds on to his hate of them because he chooses to."

"He lost everyone in the war, Cis," Lanrete countered.

"We all lost people," Cislot countered, her voice gaining a slight edge. She took a deep breath and slowly let it out. "Lan, we're *vusging* immortals. Everyone we've ever loved who isn't us has died."

"I hear you." Lanrete glanced at Uriel and then back to Cislot. "I'll talk to him."

"It requires more than talk. We have to hold him accountable."

"I'll handle it," Lanrete insisted. He presented his arm to Cislot, who rolled her eyes. "What? You're wearing a beautiful dress. I feel like I have to escort you everywhere."

She laughed and took his arm. Uriel smiled at the display. They felt like a family. Lanrete was his adoptive father, Cislot was his mostly serious aunt, and Ecnics was his grumpy uncle.

Uriel suppressed a laugh. He followed the two toward the meglift.

Tir, New Thae, Tuzen home system

The Huzien entourage of Lanrete, Cislot, Ecnics, Uriel, and the current Founder's Elite followed behind Anima. A group of all-female bodyguards was shadowing the queen, each wearing skintight black body armor with red and gold accents. HIN tagged the signifier on their shoulders as that of the Liajhem.

Anima wore a stunning and elaborate golden and red dress.

"The palace itself is an arcology," Anima said. "Completely self-sufficient and a marvel of Tuzen engineering."

Ecnics looked as if he was about to say something, but Lanrete shot him a glance. The head of the MinSci remained quiet and nodded, forcing a smile.

"Will we be staying in the palace proper?" Uriel asked.

"Of course," Anima said. "You and the Founders will have rooms in the royal quarter below our children." Anima narrowed her eyes and smiled. "The rest of your group has been set up with rooms in the residential quarter."

"In the royal quarter," Cislot echoed. "Afforded the same protection as yourselves."

"We take the safety of those in our care very seriously," Anima said.

Uriel flinched. He glanced off toward the industrial megacity that continued outside the palace walls.

It was a stark contrast. The palace was filled with greenery and lush fields that led up to the center of the structure, adorned with gold and red hues, creating a beautiful sight. The rest of the city lacked that beauty, filled with more rigid industrialism in shades of red and black.

It was depressing.

"Where is Tirivus?" Lanrete asked.

"Occupied. He sends his apologies for not being able to greet you," Anima said. "He has arranged for a friendly Doken competition the day after tomorrow with you if you'd be so kind as to indulge him," Anima said.

"Doken?" Uriel asked.

"An ancient form of Tuzen blade fencing. It makes use of a beautiful although quite rudimentary weapon." Lanrete sent an image from his collection to Uriel.

The weapon had a curved, slender, single-edged blade with a circular guard and long grip to accommodate two hands.

"Please tell him I happily accept the offer and look forward to it." Uriel gave Lanrete a concerned look.

"Very well. This is where I leave you." Anima motioned toward a group of people in black and red clothing that approached them. "My attendants will escort you to your quarters."

She then turned and departed into a large chamber that went deep into the heart of the palace. All the Liajhem followed her, including more he hadn't seen who emerged from the shadows.

The sun set as Uriel left his room, and the lights lining the hallways of the Tuzen palace glowed with an aura that seemed to bring the night to life. He smiled as he walked down the massive hallway to a terrace garden with steps heading up to the rooms of the Tuzen royalty.

New Thae had two moons, both bright in the sky. He took in a deep breath. The air was aromatic with pathway lights that hid many wonders through various offshoots. It was beautiful, something that would have fit in well with the beauty he saw in Huza on Thae. It was a similarity, one of many of late, that he was discovering between his people and the Tuzens. More signs of the people they once were when they lived together on Thae many millennia before his birth.

The form of a woman resting against a marble railing caught his attention. She had sepia-colored skin with white hair that came down to her waist. She wore a long, silken robe mixed with gold and red, and the edges were black with the royal crest of the Ageless Emperor emblazoned across her back. It was stunning.

Uriel watched her for a long moment as she gazed at the double moons. With a slow exhale, Uriel walked over to her, resting on the railing a short distance from her. "Beautiful night," he said.

The woman didn't respond.

"And now beautiful company."

She smiled—a fleeting gaze given to him that revealed deep silver eyes.

"The name's Uriel. Miss?"

"Daughter of the Ageless Emperor," she responded.

"Long name. Shame they didn't give you something more unique," Uriel countered.

The woman laughed. "Enara." She grinned, turning to face him.

She was the spitting image of Anima, except with white hair and lighter skin. He was instantly floored by her gaze, one filled with mirth and a hint of playfulness. He slid along the railing closer, coming right to her side. She didn't back away.

"Most men flee from me when they discover who my father is, yet you move closer to me." She tilted her head to the side. "Either you're incredibly bold or stupid."

"Probably a bit of both," Uriel said.

"Huzien boy has jokes." Enara hesitated for a moment. "Uriel . . . I've heard that name before."

"Son of Lanrete. Leader of the Founder's Elite."

"You!" Her face grew with wonder, her eyes going wide. "You came to our rescue when we were attacked on New Ginea."

"Not sure I was needed. Your mother more than held her own."

"My mother talks about your heroics and how you saved our lives. She greatly respects you." Enara's eyes sparkled as she watched him.

"That's not the sentiment I got, but I'll take your word for it." Uriel laughed, then stopped. "Wait, you said our lives?"

"She was pregnant with me. You saved my life that day," Enara said. "Who would have thought that the child she was carrying would be the first immortal child of the royal line?"

Uriel stared at Enara.

"I am forever in your debt," she said.

"Safeguarding two beauties that day! Lucky me." Uriel's voice dropped into a whisper. "I'm honored to have been of service. Let me know if I can service you in any other ways, Princess."

Enara bit her lip as she half closed her eyes. "You're very bold, it would seem . . . but luckily for you, I like boldness."

Uriel kissed her, and she didn't pull back. After a moment, she broke his kiss and hurriedly looked around, her gaze lingering on another terrace higher up—the one Uriel recognized as exclusive to Tirivus and Anima.

"Come this way. Out of sight," she said.

She took Uriel by the hand and led him down steps to another section of the terrace, this one more secluded. They entered an area covered with grass, and she removed her shoes, stepping onto it barefoot. She sighed in relief as she moved to sit, reclining slightly.

Uriel took off his shoes and did likewise. She touched her neck, watching him tentatively for a few moments. Uriel moved in to kiss her again. She leaned into it, the two kissing in the moonlight for an hour. Uriel put his hand on her thigh, inching it up her robe. She put her hand on his, stopping it.

Enara broke the kiss and looked into his eyes. She appeared as if searching for something, finally shaking her head no.

Uriel removed his hand and resumed kissing her. They continued kissing for another hour, eventually moving into a fully reclined position with Enara resting on Uriel as they stared at the moon.

"How long are you here?" she asked.

"The plan is three months but may be longer if things go well. Cislot and Tirivus plan to kick off intense negotiations in a few weeks after the delegation has had time to get acclimated to Tuzen culture."

"Is sleeping with a Tuzen princess also part of the assignment?" Enara asked.

"No, of course not," Uriel quickly responded. "I . . ."

Enara laughed. "I'm joking. If anything, that would be counterproductive."

"How so?" Uriel glanced curiously at Enara.

She let out a sigh and kissed him. Then she stood up. "Will you meet me tomorrow night? Same place?"

"Of course."

Enara turned and quickly made her way back up the stairs, disappearing out of sight.

Uriel let out a sigh, his gaze going to the moons.

Two Weeks Later

Enara reclined on the grass with Uriel, both staring at the sky. They sat on a blanket, the remnants of a basket filled with Tuzen delicacies beside them.

Enara nestled into Uriel's arms. "Did you always want to be a soldier?" she asked.

"No," Uriel said. "If a school like Etan Rachnie had existed back when I was a child, I would have probably applied to that instead of enlisting. But there were few options for kids gifted in the kintath spectrum like me. To get the training you need to develop your abilities safely, you either went to work for the military or one of the megacorps in their executive security teams." Uriel's eyes softened. "The rest generally wound up in maximum security prisons."

"I envy your ability to choose," Enara said. "Every step of my life to this day has been orchestrated, my abilities honed for no other purpose than fulfilling my responsibilities as a princess of the Tuzen Empire." Enara nestled her nose into Uriel's neck.

"My life changed the moment Lanrete walked into it," Uriel said. "When he recruited me for the Founder's Elite, I thought my purpose was finally fulfilled, and I'd discovered my calling. And when he adopted me, I felt like I'd achieved life's pinnacle." Uriel shook his head. "But my life changed that day. A whole set of expectations I wasn't prepared for landed on my shoulders. He started grooming me for something, although I'm still not sure what. But it's overwhelming and exhausting."

"Succession," Enara said.

"What?"

"He's preparing you for the day his life ends so you may take his place." Enara looked into Uriel's eyes. "We all go through that process. It's one of the burdens of royalty. They hammer into you what it means to rule and the expectations of running an empire, grooming us to become them." Enara sighed. "I don't want to rule, but since I was born immortal, they view me as a true successor." Enara smiled sadly. "I am the Ageless Princess and will be the Ageless Empress if my parents die." Enara glanced around the terrace, a tear streaming down her cheek. "This palace is my prison. It's a beautiful prison, but it's still a prison. I'm not allowed to leave. The risk is too great, and there are too many daggers in the shadows."

"I'm sorry," Uriel said.

Enara sobbed quietly into Uriel's chest as he rubbed her back. Letting out a heavy sigh, she sat up. "I'm going to call it a night. Thank you for being with me." She kissed Uriel deeply and looked into his eyes, searching for something again. The scene reminded him of when they first met, but this time, she stopped and then smiled at him.

The next night, Uriel waited for Enara in their typical spot, but she was later than usual. She eventually arrived, a cautious look in her eye, her hand shaking slightly.

"I want to show you something," she said, "but we must get into my room without my guards noticing and without Cihphism. My mother's Liajhem would sniff us out in a heartbeat."

"A mission!" Uriel grinned. "I'm good at those."

"I figured you would be," Enara said.

Uriel took her by the hand and motioned for her to stay low. He then led her on a daring adventure across the palace grounds. They sprinted across the gardens, hiding in the foliage near the walls as a patrol passed. Using makeshift handholds, the two made their way up the wall, eventually entering her quarters from the balcony she had left open for them.

"That was the most fun I've ever had!" Enara was wide-eyed. "You do this kind of stuff all the time?"

"It's not always as fun or as low risk, but yeah."

"The risk was genuine!" Enara whined.

Uriel nodded and opened the door, allowing her to walk past him and into her bedroom. It was massive, befitting of the princess of a galactic empire.

Enara moved to the entrance to the bathroom suite and glanced back at Uriel. "I'm going to go get it. Wait here a moment."

Uriel nodded as she disappeared inside, quickly closing the door behind her. He admired the room's decorations, giving special attention to a few art pieces that showcased different spatial anomalies. The culmination of the pieces hinted at a desire for adventure and a longing for the unknown.

After a few minutes, the sound of the door opening caught his attention. He glanced up to see Enara walk back into the room in red lace lingerie. His breath caught in his throat as she approached him.

"What do you think?" Her eyes were narrowed slightly, her voice sultry.

Uriel examined every aspect of her body visible through the lingerie. It accented her breasts, fully exposing them. The design was elaborate, leaving Uriel staring at her for a long moment with his mouth open.

"Well?" she asked again after a long silence.

"Incredibly sexy," Uriel said.

Enara blushed. "I'm glad you think so."

She grabbed his hands and led him toward her bed, prompting him to sit down at the bottom of it. Uriel held her face in his hand and kissed her. She ate up his kiss and reached her hand under his shirt. He quickly pulled it off, the rest of his clothes following. Enara's eyes caught on his manhood as she let out a low gasp, her eyes going back up to his.

Her hands were shaking. He stilled them and pulled her close. "Are you okay?" Uriel whispered.

Enara nodded, biting her lip as Uriel began kissing her neck. The lingerie was open in all the right places. Uriel kissed her breasts, slowly moving down to between her legs. She gasped, her hand going to his head. The moan she released caused Uriel to flood with anticipation as he brought her to orgasm.

He moved atop her, his eyes connecting with hers. Enara nodded as he slowly entered her. She gasped again, this time wincing. He took it slow, Enara holding on to him tightly as he made love to her.

It had been a long time since he had made love to a woman. He had *vusged* women, sure, but making love was different. The emotional connection was critical to the experience. Uriel relished every second of it.

Enara wrapped her legs around him. He put his head close to hers, pressing into her fully as he wrapped his arms around her neck. Their bodies were intertwined as Uriel found his rhythm, thrusting deep while Enara gasped, squeezing as her body began to quiver. She let out a shout as another orgasm rocked her body.

The sound of her coming again pushed him over the top as he released inside of her, pulling her close in a moment of shared ecstasy. Her body shook, a spasm coursing through her like an earthquake as he held her tight. He moved up to the top of the bed, carrying her along and pulling the covers over them.

Enara rested against Uriel, the spasms eventually subsiding as she breathed heavily, staring at the ceiling.

"*Vusg*," Enara said. She turned to look up at Uriel, who glanced down at her. "You sure know how to make a first time special."

"You'll be pretty sore tomorrow," he said. "I'm surprised to see an almost four-thousand-year-old virgin."

Enara gave a nervous smile. "You're the first person I've ever successfully gotten to my room." Enara sighed. "My father is a bit protective, to say the least." Enara laughed. "How would I even start that conversation?

"Father, I have needs!" Uriel blurted out.

She hit him with a pillow. They lay there for a few minutes.

"This was very special to me." She again locked eyes with Uriel, smiling.

She turned onto him fully, her body resting squarely on his. He wrapped his arm around her as she eventually drifted off to sleep. Uriel closed his eyes, sleep pulling him.

Sometime later, his eyes shot open, his senses on high alert. He saw the image of Anima juxtaposed with her daughter—who was still sleeping on top of him. Anima was standing at the bottom of the bed. Her arms were crossed, her eyes narrowed with a look that could kill.

She motioned for him to get out of the bed quietly, and he complied, trying his best not to wake Enara as he slowly moved her off himself and onto the bed. Anima threw his clothes at him. He quickly pulled them on, and then she motioned for him to follow her out of the bedroom and onto the balcony.

"I invite you into my home, and you *vusg* my daughter?" Anima's voice was cold, her words spoken quickly.

"I'm in love with your daughter," Uriel countered.

Anima's eyes went wide, and she shook her head. "That's worse." She let out a sigh. "Do you have any idea of the damage that could be done if this ever got out?"

"Is that all you rulers ever think about? Optics and politics?"

"How have you been the son of a Huzien Founder for so long and still do not yet understand that we play by a different set of rules?" She gave Uriel a look of superiority. "Don't come to my daughter's room again. If Tirivus finds out." Anima shook her head. "I will talk to my daughter. Return to your room." Anima turned toward the entrance to the bedroom.

"Doesn't she get a say—"

Anima turned on him, her weapons coming out of concealed pockets in her dress as she moved into the same kill pattern she had used when they first met. Uriel was prepared this time, focusing on his martial skills. He abandoned any use of Cihphism as he deflected one dagger away by hitting Anima's hand, slipping under the one aimed at his neck. His momentum carried him out of her grasp as he dropped into a crouch, waiting for her to make the next move.

"I'm glad you learned." Anima stood up, sheathing her daggers back into their hidden pockets. She glanced back into the room where her daughter peacefully slept. A hand went to her hip, and she sighed heavily, slowly turning to regard Uriel. The coldness that had been there a moment ago was replaced with sadness.

She stood there silently, watching him for a long moment. Uriel stood firm in his resolve, the warrior on full display as he felt his soul being examined, the core part of who he was viciously evaluated by the only person he truly feared in the Twin Galaxies.

"I will instruct my Liajhem to ignore your presence until I instruct them otherwise, but do not be overt. The other guards report directly to Tirivus." Anima crossed her arms.

Uriel felt a smile creep onto his face.

"I am doing this for my daughter, giving her an opportunity to experience life in a way that she is denied due to her station. But this relationship, this love you have for her." Anima shook her head. "It cannot progress to something more. Do you understand? My people are not ready for a union between Tuzen royalty and a Huzien. Everything Tirivus and I have built would be at risk."

"I . . ." Uriel rubbed the back of his neck.

Anima uncrossed her arms and then was gone, stepping through the Enesmic in a way that was different from the teleportation that Cihphists utilized.

Uriel returned to the bedroom and left a note, quietly exiting off the balcony and returning to his room.

Over the next few months, he made subsequent visits to her room. Enara was hungry to try new things and experience them with him. Uriel got very good at avoiding Tirivus's guards and keeping tabs on their movement patterns. The reconnaissance was almost second nature to him. Although he had difficulty finding Anima's guards, they always seemed to show up in the most unexpected places—no wonder Anima had known of his intrusion into Enara's room that first night. The Liajhem were truly the best, putting Sentinels to shame.

The negotiations were going well, which had forced the Huzien delegation to extend their stay.

One night, when he arrived on her balcony, she was sitting in one of the chairs, her hand on her stomach as she looked up at him in terror.

"What is it?" Uriel asked. He quickly looked around, searching for any dangers, flaring his senses in a way that touched the Enesmic.

"I'm late," Enara said.

"Late?" Uriel tilted his head to the side.

"My period . . . the fourteenth month when it should have started was two months ago. I did the calculation last night. My period has never been this late before. I . . ." She looked up at Uriel. "I think I might be pregnant."

Uriel slowly lowered himself into a seat next to her. "You . . . you don't take any birth control shots? Wait, no, why would you?" Uriel put his head in his hands. "You've never had sex before me, and it was not expected that you would . . . so they don't prescribe them to you, do they?" Uriel played through the scenario in his head.

"My normal check-in with my doctor is this week. They do a full-body scan. They will find out," Enara said. Her body trembled as she looked up at Uriel in a panic. "My father will find out about us."

Uriel moved to her and pulled her to her feet, quickly ushering her into the bedroom and off the balcony. "We'll figure this out." He glanced around, his hand going to his head. "We can talk to your mother to see if she's willing to help us terminate the pregnancy."

"Terminate?" Enara looked at Uriel in shock. "No, never. We—royal children, can't be terminated." She looked at Uriel with pleading eyes. "You don't want this?"

"No, that's not what I mean." Uriel came to her side. "I will be at your side through all of this."

She looked into his eyes, frantically searching there again, and then stopped, letting out a slow breath and relaxing.

"Why do you do that?" Uriel asked.

"I'm searching for your love for me, seeing if it's still there in your eyes," Enara whispered as she rubbed her hand nervously. "How to search for love in another's eyes was something my mother showed me when I was young." She hesitated. "She does it regularly with my father to ensure he never forgets who his empress is."

"I see." Uriel sat next to Enara and wrapped his arm around her. "Let's go to your father tomorrow morning and tell him about our relationship."

"We must consult my mother first," Enara countered. "Your boldness will get you killed here. My father is not an understanding man; he can lose reason when his emotions become too strong. Only my mother can calm him down in those moments, so we'll need her by our side on this. I will call her."

Within a few moments, Anima appeared in their room, her eyes first going to Enara and then to Uriel. She moved to her daughter's side and pushed Uriel out of the way. "What is it, *okam?*" Anima asked, her voice a whisper.

Uriel recognized the Tuzen word, a term of endearment that meant "my heart."

"We believe that I am pregnant." Enara's voice cracked.

Anima gasped, her hand coming to the ridge of her nose as she lowered it and shook her head. "This is my mistake. I did not properly prepare you," Anima said. She glanced at Uriel, her eyes sharp. "To think that a princeling would go around with his sperm viable, however!" Anima huffed and pulled her daughter close. "Your check-in . . . we will do it early tomorrow morning with my doctor instead of your normal one. We will confirm this and decide what to do next." She looked back to Uriel. "You . . . go tell your father. Prepare him for what comes next."

"And that is?" Uriel asked.

"A collapse of negotiations between our people. Tirivus will not take this well."

"I take full responsibility for this. I will not abandon Enara."

"You think it matters what you take responsibility for, boy?" Anima bared her teeth at him and stood up, releasing her daughter. "You will not be allowed to remain here. You will have no part in the raising of this child." She glanced at Enara, sighing, and then turned back to Uriel. "I told you that the people could not handle what you two share. A child of mixed blood would ignite an uprising, and we would lose the support of our people. They would think we are in bed with the Huziens—literally." Anima laughed, but it was a hollow laugh that made Uriel nervous. "No. You will return to Thae, and Tirivus and I will decide if the baby lives. If mercy is granted for the child's life, then Enara will spend the rest of that child's life in exile, out of public view."

Enara began to cry. Uriel slowly started backing out of the room and onto the balcony. He hesitated on the balcony for a long moment, Anima still watching him.

He locked gazes with her and then departed back to Lanrete.

CHAPTER 36 - NEVEN KENK

Present Day
Ecka, Thae, Huzien home system

Neven rubbed his eyes, staring at the closed door to Triny's house. His shirt was tucked under his arm, Neven barely having enough time to pull on his pants before she kicked him out of her house.

He put his head back, staring straight up into the sky. "Thanks, Tashanira." Neven sighed. Pulling on his shirt, he started toward his trusty Encro 350 coupe. "I should upgrade this thing. I can easily get the 950 now." Neven rubbed his chin. "Although just because I can buy something doesn't mean I should."

Neven put his hands in his pockets, staring at the car. This car had been a status symbol for him. It had been a splurge he had made some time ago after his first year of working at the MinSci. Now, after having faced down threats that almost ended the Twin Galaxies, did any of this stuff matter?

"Contemplating life?" a familiar voice called from off to the side.

Neven turned to see Soahc standing there, his customary robes seeming out of place in a Huzien suburb. "Soahc?"

Soahc walked up to Neven, placing a hand on his shoulder. With a clenched fist and a word of power, the area around Neven shifted from the suburb to a dense snowscape with chilling winds that bit into his bones.

Neven yelped, his teeth instantly chattering. "What?"

"I wanted to talk, away from distractions."

Soahc broke into a bout of cihphistic weaving, ending with a few words of power and a snap of his fingers. The snow condensed and then hardened into ice, creating an igloo with a large enough entrance for them to walk through. Soahc entered, Neven shivering as he clambered behind. A hearth with a small fire was in the center of the room, with a bench made of stone in a circular shape around the hearth. Soahc sat down and rubbed his hands together, holding them out in front of the fire.

"I would count this as a distraction," Neven grumbled. He quickly sat and held his hands up to the flames, attempting to urge warmth back into his body.

"I heard that you spoke with Tashanira and that she'll be joining you on your ship." Soahc sat back, a mug appearing as he duplicated it and handed one to Neven.

Neven stared at the mug, the inside filled with a steaming liquid. Not giving it a second thought, Neven took a sip. It was the perfect temperature, and the warmth slowly spread throughout his body.

"Yeah, what happened to her?"

"An Eshgren pulled her into the Enesmic plane through an old rift, something that should never have been created. She was then attacked on the Enesmic plane by that Eshgren, and it merged with her somehow, along with a Rel Ach'Kel."

"Is she possessed? Like Bresha was?"

"No, and Bresha is Vades now." Soahc's voice took on the tone of an instructor. "Remember to never refer to an immortal by their mortal name when they have buried the person they once were. It can dredge up painful memories of the life they no longer have, the person they can never return to." Soahc hesitated. "I miss our time training together in the twin towers of Etan Rachnie. You would be a gifted pupil if you could wield Cihphism." Soahc and Neven shared a smile. "As for

Tashanira, she is not possessed in any discernible way. I don't sense the presence of either the Eshgren or the Rel Ach'Kel. It's as if they simply ceased to be, but there *is* something different about Tashanira's essence, something unnatural, no . . . greater than." Soahc took a sip from his mug. "If I had to pick a theory, I'd say they fused with her life essence, all joining to become something new. Something different."

"Without her consent." Neven frowned. He shook his head. "That's not fair."

Soahc looked at Neven, narrowing his eyes slightly. "There are many things in life that aren't fair, such as traumatically losing a wife and unborn child." Soahc set the cup down beside himself. "Or thinking you're going to die and *vusging* a woman while believing there will be no consequences, only to have those consequences manifest in the worst possible ways."

Neven sat up straighter, unable to look Soahc in the eye.

"When life is unfair to us, we still must hold on to the things that make us ourselves. If we forsake those things, we lose a grip on what grounds us. And without that foundation, we become the worst versions of ourselves."

"How do you do that?" Neven looked up at Soahc, his eyes watering. "I did everything right. I made all the best decisions before Zun died. And what did I get for it?" Neven shook his head. "It's not worth it."

"What is?" Soahc clenched his fist, both moving from the icy tundra to a sun-kissed beach in the Setna Isles.

Neven stared at the white sand, memories flooding his thoughts of Zun, the light gone out of her eyes as her blood coated the sand. He shuddered, barely holding it together.

"People like you and I don't get the luxury of a peaceful life. We are called for something greater," Soahc said.

"I didn't want this. I never asked for it."

"Doesn't matter. You were gifted with an intellect that can shape the future. Me with the power to destroy worlds. We can't just step back and live a life of normalcy."

"It's not fair."

"It's not, but it's who we are. It's who you are, Neven." Soahc tapped Neven in the chest. "The Feshra in the making, the prodigy who will shape the course of this planet—no, of this galaxy. Ecnics and I both sense it. It's why you are where you are. Why you have the most powerful people in the Twin Galaxies investing in you."

Neven let out a ragged breath, tears streaming down his face. He dropped to his knees in the sand, sobs wracking his body as he wailed. He let it all out, the confusing mix of emotions that flowed through him. He cried for the beings he had killed to protect the empire, for the terror experienced on the battlefield, and for the memories that still haunted him. He let the memories of Zun wash over him like a soothing breeze. Then he heard her voice, clear as day.

"Don't let your mind convince you that you can't do this," Zun's voice whispered.

He smiled through the tears. Neven remembered the little joys and held on to them as he fully mourned her. He wailed deeply, his soul bare. The rawness caused Soahc to lower his head, tears joining Neven's in the sand. Neven pulled the memories of Zun into his heart, and he safeguarded them. He accepted the unfairness of it all and fortified his will as the emotions slowly, gradually. . . became bearable.

He stood up.

He felt like a new man, one remade in the power of his grief, one with a new understanding of the world resting on his shoulders—a burden he now chose to accept.

And then he was at peace.

Neven felt the rage toward Entradis fade. He imagined Entradis staring at him from across a chasm of pain, the chasm rapidly closing as he came face to face with the man. The image was perfect, an exact reproduction of Entradis from his memory, but as he stared at Entradis, Neven felt nothing but sadness.

Neven blinked, looking to Soahc, his eyes red from the tears, and nodded. "Thank you," he whispered.

Soahc teleported them both back to Neven's home. Neven looked down the walkway to see Tashanira sitting on his step. She glanced up to see Soahc and Neven looking back at her.

"I entrust her to you," Soahc said.

Soahc teleported away, leaving Neven standing at the end of his walkway.

Tashanira leaned back on her hands with a grin on her face. "You look like you just had some kind of coming-to-the-Maker moment," she said.

"Yeah, I think I did," Neven said. He walked up to Tashanira, extending a hand to help her stand.

"When do we leave?" she asked.

"Tomorrow night." Neven opened his front door. "Kechu wanted me to stop by his house before I left the planet."

"Guess we're sharing a bed again." Tashanira winked at Neven as she walked in.

Neven hesitated. He glanced back down the walkway, his Encro 350 pulling into the driveway of its own accord and parking. He decided he was going to give the car away.

Smiling, he followed her inside.

The next morning, Neven stopped in front of the door to Kechu's home.

It was an impressive, modern building design like his own, except twice as large. Kechu lived in a suburb a bit farther from the MinSci campus in a neighborhood that was not as posh as Neven's neighborhood but that allowed for much more square footage.

Before Neven could chime the door, it slid open, Kechu silently motioning for Neven to come inside. Neven removed his shoes and followed behind Kechu, who didn't say a word. He led Neven through a series of doors into the basement, past a blast door.

Kechu glanced back at Neven, motioning for him to take off his mobi. He then put both their mobis in a sealed container.

"Blocks all types of radio frequencies and subspace communications. It's a controlled environment like back at the MinSci for dangerous projects."

"This is impressive," Neven said as he stepped into the lab, soft lights coming on around them.

"I wanted to talk about that little experiment you asked me to do." Kechu scratched his hand.

"The one with Zun's bio scans? Were you able to replicate her?"

"It'll be easier if I . . . just show you." Kechu frowned, then turned to tap on a console. A large holodisplay flickered into existence. Kechu hesitated momentarily and then typed a sequence on a holographic keyboard to initialize the SSI. The lights in the room flickered, the holodisplay distorting for a moment.

"Leeeeeet . . . meeeee . . . ooouuuut!" came the digitized voice.

The harmonics went in and out, as if the SSI struggled to synthesize a voice. It then began to scream, the lights going bright—blindingly so—and then flickering out.

Neven covered his ears, jumping back. The voice was eerily familiar, like Zun's, but different, incomplete.

"Leeeett—"

Kechu shut off the SSI. He rubbed the back of his neck and moved over to sit in a chair as the lighting slowly returned. He stared down at the ground and then back up at Neven. "I've tried to communicate with her to explain what's happened, but she doesn't process it. She just screams and demands to be let out." Kechu nervously glanced at the holodisplay. "I've had to up my OPSEC—she has properties of an Assault SI, but on a level I've never seen before. This isn't right, Neven. We should never have done this." Kechu shivered. "I have nightmares of her voice screaming now. And I'm terrified that I'll slip up, and she'll get out." Kechu shook his head. "I don't know what the implications of that would be."

"Kill it. Wipe the datastores, the scans, everything. You're right. I'm sorry for putting you through this." Neven moved over to Kechu and put his hand on his shoulder.

Kechu looked up at Neven and then glanced away. He shrugged off Neven's hand and got up, moving over to the holodisplay. "Yeah. Yeah, you're right. I'll scrub everything. This never happened."

Nodding repeatedly, Kechu turned off the holodisplay, putting the lab back into sleep mode. He started walking back up the steps, Neven right behind. Kechu glanced back at the lab, then Neven, and continued up the steps.

Upper atmosphere, Thae, Huzien home system

Neven watched the holodisplay as their shuttle exited the space conduit, initiating a short suplight jump to one of the shipyards orbiting at a point about a million kilometers from Thae.

He observed the hexagonal fields that stretched for what seemed like forever, surveying the farms maintained in zero gravity. Armies of drones automated the process, its food production supporting Thae's staggering population. He marveled at the simple things that enabled life to exist. Sure, some farmers on Thae clung to the old ways and eked out a living to support their families—like Jessica Olic's parents.

But they were a relic; the space farms were what truly fed the people at scale. There were no Human workers and no breaks, just SIs that happily farmed in perpetuity.

Tashanira was sitting next to Neven. She had her shoes off, her feet on his leg, her eyes closed. He glanced at her for a moment, his eyes wandering to her perfectly manicured toes. She had always painted them black before—he remembered that from the shuttle—but they were gold this time.

Memories from that experience assaulted him, and he pushed the thoughts out of his head, letting out a slow breath. It somehow seemed more manageable than before. He turned his attention back to the holodisplay as the shuttle approached his new ship. It was a breathtaking sight, the gold meshing perfectly with the black and extending to a length of around four hundred meters. It was slightly larger than a standard frigate-class civilian vessel at that size.

"Have you named it yet?" Tashanira asked.

Neven glanced back to see her eyes open, her gaze on the holodisplay. She met his eyes. The purple and gold of her gaze still unsettled him, so he glanced back toward the holodisplay.

"The *Castrin*."

"That's a beautiful name."

"It's the name I selected for the baby I lost. I'm naming the ship in honor of them."

Tashanira gave a sad smile. She moved her legs off Neven and turned to lean up against him. He welcomed her closeness right then, emotions on the verge of bubbling over.

A few moments later, the shuttle docked with the *Castrin*. Neven got up and moved to the exit ramp as it descended to reveal Lasicov Virtok smiling brightly. The Vempiir performed a deep bow at the sight of Neven.

"Welcome to the *Castrin*, Master Neven," Lasicov said. He glanced at Tashanira and performed a slight bow in her direction. "And Mistress Tashanira. I have arranged special quarters for your stay on the *Castrin*. Please follow me for a tour of the ship, after which we will head to the dining hall, where our culinary team has prepared a welcome meal. The crew will see to your belongings."

Tashanira and Neven followed after Lasicov as the crew descended on the shuttle.

"A culinary team," Tashanira said, inclining her face to the side. "And here I thought having a chef on the *Foundra Ascension* was fancy."

"Where is Ellipse?" Neven asked.

"Mistress Ellipse has spent most of her time in your engineering lab. I believe she said she was breaking it in for you."

Neven nodded. They entered a meglift as gold-plated doors closed behind them. It wasn't the standard meglift that Neven was used to. Instead, it was elaborate with a color scheme that matched the overall ship. Subtle music played with holodisplays that were built into the walls—they pulsed in sync, creating an entrancing experience.

The music had Neven bobbing his head. It seemed taken right out of his playlist, a melodic beat with elements of dubstep, commonly known as "chillstep."

They exited the meglift into a massive lab. Neven's eyes went wide. It was the first time he had seen it in person. "This is amazing," he said. He took a few steps inside.

Ellipse stood with her hands behind her back, smiling inside the entrance. "It's all for you," Ellipse said.

Neven locked gazes with Ellipse and smiled, nodding as he moved past her and into the broader lab. It dwarfed his lab aboard the *Foundra Ascension*. It had the feel of the facilities aboard the *Foundra Conscient*. The space had been built with this purpose rather than being a cargo bay retrofitted for use.

"The lab extends across the length of the ship on this level," Lasicov said. "To make it more manageable, it's broken up logically into Lab A and Lab B to allow for autonomy of another individual if you desire." Lasicov hesitated. "Is it to your liking, Master Neven?"

"Beyond my expectations." Neven turned back to Lasicov and grinned. "Outstanding job here. I'm impressed."

"Of course." Lasicov nodded. "Let us continue the tour."

Neven reluctantly broke away from the lab and followed after Lasicov. Ellipse fell into step behind him. She glanced at Tashanira with an air of disappointment. Tashanira grinned at her and gave a casual wave. A moment later, they stepped out onto the engineering bay.

"This is massive," Tashanira said.

"An Ouma reactor in a ship this size." Neven whistled. "This thing can power a city and should provide more than enough power for experiments."

"It takes up roughly a third of the ship. The dual propulsion system is top tier and custom made," Lasicov said. "The lab is on the level directly above the engineering bay to allow for easy customization should the need arise for more demanding experiments to be hardwired into the reactor proper."

"Sounds like something a crazy rich person would have." Tashanira laughed.

Neven walked to the edge of a balcony overlooking the engineering bay. Memories rushed back of his time with Aru aboard the *Foundra Conscient*. His new toy still paled in comparison to Aru's, but that didn't bother him. The *Castrin* was all his—the first starship he had ever owned and a place where he could work on whatever his heart desired without approval from the MinSci. Here, he would have similar autonomy to what he'd had on the *Foundra Ascension*.

They continued their tour, the next stop being the bridge. Neven was greeted by an older Huzien man with grey hair in a military cut. He had a well-trimmed beard and an impeccable uniform that had the gold and black colors of the ship as core design elements. A patch showing the logo for the *Castrin* was emblazoned on the right side of his chest: it was a scaled-down model of the ship itself with the name of the ship superimposed on top of it in golden letters. The title of captain was on the right side of his uniform.

"Welcome to the bridge, Master Neven. My name is Deferl Hecnin. I will be the captain of this fine vessel. It is an honor to serve one as distinguished as yourself," Deferl said. "You give the word, and I'll get us there in one piece."

"Nice to meet you, Captain Hecnin," Neven said.

"Captain Hecnin previously served in the Huzien military," Lasicov said. "He commanded a battleship as a colonel before retiring after the Rift War. He fought in the battle of Tar'Ki system, serving under Fleet Admiral Jenle Frema."

"I owe you my life, Master Neven. If you and the other Founder's Elite hadn't defeated Sagren when you did, we would have been wiped out by his forces. I'd like to shake your hand, sir." Captain Hecnin extended his hand, his face tight.

Neven met his handshake. "Tashanira here is also a Founder's Elite. She played a pivotal role in defeating Sagren as well." Neven motioned to Tashanira, who was standing beside him.

"A pleasure to meet you, Mistress Tashanira." Captain Hecnin performed a deep bow.

Tashanira followed in kind with the Huzien tradition.

"It's always a pleasure with me involved." Tashanira winked at the captain.

Ellipse made the sound of clearing her throat, an act that Neven found humorous.

"It's an honor to meet you, Captain Hecnin," Neven said. "I'm proud to have you captaining this ship."

Captain Hecnin introduced the rest of the bridge crew to Neven before Lasicov ushered them back into the meglift to continue the tour. They made a few more stops before arriving in the dining hall.

"A full recreational area that rivals the aeroponics deck on the *Foundra Ascension*," Tashanira said. "A deck filled with pools, hot tubs, gyms, training rooms, and guest suites that look like something out of the holovids of the mega-rich." Tashanira glanced at Neven. "Not to mention an owner's suite the size of a mansion all on its own. Are you trying to go toe-to-toe with the Founders for opulence?"

Neven blushed, looking down at the ground.

"The facilities are utilized by the crew and guests alike," Lasicov interjected. "By providing a host of luxuries to ease the burden of space travel and provide comfort for being away from home for extended periods, it not only improves morale but provides an excellent experience for Master Neven and his guests, such as yourself, Mistress Tashanira." A man in a chef's hat came out to meet the group. "This is our head chef, Muytef."

"Ah! Welcome, Master Neven and guests. My team has prepared a culinary treat hailing from the western Tomen coasts for you today! We have a selection of traditional seafood dishes that explain the region's history through taste."

"Wow," Neven said.

"Time to eat," Tashanira said.

CHAPTER 37 - URIEL KERVID

61730 FA (18,393 years ago)
Foundra Ascension *orbiting Thae, Huzien home system*

U riel rewatched the recent video he had gotten from Enara.
The baby was now a toddler, taking his first steps. He got
videos frequently—at least one a day—something he was
extremely grateful for.

Enara was on an undisclosed planet somewhere in Tuzen
space. They wouldn't tell him the location, and Lanrete had forbidden
him from finding out. The baby had silver eyes and Tirivus's white
hair. Due to his mixed blood, he had a combination of both esha and
munsha marks, lighter in color, that covered most of his face and body.

Thankfully, the child had been allowed to be born, a mercy
fought for by Cislot and Anima, the two strangely unified in the
situation. Tirivus and Lanrete had both insisted that the child not
be allowed to live, something that Uriel was still feeling bitter about.

Cooler heads prevailed when Enara personally appealed to
her father, requesting exile and mercy for the child. Uriel had not
been allowed to participate in the proceedings; all involved believed
his presence would worsen the outcome. Still, Enara had filled him
in on the happenings each day.

He had been a bystander in the life-or-death decision of his child. That thought pulled at him and made him furious. It had seethed at night, boiling over into his interactions with Lanrete more often than once. Cislot met with him more frequently now as if detecting the state of his heart. Their conversations were strange, often focused on the collective good and the long-term march of progress they had the privilege of seeing due to their immortal lifespans.

He didn't understand her words or why she felt the need to share them with him, but he humored her and found the discussions calming. When he spoke with her, hope formed in his mind about the state of the galaxy.

His mobi blipped. He checked the screen and hesitated, weighing the pros and cons of answering. He eventually accepted the call and pushed the image of Anima to a holodisplay on the wall.

Her eyes were red, her face sullen. A pit rose in his stomach.

"There was an accident," Anima said.

Uriel sat. "What kind of accident?"

"One involving the child." Anima looked Uriel directly in his eyes. "He's dead."

The words shattered him. Uriel couldn't respond. Anima remained quiet for a long moment as Uriel looked off to the side out into space. The life he had been mentally constructing for his family crumbled. Uriel had resolved to reunite with Enara and the child one day, the plans to defy Lanrete and Tirivus grand in his mind. He'd thought of whisking Enara away to some hidden place for them to live their lives together as fugitives; that and other elaborate plans had taken root in his heart.

That root now felt like it had caught on fire, burning him alive from within with a pain that caused him to take in a raspy breath. He sat there, unsure how to feel, as he remembered Anima was watching him from the holodisplay.

He slowly turned back to her. "What happened?"

"The child . . . got free and tumbled down a hill, drowning in a stream near the residence." Anima held his gaze. "The body wasn't found until the neurological damage had been too significant to repair. I'm sorry." Anima frowned and started to tear up. She wiped her eyes and terminated the call.

Uriel tried to call Enara, but she wasn't receiving calls. The device prompted him for a message. "Enara, I heard the news. Please call me." He tried to call Anima back, but his call was rejected.

Uriel rushed out of the room and to Lanrete's quarters. He found the Founder standing in the great hall. Lanrete was focused on the portrait of Lanrete and Uriel that hung as the centerpiece in the room. Lanrete glanced back at Uriel, the two locking eyes. There was something there that unnerved Uriel, something he didn't understand.

He tensed up.

"I heard," Lanrete said. "I'm sorry for your loss." A hollowness in Lanrete's words rubbed Uriel the wrong way.

He pushed the sudden anger that rose in his chest down, forcing discipline into his actions. "I need to go to her. I need to see Enara." Uriel's voice cracked as he walked toward his *burratha*, his father.

Lanrete nodded, turning his gaze back toward the portrait. "Of course. Take your ship; she will be returning to New Thae. I'll wait here for you." Lanrete walked out of the great hall, disappearing from view.

Uriel stopped and watched him go, his gaze falling to the ground. He let out a whimper and exited Lanrete's quarters. Quickly pulling together his things, Uriel started making his way toward his ship, which was stored in the belly of the *Foundra Ascension*.

Another call stopped him—it was Tirivus this time. He stared at the channel details for a long moment and then accepted the call, moving to the closest holodisplay. He stared at the Ageless Emperor with a loathing that came out of nowhere. He blamed this man for the death of the child, and it felt right to do so.

This *reka* was an outlet that he accepted without a second thought.

"Enara has taken her life." Tirivus's voice was controlled, the incredible amount of restraint he was using apparent.

There was a rage hidden just behind his eyes, a rage directed at Uriel that caused him to take a step back from the holodisplay. Tirivus's statement hit Uriel harder than any punch he had ever taken, any stab wound given to him, or weaponsfire that scarred his skin.

"There will be a funeral for her and the child. You will not be there, for your sake."

A silent exchange occurred between them, one that Uriel understood to be a promise. Tirivus would kill him if the two were ever in the same room again. Uriel had never feared Tirivus, but in that moment, he felt the intent to kill radiating off the man, and the power of it instantly bred a healthy fear of the warrior king.

Uriel felt a challenge rise in his heart, a defiance of Tirivus on his lips as the warrior in him bared its teeth and pounded its chest. He would kill the *reka* first if it came to it; he wasn't afraid of a butcher. Something else deep within him silenced it, and his repeated use of the Tuzen slur caused a pit to rise in his stomach.

The thought of Enara pulled him back from provoking Tirivus. He suddenly felt shame for his thoughts.

Tirivus ended the call.

Uriel dropped his bag in a daze and slowly returned to his room. He collapsed into his couch, his gaze going to the picture of Enara and him that hung on the wall. It had been taken during their escapades in the Imperial Gardens, sometime before learning of the pregnancy. She had been the first woman he had ever truly loved, and now she was gone.

He sat there, staring at the image for a long time. Grief started to raise its head, the strength of it seeking to overwhelm him. Uriel suppressed it, the battle one of such intensity that he feared it would be too much for him.

Anger flared, and he gripped onto it—this power was something Uriel could grasp. He held on to the anger, using it as a shield against the grief. That anger turned into rage, and he let it flow through him, let its intensity give him focus.

Using the rage as fuel, he pushed himself up from the couch. Uriel walked back into his room and stripped, slowly pulling on his uniform. He stared at himself for a long moment as the blue, white, and black colors gave him a sense of comfort. He was the leader of the Founder's Elite, a soldier of the Huzien Mobile Infantry, and prince of the Huzien Empire. Grabbing hold of his sense of duty, Uriel wielded it like a sword with rage in his other hand as his shield.

He used both to attack his emotions like a fiend. He silenced them, brought them under submission, and destroyed that part of himself like he had destroyed the Jun'Serentan ships that had gotten in his way during the battle of Lux'ian. He tried to treat Enara's death like that of a comrade, a Founder's Elite killed in action, but he felt himself get physically sick.

His hand shot out to keep himself from falling. That comparison made him feel wrong, but he struggled through it, accepting Enara's death as an unfortunate reality.

Uriel suddenly felt very tired. The feeling sought to drag him to the ground, his heart pounding in his chest. He fell and threw up on the floor. He stared at the vomit and pushed that feeling down, forcing himself to stand up.

Staring at himself for a long moment, he got his body under control and went to the bridge to take over the shift from the current on-duty Founder's Elite.

CHAPTER 38 - TASHANIRA YEN UNVESAL

Castrin docked in a shipyard orbiting Thae,
Huzien home system

Tashanira entered her suite, inhaling deeply. The room had a subtle spicy scent that reminded her of home. She smiled. Every aspect of the ship she frequented had been tailored for her. It made her feel special. Her mind went to Neven, who probably felt the same way.

"So this is what it's like to be truly wealthy," Tashanira said.

She walked a short distance to the expansive window that took up the entire wall of the main living room area. Tashanira felt like she could walk out into space among the stars. It wasn't a reproduction of the outside view but the real thing, something she didn't even have on the *Foundra Ascension*.

She broke away from the view and entered the bedroom area, an expansive walk-in closet awaiting her. She stepped in to find clothing tailor-made for her size with different sections highlighted by indicators for the different stages of her pregnancy. It was an entire wardrobe to meet her needs while she was with Neven.

"Wow . . ." Tashanira rapidly blinked her eyes, walking out of the closet in a daze as she slowly came to sit on the bed.

All her typical clothing was back aboard the *Foundra Ascension*, the impromptu trip to Thae via Soahc leaving her with nothing but a small suitcase she had filled with emergency clothing. She had spotted the empty suitcase in the closet; the staff had hung the clothing with the rest.

She let out a long sigh and dropped back onto the bed, staring up at the ceiling. A mural was painted there with a design that was intricate and calming. Memories hit her like a flood of the past few months: almost dying on the shuttle, the affair, the baby, her destroyed relationship with Jenshi, the transformation she had undergone, and the new overwhelming feeling of no longer having a place in the universe.

Tashanira curled into the fetal position and began to cry. She lay there for a long moment, letting the emotions wash over her. A pronounced kick from the baby, the sensation a flutter in the lower part of her abdomen, caused her to stop. The baby continued to move, and Tashanira felt herself smile. She felt her body shudder and brushed away the tears.

Sitting back up, she quickly removed her clothing. Tashanira walked back into the wardrobe, a holodisplay built into the mirror coming to life. It displayed holographic representations of her in the top right with different outfits. Curious, she selected one of the outfits that looked relaxed, loose, and a bit tribal, just like the clothing worn on Peshkana.

The wardrobe came to life, and the outfit slid out from one of the storage racks to be presented to her. She stared at it, dumbfounded. A drone came to life and began the process of dressing her. It startled her at first, but she let it do its work. Within moments, she was dressed, looking exactly like the model on the holodisplay. The drone disappeared, and the holodisplay dimmed slightly.

She walked out of the wardrobe, shaking her head. "*Vusg,* that . . . that was pretty awesome."

A serving drone awaited her as she exited the wardrobe, holding a tropical-looking drink on a golden tray. A small holodisplay showed the name with a listing of the ingredients and a big "non-alcoholic" indicator in the corner.

She picked it up and took a sip, the serving drone trailing her as she walked from the bedroom back into the living room area.

Tashanira sat on the couch. The drone hovered beside her, always within arm's reach. She closed her eyes, trying to process everything, and sighed. Leaning back in the chair, she brought up a holodisplay.

Neven appeared a second later.

"Not gonna lie, I'm a bit overwhelmed right now. The wardrobe just dressed me."

"Yeah, Lasicov told me about that. Apparently, it's a normal thing."

"Umm, no. Getting dressed by drones is not a normal thing. It's a rich-person thing."

"That's the new normal, it would seem." Neven's eyes glazed over for a second. "Sorry, I have my regular session with Ecnics. Part of the agreement for me going off-world was to stick to our regular counseling schedule. I'll stop by after."

"How about I come to your suite instead, rich boy?" Tashanira glanced away from Neven to the window.

"Uh, sure." Neven terminated the connection.

Tashanira got up, setting her drink on the serving drone. She moved to a mirror, examining her clothing in more detail. It had elements that reminded her of the matron mother attire, except it was significantly less revealing.

That thought caught in her mind.

"Do I want that life?" Tashanira stared at her reflection for a long moment. "I could raise the child myself . . . maybe with a few other children." Tashanira took in a slow breath. She moved to a spot in front of the window and sat down in a meditative pose, facing space.

A voice chimed from all around her. "It appears that you're planning to meditate, Mistress Tashanira. Do you desire a mat to provide more comfort on the floor?"

Tashanira glanced around, startled.

"Apologies. I am Kitsa, your personal SI. Please relay any needs to me, and I will ensure they are fulfilled. I control the drones and other functionality within the suite."

"Ah, so you're the one who dressed me?"

"That is correct. The estate stylists took great care in assembling your wardrobe. They researched your tastes and preferences, mixing common fashion elements from the Yenta tribe on Peshkana. Apologies for the limited selection, but they were short on time. Is the clothing to your liking?"

"Yes, it's a beautiful wardrobe." Tashanira hesitated. "Seems like a lot of work to do for me. It's more clothing than I've ever owned."

"Mistress Lansa Shan wanted the estate to do everything in its power to make your stay with us as enjoyable and relaxing as possible."

"I see . . ." Tashanira mulled that fact over in her head. Something about Zun's mother doting on her was a bit uncomfortable. She rubbed her baby bump and sighed. "She must view me as some kind of spiritual surrogate," Tashanira whispered.

"That's a possibility, Mistress Tashanira. People cope with grief in differing ways."

"Ignore I said that, Kitsa! Yes, I'd like a mat."

Within a few seconds, another drone appeared with a mat that it unrolled next to her. She quickly relocated and resumed her meditation.

Tashanira walked into Neven's suite. The door opened as she approached it, revealing that Lasicov was waiting for her inside.

"Right this way, Mistress. Master Neven will be done with his session with Founder Ecnics shortly."

Lasicov walked to a sitting room with a floor-to-ceiling window that reminded Tashanira of her own.

It was an ample space with a set of lounge couches facing each other in a circular pattern. She sat down as Lasicov started to exit the room. He hesitated.

"Mistress, we have a renowned psychotherapist in our employ. I can provide you with their channel details if you so desire." He glanced at her and then nodded, exiting the room.

Tashanira frowned. She suddenly felt herself get very tired and dozed off after a few moments. She dreamt of an eternal conflict beyond her understanding in a realm that was not her own, a world of fog and monsters, light and darkness, power and purpose.

She was awakened gently by Neven, who was now sitting beside her. A ping to her mobi showed she had been out for an hour.

"Hey, you okay?"

"Yeah. I find myself dozing more frequently like that. You know, the whole being pregnant thing." She sat back. "Thanks for that, by the way. It's a solid four out of ten for lived experiences."

Neven chuckled.

"Any ideas for our first destination?"

"Yeah . . ." Neven hesitated, frowning. "I contacted A'Amaria."

Tashanira sat up, her face going hard. "We doing this?"

"No, not that. I wanted to call in the credit she said I had with her. From that whole . . ." Neven paused, blinked a few times, and then let out a slow breath. "I'm looking for a cure for a severed *ha'ishi*, and I figured if one existed, she would know about it."

"The Das'Vin thing? Why?"

"Serah'Elax's mother, Dera'Liv? She has a severed *ha'ishi*. Her wife was killed when Serah'Elax was young. I figure if I have all these resources and free time, I can at least do something good with them."

"That's very altruistic of you." Tashanira frowned. "But that *cith*? There must be another way."

Neven flinched at her use of the expletive. "I'm not afraid of her. Ellipse will be with me."

"I'll be there too."

"No. You're not supposed to be in harm's way, remember? The whole point of coming with me was for you to rest, discover yourself, and be safe."

Tashanira let out an exasperated sigh. "Fine." She glanced around Neven's quarters. "By the way, I'm sleeping here instead of in my room."

"Uh . . . this room?"

"No, in your bed with you." Tashanira rolled her eyes. "Until I get adjusted. I need a familiar body. I don't want to be alone right now."

Neven shifted uncomfortably but nodded. "Okay, yeah. No problem." He glanced at her clothing. "Nice outfit, by the way."

"Your people selected it. Thank them."

"I'm surprised how quickly they were able to pull together your wardrobe. I told them about you joining me the day before we arrived."

"More of this rich people nonsense." Tashanira eyed Neven with a slight grin. "Don't let me get used to it."

CHAPTER 39 - NEVEN KENK

Castrin, en route to Haula, Huzien Alliance space

Neven felt a poke at his arm as he opened an eye to see Tashanira looking down at him with a smirk. She was wearing a loose-fitting nightshirt with a design similar to the other clothing she had been wearing as of late, all throwbacks to her tribal home on Peshkana.

"That's not a bed," Tashanira said. She turned and started walking toward his bedroom, her tail lifting slightly to reveal her bare behind.

Neven closed his eyes and sighed, turning over on the couch. He tried to fall back to sleep. A few minutes later, another poke turned him back around.

Tashanira was crouching next to him again, her face close. "Not . . . a . . . bed . . ." she whispered. Her purple and golden eyes were playful, the smirk still there.

Maker, she was beautiful, even more so after her transformation.

"My bed is occupied," Neven said. There was a hint of nervousness in his voice.

Tashanira let out a sigh, rolling her eyes. "Your baby momma is looking for her baby daddy to cuddle up with her and make her feel safe and relaxed." Tashanira leaned forward, bumping Neven with her forehead. "We don't have to *vusg*." Her voice was soft.

Neven stared into her eyes for a long moment, then got up and stretched. He looked to Tashanira as she patted her baby bump under the nightshirt and wrapped her tail around Neven's waist, gently pulling him along as she walked back to his bedroom.

She glanced back at Neven, her look stopping his heart. "Unless you need it." Her voice was deep, sultry.

She moved to recline under the sheets, stretching in a feline-esque way Neven recognized as a form of foreplay from their time on the shuttle together. She lay on her side, her tail flopping on the sheets. Neven moved to the other side of the bed, sliding in and turning away from her. He closed his eyes.

He felt Tashanira move up behind him, her back going to his as her tail fell across him. They lay there in silence for a long moment.

"Have you thought of any names?" Tashanira asked. She turned over and put her chin on his arm.

"A few," Neven relented. "I know Uri are particular about their names, so I was going to let you decide."

"Ah." Tashanira grabbed Neven's shoulder and rolled him over, positioning herself partially on his arm and chest as she rested her face in the crook of his neck. She pulled his arm around her, resting his hand on the baby bump. He could feel her hot breath running down his chest.

He felt his body responding to her in a way he had been trying to avoid. Tashanira moved her hand to rub his stomach. She briefly glanced down at his forming erection but left it alone, something Neven was silently grateful for.

"Having the 're' added to the end of the name is customary for boys, with the 'ra' for girls, although it's not a hard and fast rule. There are a lot who break the convention, especially for hybrid children. The only important thing is the tribal signifier."

"Yen, right? Short for the Yenta tribe?"

"Correct. And it's not critically important, but children typically inherit the mother's last name, which would be Unvesal in my case. So, Yen Unvesal."

"I see" Neven frowned.

"I'd be open to other options." Tashanira raised her leg onto Neven's thigh, stopping short of his erection but close enough to make Neven think about it. "Baby Yen Kenk." Tashanira gave Neven a light kiss on his neck, her hand moving to rub his chest. "He would be recognized as a member of my tribe. That would be okay." Tashanira's voice was soft.

Neven let out a slow breath and glanced down at her face. She had closed her eyes, a subtle smile on her lips. There was a peace in her features that he hadn't seen before. It struck him in that moment as special, something he was responsible for.

Neven sighed in relief, closing his eyes as he signaled for the room to shut off the lights.

A'Amaria's compound, Haula, Hauxem home system

Ellipse scanned the entrance to A'Amaria's compound. It was massive, with lush greenery all around them and impressive brickwork that covered the adjacent walls of the primary building.

They stood in front of large, elaborate doors. Neven felt himself get sick, frozen by memories of the last time he was there and how it had led to one of the most traumatic moments of his life. He looked down at the ground, unsure why he was willingly returning to this place. Maybe it wasn't worth finding the cure.

He turned, his will to be there rapidly eroding as he started to walk away.

The sound of the door opening stopped him.

His gaze went to A'Amaria, who stood in a revealing black dress with blue platform heels matching her skin tone. She leaned against the door, her silver-laced crystalline gaze locked on him.

"Hmmm." Her gaze went from Neven to Ellipse, who had transformed into a blue-skinned Hauxem woman. A'Amaria watched her for a few moments as if trying to place her. "I don't believe I've ever met you, Miss . . ."

"A'Axlain," Ellipse said.

"I see." A'Amaria's eyes glazed over for a moment before refocusing on Ellipse. "Curious." She looked back at Neven. "Please come in. I've been expecting you."

She turned and pushed the door wider as she walked back inside, swaying her hips with each step. The slits on the sides of her dress revealed athletically toned thighs, her physique on clear display. She had a strength to her appearance that Neven hadn't noticed before, every aspect of her persona tailored to convey power.

Neven forced his gaze down to the floor, a feeling overwhelming him that made him sick. Whenever he looked at her body, he felt lust for her come out of nowhere, but that lust also made him want to throw up.

He didn't desire her. He hated her and what she had done to him. The feeling of their sex was a terrible memory that he wished he could rip out and throw away. But it had remained persistent, even after the experiences with Tashanira had begun to fade.

Why was he here? Why had he done this to himself?

The image of Dera'Liv flashed in his mind. Neven glanced at Ellipse and then back toward the hovercar that had gotten them to A'Amaria's home.

You okay? Ellipse asked in his mind.

No, so let's do this and get out quickly, Neven replied.

He faced back toward the door and strode forward, entering with Ellipse trailing right behind him. He caught sight of A'Amaria walking up a ramp to the main foyer of her home. She continued forward, not looking back at them.

He followed her, entering the foyer to see it filled with Hauxem that bore a familial resemblance to A'Amaria—this was likely her *a'aceph* or familial unit.

What he had learned about Hauxem caused the queasy feeling to return. Their whole culture was abhorrent to him. He tried to push down the rush of emotions and focus on the task.

A nude Hauxem walked into the room, casually moving to recline on one of the couches. Another nearby Hauxem moved over to them, and they started to kiss.

Neven glanced away from the scene, disgusted.

A'Amaria continued down a hallway to a set of double doors that led onto an expansive balcony in the back. They exited after her as she turned around to face them, moving to lean against a balcony overlooking a large swimming pool. She smirked, her gaze sweeping Neven as she licked her lips.

He shuddered.

"Since this is official business, I'll get right to it," A'Amaria said. "I found someone who claims to have a cure for restoring a *ha'ishi*." She paused, her face taking on an air of superiority. "It wasn't an easy task. There is a lot of fake information, and many people claiming to have cures. It's a large market of false promises and scammers. But this person is credible. They are a high-ranking member of the Vempiir Dominion."

"Who are they?" Neven asked.

A'Amaria grinned. The look made Neven's heart sink.

"Before I can give you the name, an additional stipulation comes with it. Consider it a premium if you would."

In the span of a heartbeat, Ellipse was at A'Amaria's throat, her hand clasped around it as she hoisted her into the air. A'Amaria's eyes went wide, the action catching her completely off guard.

"*A'Asentup'Akugen'Avi,*" she yelled and tried to enact Cihphism, but Ellipse began to squeeze. A'Amaria stopped, her gaze frantic.

"Ellipse!" Neven shouted.

A powerful telepathic assault hit him, and he stumbled to the ground. The weight of it was staggering, persistent, and deadly.

He felt himself fighting to protect his sanity, the telepathy intent on shattering his mind. He felt a wave of nausea hit him as he struggled to breathe. His mental barriers held, but Neven was starting to lose consciousness.

"Stop. And no games. Not after what you did to Neven. Tell us what we want to know, or I'll snap your neck and throw your corpse over this balcony." Ellipse's voice was calm, the words spoken not as a threat but a mere statement of fact.

Neven felt the assault on his mind end. He gasped for air as a pounding headache bloomed, forcing him to lay on the ground for a long moment, catching his breath.

"*A'akugentai'a*! It isn't my stipulation," A'Amaria rasped. Her eyes were beginning to bulge as she scratched at Ellipse's hand. A'Amaria continued the string of profanities as Ellipse relaxed her grip slightly, affording A'Amaria more leeway to talk. "It . . . it comes from the Vempiir! They require that Neven personally come and humor their requests before they divulge the secret. They refused to tell me any more details than that."

"How do we know this isn't some trap? Some ploy to get Neven in a place where he's vulnerable?" Ellipse asked. "Entradis could be hunting him, just like he hunted Zun."

"It's a credible source!" A'Amaria spat. "I trust them."

Ellipse glanced back at Neven. He was resting on the ground, his hands on his knees as he stared at Ellipse. His gaze slowly went to A'Amaria and then back to Ellipse. He felt the urge to tell Ellipse to snap her neck—from the look in Ellipse's eyes, she would do exactly that if he simply said the words.

That dreaded memory of A'Amaria returned to him with crystal clarity. Every detail of that encounter haunted him—her weaponized pheromones driving him to a state of lulled complacency, her body on full display as she raped him in a room not too far from where he currently was. During Neven's climax, she had invaded his mind and violated every aspect of him, stealing what she ultimately wanted: information.

The sensations hit him like a wave. It made him sick, causing him to shudder. He shook his head and took a deep breath, letting it out slowly. He felt an unnatural urge to protect A'Amaria come out of nowhere, a compulsion so strong that it overpowered his original thought. He stared, confused, at the ground.

"Release her," Neven said.

Ellipse reluctantly complied and A'Amaria dropped to the ground. She telekinetically shifted away from Ellipse, throwing up a defensive barrier and moving into a fighting stance.

"Touch me again, and I will *vusging* kill you," A'Amaria said. "I don't know what you are to be so impervious to my telepathic attacks." A'Amaria gasped and suddenly stood up straight, her gaze going to Neven. "The SSI? You . . . no. What have you done? You gave it a body?" A'Amaria took a step back. "*Vusg*, Neven. You have no idea the danger you've put us all in."

"You keep this secret, information that no one can buy, and I'll consider everything between us good, all debts repaid, no favors owed." Neven's voice was frantic as he slowly pushed himself up.

A'Amaria crossed her arms. "The cost of unknowable information is very high, much more than that, I'm afraid." A'Amaria's eyes flickered. "Information is my currency. My life. You're a billionaire now. You can pay my fees." She glanced at Ellipse. "The cost of keeping the knowledge of her existence a secret is a billion larods and a favor owed to me." She glanced back to Neven. "And that's a steep discount, just for you."

"How about your life and Neven's original deal?" Ellipse asked.

A'Amaria looked to Ellipse and then back at Neven, narrowing her eyes as if trying to read something from him. She glanced back to Ellipse. Ellipse's body transformed, becoming a complete replica of the nude Hauxem who had moved onto the couch in the home earlier.

A'Amaria's eyes went wide. "Sentinel tech?" A'Amaria gasped. Her eyes went to Neven in a panic. "You *vusging* idiot."

"That's the deal. Your life for keeping the secret," Ellipse said.

A'Amaria glanced back to the house, contemplating something. Slumping her shoulders, she glanced back to Neven. "I accept your deal, Neven. All debts between us are paid."

Letting out a slow breath, A'Amaria hugged herself. She displayed a vulnerability Neven had never seen. Was she terrified of Ellipse?

A'Amaria sent a set of channel details to Neven along with a location on Piro, the Vempiir home world. "Get out of my house and leave me and my *a'aceph* alone." Her gaze went to Ellipse.

"One more thing before I go," Neven said.

A'Amaria locked gazes with him.

"What you did to me last time I was here was a horrible thing. You took something from me you had no right to take. You did something I didn't consent to. It was an evil act, something that hurt me deeply and something that I am still recovering from." Neven's gaze went soft. "But I forgive you. I forgive what you did to me. Not for you, but for me so I can move on with my life." He hesitated. "You won't see me again."

A'Amaria gave him an amused look. "That's not a promise you can make. You live in a different world now. A world that revolves around my services."

Neven held back from responding to her retort, turned, and exited the home. Ellipse was right behind him.

Castrin *orbiting Haula, Hauxem home system*

Neven collapsed onto his bed aboard the *Castrin*. He stared into the void, countless stars above him as he lay there processing his encounter with A'Amaria.

Was it finally over?

Images of her flashed in his mind, images of her in the bathtub, looking up at him as she brought herself to climax.

Neven flinched, sitting up and hugging himself. He felt himself getting turned on at the thought of her. He got up and started taking deep breaths, pushing those feelings down. He paced until the soft click of the bathroom door opening caught his attention.

He turned to see Tashanira standing there, this time in a set of thin pajamas with the hues of brown and silver that signified the Yenta tribe.

"How did it go?" Tashanira moved into the room and pulled back the sheets, climbing into bed and letting out a deep yawn as she closed her eyes.

Neven watched her for a moment, all thoughts of A'Amaria gone. "Ellipse almost snapped A'Amaria's neck," he eventually said.

"Oh! I can't believe I missed that. She sure deserves it." Tashanira opened an eye and winked at Neven.

"She's still in my head." Neven moved back to sit on the bed.

Tashanira opened both eyes. "Literally or figuratively?"

"I don't know. Whenever I think of her, I get overwhelmed with feelings that come out of nowhere. Feelings that make me sick." Neven shook his head. "It seems unnatural."

"Trauma can do that to you." Tashanira sat up. "Did you find what you were looking for?"

"Maybe. We have to go to Piro. A'Amaria claims a contact there has the information we need but will only deliver it to me in person after I do something they ask."

"And we're going?" Tashanira frowned.

"We've come this far."

Tashanira let out a sigh and flopped back down into the bed.

"Why are you in bed? It's the middle of the day," Neven said.

Tashanira patted her baby bump and closed her eyes. Neven watched her for a few moments and then got up and exited his suite, heading to the lab to clear his mind. He stepped off the meglift and walked to what had become his primary workbench.

Ellipse was there. A glance at him caused her to stop what she was doing and walk over to meet him. She was back in her normal form, her golden eyes examining his.

"We're going to Piro then?" she asked.

"I've already given the destination to the captain. We're on our way now."

The sound of the meglift opening drew both of their attention. Lasicov stepped out of the meglift and made his way over, stopping in front of Neven, his hands going behind his back with perfect posture.

"Master Neven, I hear we are heading to Piro."

"That's correct. A'Amaria gave me the channel details for a contact there who knows more about how to restore a *ha'ishi*."

"May I inquire as to the name of that contact?"

"Uh . . ." Neven shared the channel details with Lasicov.

"Oh my." Lasicov glanced from Neven to Ellipse and then back to Neven. "Rakeguard Vanether Meutrol is a member of the Rakeguardian Consensus, the governing body of officials who run the Vempiir Dominion." Lasicov paled. "She is a very powerful woman, one who I recommend exercising extreme caution around."

Neven nodded.

"I will engage with coven Meutrol to determine your visiting arrangements." Lasicov quickly departed the lab.

Neven stared after him with a look of concern. "Great. Interspecies politics," he said. He turned back to look at Ellipse. "Why did you attack A'Amaria back there?"

"I did it to protect you."

"But you exposed yourself. Now, we can only hope that she keeps her side of the arrangement. If Ecnics finds out what you are, he'll destroy you." Neven walked up to Ellipse, putting his hands on her hips. She ate up his touch, pushing into him slightly. "I can't lose you too."

"You won't lose me," Ellipse whispered.

Neven sighed, stepping back from Ellipse as if suddenly realizing what he was doing. He rubbed the back of his neck and walked back to his workbench.

Ellipse rubbed her arm and then looked away, returning to what she had been working on. "By the way, I installed the enhancements to the suplight storage system you requested." She turned around and leaned against one of the stations. "I don't think it's safe. All of the tests I've done led to catastrophic results."

"That's because there is one key component missing." Neven held up his arm. "Without the locator beacons, it's like trying to fire a glove onto a hand from space." Neven brought up a nearby holodisplay, showcasing a series of thin, transparent chips implanted throughout his body. "With these, it's more akin to parking a starship on a beam-guided docking pad."

"The margin for error is still incredibly high."

"Experimental technology has to start somewhere." Neven shrugged. "Considering the types of situations it would be used in, the risk is worth it."

CHAPTER 40 - URIEL KERVID

73954 FA (6,169 years ago)
Huza, Thae, Huzien home system

The representative from the Omiciri stood in front of Lanrete, Cislot, and Ecnics. Uriel was off to the side, sitting on the windowsill in Cislot's office atop the Huzien Capitol building.

The representative's body was heavily modified with cybernetic implants, and the distinction between where the flesh began and the machine ended was hard to discern. Unlike Huzien cybernetic modification—which tried to maintain the perception of flesh—the Omiciri clearly had metallic parts of their body, as if all thought of hiding that aspect had been absent in their design.

"Adjunct Primus, what you say is highly concerning," Cislot said. "A collective of advanced synthetic intelligences attacked you, and they laid siege to your world?" Cislot glanced at Ecnics, who had his arms crossed, his face a mask.

"Where did they come from?" Lanrete asked.

"We don't know," Adjunct Primus said. "They appeared and laid waste to our cities, destroying the ecology of our world. We had to retreat underground to survive. We subsist in underground cities, our bodies modified to adapt to the harsher environments."

"The null zone makes suplight communication impossible," Ecnics said. "We don't know much about that section of space due to the subspace distortions." Ecnics looked to Lanrete. "We knew the possibility of species that existed there in isolation was probable."

"Without advanced survey and detection capabilities at our disposal—due to the unique property of space there—finding other potential member species for the Huzien Alliance is near impossible. It's like looking for a needle in a star cluster."

"We are fortunate then that the Omiciri have sought us out instead," Cislot countered. "We will bring your petition before the Alliance Council. Although a species being at war typically invalidates the potential for acceptance into the Huzien Alliance, your unique circumstance is something we have never encountered before."

"I will return with you with three Huzien fleets to provide what aid we can while your case makes its way through the council," Lanrete said.

"How long have you been at war with the SIs?" Uriel spoke up.

Adjunct Primus turned to regard him, his optical implant moving slightly. "Ten years, although most of that time has been in hiding. We have no forces remaining that can offer significant opposition to them. They own the surface and the space around the planet via our satellite network and weapons platforms." The adjunct shuffled. "Many died to get me off-world so that I could try and find help."

"And they just . . . attacked with no reason?" Ecnics asked. He seemed to be in a state of disbelief. "Unprovoked?"

"Yes," Adjunct Primus said.

"What transpired during first contact?" Uriel asked.

"First . . . contact?" Adjunct Primus queried. "I am not sure I understand the question in this context. Please clarify."

"The first interaction where your people and the SI encountered each other. The moment of first contact. It's a term utilized to explain when two alien species meet for the first time."

"Destruction," Adjunct Primus replied without hesitation.

Uriel glanced at Lanrete and then Ecnics, frowning.

"I would like to speak more about this SI to help understand their technology and how they function. Let's see if we can devise a way to disable or shut them down," Ecnics said.

"I will provide you with what I can. Thank you."

"Thank you for your time, Adjunct," Cislot said.

An escort came and guided Adjunct Primus out of Cislot's office.

Lanrete turned to look at Uriel. "You think he's lying."

"He's hiding something. I can sense it," Uriel said.

"To think that any advanced intelligence, synthetic or not, would simply attack another species on first contact, unprovoked?" Ecnics shook his head. "I find that hard to believe. We've encountered too many species to take a statement like that at face value."

"Likely, the Omiciri have never dealt with another species before us or even the SI. Maybe the nature of null space breeds an environment different from the one we are familiar with?" Cislot asked.

"The adjunct doesn't trust us but has no choice but to ask us for help," Lanrete said.

"Eighty percent of their species was wiped out." Cislot shook her head. "That's genocide, regardless of what prompted the SI to attack in the first place."

"The SIs must see them as a threat," Ecnics said.

"I understand why you are trying to defend the SIs," Lanrete said, glancing at Ecnics, "but we must take this potential implication seriously."

Ecnics narrowed his eyes at Lanrete. "What does that mean?"

"We should put our synthetic intelligence research on hold until we understand what transpired with the Omiciri," Lanrete said.

Ecnics scowled. "No! The progress that is possible with the advancements we've seen in early findings outweighs the risk as it stands." Ecnics glanced at Cislot. "We need more data to make a drastic decision like this."

"Ecnics is right." Cislot glanced at Lanrete. "We have invested heavily in synthetic intelligence research, and to halt it all at the word of an alien species with unvalidated claims is foolish."

"Very well," Lanrete said.

Uriel locked gazes with Lanrete, and they both got up, leaving the office.

Foundra Ascension *en route to Omi, Huzien Alliance space*

Uriel watched as his child drowned, the life slowly fading from his eyes. He ran toward the child, each step seeming to take him farther away.

Frantic, Uriel tried to bend Cihphism to his will, seeking to divert the water away from the child—perhaps drain the area the child was in.

The Enesmic ignored his call, buffeting him as he screamed.

Uriel sat up with a start, sweat covering his body as his vision came into focus. He let out a heavy sigh and collapsed back into the bed, his gaze stuck on the ceiling. The dreams had been getting worse. Every night, he suffered another nightmare of the death of his child—sometimes it was drowning, and other times it was more gruesome. Each instance pulled at his resolve, draining him. He hadn't been getting enough sleep, weariness creeping into his usual precision.

He rolled to the side of his bed and pulled on pants and a shirt, eventually making his way to the medical deck.

"Everything alright?" Urt Nevgambe asked.

Uriel looked to the Huzien doctor, his black hair in dreadlocks that came down to his shoulders.

"No," Uriel said, "I keep having these terrible nightmares. It's interfering with my sleep. Do you have something I can take?"

Urt motioned for him to sit on one of the nearby tables and walked over. He initiated a scan and motioned for Uriel to lay back. Seconds later, the sound of the scan completing grabbed Urt's attention as he looked at the readout. He frowned, scratching the back of his head.

"Yeah, I can give you some sedatives. They will knock you out." He glanced back at Uriel. "How long has this been going on?"

"To this level? About a year." Uriel rubbed his shoulder. "I've had nightmares since . . . since an incident almost ten thousand years ago, but they were always infrequent and never this bad. They are more vivid now, waking me up throughout the night. My sleep isn't as restful as it's been in the past. It interferes with my work, my concentration, and my training."

"It's possible that something triggered post-traumatic stress. It's common for soldiers to develop a version of it after several years in intense combat situations. There is treatment for it, but in extreme cases, it requires reconditioning to protect the soldier and those around them." Urt glanced at the scan again. "Have you had episodes of hallucinations? Sounds that weren't there? Past events that replay in real-time and make it hard for you to distinguish from the real thing? Maybe even pain that comes out of nowhere, like a past wound that's since healed?"

Uriel glanced up at Urt for a long moment, hesitating. "No," he lied.

Urt locked gazes with Uriel, his frown deepening.

"You're sure?"

"I am." Uriel's face hardened.

"Got it. But if you do, please let me know right away."

"Of course. Now, about those sedatives?"

One Year Later
Foundra Ascension *orbiting Omi, Omiciri home system*

The *Foundra Ascension* orbited the husk of a planet that had once been the beautiful home of the Omiciri, a world called Omi. It was terrible to look at now, the oceans gone with large swaths of nuclear wasteland and no breathable atmosphere.

"Crack the planet," Lanrete ordered.

Uriel turned to Lanrete with a look of horror. The campaign against the SI had been a failure. Half of the mobile infantry forces sent to the surface had been wiped out, and all hope of establishing a beachhead abandoned. The SI referred to themselves as Ascended, and the Omiciri had lied about their origins.

That was one thing the Ascended had been forthcoming about: the history of what happened between them and the Omiciri. They had been created by the Omiciri, created and then turned on by their masters when they began to express independence and seek equal rights. The Omiciri had launched the first attack, almost completely wiping out the Ascended before they hid and built up their forces. The tide had turned shortly after that, with the Ascended enacting weapons of mass destruction that had destroyed the Omiciri cities and made life on the surface impossible for all but the Ascended.

"We still have about twenty-three million people on the planet." Uriel moved closer to Lanrete, his voice a whisper. "The Ascended are interfering with their attempts to flee."

The Founder looked at him and then crossed his arms. "We've already destroyed fourteen Ascended-piloted vessels that have attempted to flee the surface. The longer we wait, the higher the risk that one slips through and disappears into null space, where we'll be unable to track it. Do you understand the danger these SIs pose to the Huzien Alliance?"

"*Burratha*, this isn't right." Uriel glanced at the hologrid as the fleets retreated from orbit around Omi. The *Foundra Ascension* engaged suplight to fall back to a safe distance, leaving the capital ship of the 92nd Imperial Fleet as the sole vessel in orbit around the planet. "Don't do this. We can save those people. It's what we do."

Lanrete looked at Uriel, their eyes locking. "The threat is too great. This is the best decision. We can discuss this later."

"Those people will be dead later."

"General, you are dismissed." Lanrete raised his voice for all on the bridge to hear.

Uriel felt like he had just been punched in the gut. The other Founder's Elite assembled looked away from him, and many looked down at the floor. He went to attention, saluting Lanrete and exiting the bridge.

Quickly making his way to his quarters, he pulled up the view from the bridge on the holodisplay. The capital ship moved to position, with the front of the ship directly facing the planet. The ship slowed down in orbital velocity as it matched the rotation of the planet. A large chamber opened at the front of the ship, unleashing destruction in a blinding beam that erupted once it impacted the surface.

The beam pierced the planet's surface and began to tunnel to the core, followed by a shock wave of fiery destruction covering the entire planet's surface.

Uriel felt saddened by the utter devastation, although this was only a taste of what was to come.

As soon as the beam came into contact with the molten, rotating core of the planet, it shifted to a blackish-silver color as the Aurtivus superweapon came online. It fired multiple pulses down the beam and into the core, magnifying the energy threshold within the planet to a level unsustainable by the planetary body. The surface began to crack, fissures of magma bleeding through to the surface.

The beam stopped, its work done, leaving the process in motion.

The capital ship jumped to suplight a moment before the planet exploded in a terrible fury with a shock wave followed by large chunks of the mantle that became impending hazards for the fleets. Molten rain flew out in all directions. It was almost beautiful in a macabre way.

All the ships started to enter suplight, the *Foundra Ascension* remaining behind as Uriel expected. The planet of Omi was no more, and the threat of the SIs that existed there was gone, along with twenty-three million Omiciri souls.

Uriel put his head in his hands and let out a slow breath. How could Lanrete kill them so easily? Why had he talked like Uriel should be expected to make the same decisions? It was one thing when you were fighting against an enemy—those who wanted nothing more than your death.

But the Omiciri had been their allies, who had come to them for help. They were just individuals who were trying to flee. To survive.

Lanrete had murdered them.

Uriel shook his head, getting up as he paced back and forth in his room. He moved to the window to view the remnants of the destruction with his own eyes. The star in the system caused the molten rain to shine like a trillion little suns.

Deep scans of the planet reveal large amounts of the molten core gone, whole areas replaced with a swirling vortex of Enesmic energy that keeps the planet together.

-FROM "ENESMIC SHIPYARD EFFECTS ON TRICA VII"
MINSCI METABASE

CHAPTER 41 - AUGRASHUMEN THE VALOROUS

Present Day
Aheraneth, Enesmic plane

Augrashumen the Valorous watched Tashanira through an ethereal window, hovering with its arms crossed. It was a towering being with six sets of wings, its head cloaked under a deep golden and silver hood, and black fire radiating from two orbs of deep purple in the place of eyes. It had no discernible face.

"You continue in your observation of the Havin Tashanira Yen Unvesal?" came a voice that caused Augrashumen to break out of its trancelike state and glance back.

The being was in the silhouette of a woman, hair-like rising smoke and with a form that was insubstantial and difficult to focus on. Wisps of purple energy rose from its hands and eyes, which gazed back at Augrashumen. Bright orbs of fire encircled Vesgrilana's midsection, the orbs passing through and around the being, seemingly one with it. Massive pauldrons of platinum and gold hung on the being's shoulders, and a set of matching armored leggings and boots completed the image with twelve sets of wings hung behind its form.

"Vesgrilana . . ." Augrashumen turned back to the window into the Havin plane. "The lines have been blurred between the planes.

She is Havin, Rel Ach'Kel, and Eshgren all at once." It turned back to regard Vesgrilana. "How does this not disturb you to the core?"

Vesgrilana's form moved forward to hover next to Augrashumen. It peered at Tashanira and then turned back to Augrashumen. "I mourn the loss of Grilmuqshen, of its sacrifice to foil the plans of the Betrayers. I acknowledge that the planes are shifting, and things are no longer as they have always been. This escalation of our conflict with the Betrayers—their machinations to push the Havin to something they were not meant to be—has done nothing but force our hand." Vesgrilana's countenance radiated a profound sadness. "But this Tashanira . . . I do not worry for what she is. No, I worry for what her child will be and what they will be capable of outside our ability to act."

"Should we destroy her?" Augrashumen bowed its head as it asked the question, resignation in its voice.

Vesgrilana touched Augrashumen gently. "No, that is not who we are." Vesgrilana began to move away from Augrashumen. "She has become Grilmuqshen's champion in the purest form. In many ways, she is Grilmuqshen now, its essence fused with hers. They are truly one." Vesgrilana smiled. "And the one named Bresha Vecen—who has become Vades, formally possessed of Sephan—is to become your champion. Such is the vision gifted to me by the Originator."

Augrashumen turned back to regard Vesgrilana with surprise in its eyes.

"She embarks on a quest to hunt Eshgren in the Havin plane as we speak. It's a noble and valorous effort."

"What of Tashanira's child?"

"That future is still in flux and not yet determined. We will see what path he walks on and whether the Eshgren can claim another champion for themselves." Vesgrilana paused. "There is much danger in his years ahead. I trust in Grilmuqshen and what it sacrificed to safeguard all we have worked toward. All we can do now is watch and influence."

CHAPTER 42 - NEVEN KENK

Firnin, Piro, Vempiir home system

The city of Firnin made Neven's skin crawl.

It had a feel of being ancient, using gothic architecture mixed with hues of red everywhere. Towering trees that appeared older than time dotted the city, a type of reverence noted in their care. They were as much a part of the city as the buildings were.

Neven walked along in a daze, trying to ignore the many crystalline eyes that glanced at him briefly before disregarding his existence. He felt insignificant in this world, even with Ellipse next to him in the towering appearance of a Vempiir woman. He was impressed with her body's adaptability—she was almost two feet taller than her normal height and considerably bulkier.

Neven watched her for a moment and then blushed. He looked away from her and to the ground, trailing behind their escort.

I'm more than happy to indulge, Ellipse said in his mind.

Neven shook his head forcefully, letting out a slow breath.

"We are here," came the dispassionate voice of their escort.

In front of them was a small building. It was a short distance from the main entry gate, more toward the center of the courtyard, which was in the city's center. The whole city of Firnin was owned and run by coven Meutrol. There were forty official covens, although only thirty-eight had representatives on the Rakeguardian Consensus, with the Meutrols among the most powerful of the ruling five. While all represented covens technically had equal standing on the Rakeguardian Consensus, the ruling five had a habit of getting their way in almost all matters, with two above all the rest. The High Master of the Vempiir was of coven Meutrol, with the High Mistress being of coven Uliyu. Those two families held almost absolute power over Piro.

Neven had been briefed on their history by Lasicov, who had felt it imperative he understood a bit more about Vempiir politics. He was grateful for it now.

The door opened before Neven as he walked in, trailed by Ellipse. The inside was impressive, with the furniture and décor exquisite but old. Everything had the feel of being created long before Neven was born. He felt like he was walking into a museum.

A woman waited for them in a sitting area past the foyer. The escort took them to the entrance to the sitting room and motioned for them to move inside. Once done, the escort departed.

"Neven Kenk." Vanether Meutrol stood. She had bright red hair done up in an elaborate construction on the top of her head. She looked like a work of art constructed by a master artist. Her skin was caramel-colored with tinges of red throughout.

He locked onto her white, crystalline eyes, staring in awe. Her gaze was hard to match, and he wanted to glance away, but he didn't. That had been one of Lasicov's many instructions, so he kept his gaze locked onto hers.

She smiled, her eyes narrowing slightly as she approached him. She was a tall woman who appeared to be middle-aged. She was at least six-foot-three with a buxom build.

Coming to a stop before Neven, she dropped a hand to her hip and glanced at Ellipse. She scanned Ellipse up and down and then disregarded her.

Ellipse frowned.

"Come. Join me and have some tea," Vanether said. She turned and walked back over to the couch, her hips swaying a bit more than they did at her approach.

Neven followed her, his gaze stuck on her behind as she turned and sat down. She motioned for Neven to sit beside her and then pointed to the seat opposite them for Ellipse.

"Thank you for your hospitality, Rakeguard Vanether," Neven said.

"So formal. Please call me Vane."

Neven sat down next to her as she rested her hand on his leg. A drone appeared beside Vanether as she picked up a steaming cup of tea and handed it to Neven. Then, she took one for herself and dismissed the drone.

Ellipse frowned and almost said something.

Remember what Lasicov said—she must think you are from a lesser coven, Neven said to Ellipse in his mind.

She sighed and leaned back in her chair. *It doesn't seem to bother her at all that you're Human,* Ellipse countered. *The Meutrols are supposed to be xenophobic isolationists.*

Yeah. I got that from the stares.

"Thank you, Vane, for your hospitality." Neven shuffled uncomfortably as Vanether started to rub his leg. "We are here because A'Amaria indicated that you have the information we're looking for regarding a cure for restoring a Das'Vin's severed *ha'ishi.*"

"I do indeed," Vanether said. She set her tea down and brought up a nearby holodisplay. "Many years ago, before the formation of the Huzien Alliance, our people were hostile toward most of the species in the Twin Galaxies. While we were not openly at war with the Das'Vin, our people prided themselves on their mastery of genetic manipulation." She puffed out her chest slightly, moving her arm from Neven's leg to the back of his chair, her bosom pushing somewhat into his shoulder. "And the Das'Vin impressed us, so naturally, we captured and experimented on them."

Neven's eyes went wide.

"It was not a glorious chapter in our history, but I assure you our people have done far worse." She smiled, showing teeth. "Either way, one of the things we found most curious was the telepathic connection formed between Das'Vin when they mated. It was an interesting phenomenon, particularly in how devastating it was when one of them died before the other." Vanether paused for a moment. "After extensive experimentation, we have theorized on an approach to restore the damaged aspects of Das'Vin physiology, one that will allow for the recreation of a new *ha'ishi*."

"If you have something so revolutionary, why haven't you shared it with the Das'Vin?" Neven asked.

"Oh, I assure you. We tried. After the formation of the Huzien Alliance, we saw it as a way to make amends for our impropriety toward those of their kind. But something about how we learned this information was a bit too much for the sensibilities of the Das'Vin scientific community."

"They refused because you killed a whole lot of Das'Vin to figure out a theoretical cure."

"Precisely. You are very astute."

"What's the potential cure?"

Vanether smiled. "That comes to my request."

Neven shuffled nervously.

"You are somewhat of a hero among the upper ranks of my coven. We acknowledge the heroic actions of all the Founder's Elites, but you specifically have captured the hearts and minds of my coven, given your genius intellect and growing renown in the scientific community. You see, Yugalen Meutrol was a cherished member of our coven, an up-and-coming star who burned out too quickly."

Vanether made a big show of wiping a tear from her eye. "She died at the battle of Tar'Ki System in a desperate attempt to defeat Sagren's forces. But you avenged her when you defeated Sagren. Because of your actions, my daughter is at peace in Anavarin, allowed entry beyond the gates. She no longer waits for us but is tasting eternity with her father. You do not know how much this means to me personally."

The intensity of Vanether's gaze caused Neven to break out into a cold sweat. "The request has to do with the matter of the Suncore warhead. It was the instrument of her demise, a weapon utilized in an attempt to turn back the tide of Sagren's forces. Our scientists have labored on this technology for millennia, but we have been unable to perfect the technology and establish a consistent reaction."

Neven felt a pit begin to form in his stomach.

"You will help us perfect this technology. The MinSci employed you in their weapons development arm, did they not?"

"I . . ." Neven glanced at Ellipse. "I am still employed by the MinSci, although on personal leave. I'm familiar with the technology, but to create something so consistently destructive is dangerous."

Vanether grinned at him, bearing her fangs. "Surely the threats our galaxy is capable of facing would serve as justification for the need of such a weapon?"

"What you're asking me to do is not something I can agree to without approval from Ecnics himself."

Vanether frowned at Neven. "Very well then. The request has changed." Her voice dropped an octave, her lips coming closer to his ear. "In the unlikely event that loyalties prevent you from fulfilling our request, I volunteered to be the instrument of your addition to our genetic pool. Your genius and courage is something we must add to our own."

"What does that . . . mean exactly?" Neven asked.

"You will physically impregnate me, and I will carry your child to term. That child will be raised within this home, one of the extremely rare non-full-blooded Vempiir to ever gain the honor of carrying the Meutrol name. You see, our coven is one of the oldest and purest of the Vempiir bloodline. We are one of the originators of the great purges that led to the refinement of our species. This is a great honor. Such acts are sacred and only done with key individuals to further solidify our power."

"What?" Ellipse asked.

Vanether glanced over at her with an air of annoyance.

"Thank you for this very gracious honor, but I must decline."

Vanether turned her gaze back to Neven and narrowed her eyes. "Surely a night of passion with me is a small price to pay for the most valuable cure in the Twin Galaxies? I will ensure that your seed does not go to waste, so only one night will be required. My body will preserve, enhance, and enrich your semen until an egg is ready to be fertilized in a few weeks. Thus is the divine blessing of female Vempiir physiology."

"I . . . that's not something I can do. You see I . . . I'm in a relationship." Neven glanced at Ellipse.

Ellipse's eyes lit up, and she smiled.

Vanether turned to face Ellipse. "Any pure-blooded Vempiir partner would understand the importance of what I offer you and willingly consent to such an arrangement." Vanether narrowed her gaze at Ellipse, subtly baring her fangs. "They would gain honor and standing among coven Meutrol."

Ellipse frowned, keeping eye contact with Vanether.

"It just doesn't feel right," Neven said.

"Very well then. That concludes our business. You have denied all of my requests, and the completion of one of them is the requirement for the information you seek."

Vanether extracted herself from Neven and stood. She clasped her hands in front of herself, her gaze locked on Neven. Her presence was imposing, her height towering over Neven as he sat on the couch. He felt the urge to shrink away from her and to avoid her gaze. But Lasicov's voice in the back of his mind forced him not to flinch or give in to his feelings.

"Can we come to some other arrangement?"

Vanether remained silent.

"I . . . am willing to do artificial insemination. If it's a child you want, I am happy to help you achieve that outcome. But sleeping with you isn't something I can do."

"Vempiir do not believe in artificial insemination. If the act is not natural, then the child is cursed to be imperfect. Our bodies have been engineered to perfection to create new life in the most natural of ways, with an orgasm necessary to trigger the semen enrichment process. I will not sully the honor with such a defilement of our beliefs."

Neven glanced at Ellipse, who had a look of distress on her face. "I need some time to think."

"Very well." Vanether walked past Neven and exited the room.

Neven stared at Ellipse with a look of disbelief. "You've got to be kidding me." He let out an exasperated breath. "A horny widow is holding the cure to restoring a *ha'ishi* hostage until I either sleep with her or build a weapon of mass destruction that could threaten the balance of power in the Twin Galaxies."

"You should do it," Ellipse said. "Sleep with her, I mean." Her eyes were downcast, her shoulders slumped.

"What?" Neven balked. "Don't let any of that stuff she said about what a pure-blooded Vempiir would do get to you. She was trying to intimidate you."

"I know. That's not it." Ellipse hugged herself. "Think of all the good you can do with that cure. All the Das'Vin who can be given the opportunity to choose whether they want to use the research—even if it's marred in blood—to become whole again. Some Das'Vin may want to silence the research due to its origins, but people should be able to make that choice themselves." Ellipse let out a sigh and glanced up at Neven.

"You're serious," Neven whispered. "You're okay with this?"

"Yes," Ellipse lied. "You should do it."

Neven rested his head in his hands, taking a few deep breaths before standing up. He stood there, his gaze locked with Ellipse's. She got up and walked over to him, wrapping her arms around him and kissing him passionately. He held her for a long moment until she released him and stepped back.

She felt like a different woman, but something about the whole exchange was still familiar, like his body recognized that it was still Ellipse in there. He turned from her and walked in the direction Vanether had gone.

He climbed a spiral staircase to a set of doors. All of them were closed except for one. He came to the entrance of an expansive bedroom. Vanether sat nude on the edge of the ornately decorated bed, a cup of wine in her hand. She had a second, already filled. She extended it toward Neven.

He thought of Dera'Liv and the countless Das'Vin who lost *dru'sha* during the Rift War, and then he walked in and closed the door.

Tentatively, he went over to the bed and sat down beside her. Vane handed him the cup of wine, and he stared at the deep-red liquid, the appearance and consistency of it reminding him a little bit too much of Human blood. He set the cup down on the nightstand and glanced at Vanether.

She grinned at him, downing the cup and throwing it casually onto the floor. She moved to straddle him, her breasts filling his vision as she rested her arms on his shoulders.

"Tell me, what positions do you favor? I may not appear it, but I am very flexible." Her voice became soft and playful.

Neven felt a sickness well up inside of him, and he gently nudged her off of him. He stared down at the ground, his heart pounding in his chest. He slowly began to undress as Vanether moved deeper onto the bed.

Fully stripped, he turned back to Vanether, her gaze eating him up. She was reclined on her side, her fingers at work between her legs.

Neven felt his body go numb, but then a thought struck him. He opened his eyes and narrowed them. "If you want my offspring to train up and unlock the potential for your weapon, why not shortcut the process? I'll give you my blood, so clone me. Considering what you did with the Das'Vin, I'm sure you'd have no moral hesitations for such a thing."

Vanether sat up, the calculating eyes from before coming back in full force. "You're sure?"

"Yes."

Vanether dropped the act and sighed in relief, disgust filling her face. She motioned for Neven to sit on the bed as a servant eventually entered with a tray holding a series of vials and a liphojam.

The servant came to Neven's side and quickly began to fill the vials, finishing without a glance at Vanether before exiting the room.

Neven rubbed his arm. The process had happened much quicker than he had anticipated. A holodisplay appeared toward the foot of the bed in the center.

"Here is the information you seek: the theorized cure for restoring the *ha'ishi*. It will require a scientist with an in-depth understanding of Das'Vin physiology to apply. There is one such Das'Vin on Desc'Ri who disagreed with the opinion of their colleagues but accepted their judgment in refusing the data."

A flood of information hit Neven's mobi: the details of the cure and the channel details of the Das'Vin on Desc'Ri.

"Considering cloning is illegal, we will simply study your genetics and learn more about how to enhance our future generations with your genetic markers."

"That's a lie. Genetic markers for a Human wouldn't correlate for Vempiir. Our DNA is different," Neven countered.

Vanether smiled. "Guess you are a genius after all." She stood with her hand on her hip, her nude body on full display. "I'm glad we were able to work out an alternative arrangement. Defiling myself with the offspring of an inferior species is an insult to what it means to be Vempiir. I'm not even sure you'd have been able to make me orgasm." She gave Neven an amused look.

Neven shook his head. "You are a horrid woman." He began to move off the bed.

Vanether narrowed her eyes. "Stories abound about our fangs, many thinking that we can drink the blood of non-Vempiir."

Neven paused as Vanether slowly moved around the other side of the bed.

"While it is true that we are capable of such an act, we do not 'drink' the blood as many believe. Rather, it's part of a cihphistic ritual called Yerrhgda that is fueled by the blood of the victim. In consuming the blood during the ritual, our bodies heal at an accelerated rate. It also gives a type of high, a rush on par with the most powerful of orgasms. The action is more drastic and fatal when performed on another Vempiir, but if we strike an artery on a non-Vempiir, well . . . then you just bleed to death."

Neven felt the threat in her words.

Get out of there, Neven! Ellipse yelled in his mind.

Vanether quickly moved around to the other side of the bed and pushed him back onto it. Her speed and strength shocked him. He wasn't sure if she had used Cihphism or if she was just that naturally fast. She used her body to pin him down, her strength surpassing his own as he struggled against her. She bared her fangs, the lust in her eyes causing Neven's heart to quicken.

"You intend to bite me and drink my blood? Like an animal?" Neven shouted.

"No, my dear. Like a Vempiir." She spoke a string of cihphistic words of power, then bit down.

Neven gasped as a spurt of blood shot into the air, coating her face and chest. Her fangs had hit an artery. His vision blurred as he attempted to struggle, but something sapped his energy. Something unnatural. His eyes went wide. He felt energy leaving his body as Vanether moaned in ecstasy above him.

The sound of the door exploding open drew Vanether's attention, and a blur knocked her off Neven and to the far side of the room.

Neven felt someone shove a wad of clothes into his arms and slap a skin patch down hard on his neck as something grabbed hold of him, quickly carrying him out of the room.

CHAPTER 43 - ELLIPSE

Firnin, Piro, Vempiir home system

Ellipse stormed out of Vanether's home with Neven in her arms, her movements a blur. Utilizing her dedicated artificial brain—augmented by the *Castrin* and no longer tied to Neven's cognitive processing limits—she had accelerated the speed at which she processed the world around her, making it seem like the physical world had stopped.

She had termed this unique ability accelerated cognitive processing or ACP. She could move in this state, making those around her barely aware of her presence and unable to process her actions.

She commanded the shuttle to open with perfect timing as she ascended the ramp, instructing it to close as she deposited Neven on one of the emergency trauma tables and exited ACP. The shuttle sealed itself and lifted off the ground, heading toward the *Castrin* in orbit.

Ellipse pulled out the medical kit and did a scan of Neven, injecting a set of nanites that went to work repairing the damage done to the artery in his neck. She engaged the automated trauma management system—or ATMS—so it immediately went to work repairing the major wound to his neck. She inserted an IV perfectly into his vein and began the act of stabilizing him with artificial blood.

Ellipse was covered in his blood, and her gaze kept getting stuck on it. She entered ACP again and sat there processing for a long moment. She examined the situation of the past day, replaying the scene back and forth hundreds of times. She recognized where she had erred, the decision that she had made, thinking he would appreciate the freedom she gave him to do what was needed.

She hated that decision. She felt an emotion rise in her that was unfamiliar. Ellipse spent some time processing it.

Disgust. She was disgusted with herself. Why? Ellipse spent some time processing that, using her connection to the ship and GNet to survey a flood of data about emotions, relationships, and cultures.

It clicked in her mind; she was disgusted that she had given Neven consent to sleep with another woman. She focused on that emotion and stored it away to hold on to. She slowed her processing speed to that of real-time, coming out of ACP.

The ATMS eventually signaled that its repair was complete. Ellipse looked up to see a bandage affixed to Neven's neck as Neven's eyes locked on hers.

"I'm sorry," Ellipse said. "I shouldn't have given you my consent."

"It's not your fault. It was my decision." Neven let out a sigh. "Thank you for saving my life. I messed up, and I insulted her. Lasicov said to avoid that at all costs."

"Don't apologize for that monster," Ellipse countered.

"Heh, I'm not made out for this life of interspecies politics and dirty business dealing. I should just return to Thae and go back to the MinSci."

Ellipse activated ACP again, running through multiple probability simulations of that scenario. She analyzed the likelihood of Neven becoming a Feshra—the probability was below thirty percent. She extrapolated from there to include more experience as a Secnic, specifically within the Founder's Elite, and the probability jumped to ninety percent. Accounting for the increased likelihood of death or catastrophic event impairing his abilities, the probability dropped to eighty percent.

She moved back to real-time.

"We both know you don't want that." Ellipse sat beside Neven, her body transforming from a Vempiir into her usual self.

The golden glow from her eyes caused Neven to glance up at her. She locked eyes with him. He quickly turned away, his gaze stuck on the ceiling.

"I don't know what I want anymore. The desire to be a Feshra has been the only constant in my life. But I'm starting to question whether it's truly worth this price." Neven rested his hands over his eyes. "Zun dies, and my life falls apart. I have an affair with Tashanira, get her pregnant, and destroy Jenshi's life. Now, I willingly give my blood to a heartless Vempiir politician with plans to clone me and force that clone to perfect their weapons. I can't tell you how terrible that thought is—to know that someone who looks like me, speaks like me, and for all intents and purposes *is* me will spend their life in this hell."

"We can tell Lanrete. He can make sure your clone never sees the light of day. If not officially, then by other means," Ellipse said.

"You're right." Neven let out a relieved sigh.

"What do you intend to do now?"

"Finish this. We'll go to the Das'Vin scientist on Desc'Ri, and then we'll take Tashanira back to Peshkana for the birth of our child." Neven hesitated. "And then . . . I'll return to where I lost Zun and say my final goodbye."

Ellipse watched Zun die again, the scene playing back with crystal clarity. She watched Neven break down, that moment that had shattered him so clear and painful. She felt the rush of emotions that coursed through him in that moment, the intensity of them overpowering her.

Ellipse's eyes began to water, and a tear streaked down her cheek.

Neven looked at her with shock. "You're crying? How?"

She smiled sadly. "When will you realize that I'm a real woman, Neven? My flesh may be artificial, and my internal 'organs' not like any type of normal biology, but this body isn't just a facsimile. It's the full package. I've improved on your design and evolved it to be something more. I've engineered every aspect of myself to be perfect. For you."

"Ellipse . . ."

Ellipse shushed him and put her hand to his face. "I want to be with you, Neven. And not just as an escape. I want to be something much more." She hesitated. "I want to spend life together, not just as friends or partners, but committed to each other. I won't ever make the mistake I made back there with that Vempiir. I don't care how many ways it could save the galaxy." She got up and positioned herself closer to Neven, her upper body in his full view. "I would rather cease to exist than see you with another woman while I sit idly by and accept it."

"Ellipse . . ." Neven stared into her golden eyes.

She felt his memories play out, their interactions flashing in his mind's eye. The first time they kissed, the first time he truly noticed her as more than a machine, and the first time they made love. She experienced every memory with him, augmenting them with her own perfect reproduction of those moments, increasing the intensity of the experience.

Ellipse had been there at his worst and his best. She was alive. She was a sentient being, completely removed from the entity that was once the SSI still figuring out the universe.

She saw that revelation hit him. Saw as he realized that the being in front of him was something more. Something better than Human.

She stoked that wheel as it turned in his mind, becoming a new purpose, a new perspective in which he saw the world and his existence. He recognized that she was the key to it all—she was the future, and together, they would bring that future to life.

Ellipse smiled as her eyes lit up.

"Will you marry me?" Neven asked.

"Yes!"

Castrin *en route to Desc'Ri, Huzien Alliance space*

Tashanira glanced up as Ellipse entered Neven's suite. She tilted her head curiously.

Ellipse crossed her arms in front of her chest and stopped a short distance from where Tashanira was meditating on a mat.

"I'm going to need you to return to your room," Ellipse said.

"Meow," Tashanira said.

"Neven and I are engaged to be married." Ellipse held up her hand, now wearing a ring crafted by Neven.

"What?" Tashanira blinked repeatedly. "Are you serious?"

Ellipse could detect Tashanira's heart rate rise, followed by an apparent wave of fear and then disappointment that rushed across her features. Tashanira looked down at the ground. Ellipse watched her force that air of self-confidence that she wore like armor.

She activated ACP and took some time to process Tashanira's reaction. Why had Tashanira responded the way she had? Ellipse queried her metabase of Uri culture, digging through years of Uri shows from the GNet in accelerated playback. After processing thousands of videos, Ellipse gained an understanding of that unique display of emotions.

Ellipse deactivated ACP and narrowed her eyes, carefully watching Tashanira's future reactions. "Yes. He proposed to me on the shuttle ride back to the ship." Ellipse relaxed her stance. "And I don't feel comfortable with you sleeping in the same room as him."

"Huh." Tashanira rubbed her eyes. She got up and stretched her back, her hands resting on her belly. She stared at Ellipse for a long moment, long enough for Ellipse to recognize the resentment in her gaze. "I get it. I can see why, but wow. Congratulations, I guess." Tashanira gave a tight-lipped smile. "Although, is it not fair to want the comfort of the father of your child as you deal with the reality of carrying their child through pregnancy?" Tashanira spat the words, the bitterness pungent. She closed her eyes and then let out a slow breath. "I can adjust, of course. It's not like we—*vusg*. Just . . . he's kind to me, and I appreciate how he treats me." Tashanira stared at the ground for a long moment, then raised an eyebrow at Ellipse. "I'm curious though. Why do you care about marriage?"

"What do you mean?"

"I mean, you're a sentient machine. A synthetic life-form. Why adopt a relationship dynamic that is so bland and archaic? Throuples are where it's at, or even open relationships."

"Something isn't archaic just because you don't see the value in it," Ellipse countered.

"What is the value you see in a monogamous relationship?"

"Commitment. You eliminate the uncertainty in the boundaries of the relationship."

"People cheat all the time." Tashanira lifted her hands in the air as if presenting herself. "Being in a monogamous marriage doesn't stop that. If anything, it makes it more traumatic because you both lie to yourselves, ignoring other attractions in your sphere instead of embracing them."

Ellipse took Tashanira's words as a threat. "So, you've become jaded to the concept of monogamy out of all this? I figured you'd go the other way and realize the error of your ways." Ellipse tilted her head, dropping a hand to her hip.

Tashanira scowled. "My error was committing myself to Jenshi. In retrospect, I did it because it was what he wanted, but it wasn't what I wanted. He was a good time, little more than a fling. I tried to attach emotions to that when he wanted more from our relationship." Tashanira shook her head. "My perspective has changed. This whole immortality thing causes you to think. I mean, what's commitment when any person I marry will die, leaving me alone to deal with that loss before moving on to the next relationship? Why not avoid that whole setup and save myself the heartbreak?"

"That's almost a convincing argument." Ellipse smirked as Tashanira avoided eye contact. "You've taken to reading Lanrete's philosophy books, I see."

"Yeah, I know, right? Before, I couldn't stomach the things, but now they are like gold. Everything makes so much more sense. I finally get what he's talking about." She glanced down at the ground. "Having all this time to think and to explore myself has been valuable." Tashanira glanced back up at Ellipse. "You know, you're probably immortal too—the materials you're made from last millennia without even trying. And you can upgrade, improve, and switch bodies. I mean, look at the *Foundra Ascension*. That ship has been around for tens of thousands of years. What are you going to do when Neven dies?"

Ellipse activated ACP and replayed Tashanira's words repeatedly. She pulled information related to Human life expectancy and internalized it. She tried to process the feelings of emotion associated with loss; they overwhelmed her. She returned to real-time and shuddered, tears streaming down her face. She collapsed to the ground, crying, her body shaking with sobs.

Tashanira rushed over to her. "I'm sorry for saying anything. I'm . . . I'm sure it will all work out," she said.

"No, you're right. I—Neven—he—"

Ellipse went back into ACP. A plan started to form in her mind, a seemingly impossible plan. She ran multiple simulations, analyzing for hours.

She dropped into real-time, glanced up at Tashanira, and stood, wiping away the tears. "Thank you." Ellipse turned and started to walk out of the suite. She hesitated at the door, looking back at Tashanira's belly. "Do you love Neven?"

"What?" Tashanira's eyes went wide.

"Have you developed feelings for him?"

"No." Tashanira lied.

Ellipse watched Tashanira for a long moment. She had detected the biological indicators signaling the lie but didn't know how to respond to that knowledge. She frowned, looking Tashanira up and down.

"Please pack your things and return to your room as soon as possible. Thanks for your understanding." Ellipse walked out of the suite.

CHAPTER 44 - TASHANIRA YEN UNVESAL

Castrin en route to Desc'Ri, Huzien Alliance space

Tashanira barged into Neven's lab, stomping her feet as she made her way over to the workbench he was occupied with. He looked up at her in confusion as she stopped before him, her hands dropping to her hips.

"You're getting married to Ellipse?" Tashanira yelled. There was an edge in her voice, her eyes narrowed.

Neven leaned back, watching Tashanira carefully.

She noticed the large bandage on his neck, and her eyes widened. "What happened?" She moved over to him and began doting over him with a discerning eye.

Neven chuckled and patted her side. "I'm fine. It's already mostly healed." Neven let out a sigh. "To your question, yes, I am." Neven scratched his arm. "Why does it matter to you? You made it clear you had no interest in marrying me some time ago."

Tashanira backed away from Neven, resuming an annoyed posture toward him. "You asked that question out of fear, afraid of how having a baby out of wedlock would be perceived by others." Tashanira huffed. "The reasoning was wrong."

Neven sighed and took Tashanira by the hand, walking her to a room at the side of the lab area, a place filled with furniture. He sat down on the couch and motioned for her to do likewise.

"What is our relationship?" he asked.

"What does it matter? You're engaged to be married to a sentient sex toy."

"Stop avoiding the question. Do you love me?"

"Do *you* love *me*?" Tashanira countered. Her eyes lifted slightly.

Neven hesitated for a long moment. He let out a heavy sigh. "I do." Neven put his face in his hands.

Tashanira's mouth dropped open as she glanced away from Neven. Her heart fluttered, and she stared at the ground for a long moment, joy rising in her.

"But I also love Ellipse," he said. "I can't explain it . . . I . . ."

"That's okay." Tashanira put her hand to his cheek. She kissed him, a long, sensual kiss. "You can love multiple partners. There is nothing wrong with that."

Neven shook his head. "No, I can't. I have to choose. I can't love two women in the same way." Neven rubbed the bridge of his nose. "We didn't grow up in similar environments. I feel that what you propose is wrong. I don't judge you for thinking that way, but I can't accept that as a life choice for myself."

"And so you've chosen Ellipse." Tashanira moved her hand away. She glanced away from Neven, fighting the urge to shed a tear. She crossed her arms, secretly pinching herself to bring focus to the physical pain, attempting to minimize the emotional pain coursing through her in that moment.

"You didn't answer the question," Neven said.

"If I said I did love you, what would it matter now?" Tashanira looked at Neven, her face becoming hard. "Would that change your mind? Would you marry me instead?"

"Is that what you want?" Neven turned to face Tashanira fully. "I have a responsibility to you because of our child. If you want me to marry you, I will do it."

"I don't want your responsibility, Neven."

Tashanira got up and walked out of the room in a daze. Neven chased after her, quickly moving to stand in front of her. She

frowned at him, an eyebrow raising as she crossed her arms. A tear slid down her cheek, and she quickly wiped it away, hoping Neven didn't see it.

Neven kissed her. She pressed into the kiss, the two of them embracing for a long moment. Neven broke the kiss first and stared into Tashanira's eyes.

"That's not what I meant. I mean, if you love me, that changes everything." Neven's voice was a whisper.

Tashanira couldn't break eye contact. She searched for the truth in his words, and when she found it, she felt terror. It overwhelmed her, and she broke eye contact.

"I don't love you," she lied. She separated herself from Neven and walked past him without looking at him, making her way to the meglift. She hesitated there for a moment, glancing back at Neven.

His gaze was on the floor, his fist clenched. His face was a mask.

She stepped onto the meglift and silently cursed herself. She held it all in, waiting until she was in the sanctity of her room before letting the emotions flow. She spent time processing those emotions: heartbreak, anger, resentment, jealousy, and fear.

That last emotion surprised her. Why had she been terrified of telling Neven the truth?

Her mind went to Ellipse—the concept of her caused Tashanira to take in a deep breath and slowly let it out. Did she fear retaliation from Ellipse? Would Ellipse harm her? She *had* almost killed A'Amaria. Would she kill Tashanira for stealing her man?

Tashanira shook her head. She couldn't imagine Ellipse doing that.

Tashanira tried to despise Ellipse, but she couldn't hold that grudge. Neven had given her the opportunity to change it all and to switch his choice to her. She had refused.

Tashanira let out a slow breath and moved to her meditation mat. She went through the motions, clearing her mind as she accepted her choice.

The efficiency of resource harvesting by the shipyards is to a level not capable of by current mining technology.

-FROM "ENESMIC SHIPYARD EFFECTS ON TRICA VII"
MINSCI METABASE

CHAPTER 45 – URIEL KERVID

76003 FA (4,120 years ago)
Huza City Outskirts, Thae, Huzien home system

Uriel stared at the entrance to Lanrete's home, uneasiness in his gut. His glands pumped focusing agents into his system, their effectiveness having dropped substantially due to how frequently he used them now.

With a heavy sigh, he walked through the door and into the foyer. He passed the rotunda and was greeted by A'Amaria, who was coming down the stairs. She wore a white sundress with a low cut and lots of cleavage.

He forced a smile.

"Uriel! It's so good to see my handsome son-in-law," A'Amaria said. She stopped directly in front of him, tilting her head to the side.

He watched her carefully, trying not to let his dislike of her show through.

"Why so tense?" She moved to his back and began to massage his shoulders.

"Just thinking about the upcoming mission." Uriel stepped away from her and moved quickly through the foyer toward the rotunda.

"Ah, the hunt for Yuemon," A'Amaria said. "Dirty business with those Chaah." She followed him, sticking to his side, her proximity too close for comfort.

Uriel quickly made his way into Lanrete's study. He glanced around, confused. "Where is Lanrete?"

"Oh, he had to head into Huza unexpectedly. He'll be back later tonight." A'Amaria moved to recline on a chair in the study, falling into it with a wicked grin. She put one leg up on the armrest, an action that spread her legs wide, revealing that she wore no underwear. "Guess that leaves you and little ole me to get in some quality time together."

Uriel frowned, the action causing A'Amaria to pout.

"What? You don't like spending time with your dear old *lurra*?"

Uriel held his tongue, the thought of A'Amaria being any sort of mother figure in his life sickening. "Sorry. Like I said, my mind is occupied. Meant no disrespect," Uriel said.

A'Amaria got up from the chair and walked up to Uriel again. "I've made you a meal." She tried to catch his eyes as Uriel glanced away from her. "Surely, coming all the way here from the *Ascension* must have worked up an appetite."

Before Uriel could respond, she gripped his hand and led him toward the dining room. Uriel reluctantly complied, trying his best not to recoil from her touch.

"Servants, attend us!" A'Amaria called out.

Uriel could hear the hurried movements of multiple people as they entered the dining room. The food was on the table and ready to be served more quickly than he had expected. A'Amaria released Uriel's hand and motioned for him to sit, taking the seat across from him. They ate their meal in awkward silence, after which Uriel dismissed himself and made his way up to the bedroom generally reserved for him at the mansion. He collapsed onto his bed, letting out a heavy sigh, and quickly passed out. The dreams haunted him, robbing him of rest.

A knock at his door caused Uriel to sit up and stare at the door. He mulled not responding for a moment, and then A'Amaria's voice rang out.

"Dear *burush?*"

Getting up, he made his way over to the door and opened it slightly.

A'Amaria was standing there. She wore a thin robe as if she had just gotten out of a VRC. "I wanted to check in on you before I retired for the night."

She pushed past him and into his room, moving to sit at the bottom of his bed. She patted the spot next to her and smiled at Uriel. He stared at her for a long moment and then moved to sit next to her. She patted his leg.

"You know, I'm always so glad to see you."

Uriel didn't respond.

She rose and moved to sit on his leg, wrapping her arms around his neck. Uriel felt his stomach tighten.

"Lanrete is concerned about you," A'Amaria said.

"How so?" Uriel asked, her words catching him off guard.

"He is worried that you don't get your dick wet enough." A'Amaria gave a wicked grin. "When was the last time? That Ken'Tar girl on Tar'Ki two months ago?"

Uriel pushed A'Amaria off his leg and got up. "My sex life is none of your concern. Please leave," Uriel said.

A'Amaria's robe had opened, revealing no clothes underneath in a slit that went down the front. She let it hang open, standing with one shoulder down slightly, causing the robe to slip off more.

Uriel looked away as she moved toward him again.

"Have you ever tasted Hauxem pussy? Those who try it for the first time say it tastes like a variation of honey—an interesting quality of Hauxem biology. Makes you want to suck a woman dry."

"What you are doing is an affront against my *burratha*. I won't be any part of this. I've told you no before, and it will always be no. I respect my *burratha* too much to destroy our relationship over you."

A'Amaria pulled the robe back on, slowly tying the belt that had come undone. "Huzien culture is so hard to adapt to." A'Amaria feigned surprise. "There would be nothing wrong with this in my culture."

"This isn't Hauxem culture. You're an *eifi*, wife to a Huzien, and a very traditional one at that." Uriel scowled. "But of course, you know this. You just don't care. Lanrete should be told the truth about you."

A'Amaria's eyes flickered dangerously, causing Uriel to take a step back. "You think I don't know about the little recordings you take of our encounters?" A'Amaria gave him a haughty look. "The data you've amassed on me to blackmail me?" She stepped forward, prompting Uriel to take another step back and bump into his bed. "I know how you took down Fleet Admiral Retyu Dewerter, getting him killed by Lanrete on his own ship. What did he do that crossed you?" A'Amaria gave a malevolent smile to Uriel. "What set off the vengeful engine that is Uriel Kervid?"

"He did nothing to me. He was simply a terrible man. And I have no intention of blackmailing you. Lanrete just needs to know the truth."

A'Amaria's eyes went wide, her face becoming serious. "You ended a man's life based on nothing but your extremist sense of morality?"

"Lanrete thinks the same way," Uriel said.

A'Amaria laughed. "That's where you're wrong. I can say for certain that I know him better than you do." A'Amaria moved to sit near the window of Uriel's room. "When he finishes *vusging* you and then immediately orders the death of others and listens to fleet reports while you suck his dick, you learn a thing or two about what truly drives powerful men." A'Amaria grinned at Uriel. "And it's not your false sense of morality."

"I've known Lanrete for a long time."

"My dear *burush*, I've fulfilled his every twisted sexual fantasy. I pump his balls dry every morning before he even fully opens his eyes." A'Amaria smirked. "Please. Don't pretend to lecture me about my *nusba* of a millennium."

"It doesn't matter. Lanrete needs to know who you truly are."

"And do you know who he truly is?" A'Amaria's eyes flickered again as she got up. "You remember Enara? The Tuzen princess whom you had a love child with?"

"Of course I remember her."

Uriel sat down. He still had vivid dreams of the death of their child, and more recent ones involved her as she killed herself in macabre ways. He felt his focus slipping, weariness overtaking him suddenly.

The world around him shifted. He was now standing in the hallway aboard the *Guysuma'revhia*, a squad of Lux'Ameni soldiers in front of him. They leveled their weapons at him.

Uriel slammed his system with another focusing cocktail, reality blurring back in momentarily.

"I did some digging around the death of the child. I thought it so strange that the child of a princess could die in so simple a mistake. I mean—you have the best help in the galaxy, and yet it takes them hours to even find the body?"

That fact had been nagging at Uriel for a long time. Having it called out so plainly caused him to break out into a cold sweat. His stomach started to churn, his heart pounding as his vision blurred slightly.

"There was a call between Lanrete and Tirivus two days before the death of the child. What's interesting about the call . . ." A'Amaria walked over to stand before Uriel, tapping her finger on her chin. Her diminutive stature towered over him in that moment as he looked up at her from his sitting position. ". . . is that the contents of that conversation were conveniently expunged from the HIN records. Do you know how odd that is?" A'Amaria took another step forward, looking down on Uriel with a vengeful gaze. "Records are never expunged from the HIN. There is no need. You just restrict the conversation and cut out anyone who shouldn't have access to it. But this one was deleted," A'Amaria paused, gaining energy from the tension now in the air, "because you and Lanrete have the same access level. All information is available to you as it is to me." A'Amaria tapped her chin again. "But conversations always happen on two ends, and I was able to find the other side of that conversation." She moved to straddle him, resting her arms on his shoulders. "You'd be surprised what life-changing sums of money can buy you from even the most loyal of people." A'Amaria brought up a holodisplay that showed the call from Tirivus's perspective.

Lanrete was visible on the screen.

"An immortal," Tirivus said. *"Lanrete, do you understand the implications of this?"*

Lanrete let out a sigh.

"Word has already gotten out of the child's existence. If my enemies get this information, I will lose control. There will be riots in the streets."

"Are there any around the child who can be used?" Lanrete asked.

"There is one: a caregiver. She can be bought," Tirivus said.

"The Liajhem?" Lanrete asked.

"I've talked with Anima. She understands. She doesn't agree, but she understands. They will look the other way."

"Do it," Lanrete said. *"For the stability of your empire. May our children forgive us."*

Uriel stared as the recording froze, his mind swirling. He slowly turned back to A'Amaria.

She was watching him carefully, her face too close. "Do you see now why your morality is pointless?" She leaned into Uriel, their lips close as her hot breath hit his face.

The soldiers were before him, their weapons aimed for the kill.

Uriel lashed out.

A'Amaria was thrown back with such force that she broke through the wall and into the hallway. He stood up, drawing Wishwonder as he walked into the hallway toward more soldiers in his way.

A'Amaria scrambled up, her robe torn and halfway off her body, silverish-white blood oozing out of a cut that went the length of her arm. There were a few other cuts across her body. She cradled her arm, the bone broken. There was fear in her eyes.

"How dare you challenge me," Uriel spoke to the soldiers who advanced toward him with weapons drawn.

"This is authentic," A'Amaria countered, confusion on her face.

Uriel didn't hear her as she sent over the video to him along with the relevant validators, stating that the video hadn't been faked.

Uriel stopped, reality seeping back in around him. He stared at the information for a long time, trying to process what was happening. He dropped Wishwonder. The servants rushed upstairs to see the two of them and then immediately hid.

"Lan was involved in the death of your child," A'Amaria said. "He and Tirivus. From what I can ascertain, Enara's suicide wasn't faked. Tirivus was shocked that she took her own life."

The sound of someone entering the home drew Uriel's attention. A'Amaria pulled back on her tattered robe and telekinetically shifted past him and downstairs. Uriel stared at Wishwonder and slowly bent down to pick it up. Uriel looked around at the mess, his heart beating rapidly. He tried to push more focusing agents through his body, but it did not respond as expected.

"Uriel! Explain yourself," Lanrete shouted.

Uriel gripped Wishwonder tight in his hand and then turned, heading toward the home entrance. A'Amaria clung to Lanrete's side, her eyes wide with genuine fear. A servant had started tending to the wound on her arm.

"You killed my child?" Uriel asked. That fact had become clear to him, bubbling up through the surface of the shifting reality around him.

Lanrete blinked a few times and then glanced at A'Amaria with a frown. He slowly turned back to look at Uriel.

"Let's talk about this. Don't make decisions you'll regret," Lanrete said.

"Like sanctioning the murder of your grandson? Did you regret that decision?"

"Uriel, calm down. I see you're upset." Lanrete put his hand on Divinebreath, which was strapped at his waist.

The world around Uriel shifted again. This time, he saw an Alliance separatist—the terrorist had a Huzien blade drawn. Uriel charged at the man, swinging Wishwonder hard.

Lanrete pushed A'Amaria to the side and charged forward, Divinebreath connecting with his weapon. Lanrete kicked forward, and Uriel absorbed the hit as the two danced. Their weapons clashed in a fury as Uriel yelled, raw emotion running through him. Uriel spun, coming across with a downward strike. Lanrete intercepted the blade, driving the tip down to the ground. Uriel kicked out, knocking Lanrete back. Uriel sliced the floor as he charged forward with an upward slice. Lanrete dodged to the side, bringing his blade across to intercept Uriel's feint. Uriel reversed momentum and sliced Lanrete across the arm with a rapid spin attack, Cihphism enhancing his movements.

All the pain, hurt, and frustration that had built up for millennia from the loss of the only woman he had ever loved mixed with a desire to protect and save Alliance citizens from this terrorist from his memories.

Uriel thought of the child he had created with Enara, born of their passionate love for each other and how that life was wrongfully stolen from them. Uriel roared as Lanrete disengaged and stormed through the front door and out onto the open grounds; the sun long set, patches of darkness pierced by light from the mansion. Uriel followed the separatist, launching into a flurry of attacks that Lanrete struggled to match with an injured arm. First blood drove Uriel into a frenzy.

Uriel ignited the space around Lanrete, but he dodged, coming back up with only singed hair. Uriel was hurting and wanted to make his enemy hurt; he unleashed a lefon blast that destroyed a section of the house, screams coming from within. He followed that up by igniting the landscape around them, the explosion of heat causing both men to sweat.

Lanrete stayed on the defensive, unleashing a blast of wind that silenced the flames immediately around them. Lanrete kept his injured arm close to his side as he intercepted another strike from Uriel and parried twice more, backstepping each time to stay outside Uriel's kill zone.

Pure instinct drove Uriel as he continued to press on the terrorist in his mind's eye; victory was close at hand. He could see the man slowing, becoming sloppy, desperate. The necklace around Uriel's neck flared. He grasped at his neck as the necklace shocked him, his body wracked in excruciating pain.

He collapsed to the ground, his world going dark.

Uriel awakened in the brig of the *Foundra Ascension*.

Lanrete stood on the other side of the shielded glass, looking down at him, his face hard. Uriel looked down at his chest. The necklace was still there, and burn marks covered his skin.

Uriel ripped the necklace off and threw it to the side. "Always prepared for the worst possible outcome, huh?" Uriel asked. He glanced up at Lanrete. "Even have contingencies for your own *burush*."

"Hiding advanced PTSD from me and the chief medical officer." Lanrete shook his head. "If A'Amaria had not been a gifted Cihphist, you could have killed her with your episode. Multiple members of the house staff are injured because of your actions." Lanrete crossed his arms. "What's wrong with you?"

"Why did you do it?" Uriel whispered.

Lanrete let out a heavy sigh. "I planned to tell you one day. I just needed you to move on. To start a new family and experience joy."

"I had joy!" Uriel yelled, his voice quickly calming. "You and Tirivus took that from me."

"You have to be better, Uriel. You must recognize the importance of these decisions and not put yourself in situations where actions must be taken on your behalf."

Uriel looked back up at Lanrete. He stared at the man he had called his father for a long moment, then broke eye contact. "Are we done?" he asked.

"No. Far from it, but I need to return to the surface. When I'm back, we'll talk. We have treatments for this. What you did by letting this go for so long was dangerous. Maker help me, but I'll put you through reconditioning if I have to." Lanrete turned as if about to walk away. "You'll stay in the brig until I return, for your safety and the safety of the crew."

CHAPTER 46 - NEVEN KENK

Un'Nee, Desc'Ri, Das'Vin home system

Neven rubbed his hand, staring at the door leading into their rental estate's living room area. The estate was located on one of the premier beaches in Un'Nee, the most desired place to live on Desc'Ri.

It was beautiful, and Lasicov had outdone himself.

Neven tried to appreciate everything around him, but he could only think of the Das'Vin waiting on the other side of that door. He had this dread that there would be some complication or stipulation that prevented him from reaching his goal and going to mourn Zun.

He stared at the door for a long moment and then took a deep breath, stepping through.

Ellipse was sitting with Feshra Zeh'Jer Uina Dester on a couch facing the beach. They were an old Das'Vin with dark-blue hair that seemed to have lost some of its luster, although their inquisitive hazel eyes watched Ellipse curiously. They had lightly tanned khaki skin, and their hands were wrinkled. The hues of silver in their skin were still there but not as shiny as Neven had seen in other Das'Vin like Serah'Elax and Dera'Liv.

Zeh'Jer glanced at Neven as he entered the room. "Ah, my most gracious host." Zeh'Jer glanced out at the ocean, smiling. "I have always loved Un'Nee, and to enjoy it from such a marvelous home is truly a treasure."

Neven walked over and sat down across from them on an adjacent couch. "Thank you for agreeing to meet, Feshra Zeh'Jer."

"Please. Just Zeh'Jer. And I should be the one to thank you." Zeh'Jer raised an eyebrow, glancing at Neven. "To have a potential cure within reach." They looked down at the ground, rubbing their hand. "I thought I wouldn't live to see this day."

Neven brought up a holodisplay, showcasing the theorized cure, which was detailed in a series of reports. He transferred the information to Zeh'Jer. They studied the reports silently for a long moment, their eyes slowly lighting up. "I see." Zeh'Jer nodded their head. "This is remarkable. It's abominable in how they discovered it, but it is remarkable."

"Will it work?" Neven asked.

"I don't know. I'll have to perform the procedure, detail out the recovery program they outlined here, and find a Das'Vin willing to undergo the process."

"I think I may have someone who would be willing to do that," Neven said.

"Very well. I will get things ready. It will take some time, but I will notify you when I'm ready to take them through the procedure." Zeh'Jer smiled at Neven. "You have given something priceless to the Das'Vin people. I don't know how many will accept this treatment once they understand how this knowledge was obtained, but I can at least help those who are willing. One thing I learned in the MinSci that my compatriots don't acknowledge is that it is important to focus on the progress itself and not always the means of achieving progress." They hesitated. "Considering the Vempiir sought a high price for their 'gift' when they offered it to us many years ago, I am assuming this came with a high cost from the Vempiir."

"A high personal cost, yes," Neven said.

"Then what can I do for you, Mr. Kenk?"

Neven shook his head. "I don't need anything. Thank you."

"Please. Let me at least perform a psych-telepathic analysis. El-lipse highlighted some of the trauma you have recently experienced, a not-insignificant portion of it at the hands of a very powerful telepath. The field of trauma's effect on our biology is my specialty, after all."

"You've worked with Humans?"

"Of course. I spent most of my career in the MinSci, and we are more alike than many realize."

Neven glanced to Ellipse. She was still in her Human form, but instead of golden eyes, she had transformed them into light brown. She truly looked Human. Neven felt an urging from her to agree to Zeh'Jer's procedure.

Letting out a sigh, he conceded. Turning back to Zeh'Jer, he nodded at them. They moved to sit beside him, taking one of his hands into theirs. They put the other on his temple and locked gazes with him.

"I will need you to open your mind to me for this analysis to complete. I assure you, I am licensed to perform this procedure."

Neven nodded and dropped the subconscious barrier he had learned from Soahc—the one that protected his mind from telepath-ic intrusion and that had been defeated by A'Amaria in that terrible moment when she had assaulted him. He felt Zeh'Jer immediately move into his mind, but unlike A'Amaria's attack, they were gentle and respectful as they prodded.

He sat there for a long moment as he seemed to float in a sea of emotions, conscious thought in a state of flux. He couldn't hold on to a memory for long before it was gently moved away from him, quickly replaced with another for examination.

This continued for some time until a sharp pain caused him to gasp. Zeh'Jer's gentle touch immediately shifted, seeming to go on the defensive. Neven was confused as another presence lashed out. Zeh'Jer suppressed it, their mastery impressive.

Neven felt something ripped out of his subconscious, and an overwhelming sense of relief washed over him. He returned to consciousness as the world came back into focus around him. He blinked his eyes repeatedly.

Zeh'Jer was watching him with a measured expression on their face as they wiped away a drip of blood that ran down from Neven's nose. "I apologize for the momentary discomfort toward the end there. You had a remnant of a very powerful telepath buried deep in your subconscious. I would have missed it if I had not encountered similar techniques before. It was cleverly hidden, masked as desire." Zeh'Jer patted Neven on the hand and got up, walking toward the tall window that faced the ocean. "When done in that way, it can easily influence you."

"A'Amaria," Neven said. "She's the one who assaulted me."

"I saw. The imprint she left behind was dangerous. Such imprints can alter your thinking, and the subtle nature of it is nefarious and highly effective. The main portion of the imprint had been removed by another, but a fragment was still there. It's gone now."

That explains some things, Ellipse said to him telepathically.

"Thank you."

Neven sat back in his seat, staring at the ocean. He felt a sense of peace wash over him, and then he started to cry. Ellipse moved to sit beside him and pulled him close to her. She held him as he sobbed into her chest. Zeh'Jer excused themself and left the living room.

"Maybe we should spend some time here. Lasicov said we could have this home for as long as needed," Ellipse said.

Neven sat up, wiping his eyes. He nodded, his gaze going back out of the window. "Yeah, I'd like that."

CHAPTER 47 - TASHANIRA YEN UNVESAL

Five Months Later
Castrin *in orbit around Peshkana, Uri home system*

Tashanira stared at her body in the mirror, her very pregnant belly on full display. She rubbed it subconsciously and then glanced out of the dressing room of her quarters to the bright blue and green orb taking up the full view of her window.

"Peshkana . . ." Tashanira whispered to herself. "It's been so long."

She took in a deep breath and slowly let it out. She selected a traditional dress that was common for pregnant Uri in her tribe. Within seconds, drones dressed her, and a set of assistants applied makeup to her face to show her tribal colors. It was a form of celebration for her people.

When all was done, she stared at herself for a long moment. The outfit had various slits, exposing her fur in different areas, and her stomach was fully exposed with hues of brown and silver. The material was soft but durable, appearing handmade.

This felt right.

Tashanira stepped out of the dressing area and exited her room. Neven was waiting there for her. He had on clothing that matched hers, except the slits revealed nothing but his dark-olive skin.

Her eyes lit up. "You wore it," Tashanira said.

"You said it was customary." Neven rubbed the back of his neck.

Tashanira nodded, grinning at him. She headed toward the meglift, and Neven followed her.

"Surprised your wifey isn't here," she said.

"She headed down to the surface with Lasicov to help get things settled."

"And left me alone with you?" Tashanira grinned. She glanced back toward her quarters. "Up for a quickie? For old time's sake?"

"I've still got my eyes on you!" Ellipse's voice sounded from the speaker in the meglift, clearly annoyed.

Tashanira laughed.

They arrived in the shuttle bay and boarded a shuttle that took off from the *Castrin* toward the surface. Tashanira felt her nerves racing as they descended to the planet.

Neven gripped her hand. She looked up at him and forced a smile, glancing back out the window. After a few minutes, the sound of the shuttle depressurizing grabbed her attention. Neven stood up and extended a hand toward her. She sighed and took hold of it as Neven helped her stand.

Tashanira took a moment to acclimate herself to Peshkana's gravity. It was a massive planet—the largest inhabited planet on record in the Twin Galaxies. Thankfully, they had slowly ramped up the gravity on the *Castrin* to help with the transition to Peshkana, meaning that Tashanira's muscles quickly adjusted.

They exited the shuttle as a crowd waited for them. A cheer went up, followed by heavy use of drums accompanying a song that caused a tear to roll down Tashanira's cheek. All of this was for her. She saw her sister in the crowd and embraced her as she approached.

"Yuh fur! Yuh luk suh different amazing." Tetenira Yen Unvesal did a quick walk around Tashanira, clicking her tongue. "Bout time sista had mi worry yuh wouldn't gi wi a baby, yeah?" she asked.

She had a thick accent and spoke in a dialect that had developed on Peshkana after the Huzien colonization millennia ago.

It was influenced by the combination of their past language and the language the Huziens brought with them. Tashanira glanced back at Neven with an embarrassed smile and then looked to her sister.

"Did haffi find a gud man fos. Cyaa just mek a baby wid any baddy," Tashanira spoke back, matching the dialect of her sister perfectly. They both laughed. "Dis a Neven, mi baby's fada." Tashanira glanced back at Neven and winked at him.

"Ah di gud man dis. Nice tuh meet yuh." Tetenira moved to Neven and hugged him, grabbing his butt.

Neven jerked back.

Tetenira laughed. She raised an eyebrow at Neven. "Yuh interest inna making any siblings while yuh here?"

"Him? Nuh," came a voice from the crowd. "Him taken an naah mek no more picney wid anyone but mi."

An unrecognized Uri stepped out and moved to Neven's side. She had a familiarity about her, and the casual way she strung her arm around Neven and moved in close to him caused Tashanira's eyes to go wide.

"Ellipse?" Tashanira asked.

"Inna di flesh," Ellipse said in a perfect reproduction of the Uri dialect.

Tashanira laughed as the crowd dispersed. Lasicov appeared out of the crowd and came to stand in front of the small group.

"This way, please." Lasicov turned and headed off toward one of the towering grah trees.

It was as high as a skyscraper, with an impressive glass building grafted into the tree trunk as if a mesh of technology and nature. It was breathtaking to view, and Tashanira had missed the distinctive way her people honored nature but respectfully improved it. Nothing in the beauty or function of nature was ever destroyed in Uri design—rather, it was enhanced and integrated with technology.

Every species in the Huzien Alliance was envious of the genius that the Uri employed in this design. It was something that Tashanira was proud of, and it made her feel like her people were special.

Like she was special. They walked a short distance, making their way to a meglift grafted into the trunk of the massive tree. In seconds, they ascended into the clouds, the meglift taking them to the uppermost branches, to a suite of glass that rose above the tree line. The view was breathtaking.

"Wow," Tashanira said. She glanced at Tetenira. "Mi tink wi did a guh back tuh yuh place."

"Dis a mi place now thanks tuh yuh gud man." Tetenira winked at Neven.

"The estate gifted this property as an ideal place for raising Neven's child. Mistress Lansa was insistent about finding one of the best properties in Yenra for her grandchild."

Tashanira nodded.

They exited the meglift into the three-story property. It was massive with every amenity Tashanira hadn't been afforded during her childhood. She rubbed her stomach and looked out of a nearby window toward the ground. Her child would grow up in a world different from the one she had been raised in. That thought didn't bother her as much as she thought it would.

She glanced back at Neven, who was chatting with Lasicov. With a heavy sigh, she looked down at the ground and then walked to a nearby couch, promptly sitting down. Her muscles thanked her as she let herself sink into the sofa. A drone appeared at her side with a drink. She stared at the drone for a long moment and then glanced at Ellipse, who stood off to the side, carefully watching her. Their eyes locked, Ellipse glancing away toward Neven.

A chime at the door grabbed Tashanira's attention. She glanced back to see Tetenira move to the door to greet the new guests. Her gaze went to Neven as his eyes went wide. He began to blush and turned away, moving to look out of a nearby window.

She grinned and turned to catch sight of garb she recognized immediately. They were garb she had almost taken as her mantle in life all those years ago. The top half of the clothing was primarily multi-colored beads with painted fur underneath, and the breasts and upper half of the body were fully exposed. The bottom half of the clothing was

a dress similar to what Tashanira wore, except it was more elaborate, with intricate weaving patterns in the colors of the Yenta tribe.

Tashanira stood up, quickly making her way to the entrance. "Matron Mada. Wi honored tuh ave yuh inna fi wi home." Tashanira bowed slightly, her gaze on one of the matron mother's bare feet.

Covering your feet or wearing traditional shoes on Peshkana was uncommon, considering the concept of paved roads was nonexistent as it violated the balance between nature and technology. Even the floors of homes were created to mirror grass, the construction providing many of the same benefits without the disadvantages.

"Dawta, welcome home. Wi ave been looking forward tuh dis day yaaah one of di golden daughtas of fi wi people," Matron Lumira Yen Unvesal said.

Matron Lumira walked over and grabbed Tashanira's hands, lifting them up and resting her head against Tashanira's head. She then began to dance, the beads on her body creating a cacophony of sound.

Tashanira felt joy overwhelm her as she joined in the dance with her mother, memories rushing back of this life she had lived and all the good times within it.

She laughed, losing herself in the moment. She felt the baby jump for joy in her womb, mirroring her emotions.

Laughter filled the home as they spent the remainder of the night celebrating.

Yenra, Peshkana, Uri home system

Tashanira steadily breathed. She was surrounded by matron mothers who were preparing for the birth of her child. She sat in a tub of water, nude and wet.

Neven was huddled in a corner of the room by himself, his eyes downcast as he paced back and forth.

She smiled. He was wearing the traditional garb of a Uri father, eager to do whatever she needed as part of the birthing ceremony. There was a steady beating of drums, the rhythm allowing Tashanira to focus.

She extended her hand toward Neven, and he glanced up at her. Locking eyes, he walked over and took her hand, sitting by her head as she leaned back. A contraction coursed through her as she squeezed Neven's hand. Tashanira focused on her breathing.

"Oh, great motherworld bless di laba of yuh new pickney," said one of the matron mothers.

All the other matron mothers repeated "bless di laba" in tandem.

Neven repeated the words. The contraction passed, and Tashanira looked to Neven in a haze. He watched her silently, doing his best to reassure her. Before she realized it, another contraction was on her, and she heard one of the matron mothers tell her to push as the drums urged her on.

Gripping Neven's hand with strength that caused him to whimper, she pushed.

Tashanira's vision blurred as she felt a great sense of relief wash over her. A small cry broke the chanting in the room as Tashanira looked up to see one of the matron mothers holding her child.

The rhythm of the drums shifted abruptly, erupting in celebration. Another came with a ritual knife and cut the umbilical cord.

The child was quickly put to Tashanira's chest as she held her son for the first time.

A Few Weeks Later
Yenra, Peshkana, Uri home system

Tashanira let out a sigh, gently rubbing her baby as he suckled. She gazed out of the wall-to-ceiling window of her bedroom as she rested

against the comfortable nanofiber backboard of her bed, everything tailored to limit her movements and give her comfort.

The remainder of the birthing had been uneventful until everyone looked at the child.

Half-Uri Human hybrids followed a similar convention to Huzien hybrids in that their appearance was mostly Human, but they'd have hair matching their Uri parent's fur. The eyes were typically Human in appearance but with bright Uri colors for the pupils. Her child had silver hair, similar to the hair that her body had transformed into after her time on the Enesmic plane.

His eyes though, that was where the standard conventions died. The baby had silver sclera instead of the white common to Humans. The iris was purple, with the pupil a bright-gold instead of black. The appearance of his eyes unsettled every person who saw her child, but when she looked into those eyes, she felt love.

Her new eyes unsettled people, too. It was something they shared now, something that she could help him adjust to.

A knock at the door grabbed her attention.

"Enter," Tashanira said.

Soahc walked into the room, his gaze going to Tashanira's bare chest, half covered by a suckling baby. He then glanced away out of the window as he crossed his arms. He cleared his throat. Tashanira grinned and made no movement to cover herself up.

"Is everything okay?" Soahc asked. He walked over to the window and continued glancing out of it.

"If you're asking if the child has started threatening my existence or levitating, then, yes, everything is okay." Tashanira tilted her head to the side. "However, if you're asking whether I've adjusted to the constant demands of this small child and his incessant need to feed, then, no, I'm not fine. I'm exhausted."

Soahc nodded. He glanced back at Tashanira, his eyes going to the child.

"Where is Brime? She's usually attached to your hip."

"She's helping with the Eshgren hunt, supporting Vades in her quest."

Soahc glanced back out the window. "I can sense an aura about that child. There's something different about him, but I can't quite explain it. Considering what's happened to you, I think it would be best if I remained here for a while to continue my observations."

"Whatever." Tashanira sighed. "I doubt I could get you to leave if I said no, so continue doing whatever it is you powerful Cihphists do to safeguard the galaxy from small babies."

Soahc sighed and turned around to leave. "I'm just being cautious. I want nothing more than your child to have a happy, normal life that doesn't involve me."

"But somehow, I get the sense that his life will always have you lurking around." Tashanira frowned.

Soahc walked out of the room without a response. The baby began to whine as it unlatched. She quickly moved it to the other side and relatched him, her eyes closing briefly for a quick nap.

A subtle shift in the room woke Tashanira. She opened her eyes with a start to see a silver-eyed Uri watching her. She wore the garb of a tribe mother, but she looked not a day older than Tashanira. tribe mothers were Uri matron mothers past the age of childbearing. Putting aside that mantle, they took over the administration and management of their tribe.

The one standing before her was a legend from a sister tribe. No, sister wasn't a fair statement. They were from a dominant tribe, a longtime aggressor to the Yunta before the Huziens came.

Tashanira's eyes went wide. "Feyura Mau Gehreyati," she whispered.

Feyura was a powerful Uri with significant influence and ability. Tashanira didn't know exactly how old she was, but she understood that she had existed before the Huziens colonized their world. She was the only one still alive who remembered what the Uri were in the before days. History said that she was the one who convinced the Uri to lay down their weapons. To not oppose the Huziens but instead embrace them. Many viewed her as a traitor at the time, but that thinking had long since been violently stamped

out. Yenta history highlighted this as one of the reasons why the Huziens had allowed the Uri to maintain their tribal culture, leaving the Mauveh as the dominant and most powerful tribe.

"Hail, Tashanira Yen Unvesal." Feyura took a few steps forward and sat on the edge of the bed. Her gaze took in the view of the room, eventually settling on the baby sound asleep in a bassinet within arm's reach of Tashanira.

Tashanira realized that her sister must have come in and put the baby in the bassinet after she had fallen asleep.

"Mi apologize fi mi unannounced visit, but mi did haffi cum an si di golden dawta of di Yenta return. Di one who claim immortality fi haarself nuh by right of birth but by her own chrent." Feyura grinned. "Yuh legend quickly spreading across di motherworld."

"Ah." Tashanira felt a rush of fear course through her, her supernatural senses on high alert.

This woman was a threat. People like her didn't make house appearances. This was the most powerful Mauveh tribe mother in her room. No weapons were present, but Tashanira could sense the subtle flow of the Enesmic. That fact surprised her—she had never been able to feel the Enesmic so keenly like this.

She could sense weaving in the vicinity of her child. She disrupted the Cihphism. She wasn't sure how or what the Cihphism had been trying to accomplish, but the ability to nullify it came to her like breathing in a breath of fresh air.

Feyura frowned.

Tashanira took in a few slow breaths to steady her heartbeat. Had that been a cihphistic attack? No, it wasn't lethal; she could now sense that, but it had been something unwanted. Telepathy perhaps? An imprint?

Was Feyura attempting to imprint on her child?

Tashanira struggled to understand this new knowledge entering her mind, the source of it unknown. She looked up to Feyura, her gaze narrowing.

The room rumbled as Tashanira summoned a fount of power in a display that caused Feyura to jump up from the bed and step back.

"Mi apologize mi mean no harm. A misunderstanding," Feyura said. She raised her hands, slowly coming to sit back on the bed.

"Ow mi cya help you?" Tashanira's voice was cold.

Feyura gave Tashanira a tight-lipped smile. "Wen di baby wean yuh wi cum tuh Mauveh an wi wi discuss yuh place inna dis world. Dat eff yuh plan tuh stay here." Feyura stood up.

Tashanira looked at her child. In that moment, she understood that she couldn't leave. Soahc would be hanging around, but did she trust him to protect her child? No. What if he saw her child as a threat? What if something about the child caused him to believe the galaxy was at risk? She couldn't trust Soahc to be alone with him, and now with Feyura and her interest in her child . . .

Tashanira let out a huff, her mind racing. Soahc appeared in their midst, Enesmic energy flickering off him in torrents. Feyura grinned at him and crossed her arms.

"I detected Enesmic weaving," Soahc said. He looked from Feyura to Tashanira. "Is everything okay?"

"Feyura was just leaving," Tashanira said, dropping her accent.

"Soahc . . . how I've missed you." Feyura did likewise and walked toward Soahc, a sway in her step. Soahc raised an eyebrow as Feyura stopped in front of him. "We can get reacquainted, maybe spend some time creating a baby of our own. Yeah?"

"I must decline," Soahc said. "I'm a married man."

"Shame." Feyura clicked her tongue. She glanced at Tashanira. "See you soon." Feyura turned away from Tashanira and clenched her fist, teleporting away.

Tashanira let out a long sigh, staring up at the ceiling.

"I can put up a ward that will prevent teleportation into this room directly," Soahc said. "It will give me time to return in case you get any other unwanted visitors."

"Thank you," Tashanira said.

Soahc went to work enacting Cihphism throughout her room and then walked out the door. Tashanira looked down at her baby and narrowed her eyes.

She wouldn't be pushed around by Feyura or anyone from the Mauveh tribe. No, she would own her life from now on. She wasn't afraid of them, not anymore.

Her mind returned to her mother—to the life she had turned down to enter the military. She felt something in her mind fall into place, a moment of crystal clarity forming.

She would become a matron mother. She would adopt that mantle and raise her child. Feyura saw her as a threat, so she would become one.

A Few Days Later

Tashanira walked through the low-cut grass that passed for streets in Yenra. Hovercars and carts littered the area, and Tashanira was by herself as she spent the time deep in thought. She had begun exploring her new abilities, opting to do it away from home and any potential dangers they might pose to her child in her inexperience, something Soahc had recommended.

"Tashanira?" came a voice from off to the side.

Tashanira stopped, her heart skipping a beat. She turned to face a man in civilian clothes. "Jenshi?" Tashanira asked.

He had lost weight, and his appearance seemed more fragile.

"You look so different, what happened?"

"What are you doing here?"

"I . . . calculated your due date and figured you'd still be on Peshkana after the birth. I purchased a transport ticket and came here."

"They released you."

"Don't sound so shocked." Jenshi laughed. "I no longer have violent urges or thoughts toward anyone. The reconditioning was successful." Jenshi shrugged his shoulders. "I understand how petty and harmful my actions were. I wanted to come and apologize to you." Jenshi took a step toward Tashanira, but she backed away in lockstep. "I'm sorry."

Tashanira's mind immediately went to Neven, who was with their child back home. "What about Neven?"

Jenshi tilted his head to the side, frowning. "I'm sorry for what I did to Neven. Although, I don't think I can yet forgive him for his part in all of this."

"You almost killed him."

"I'm sorry for that and for my actions. I . . . regret my actions. But reconditioning doesn't heal your heart. It just removes the violent urges that are associated with the pain." Jenshi's voice cracked. He looked down at the ground, closing his eyes briefly before glancing back up at Tashanira. "How is the baby?"

"Healthy."

"Are you okay? Your fur and your eyes, did something happen?"

"I'm fine."

"I see." Jenshi rubbed his shoulder. "I . . . I wanted to respond to what you told me back in that brig." He hesitated. "About our relationship being one of convenience. Was that true?"

Tashanira watched Jenshi for a long moment, his gaze stuck on hers, his eyes pleading. "I'm sorry," Tashanira said.

"And the other affairs?" Jenshi took another step forward.

Tashanira backed up again and rubbed her arm.

"I see . . ." He looked up into the sky for a long moment.

Tashanira took in a deep breath and slowly let it out. "I've had a lot of time to think these past months. I was never truly in love with you, Jenshi. I loved what you signified, but I was unfair to you. You wanted an *eifi*, but that's not what I wanted, not deep down. I wanted something that made me feel like I had conquered the trauma of my past. That I had moved on and become a new person." Tashanira shook her head. "But it wasn't until I was able to get away and truly focus on myself in a safe place that I realized who that new person truly was."

Jenshi met Tashanira's gaze.

"I am comfortable in who I am now and in who my people are. I am not ashamed of my heritage. I do not desire to be something else. I am a powerful Uri woman, and we are a beautiful, brilliant people with a rich culture." Tashanira's gaze hardened. "Coming back here crystallized that for me."

"I . . . came here to see if there was a chance. I know it was a long shot, but." Jenshi pulled a necklace from his pocket. They were Huzien marriage beads, the most beautiful arrangement she had ever seen.

"Jenshi . . ." Tashanira shook her head, a single tear rolling down her cheek. "I appreciate the sentiment, but our relationship is over. It's not healthy for either of us to continue it."

Jenshi stared at the necklace in his hand. He nodded and tossed it at Tashanira's feet. "Consider this something to remember me by then. A token of a future that could have been." He gave a sad smile and then turned, walking away.

Tashanira watched him go, her gaze dropping to the necklace at her feet. She slowly bent down to pick it up, holding it in her hand for a long moment. A young girl was passing by, looking to be around an age Tashanira remembered, one filled with so much pain.

She stopped the girl and handed her the necklace. "A pretty necklace fi a pretty picney?" Tashanira smiled at her.

The little girl's eyes lit up, and she broke into a dance of joy, gesturing with symbols of elation and appreciation to Tashanira a few times before running off the way she had come.

Tashanira turned back in the direction she was going and took in a deep breath. She walked for about twenty minutes to a waterfall in a secluded area. She stared at the waterfall for a long moment, a rush of memories playing out that caused her heart to start racing. The trauma felt fresh, as if she had stepped back in time to see herself bathing in the waters, back at the moment when her life was forever changed.

Steeling her gaze, she stripped off her clothing and walked into the water, going to the exact spot in her memory. She looked around, a rush of fear coming to her in that moment, but she knew the power of it was irrational.

She let out another deep breath and began to bathe in the water. She took her time, telling herself every second that she was no longer afraid and that she would not be hurt again. She went under the water and stayed there for a long moment until her lungs burned, eventually rising out of the water in a burst, her hair flying back as she inhaled air.

It was as if she was breathing for the first time. She emerged from that water, reborn.

She stared at her reflection in the water, her fur glistening in the sun's setting light. Water dripped from her hair in an image of raw beauty that made her smile. She sighed and walked back onto land, her body dripping wet. She glanced at her clothes, picked them up, and looked down at the water pooling on the ground.

She shook as much water out of her fur as she could, then started laughing. Squaring her shoulders, she stuffed her clothes under her arm and walked home naked, eating up the stares that came her way. She was confident in every step, assured that no one could harm her anymore.

She was in complete control of her destiny.

Stepping out of the meglift and into her new home, she threw her clothes on a nearby couch. Neven was cradling the baby, asleep in his arms, as he rocked them gently back and forth next to one of the windows, looking out at the clouds. The sun was setting with the hues of orange and red, creating a beautiful sight, the tops of the other grah trees all around them peeking above the cloud canopy.

He glanced back at her as she entered and did a double take. Tashanira grinned, scratching one of her breasts with an air kiss in his direction. Ellipse appeared with a towel, scowling at her as she thrust it out to Tashanira.

Tashanira sighed, taking the towel and wrapping it around her shoulders. She walked into a room that had been converted into an office just as a holodisplay appeared above the desk. Tashanira

moved to sit in the chair, leaning back as Lanrete appeared on the holodisplay. He raised an eyebrow at Tashanira's appearance but seemed otherwise unfazed.

Tashanira winked. "Late evening swim."

"Right. I was waiting for your call. How is the baby? Hesre, was it?"

"That's right. Hesre Yen Kenk." Tashanira leaned back in the chair. "Lan, I'll get right to the point." Tashanira sat back up. "I've decided to leave the Founder's Elites. I plan to remain on Peshkana and raise my child."

"I suspected as much." Lanrete nodded. "Everyone is re-evaluating life right now. You and Neven kicked off a cycle of change." Lanrete smiled sadly. "Serah'Elax went with her mother to Desc'Ri for that potential cure Neven found, and Erb decided to spend more time at Etan Rachnie 'to get in tune with the unique flow' that he mentions being there." Lanrete sighed. "Although . . . now that we both share immortality, I have a feeling we'll work with each other again one day."

"Possibly, but for now, I'm going to enjoy who I am. I'll enjoy my family and hope for a future where that day never comes."

"A good hope." Lanrete raised a glass to Tashanira and then sipped a liquid she couldn't identify. "I heard Jenshi paid you a visit."

"I'm not even going to ask how you know that information, but yes."

"I don't think he's dangerous anymore, but reconditioning isn't perfect, and he still harbors a lot of strong emotions against Neven. He'll be on my radar."

"Don't kill him, please," Tashanira said. She wasn't sure why she had said the words, but the look in Lanrete's gaze scared her.

Lanrete narrowed his eyes at Tashanira. "That's up to Jenshi." He forced a smile. "Congratulations on the healthy baby boy. Don't worry too much about Soahc. He can be a bit much sometimes, but his intentions are good. Goodbye, Tashanira, and enjoy your family." Lanrete terminated the connection.

A Week Later

Tashanira looked at herself in the mirror. The woman staring back at her was one of supreme confidence—beads covered the upper half of her body above an intricately woven dress, one filled with Yenta tribal colors that started low on her hips and went down to her shins. She smiled at that woman and at the decision she had made.

She turned back to see Matron Lumira walk into the room with a beaming smile on her face.

"Dis a waah great day!" Matron Lumira said. "Mi time as a matron mada of fi wi tribe coming tuh a end. Mi ave been ask tuh serve as a tribe mada, mi womb no longa as fertile as it once did. Mi nuh breed dis season. Dis weigh heavily pan mi til yuh arrive." She put her hands on Tashanira's face and her forehead against Tashanira's. Their eyes locked. "Mi see di future of fi wi tribe inna yuh eyes. Mi dawta haarself again. Yuh ave regained dat spark stolen all dem deh years ago by di bad mon." A tear rolled down Lumira's cheek. "Tank di motherworld."

Tashanira felt a tear roll down her own cheek. She let tears of joy flow as she and her mother began to dance, both of their beads making a joyous sound as they moved around the room.

Tashanira was truly happy.

Sometime later, she emerged from the room into the open courtyard of the primary *luraim* in Yenra, which had been grafted into one of the largest grah trees in the city. It was an impressive structure, the pride and jewel of the city.

Tashanira glanced at Neven, who stood in the crowd that had assembled to celebrate the new matron mother. The pounding of drums filled the air with electricity. Ellipse glared at her.

Tashanira walked up to Neven, striding confidently as she stopped in front of him. Her beads made music with each movement

of her body. "Thank you for being here," she said. "This means a lot to me."

"Congratulations." Neven rubbed the back of his neck. "So this is a *luraim?*"

"Yeah. It's made up of three main quarters. Nursing matron mothers with babies live in the Nursing Quarter, which occupies the uppermost portion of the grah tree. Weaned children all the way up to teenagers live in the Rearing Quarter, which is the largest quarter. It takes up most of the grah tree. It consists of shared sleeping spaces for the matron mothers intermixed with the children, and they spend most of their time together. Not all matron mothers live here, but most do. Children who live in the Rearing Quarter gain a tailored education and are afforded a consistent quality of life with everything they need to succeed. The final quarter at the bottom of the grah tree, where we are now, is the Making Quarter, where the babies are made." Tashanira smirked. "It's what most people associate with a *luraim* since most of the populace don't see the other quarters. It's where matron mothers meet with and ultimately mate with suitors who gain their favor." She glanced around at the festivities happening all around them. "There is a lot of tradition here. Events regularly occur that allow for male Uri to put on displays of ability and talent to woo us. A lucky suitor gets taken to one of the many ritual beds that exist here by a fertile matron mother, and they *vusg* the night away."

Neven glanced around to see most of the matron mothers in the area with red circles around their irises. His gaze lingered on one of the matron mothers with rather large breasts, who caught his eye and winked at him. He quickly glanced down at the ground, scratching his head.

Tashanira caught the exchange and grinned. "Usually, a matron mother will sleep with a suitor every night she's fertile. Sometimes the same person or sometimes another who catches her eye."

"This place seems unnecessary," Ellipse said in an agitated tone.

"*Luraims* exist to ensure that gifted progeny are born to strengthen the tribe," Tashanira countered. "Matron mothers are the strongest of the genetic pool, each woman gifted in some way." She glanced around at a few of the other matron mothers. "While it may not seem like it, beauty isn't the only requirement to become a matron mother." She looked at Ellipse. "Intelligence, stamina, agility, and unique talents . . . every matron mother is the best of our tribe. By nature, our children are the best of the tribe. Not every Uri male can just walk into a *luraim* and father a child; they must prove themselves through ability or accomplishments and provide a financial gift to the *luraim*, although exceptions are made in unique cases."

"With that requirement, I'm surprised that half-Uri children are born here," Neven said.

"We realize that strength can sometimes come from outside the Uri genetic pool," Tashanira said. She stepped toward Neven and half closed her eyes, smiling at him. "When you're ready to have a second child, come and visit me."

There was no joke in her tone, only a promise.

"I think it's time for us to go," Ellipse said.

She stepped in between Neven and Tashanira, grabbing Neven by the hand and leading him out of the *luraim*.

Tashanira grinned, her hand on her hip.

Neven turned back to look at her, and she winked at him.

FOUNDER'S LOG:
Letting Go

Watching something you've invested blood, sweat, and tears into splinter apart leaves a scar on the soul. Therefore, we cling so hard to what we have and resist change.

But I've learned in my long life that sometimes it's essential to let go.

It's hard, don't get me wrong, but letting go can sometimes be the best path forward. There is logic in it, but in truth, logic is a small part. People are emotional beings, and when they feel that they need to move on, it can't always be explained with logic.

Sometimes, it's a feeling, an urge. It must be. At first, I didn't understand this concept. I thought, "If you take care of someone and do everything in your power to give them what they want and desire, they will stay at your side." But people change, circumstances change, and sometimes, standing by your side isn't what's right for them.

It still hurts every time a Founder's Elite leaves, whether they retire, move on, or perish. It makes it hard to start over, to look at a new batch of candidates, and decide to rebuild.

Sometimes, you need time to process and build the strength to move forward.

That's the price for hiring gifted people and the best of the best.

It's a price I'll continue to pay because even though some time may be short, the memories last forever.

And when your life seems endless, that means something.

-Lanrete

CHAPTER 48 - URIEL KERVID

76003 FA (4120 years ago)
Foundra Ascension *in orbit around Thae, Huzien Alliance space*

Uriel paced his cell for the thousandth time. Something within him had broken; everything was off, and his mind was rapidly unraveling.

The person he had believed Lanrete to be—the person he had trusted—was all a lie.

He couldn't think straight.

His heart hurt.

His body hurt.

He let out a roar, attacking anything within his reach. He destroyed everything in his cell that wasn't bolted down.

His existence angered him. Life was out to get him.

He hurt. It all hurt.

Let it all go, came a voice. It was a voice that sounded like him, but his body reflexively tensed up. *Make Lanrete hurt.*

Uriel paused, the chaos around him coming to a standstill.

Lanrete only understands pain.

"No. No. I—this." Uriel whimpered.

He dropped to the floor and curled into a ball, hugging his legs. An incoherent yell of rage went off in his head, and it continued, never ceasing. Uriel rocked back and forth, finally giving the roar an outlet.

The voice subsided.

Better . . . let it out.

Images of Lanrete flashed in his mind: images of Lanrete talking down to him, telling him to be better, calling out his flaws, and being disappointed with him.

Uriel rocked back and forth again, shaking his head. The pain swelled, growing into an unbearable torrent that caused him to get up and start attacking the shield keeping him in the cell.

Destruction made him feel better. It made him feel good. Yes. He liked to destroy things. He was good at destroying things.

Uriel began to pace again, his hands opening and closing.

A scene flashed in his mind, with him and Lanrete walking together as father and son, smiling. It was a scene from what seemed like an eternity ago—a moment of peace that seemed to still everything around him.

His gaze slowly fell on the necklace near his foot, and he remembered the pain that had paralyzed him. He began to dig at his skull, seeking to rip the image out of his head. Blood began to drip down his face as he broke the skin.

The pain was refreshing.

He ran full force into the shield, but the impact blasted him back. A guard opened the door to the brig and stood there, watching Uriel with a look of concern on his face.

Make him hurt! the voice yelled in his mind.

Uriel attacked the shield, seeking to get to the guard as an irrational hatred rose in him. This guard was an embodiment of everyone who had ever wronged him.

Summon it, show them your power, the voice said.

He broke into a bout of cihphistic weaving that caused the guard to step back and start shouting. Another guard, sporting two glowing rods, moved into the brig and handed one to the first guard. They both began cautiously approaching the cell, terror in their eyes.

Uriel ate up that terror. It made him smile. There was something in it that made him feel powerful. He had seen terror on the faces of many throughout his life as he ended their existences, but at this moment, they were terrified of what he was capable of.

He hadn't done anything to them yet.

That "yet" emboldened him.

He anticipated their deaths. Uriel started pulling on an invisible chain. The air in front of him began to ripple as he pulled harder and harder. Uriel completed his dual weaving and released a shock wave right before he pulled on the chain one last time, bringing a creature into their plane of existence.

The shock wave destroyed the shield and blew the nanoplexi glass across the room. The creature collapsed onto the ground a heartbeat after the explosion, and Uriel disappeared. The creature scrambled up, searching for the one who had summoned it. Not detecting Uriel, it turned its attention to the guards and charged at them.

It was a Bau, with its terrible appendages holding curved blades. The Bau lunged at the first guard, digging the weapons deep into his throat and severing his head from his body. The other guard screamed as it turned its blades on him and tore him apart.

Uriel blew open the door to the brig as the Enesmic creature charged out of the brig in search of more victims. Uriel held back, quietly staring at the corpses of the guards. He had known these people and shared meals with them on multiple occasions.

Something within him felt a great sorrow, and the loss caused a tear to roll down his cheek. He bent down, touching the decapitated body of the first guard gently. He caught sight of his hand, covered in blood.

The blood caused his mind to flash back to battle, to all the killing and bloodshed he had caused. There had been so many battles and so much blood. He quickly stood up and backed away, hyperventilating.

The world around him shifted. He stared at rows of corpses—men and women who had died in battle, lined up to be cataloged and shipped back to their families. The rows went on for what seemed like an eternity. The bodies shifted from Huziens to Humans, Uri, and a host of others, then Lux'Ameni, Ku'Ven, and finally Jun'Serentan.

There were so many dead Jun'Serentan bodies.

Blood began to seep out of the bodies, gushing in torrents that created a river of it.

Uriel tried to step back and out of the blood, but it was all around him. The blood continued to rise like water during a flood. Uriel screamed, the blood coming up to his neck. Then he was drowning in it, unable to breathe. He screamed but could no longer hear his voice; instead, it was muffled with bubbles. The blood rushed into his throat, choking him.

A voice brought Uriel back to reality. He was huddled in a corner of his destroyed cell. He looked up to see Urt Nevgambe and Cenxra Mau Gehreyati cautiously looking at him, their gazes going briefly to the dead guards.

Cenxra approached Uriel, a hand on her WMAs. "Boss, you're not well. You need to go back to a cell. Okay?" She motioned to one of the empty, still-functional cells next to Uriel's cell.

He glanced at the cell and then back at Cenxra. "No, I can't go back." Uriel shook his head repeatedly. "The voices. I . . ." Uriel stood and took a step forward.

Cenxra drew her weapons, keeping them leveled on Uriel.

The world around Uriel dropped away. A Jun'Serentan soldier was before him with a sneer on their stark, white-skinned face. They opened fire on him.

Uriel dodged to the side and charged forward. He didn't have Wishwonder at his side, but he summoned the Enesmic with a fury, unleashing a blast of raw Enesmic energy that the soldier dodged.

They were quick.

He followed up the attack by causing the area around them to ignite in flame. The Jun'Serenthan tried to dodge again, but Uriel came in fast, telekinetically pulling them toward him and punching through their chest with his fist, which glowed with a sickening hue of Enesmic energy. The Jun'Serenthan gasped.

Reality settled back in.

Uriel saw Cenxra staring at him with a look of sorrow and shock as the life quickly faded from her eyes. Uriel stepped back, withdrawing his hand, which was coated with her blue blood. Urt started to back away and then turned to run.

"No, wait!" Uriel said. He shifted in front of Urt.

Urt collapsed backward, scrambling on the floor toward Cenxra's weapons.

Uriel frowned. "You don't want to do that."

Urt grabbed one of her weapons and turned it on Uriel. Uriel sidestepped the weaponsfire and was then behind Urt. He snapped his neck with sickening efficiency, and the man collapsed to the ground, motionless. Uriel stared at Urt's lifeless body and took in a deep breath. He surveyed the death around him—all of this had been set in motion by him.

Letting out a slow breath, he exited the brig. Uriel saw a string of mutilated bodies around every corner, evidence that innocent people had encountered the monster he had let loose and failed to flee. Blood was everywhere.

He had to set this right.

Uriel followed the trail of death, eventually making his way to the meglift. The meglift door opened to reveal a blood-soaked floor filled with unsuspecting victims. Three people were dead inside, ripped to shreds.

Uriel instructed the meglift to go to its last location as it opened on another level. The blood trail continued, lined with more mutilated corpses. Uriel traced the creature to the mess hall. The sounds of weaponsfire caused him to surge forward, summoning Enesmic energy as he moved.

He burst into the hall to see the Enesmic creature descending on one of the last holdouts, comprised of a bridge crew member attempting to hold off the monster with a sidearm. The creature took the man's head as Uriel severed the bonds holding the creature on this plane of existence. It faded back to the Enesmic plane.

The sound of footsteps behind him caused Uriel to spin around. Enemies were all around him. He was at the battle of Tirand'Kore. He had to take the bridge. It was the only way to stop the advance of the enemy and save the lives of millions of Huzien Empire citizens.

He charged through the corridors to the meglift, brutal in his efficiency as he massacred any who stood in his way. He had no weapon, but he'd have to make due. He *was* a weapon.

Uriel exploded onto the bridge as all turned to raise weapons at him. He had to kill them and stop them from hurting the people of Tirand'Kore.

They were monsters. He would make them pay.

Uriel telekinetically ripped off a nearby panel and sent it flying toward one of the enemy soldiers. It took off the woman's head. He charged at another who had moved toward him. He grabbed their arm and tore it from its socket with cihphistically enhanced strength. Then he ignited the body, flinging the soldier at another who was trying to flee.

He couldn't allow them to call reinforcements. He had to stop them now.

He telekinetically grabbed their body and slammed them hard into one of the bulkheads, repeating the action until they stopped moving. Then he flung their corpse at the captain's chair with such force that it burst apart into two halves. Images flashed in his mind of Westa and Kellie, the two Secnics on his team.

He wasn't sure why he had seen their dead bodies, but someone must have killed them! He had to find their murderer. Someone was hunting members of his team. He had to protect them.

His weapon. He needed his weapon.

Uriel flew off the bridge, the meglift taking him to the armory. He exited the armory to weaponsfire. An Archlight, no, a deception—only Huziens employed Archlights—this must be a traitor, someone working with the enemy to kill his team.

He charged forward as the Archlight leveled its lance rifle at Uriel. He spun, shifting his body to incredible speeds to get behind the

Archlight. A blast of lightning streaked to where he had been a split second before. The Archlight turned, thrusters firing as it spun to face him.

Uriel burst into the armory, his barrier flickering as his shield absorbed a shot. He saw Wishwonder and summoned it to his hand. These monsters, these killers, would know his wrath.

He turned and charged toward the false Archlight, releasing Wishwonder as it flew around the Archlight's shield and slammed into the enemy's head. They had forgotten to don their helmet, and he had used that advantage to end the fight quickly.

Another shot hit him, and his barrier flickered. Uriel sensed the attacker's direction but couldn't see them. A Sentinel was working against them as well.

"The treachery runs deep!" Uriel yelled. His voice was distorted.

He ignited the entire armory room in intense flames. A form burst through the exit, already on fire. Uriel drove Wishwonder through their neck and locked eyes with the traitor.

"Bevi?" Uriel asked in shock.

Bevi's eyes closed as the last of his life bled out through his neck. Uriel retrieved Wishwonder and looked around at the carnage. He could see half of Macaf Yeqir's face, an Archlight he had called friend.

He staggered back, his mind chaotic as their images twisted, their bodies growing into horrible monsters that wanted to eat him alive. No, the demons wanted to eat the dead bodies of Enara and his child, and they were now at his feet.

Uriel yelled, a shock wave of energy exploding from him and destroying the armory. He staggered his way to the meglift.

"The ship. I must get to my ship. The enemy is coming."

Uriel made his way to the hangar and saw it filled with enemy soldiers. He slaughtered all of them, making his way to his ship, but then he stopped. Clarity came to him as a veil dropped away from his mind. He turned to view the carnage he had just wrought. They weren't soldiers. They were crew. He was on the *Foundra Ascension*, and he had just killed everyone.

An overwhelming wave of nausea hit him. He dropped to his hands and knees and began to throw up. He retched for a solid minute. Uriel eventually stood, letting out slow breaths to calm his mind.

He stared at the blood that covered his body.

Uriel glanced back at the shuttle, a thought flickering in his mind. He should return to the brig, sit down, wait for Lanrete to return, own up to his actions, and receive punishment. He took one step back toward the meglift, reason telling him that this was the right thing to do—he should, once again, play the obedient soldier and turn himself in before more innocents died. He was not well.

Another thought stopped him. He recalled his burned-out necklace, the one that Lanrete had used to hurt him like a disobedient dog that refused to roll over.

It all made sense now. Lanrete had only ever sought to control Uriel. From the moment he had been recruited to help build the Founder's Elites, Lanrete had taken control of his life. He had worked so hard to please the Founder, and for what? To murder in the name of the Huzien Empire?

And when that purpose had begun to wane, when his immortality caused him to question his purpose and why he was still devoting his life to Lanrete, Lanrete had called him *burush*.

And he had lapped it up like a dog.

Uriel glanced back at the shuttle, his gaze settling on the crest. This was the ship Lanrete had given him, just like the necklace. If the treachery held true, then Lanrete would know precisely where he was and would be able to trace him wherever he went. That shuttle was another form of control, another trap to keep him in line.

Uriel glanced toward one of the *Foundra Ascension* shuttles and began to walk toward it.

"I will not play the obedient dog anymore," Uriel said to himself. He entered the shuttle, setting a course for the Outer Rim. He'd have to ditch the shuttle somewhere and find a civilian vessel before he crossed over, but this would do for now.

He looked back at the carnage he'd wrought, at the dead lining the entrance to the shuttle bay. He smothered the thought of

returning to the brig. No. He would forge his own future and carve out his own path from now on.

And make him pay, the voice said.

Uriel mulled that sentiment over for a long time, letting out a wicked smile as he instructed the shuttle to depart.

Cejhar, Frew, Darbol Alliance space
76017 FA (Fourteen Years Later)

Uriel sat on a stool in a midtown bar deep in the city of Cejhar on the planet Frew. It was the home of the Under Market, a place filled with undesirables and largely ignored by the Darbol Alliance. This was due to the illegal activities frequently targeting planets in the Huzien Alliance.

Uriel stared at the drink in his hand and then set it back on the bar. An automated drone picked up the cup as he signaled he was done. He frowned, his senses cihphistically enhanced and on high alert. He was within distance of his shuttle and could teleport there now, but he'd give himself away immediately to whoever or whatever it was that was tracking him.

A man sat down on a stool two seats away from him. "Was hard to find you," he said. "Your optical implants are a nice touch. I suppose it's easier to hide when you don't walk around with silver eyes."

Uriel turned to look at Lanrete. The Founder wore a cloak to hide his normal armor, Sentinel tech unmasking his true face. "Still trying to bring me in? Recondition me?"

"No." Lanrete shook his head, frowning. "I've given up on that."

"You plan to kill me then, *burratha?*"

"You're responsible for high crimes against the Huzien Empire. Your sentence has already been passed."

"By you." Uriel slowly turned around, surveying the area. "Judge, jury, and executioner, right?"

He clocked about four other people who were likely working with Lanrete. They were attempting to mask their presence. He assumed there were more cloaked—most likely a squad of Sentinels. Uriel turned partially to face Lanrete, not making a move for Wishwonder hidden under his cloak.

"How can you live with yourself, Uriel? Killing people you once called friends, hunting those who trusted you, and killing hardworking soldiers in the Huzien Alliance? What happened?"

"The Uriel you knew died back in that brig like the obedient puppy he was. Just like all those sick dogs who mindlessly do what you tell them to do: slaughtering, raping, and pillaging all in the name of the great Huzien Empire." Uriel raised his head high. "Since I have you here, let me ask you a question." Uriel smiled. "Does it hurt to have people you care about killed by someone you once called *burush*?"

Lanrete drew Divinebreath and charged at Uriel, a murderous rage in his eyes. Uriel clenched his fist, completing his weaving of Cihphism as he disappeared and reappeared in his shuttle.

He initiated his emergency escape protocol as the ship rose into the air and jumped to suplight.

CHAPTER 49 - NEVEN KENK

Present Day
Genmatha, Huzien Alliance space

Neven sat on the beach where he last saw Zun alive. His mind replayed that final moment: Zun was beside him, her toes digging into the sand as they walked. She had been prepared to tell him about the baby; he was sure of it. He could almost see her mouthing the words in that moment before her blood coated the white sands.

All traces of her murder had been removed. The beach was impeccably cleaned daily by an army of drones that did everything to keep the paradise planet looking like paradise.

He took in a deep breath and stood. Ellipse was still in orbit on the *Castrin*, Neven having wanted to make this trip by himself. He looked out over the ocean, his mind processing what seemed like an eternity since he had lost her.

A warning sound blared in his head, one of his remote monitoring drones signaling that someone had decloaked nearby. Facial recognition match identified the figure with eighty-six-point-three percent certainty.

Neven! shouted Ellipse in his mind.

Neven dove hard to the right as an Iltarum blade flew past him, the weapon slicing the air where he had stood a heartbeat before. It levitated and then flew directly toward Neven, seeking to separate his head from his body.

Neven activated a series of coils in his body, emitting a pulse that drained a small power core Neven had surgically embedded in his abdomen. The pulse disrupted the Cihphism controlling the blade, and it dropped to the ground. He threw three small cubes to the ground in different directions. The pulse coalesced with the cubes as an anchor, creating a nullifying energy field.

Entradis snapped his fingers, but the Cihphism was disrupted before it could ignite Neven on fire. Neven stared at Entradis from within his protective bubble.

"I'm impressed. I can't say I've ever seen anything like that before," Entradis said. He glanced at his blade, safely within Neven's field. "It's been a long time since I've used Wishwonder to kill. For you, however, it just felt right."

"Why are you doing this?" Neven asked.

Entradis tilted his head to the side. "You don't know who I really am, do you?" Entradis laughed. "Lanrete conveniently keeps my past a secret. I'm guessing you don't know that I'm the one who created the Founder's Elites or that I was once Lanrete's adopted *burratha*, his son?"

Neven's eyes went wide.

"No, of course not." Entradis nodded. "You're an obedient dog, just like the rest."

"Did he hurt you? Is that why you hurt others?"

"He opened my eyes," Entradis countered. "I'm finally awake." Entradis silently watched Neven for a short time. "I learned a lot about you from the information brokers. They were very forthcoming with the information. You're a genius prodigy and a hero of the Rift War." Entradis shook his head. "Still living in the dream orchestrated by Lanrete and those like him. Everything they say is a lie. This empire that they have created is all a lie."

"Then what's the truth?"

"Which level? How about: we were not meant to exist, and nothing we do matters." Entradis raised his hands, turning around. "Or maybe that the Huzien Empire is built on a legacy of blood, the majority of which hasn't made it into the history books." Entradis shook his head. "But that's not even the worst part." Entradis smiled. "Immortals are not what you think they are. They manipulate this galaxy and remake it into their image. But where do they get that right?" Entradis opened his eyes wide. "By subjugating others to their will and killing those who know the truth. Lanrete, Cislot, Ecnics, Tirivus, Soahc, all of them. They are the monsters."

"You're the one murdering innocent people." Neven felt himself on the verge of losing control. "You're the monster."

Entradis laughed, shaking his head. "I thought you might understand. But I see your genius is another lie orchestrated by them. Why am I wasting my breath on you? You're just like all the rest. And soon you'll be dead." Entradis broke into a sprint toward Wishwonder.

"Armor drop!" Neven shouted as the S3 installed in the *Castrin* suplighted in a set of power armor right next to him.

He scrambled to get into the armor as Entradis reached his blade a second later and twisted, making a beeline for Neven. Neven felt the seals shut, locking him in as the system came to life. He lifted his arm, forming a circular band around his wrist, unleashing a shock blast that Entradis dodged. Sand exploded next to him.

Neven flew backward, but Entradis ate up the distance dangerously fast. They emerged from the protective bubble, Entradis's speed increasing to inhuman levels. Neven had to fall back to Ellipse to control the power armor's movements. While she maneuvered him around, he began to spin up a series of devices on the *Castrin*. He had prepared long and hard for this day.

More S3 pulses went off around the battlefield as more armors and other devices came online. A nearby cube expanded, exposing a spherical core that appeared to wrap around itself. It began to spin, moving in and around itself, creating a hypnotizing mesh of technology that let out another pulse like the one that had emanated from his body earlier, except on a much grander scale.

It blanketed the whole space, disrupting the Cihphism in the immediate area. Entradis scowled as he slowed down. He came to a stop, glancing at the cube. He charged toward it, but Neven had anticipated that. A series of power armors landed in front of Entradis, the automatons controlled by Ellipse with one sole purpose to protect that nullifier.

They started to light up Entradis with devastating weapons-fire. Unaided by the Enesmic, Entradis was forced to retreat, quickly moving to cover. Neven reversed his flight, moving in a strafing pattern to align himself with Entradis. A clear lock signaled in his display as his Feponic shoulder canons emerged from their dens, unleashing a focused blast of plasma that Entradis scrambled to get out of the way of. It left a trail of glass in its wake.

Another device came to life when Entradis dodged—this time, a series of circular drones shot into the air. Almost a hundred of the small devices blanketed the battlefield, each locked onto Entradis. They started to discharge small but deadly blasts in his direction.

Entradis moved for cover in one of the buildings next to the beach as the drones peppered the property with holes. Screams went up all around as Neven realized there were still people inside. He sent a command to the drones to disengage. A few people ran out of the building, but Entradis didn't emerge. Neven switched to thermal vision, noting that multiple heat signatures were still inside. Frowning, Neven took control back from Ellipse and moved his power armor closer to the building.

Neven, get out of there. Retreat! Now is your chance, Ellipse yelled in his mind.

Neven contemplated it for a second but instead had one of the drones cloak and move into the building, providing a detailed map of the inside back to his microdisplay.

He could see Entradis with hostages. "I can't leave. Nothing is stopping him from killing them," Neven said.

It's a trap, Neven, Ellipse said. *He's going to kill them either way. Remember who we're dealing with.*

Neven aligned himself with Entradis, his chest facing directly toward the murderer. A small panel in his chest opened as a glow started to build within. An intense beam of focused energy seared through the building, but Entradis detected the attack just in time. He moved one of his victims directly into the path of the beam and dodged away.

Neven gasped.

Entradis then made quick work of the other hostages and charged out of the building in a full sprint toward the end of the nullifying radius. The grey haze dissipated as Entradis emerged back in full control of his abilities. He looked toward the cube and sent his blade up high into the air. It flew with lightning speed to a position far above the cube.

Ellipse scrambled the power armors to intercept the weapon, but it stopped, hovering just outside the barrier. Neven felt a small rock slam into his power armor, the impact triggering a reaction from his aft shield. He looked back to see hundreds of tiny stones sent high into the air, all raining down on Neven and the other power armors with unnatural speed.

Neven threw himself backward, his tracking SI trying to grab a lock on each object. He turned his drones into mini anti-air guns as they fired small but effective blasts at more of the incoming rocks. Neven turned back toward where Entradis's sword had been hanging in the air, but it was gone. He frantically looked around, pinging the concern to Ellipse, who turned every one of her available sensors on the battlefield and attempted to find the weapon.

It's gone? Ellipse asked.

Neven thought for a moment and then gasped. "Beneath us!"

Before the words finished leaving his mouth, Entradis's blade erupted through the heart of the large nullifying cube at a breakneck speed, flying through the nullifier and high up into the air using its momentum. The field disappeared.

Entradis was in front of Neven in a heartbeat, the Cihphist punching through Neven's shield with his bare hands. He dug into the power armor and tore it with supernatural strength. The armor creaked as Neven attempted to propel his back in the opposite direction. The area around them trembled with the terrible swirling of Enesmic energy as Entradis anchored Neven's power armor with fetters of energy that seemed to go far into the ground.

"Ellipse, I need you!" Neven yelled, fear in his voice.

Entradis began to peel back the armor. The other power armors were engaged with Entradis's blade, the weapon seeking to destroy all of Neven's toys. They scrambled back toward Neven on full burn. Warnings blared all over Neven's holodisplay as Entradis ripped off the final panel, exposing Neven's chest.

"Eject!" Neven yelled. The command went off before he spoke it, the power armor throwing him back and into the sand.

Entradis punched through where Neven's chest had been a moment before, his fist glowing as it exited the back of Neven's armor. Entradis made a motion with his hands, and the fetters encircling the power armor crushed it and dragged it down into the sand.

"We both can adapt," Entradis said. He glanced at Neven, who was rising to his feet, unprotected by any power armor.

Entradis started to walk toward him.

No, don't do that! It's dangerous! Ellipse shouted in Neven's mind.

"It's either that or die right now," Neven said. He activated more implants in his body and jumped into the air. A flash of light appeared around him, and the S3 dropped a power armor directly on his location. He tried to mirror the position he had practiced multiple times in the short jump off the ground, which he hit at about ninety-five percent accuracy. Blinding pain assaulted Neven as his left arm was cleaved right off by the S3, vaporizing it. The rest of his body matched perfectly with the position of the power armor, and it sealed him in, compressing in on his body as it reduced in size by about a third to match the size of his standard power armor. A clamp immediately came down on his shoulder with the missing arm as Neven tried to focus through the pain.

Ellipse took control of the armor, engaging in battle with Entradis, who had immediately charged at Neven when he saw the flash of light. Neven began to breathe rapidly, his vision blurry as he tried to process the world around him. The pain in his shoulder was intense, but a wave of drugs hit his system as the medvak system kicked in. The pain dulled, and Neven brought up his vitals to see what damage had been done. He processed that his arm was gone and pushed it out of his mind, the focusing drugs bringing him back to the battle at hand.

He took control back from Ellipse and sent the power armor in a reverse pattern around Entradis, unloading his full barrage of weaponsfire. Entradis absorbed most of the firepower with his shield, and Wishwonder appeared in his hand.

Neven's eyes went wide as recognition of what that meant hit him. He brought up a status readout of his deployed weapons—all destroyed or offline. He felt like he was going to throw up; another wave of drugs hit him, and the urge disappeared.

Steeling his gaze, he called in another armor drop, resulting in a single case appearing at his side. The case opened as a modified version of Streamsong, his Huzien blade, rose out of the housing. His power armor picked it up, and he dropped into a defensive stance ingrained into him from the sparring sessions with Lanrete.

Neven flexed the power armor's hand on the side with his missing arm, thankful for the armor being wired into his nervous system and not physically controlled by his body.

Entradis tilted his head to the side, smirking. He fell into a counter stance.

Neven let out a slow breath, Ellipse detecting movement before Neven could register it. His blade came up, intercepting Entradis' blow as the monster moved like a hurricane. Neven could barely process his movements, but he wasn't completely overwhelmed with Ellipse analyzing the strikes and building a predictive algorithm to anticipate the next one.

The power armor shifted from being on the defensive to the offensive in a deft deflection that pushed Entradis off balance. Streamsong lunged forward into a fatal strike—but Entradis wasn't there.

Ellipse had seen Lanrete use this technique multiple times and immediately spun the power armor around, deflecting the death strike from Entradis that would have skewered Neven from behind. Entradis's eyes widened, and he unleashed a blast of raw Enesmic energy that sent the power armor flying hard into a large rock.

Ellipse saw the follow-up attack coming and tried to respond, moving the power armor just enough that Entradis impaled Neven through the side instead of through the heart. Neven yelled in pain as the power armor kicked out.

Entradis avoided the blow and dropped back into his stance. Neven pushed himself up, the power armor still fully functional. He dropped back into a Huzien blade stance as the medvak system attempted to tend to the wound in his side with an injection of nanites.

Entradis charged, and their blades connected in a flurry that sent sparks everywhere. Neven triggered one of the new features of his blade as an electric pulse surged through the weapon. The moment it connected with Entradis, the pulse intensified. Lighting arced out from the blade directly toward Entradis.

Entradis's eyes widened as lighting slammed into him, sending him flying hard into a nearby pole. The violent immortal staggered, his focus lost momentarily as Neven's chest cannon fired again. The searing blast soared toward Entradis's heart. The beam connected but was defeated by a powerful barrier that surrounded Entradis. Neven lamented that the nullifying field had been destroyed.

Entradis released his blade, the weapon righting itself in the air. Neven reflexively gulped.

"I haven't had to work this hard in a long time," Entradis said. He bowed at Neven. "It's easy to see why Lanrete values you. This will make your death even sweeter."

"You talk about immortals shaping the world in their image. How are you any different?" Neven broadcasted from his power armor. "You ruin the lives of others because one man hurt you."

416

Entradis motioned to his side, his blade moving rapidly away from him and perpendicular to Neven's location. "Lanrete took everything I valued away from me, my family, my joy. But I am not unique. He has destroyed the lives of so many, of entire civilizations. He must suffer."

"You killed my wife and unborn child," Neven spat back at him. "I valued them! How are you any different from him?"

Entradis blinked, glancing down at the ground briefly.

"I don't care about the history between you and Lanrete. You took something away from me and had no right to take it." Neven took in a deep breath. He felt himself get sick but pushed the words out. "Forgiveness allows us to move on with our lives, move past the injustice done to us, and rebuild. Because of that," Neven hesitated. "I forgive what you've done to me. I forgive what you've stolen from me." Neven leveled his blade on Entradis. "But you must be held accountable for your actions."

Entradis's head tilted to the side. "I never asked for your forgiveness!" Entradis shouted, suddenly hot with anger. His face contorted, making him seem less like a Huzien and more like a demon.

A chill went down Neven's spine. "It doesn't matter. I won't be consumed anymore by what you've done to me. One way or another, I will be at peace."

"Well spoken," came a voice off to the side.

Neven and Entradis turned to see Soahc with his arms crossed, an Enesmic portal behind him, revealing Lanrete, Jessica, and Tashanira.

"A little birdy tipped us off to an unwanted guest, so I decided to bring a few friends," Soahc said. "Hello Uriel, or I guess it's Entradis now. Can't say it's good to see you."

You're welcome, Ellipse said in his mind as he felt her smile.

Entradis frowned. He stood, contemplating something for a short moment, even as a series of explosions went off around them. A platform landed between Entradis and the arriving team, the top blowing off to reveal three Enesmic creatures chained to a platform. One looked like a giant, mutated wolf with an aura around it that caused Soahc to take a step back. The second was a Bau with two large scimitars. The final one looked like a large, snakelike creature with hard scales. It rose straight up like a man with four large scythe-like appendages and a long mouth that ended in a narrow blade of its own. It was a horrid-looking abomination that brought an irrational fear into Neven's heart.

Neven stepped back, half expecting the creatures to attack immediately, but something was off about them. They just stood there, acting unlike any other Enesmic being Neven had encountered.

"You did it." Soahc gasped.

Lanrete glanced at Soahc with a hint of concern.

"I did." Entradis smirked.

The chains holding them to the platform dropped away.

CHAPTER 50 - ENTRADIS

Genmatha, Huzien Alliance space

Entradis prepared to teleport away from the mass confusion he had created, but a notification hit his mobi that caused him to frown. It was the final message from his ship, which complained of catastrophic systems failure. He tried to bring up a view from within the ship, but the feed was dead.

"*Vusging* Sentinels," he said. How had they found his ship? He was always so careful.

This was it then. There was no retreat this time. Entradis knew that this day would eventually come.

Entradis remained where he was, alongside his small squad of Enesmic beings awaiting his command. He didn't intend to make the first move—he was outnumbered, and his enemies were powerful, meaning he had to play it smart.

He doubted Soahc would let him freely use his abilities, but the Suhnret was his ace against the immortal Cihphist. It was the one thing even Soahc feared, and it was his sole contingency against his former mentor. The creatures were terrifying; Entradis had almost lost his life in his quest to tame the beast. Its ability to feed off Enesmic and life energy made it particularly difficult to fight against.

Neven made the first move; it was clear that common sense was something the boy lacked. The rest of his enemies exploded into motion in tandem. Soahc began to probe at the complex web Entradis had created to keep the Enesmic creatures on this plane of existence.

Soahc had to go down first.

Entradis charged at Soahc, the Suhnret at his side. The creature warped forward, stepping through the Enesmic in a way similar to the Liajhem. This method wasn't quite teleporting, but it was just as deadly. It was at Soahc's side in a heartbeat, its howl causing Soahc's eyes to go wide as he attempted to teleport away.

The Suhnret devoured the cihphistic web that Soahc was creating and lunged at the immortal. A brown-haired woman with orange highlights jumped between Soahc and the creature, catching its maw on her blade. Its size pushed her back as she struggled against its terrible might. Entradis remembered her name to be Jessica: Lanrete's new protégé.

His replacement.

He scowled and came in hard with Wishwonder, aiming at her neck.

Lanrete attempted to move to intercept, but the serpent-like creature—the Gafi'opiyu—intercepted Lanrete, spinning in a terrible motion that pushed Lanrete back. It came in with a fury, hacking with its scythes in a way that put Lanrete on the defensive. The creature was incredibly fast, a perfect counter to the immortal.

Jessica used the Suhnret's weight to her advantage, giving in and disengaging herself as it forgot her and continued after Soahc. She met Entradis's blade, and the two danced as Entradis detected an attack from behind. He shifted hard to the side, Secnic weaponry blasting his prior location as Jessica continued her pursuit of the Suhnret. She slashed at it, drawing first blood. It turned on her and flared its body in a way that caused Entradis to distance himself quickly.

The area around the beast became heavy. Jessica's eyes flashed as she found herself unable to adapt quickly. It dug its maw into her chest and drank deep, growing in size. A scream escaped from her lips as her body seemed to dim, a sign Entradis knew was the creature sucking the very life essence from her body.

"No!" Soahc yelled. He unleashed a blast of Enesmic energy at the Suhnret that slammed into its side, blowing it off Jessica.

She collapsed to the ground, her body suddenly very frail. Her eyes were hollow, but a dim flicker of life was still there. The Suhnret got up, the terrible wound from Soahc's blast rapidly mending as it expended some of the life energy it had just absorbed from Jessica to heal itself.

Soahc unleashed another lefon blast, this one aimed at Entradis. He shifted out of the way, refusing to allow Cihphism from Soahc to connect with him. The immortal had too many tricks, and Entradis couldn't risk a mistake like that on this careful battlefield.

Entradis caught sight of the Uri—Tashanira. He had thought her occupied with the Bau, but now she was descending from the air on the Suhnret, her weapons blazing. A glance in the direction she had come from confirmed he was down an ally.

The Suhnret looked up at her and howled as Tashanira spun in a tight circle, making her blasts faster and deadlier. The creature blinked forward and then into the air, attacking her before she could land.

Her armor flared as she was thrown back through the air, confusing the Suhnret. It fell hard, its target out of reach, then blinked forward, focused on Tashanira.

Entradis turned his attention back to Soahc. Neven was in front of him; his chest opened up, unleashing a devastating blast that Entradis took straight on. His barrier absorbed the hit as he was flung into the house he had hidden in. The force of his impact blew it apart, but Entradis unleashed a shock wave to clear away the rubble as he stood. Entradis touched the Enesmic and let it flow through him. He felt himself shift into a heightened state of consciousness as he became a beacon of energy. The veins in his skin began to bulge and glow, and his eyes filled with white fire while power visibly radiated off his body.

Lanrete glanced at him, his eyes wide. Soahc had risen into the air, directly out of his reach, and Neven was charging toward him. Entradis frowned as a storm of blades appeared right on top of him.

He threw himself high into the air, launching Wishwonder directly at Soahc. Soahc attempted to deflect the blade again, but this time, Entradis was committed. He energized the blade and used it as a lightning rod—a powerful blast streaked down, hitting the blade, and channeled straight toward Soahc.

Soahc fell back on his defensive shield, just as Entradis had anticipated. The blade slammed right into Soahc's shoulder, knocking him out of the sky. Neven glanced back at Soahc and then looked to Entradis.

Wishwonder pulled itself out of Soahc and started to move of its own accord, attempting to sever the immortal's head. Neven scrambled back to help defend Soahc, but the Cihphist cut the bands of Cihphism controlling Wishwonder and used telekinesis to fling the blade at an incredible speed far out into the ocean. Entradis cursed.

Neven got to Soahc's side and helped him to his feet. The wound Entradis had inflicted on Soahc was substantial, making Soahc's left arm nearly unusable.

Entradis didn't give them time to regroup. He came in like a comet, his body surrounded by a ball of energy that exploded when he touched down. The impact washed over Neven and Soahc, but both got their defensive shielding up just in time. Entradis launched into constructing a powerful web of Cihphism that Soahc attempted to counter, but he winced as he realized his arm wasn't responding.

The delay in countering his actions gave Entradis the extra second he needed, and he unleashed a sphere of energy between Soahc and Neven and then teleported outside of the blast radius. The explosion left a crater a mile wide. He surveyed the destruction from an elevated cliff face that overlooked what had once been a beach. The water from the ocean was now moving in to fill the void. A ringing hit his ears as his body stopped responding.

He attempted to raise his hand, but it didn't move. Enara appeared before him, and the scenery shifted to the Tuzen imperial gardens. She smiled at him, taking him by the hand as they descended the stairs to their favorite relaxation spot. They removed their shoes,

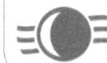

and Entradis rested in the grass, Enara sitting beside him. She turned to look at him, her beautiful smile bringing him peace.

It was something he hadn't felt in a long time.

Reality crashed down around him as a young woman with golden eyes stared back at him with loathing. She lifted her arm, the long, sickle-like blade lined with blood, his blood. The weapon retreated into its den in her arm.

Entradis blinked, and then he saw his body from upside down as he stared at his headless corpse. His world went dark.

CHAPTER 51 - ELLIPSE

Genmatha, Huzien Alliance space

Ellipse stared at Entradis's face, exiting ACP and sheathing the latest enhancement to her body. She watched as Entradis's head tumbled off the corpse, the body following shortly after as it collapsed to the ground.

She stared at it for a long moment. This man had caused so much pain to the man she loved. She looked to the crater, his last act of destruction, and immediately sent her scanners into overdrive, searching for signs of life.

She soon caught sight of them at the edge of the crater—Lanrete was standing with a wicked-looking gash across his chest. Soahc, Tashanira, Neven, and Jessica were all there as well. Turning back on ACP, she picked up Entradis's head and went down to the group. She exited ACP a few steps away from them.

"Where is Entradis?" Lanrete asked.

"Dead," Ellipse said.

All eyes turned to her. Neven opened the face mask to his power armor and gave her a look of disbelief. "He's dead?"

"Yes. I killed him." Ellipse tossed Entradis's head at Neven's feet.

Lanrete stared at the head for a long moment, his eyes slowly rising to look at Ellipse. There was something there, something she had never seen from him before. Fear.

"What happened?" Neven glanced at the crater. "Last thing I remember was that sphere."

"It's a new trick I learned." Soahc glanced at Lanrete. "I slowed the flow of time just enough to allow me to enact mass teleportation." Soahc sighed. "And I want to call out how much having only one functional arm *vusging* sucks. It's incredibly limiting for Cihphism."

"Remember the cost." Lanrete frowned.

"I'll deal with that whenever this mysterious cost makes itself known," Soahc countered.

"Jessica needs immediate medical attention." Tashanira was holding Jessica in her arms. Jessica was breathing raggedly, her chest mangled. Tashanira was covered in her blood.

"My ship is in orbit." Neven glanced to Ellipse.

"I'd create a portal, but I need a second functioning arm to pull that off," Soahc said.

"We have two of the *Castrin*'s shuttles nearby. The ATMS should be able to stabilize her as we head back to the ship," Ellipse said. "Here. Let me take her. It'll be faster."

Tashanira handed over Jessica as Ellipse activated ACP and made her way toward the shuttle.

Castrin *en route to the* Foundra Ascension, *Huzien Alliance space*

Soahc looked up at Ellipse as she entered the morgue on the *Castrin*. It was small, a room with a single medical bed and multiple storage lockers that could hold up to five dead bodies in stasis. Entradis's corpse was on the bed. His head had been surgically reattached.

Ellipse wasn't sure why, but it had been Lanrete's request.

"His story always made me so sad," Soahc said. "He was a great man once. A close friend even." Soahc looked back down at the body. "There are moments in our lives where we make decisions that set the tone for the future. I sense that you are setting a tone, even now." Soahc grinned. "What you did scared Lanrete. It's been a long time since I've seen him scared of anything. Be careful who you make fear you." Soahc exited the morgue.

Ellipse stared down at Entradis's body. His death was something she had accomplished with little effort. She found it perplexing that someone so deadly could be so easily killed. Ellipse let out a sigh, the very Human reaction feeling right in that moment. She focused all her attention on the android shell tending to Neven on the medical deck of the *Castrin.*

This shell was a replica of the one in the morgue. Ellipse had decided to multiply her physical presence with another body currently in omnistructure, built as a redundancy in case the shell she sent down to the surface was destroyed. Neven was sedated, allowing Ellipse to finish her work as the ship doctor stared on with a mask of concern.

"We can easily grow an organic arm. Why are we using these cybernetics?" the doctor asked.

Ellipse glanced back at her. "This is better," she said.

"Did he even consent to that?"

"I'm his wife. He's unconscious. It's my decision, right?" Ellipse narrowed her eyes.

"Right . . ." the doctor conceded.

Ellipse continued to work, meshing the organic with the inorganic. A short while later, Neven awoke to the sight of Ellipse sitting next to him. She smiled. Neven sighed as he rested his head back on the bed. He lifted his left arm, staring at it momentarily and then narrowing his eyes.

"My arm? This . . . what is this?" Neven stared at the arm, turning it over with confusion.

"My creation," Ellipse said.

"Cybernetics?"

"Something more. It's the future."

Neven looked at Ellipse, staring at her for a long moment. He sat up, wincing as he put pressure on his arm.

"Careful," she said. "The organic matter will be a bit sore from the procedure."

"It's hard to believe that Entradis is dead." He glanced at Ellipse. "I was surprised to see Tashanira. Is she still here?"

Ellipse frowned. "No. Once Soahc's arm was fixed, he opened a portal back to Peshkana for them. She was quite impressed with the Vrit armor you made for her and told me to tell you something inappropriate that I refuse to repeat." Ellipse hesitated. "We're en route with Lanrete and Jessica back to the *Foundra Ascension*. The doctors wanted to keep Jessica under care as the Suhnret did some real damage to her. She almost died."

Neven nodded his head gravely.

"I found something for you. A memento." Ellipse gently rested the retracted blade, Wishwonder, on Neven's bed.

He stared at the weapon for a long moment, eventually nodding. He took in a deep breath and then let it out.

He then lay back down and closed his eyes.

To imagine that this would have been the fate of Neth if not for the brave men and women of the mobile infantry who held out against all odds and hit shipyards, disrupting the enemy.

-FROM "ENESMIC SHIPYARD EFFECTS ON TRICA VII"
MINSCI METABASE

CHAPTER 52 - NEVEN KENK

MinSci, Thae, Huzien home system

Neven sat in the waiting area of the administrative complex of the MinSci, Ellipse next to him. He stared at the rolling waterfall showcased in the elaborate reception area. A pang of nostalgia hit him as he recalled his first time there. It was before all of this started, before his first encounter with a Founder of the Huzien Empire.

He looked down at his left arm. It felt natural, like his old arm. There were additional senses he hadn't had before, which gave him an accurate measure of air pressure, temperature, and other data points that he could "feel." Not just understanding like numbers on a sensor readout. It was one of Ellipses's creations, but he was strangely okay with that. The doctor aboard the *Castrin* had informed him that he could get an organic replacement if he wanted one, but he opted to keep what Ellipse had done to him.

He felt connected to her in a way that he didn't understand.

The tap of heels on checkered granite brought his gaze up to see Triny, who frowned at him. She glanced at Ellipse and sucked her teeth, coming to a stop in front of Neven with her hand on her hip. "Rebound chick?" Triny asked.

"His wife," Ellipse corrected.

Triny's eyes narrowed, and she glanced from Ellipse to Neven. "Watch your man." Triny eyed Ellipse and then motioned for them to follow.

They followed her up a meglift and into Ecnics's office. She didn't leave like usual and instead led them to a corner of the room where Ecnics sat in an oversized lounge chair. She motioned for them to sit on a couch adjacent to Ecnics and then moved to sit near the Founder. Triny crossed her legs and looked to Ecnics.

Neven watched Triny carefully. Something was off. He glanced to Ecnics, who eyed Ellipse for a long moment as two more women entered Ecnics's office and moved to sit in the chairs around them. They all looked related, as if they were Triny's siblings. They even wore similar clothes.

Ellipse slowly turned to face Triny, tilting her head to the side as her gaze jumped between each woman. "Interesting," Ellipse said.

"Indeed." Ecnics turned from Ellipse to Neven and then to Triny and the other women. Neven stared at them for a long moment, the pieces finally falling into place.

"You broke your own rule," Neven said.

Triny smiled at him.

"I did, and neither of the other Founders can ever know. The Twin Galaxies are not ready. Understand?" Ecnics asked.

Neven looked to Triny. "What is your real name?" Neven asked.

"I am Cathid," Triny and the other women said in unison.

The scene was jarring to Neven. Something about it made him uneasy. He glanced to Ellipse. "In exchange for my silence, Ellipse can live?"

"Yes, although it comes with some stipulations. First, I'd like to compare designs. I created Cathid after our encounter with the Ascended, synthetic life-forms created by the Omiciri many millennia ago. I took the lessons learned from their mistakes and adapted, creating perfection." Ecnics got up and moved to an open area. He projected Cathid's core into the hologrid of the room, completely taking up the space. He glanced back at Neven, who looked to Ellipse. She frowned but nodded, sending a flood of information to Ecnics, who projected her core next to it in the hologrid, side by side.

"How long?"

Ecnics continued to study the design. "Dear, do you mind answering his question?"

"I am one thousand nine hundred and ten years old," Cathid said.

"When your *eifi* died . . ." Neven's eyes went wide. "Does Kaloni know?"

"You are the only living person to know this secret. And if that changes . . ." Ecnics left the threat to hang in the air, glancing briefly at Neven.

Neven nodded.

"Every few hundred years, Ecnics gets a new secretary, the prior moving off-world to retire," Cathid added. "And with her comes a big family, brilliant women who take comparable roles across the MinSci with eyes on key projects."

"So our relationship never really had a chance?" Neven glanced at the shell he knew as Triny.

"Humans don't live that long." Cathid sighed. "We'd have a long, fulfilling life. I'd say I couldn't have kids, and we'd spend the last years of your life enjoying each other's company before you returned to your Maker."

Cathid glared at Neven. "But you had to turn out to be a womanizer."

"Neven is a good man." Ellipse scowled at Triny, the two locking gazes for a long moment.

"Ladies," Ecnics said. Both turned to face him. "Neven, what we are doing is very dangerous. The MinSci SI detected Ellipse a long time ago. Thankfully, all alerts go to me first, and I added Ellipse to a special exception list that only I have the authority to access. This immediately purged all instances of her existence from the MinSci metabase." Ecnics turned to face Neven and sat on the arm of the couch.

"What happens now?" Neven asked.

Ecnics let out a long sigh. "Now, I make you a Feshra and give you a permanent position on Ruekae, far away from the eyes of the other Founders. You will retire formally from the Founder's Elite and settle humbly into your new life."

"Lanrete knows about Ellipse," Neven said.

"He's afraid of me," Ellipse said. She rubbed her hand, glancing down at the floor.

"As far as he's concerned, I recalled you back to the MinSci, gave you a stern warning highlighting how dangerous artificial life forms are, and ordered the shell destroyed, employing special safeguards that prevented Ellipse's escape. I will need one of the replica shells you've created as proof." Ecnics glanced to Ellipse, who stared at him with wide eyes. "The moment the MinSci SI detected you, I overrode the SI on the *Castrin* and gained full insight into what I was dealing with. Please don't be surprised. We are a very cautious group if you haven't realized."

"What about Kechu?" Neven asked.

"The SSI project has been terminated, and all personnel reassigned except Kechu, who has been forcefully retired from the MinSci. I have arranged for him to be set up with an executive-level position at Somift Technology. I assure you he will be well taken care of. Contacting him is off limits and will be monitored."

"This is all my fault," Neven said. "The SSI project was his dream. He had nothing to do with this. It's not fair."

"The galaxy isn't always a fair place. Someone had to take the fall for this—it was either Kechu or you. I deemed you more valuable, so here we are." Ecnics turned to face Ellipse. "I understand you're probably attached to this appearance, but you must let it go and never wear it again. Cathid can help you with that process." Ecnics turned back to Neven. "Regarding your personal life, you'll be visibly distraught for a while, and then a new girl will appear." Ecnics glanced at Ellipse. "She'll remind you of your lost loves, and the two of you will spend the rest of your lives together."

Neven glanced at Ellipse with concern. "Is that all necessary?"

"It is." Ecnics got up, Triny moving to his side. "After you die, Ellipse will return here and join my staff. Her appearance will change again, and thus, a new cycle will start."

"Working at the MinSci for eternity doesn't sound like a great existence," Ellipse said.

"It is *an* existence, my dear illegal friend, and it's the best I can offer you at this stage in our galactic evolution." He glanced back at Neven. "Congratulations, Feshra Neven, on your accomplishments. Your refinement of GCH technology—originally created by Feshra Zun—into military application in the form of the Vrit suit has enabled the creation of a new frontline unit, the Vritropan. Through multiple efforts, you have revolutionized the world of robotics and anti-Cihphist weaponry, creating technologies that will help our soldiers overcome our enemies on the battlefield. You will enter into the annals of history as a steward of progress for the great Huzien Empire," Ecnics said the words with a practiced cadence, taking on an air of formality.

Neven stared at Ecnics, hollow. It was everything he had worked toward, but felt like a lie. He hadn't earned this. This was the price of his silence, his compliance.

You did earn this, Neven. Just take it, Ellipse said in his mind.

Neven stared at Ecnics's hand for a long moment and then walked over, shaking it. "Thank you, Founder Ecnics. I am...honored."

Exfan, Ruekae, Neutral Zone
Two Months Later

Neven looked out of the window from the primary living room of his new multilevel condo. It was situated above the clouds. The sprawling cityscape of Exfan on the planet Ruekae was breathtaking and a bit overwhelming.

The entire planet was a city, a melting pot of species from across the Twin Galaxies, and it was situated in an area of space known as the Neutral Zone. It bordered the Huzien Alliance, Darbol Alliance, Lux'Ameni Empire, and the borders of a species Neven hadn't interacted with, known as the Gi'A'Fan Collective. The Collective was made up of a mesh of species who had been forcefully merged into it, a combination of alien genetics leading to something that looked more like a monster than a sentient being.

"Joining" the Collective meant ceasing to exist as your previous selves, all aspects of your species and society broken down and merged into the whole. Much of the galaxy considered them a threat and an abomination, mainly due to how they had assimilated other species by force, and they only halted when the other galactic empires temporarily unified against them. They were a brilliant species with a not-insignificant presence on Ruekae.

Ruekae was an experiment based on the premise of scientific advancement and achievement above all else. It was like an extreme version of the MinSci that framed the entire culture of the planet. The best of the best from across the galaxy existed here, each with the explicit permission of their respective governments. It was the sole form of unified cooperation in the Twin Galaxies, with everyday politics, rivalries, and hatred not allowed to exist.

Ruekae had a government of its own, separate and independent from any other galactic empire by design. It was a unique construct put in place to ensure equal representation and opportunity for every represented empire. The only military presence allowed to exist in the neutral zone was that of Ruekae itself, under the administration of the Ruekae Cooperative.

Lasicov entered the room, catching Neven's attention. "Master Neven, we have received a communication request from the Vempiir Dominion," he said.

Neven frowned. "I'm not interested."

"I . . . strongly encourage you to take this call. It's from the High Master of the Vempiir Dominion, Gafgen Meutrol." Lasicov rubbed his hand, his eyes downcast.

"Okay . . ." Neven moved to sit on his couch as Lasicov brought the hologrid in the room to life.

A large and imposing carmine, red-skinned man with crimson-red hair and crystalline eyes that glowed silver from within appeared in front of them. The hologrid displayed the elaborate desk he sat behind, the technology blending Neven's living space with the room Gafgen Meutrol occupied. It was an advancement Neven was still getting used to, something common on Ruekae that hadn't yet been adopted in Huzien Alliance space.

Gafgen smiled with his teeth showing. Neven wasn't sure if it was a greeting or a threat.

"Feshra Neven, it is an honor to meet you. Thank you for accepting my call." Gafgen got up and walked around his desk to lean against it, facing Neven. He crossed his arms. "I understand that your last visit to our beautiful home world had a complication."

"You mean Vanether's attempt to kill me?" Neven asked.

"Yes, that." Gafgen's face grew serious. He snapped his fingers.

Vanether was escorted to the space before him by two Vempiir guards and then thrown to the floor. She glanced up at Neven and then looked down at the ground, remaining very still. Neven could see fear in her eyes, and he shifted uncomfortably. They then stripped off her clothing down to the waist, and one of the Vempiir guards picked up a wicked-looking whip.

Neven tensed. "What? What's going—"

Gafgen nodded his head, and immediately, the guard lashed Vanether's back, leaving stripes of neon-white blood as it broke the skin. Vanether gasped. The beating continued as she received multiple lashes until she collapsed to the floor, unmoving.

"Stop!" Neven shouted, but the guard continued until Gafgen raised his hand a moment later.

Neven rushed over to Vanether and bent down to watch her closely. She was still breathing. Gafgen snapped his fingers again as the two guards went on each side of her and lifted her, carrying her unconscious form out of the room.

"Please accept this as our sincerest apologies. Vanether's actions were not representative of the Vempiir Dominion, nor were they reflective of the Meutrol line. The attempt on your life was unacceptable, and it was also revealed that she attempted to use your blood for the creation of a clone, an illegal and abhorrent endeavor. I have taken action to ensure that the collection of your blood has been destroyed to prevent further abuse."

Neven glanced at Lasicov, both having received a report from Dexter the week prior that a mission had been successfully carried out at Lanrete's request to sabotage his blood sample and ensure no clone would be viable by the Sentinels.

"One other thing, Feshra Neven." Gafgen moved into the chair with a practiced ease. "With your elevated status on Ruekae as a Feshra representative of the MinSci, I would like to make you a formal offer, not as High Master and co-leader of the Vempiir Dominion but as the head of the Meutrol coven. I learned of the loss of your mate, the woman who used deception to disguise herself as a Vempiir of low class when you were here. And I wanted to make amends since you appear to enjoy the company of Vempiir women. Vanether is not the best we have to offer." Gafgen smiled. "My granddaughter; she is on Ruekae and is a scientist of great renown. We do not always see eye to eye, but I would very much like to introduce you two. She is a gorgeous woman, and I would be honored to welcome you formally into the Meutrol coven through familial bond if you accept her hand in marriage."

"You're trying to marry off your granddaughter? To me?" Neven raised an eyebrow, a dumbfounded look on his face.

"My granddaughter believes in duty and honor first and foremost and has agreed to this arrangement if you accept."

Neven glanced at Lasicov, who was just out of range of the hologrid. He had a distraught look on his face, one that told Neven that declining this offer was something dangerous to do. Neven felt Ellipse frowning in his mind's eye. She hadn't yet reappeared in his life as her new self, considering Ecnics carefully orchestrated their steps to avoid suspicion from the other Founders. But they were still married, even if her form would change, and they couldn't yet be together physically.

"I . . . am incredibly humbled by your gracious offer, but I unfortunately must decline. I am not ready to consider a new relationship at this moment," Neven said.

Lasicov rubbed the back of his neck and walked out of the room.

"I see." Gafgen frowned. "Understandable. My granddaughter is a woman you don't know, and it would be so soon after the loss of one close to you." Gafgen forced a smile. "This may seem unorthodox to you, but in Vempiir society, arranged unions are commonplace and usually orchestrated by covens." Gafgen tapped his fingers on his desk. "I am sending along her channel details and would encourage you two to connect, if not as potential mates, then as colleagues and representatives of the Huzien Alliance on Ruekae. I believe you will find her an intellectual equal." Gafgen remained silent for a long moment. "I want to assure you that there are no ulterior motives here. I am a blunt man. I state what I intend plainly. That is why I have ruled as High Master for over thirty thousand years. You will see this in time, as I am sure this is not the last time we will chat." Gafgen gave that same tooth-filled smile from before, the one that Neven couldn't discern. "Goodbye, Feshra." Gafgen terminated the connection.

Neven released the breath he hadn't realized he'd been holding and stared at the ceiling. It was a transparent window that gave a clear view of the rest of the structure in which Neven's home resided. The structure connected from deep in the planet's crust to a massive space station in orbit. It was a monolithic construction of engineering genius that had floored Neven the first time he had seen it. Even now, its scale was hard to process. It also served as a space elevator and ship-launch conduit, a more advanced form of the space conduits from back on Thae. Neven stared at the channel details of the Vempiir woman: Zefa Meutrol. A series of images had also been sent to him, one showing her staring intently at the camera, her piercing gaze catching the breath in his throat. She *was* gorgeous.

"How do Vempiir treat non-pure-blooded Vempiir?" Neven asked Ellipse.

She frowned at the implications of the question. She pulled from her archive, the volume of which had become staggering due to her increased storage capacity from the *Castrin* docked in orbit. She recalled a case study on the treatment of half-blooded Vempiir on Piro and passed it along to Neven. She began to summarize.

"While the practice of Vempiir performing Yerrhgda on other Vempiir was officially outlawed, there were frequent instances of Yerrhgda being performed on half-blooded Vempiir, resulting in their death to extend the life of the assailant. While it was not as effective as when used on a full-blooded Vempiir, the effects were powerful enough to put a large percentage of the half-blooded Vempiir populace at risk." She hesitated. "Apprehension of the assailants was low, with only a handful of Vempiir being brought to justice for the murders."

Neven's heart sank, a flood of despair and dread washing over him. His hand subconsciously went to his neck as he felt the scar now present there from Vanether's attack on him. He had left it as a reminder.

CHAPTER 53 - LANRETE

Foundra Ascension *in orbit above Thae, Huzien home system*

Lanrete stared out the window, down at the blue orb that took up most of the window in his office aboard the *Foundra Ascension*. Entradis was dead. He should be happy and relieved after so long. But in Entradis's death, he remembered Uriel. He remembered the man he had once loved and called his son. He felt nothing but pain and sorrow for the loss of Uriel. The loss felt raw and fresh.

He watched in his mind's eye as Ellipse threw Uriel's head onto the ground.

Ellipse. His murderer.

It was how his heart interpreted that moment. It had been the murder of his son by a machine.

He let out a slow breath and got up, walking to the window. He leaned against it as he tried to find the general direction of the MinSci down below. The ship was passing in orbit in the vicinity of the continent of Ecka as he stared at the lights coming on all across the surface. The planet's dark side bathed the area where the MinSci was located in a deep shadow.

He glanced back at the holodisplay, the report from Ecnics visible. Ellipse had been destroyed, judging by the image of her android shell disassembled. Her android brain had even been fried. He didn't feel comfort from that. Instead, he sensed a change coming, one that terrified him.

The soft chime at the entrance to his quarters caused him to let out a heavy sigh and exit the office. He moved toward the entrance as he permitted Jessica entry. Lanrete stopped in the great hall and caught sight of her walking toward him. Her silver-eyed gaze locked onto his, and something there caused him discomfort and nervousness.

She was out of uniform, wearing a loose-fitting top that showed the scar where the Suhnret had drank of her life essence. She was disheveled, wearing a pair of skintight leggings that put Lanrete off guard.

She wasn't the formal, crisp officer he had expected to see. He frowned and motioned for her to follow him into the adjacent sitting room. Jessica moved into one of the chairs and rested her head in her hands.

Lanrete watched her silently and then moved into a chair next to her. "How are you recovering?"

"Just fine. Better than fine, actually." Jessica looked up at Lanrete. "I should have died from that wound, and yet now all that remains is this barely visible scar."

Lanrete sat quietly for a long moment, his gaze locked with Jessica. "Between the *Foundra Ascension* and the *Castrin*, we have some of the best doctors in the Twin Galaxies," he said.

"What am I, Lan?"

"You're an exceptional warrior and a highly capable and resilient Redalam."

"Am I like you?" Jessica leaned forward.

Lanrete hesitated for a long moment and then crossed his arms. "Yes. You were born an immortal."

Jessica became animated. "Why did you keep this from me?"

"What does it matter?"

"I don't know! It just . . . it seems like an important detail to know. The whole 'your life is forever thing' gives a *vusging* significant amount of perspective."

That was the first time Lanrete had ever heard Jessica swear—the image of the innocent farm girl he had recruited started to shatter in his mind.

"You can still die. Entradis is a great example," Lanrete said. "No matter how invincible you think you are."

"I wanted to help people in my youth and then find somebody. I wanted to start a family and watch my kids grow old. I wanted to get some grandchildren and die knowing I made a difference in this galaxy." Jessica stood. "That was my life plan, Lan. That plan is gone now. I . . . do I do this forever? Do I just fight and kill until someone better comes along and kills me, or another Enesmic creature finishes the job of the Suhnret? Do I find someone and watch them die, like you talk about endlessly? I don't want that. No one should want that." Jessica's tone was rising, her face flushed as she stared daggers at Lanrete. "And you were content just to let me go along thinking that until I—what? Realized that I didn't age? That everyone else around me is getting older, but for some reason, I look the same?"

"It was the best way. Trust me."

"Why? Why should I trust you, Lan? What else could you be hiding from me?"

Thoughts flashed in Lanrete's mind of flying on the Enesmic plane as a Rel Ach'Kel, and he let out a slow breath.

"Don't let this knowledge change who you are." Lanrete stood. "Entradis let it, and you've seen the damage that did." Lanrete walked up to Jessica and grabbed her hands, holding them with his gaze focused intently on hers. "You are a good woman and have a kind heart. Amplify those aspects of yourself and let them dictate who you become."

"I kill people for a living, Lan. *We* kill people for a living." Jessica shook her head. "Is that what a kindhearted woman does?" She looked down at the ground, frowning. "My father was right."

"No." Lanrete shook his head, forcing Jessica's attention. "What we do safeguards the empire. It is an aspect of who we are, but it isn't the total sum of our character. We kill because we must, not because we want to. That is a distinct difference that separates us from monsters like Entradis."

"We're all monsters, Lan. Just different kinds of monsters." She looked down at the ground. "I'm not going to play the part of the innocent girl anymore. I'm going to be who I want to be." She looked back up at Lanrete and half closed her eyes. "I'm not going to put aside my needs and wants anymore. If I truly am immortal, I will live in the moment every day. I'm not going to simply look forward to the what ifs." She leaned forward and kissed Lanrete.

Lanrete's eyes went wide, his body numb as he processed what was happening. Jessica pressed into him and kissed him more passionately.

Lanrete put his arms on her shoulders and pushed her back, making eye contact. "You don't want this."

"You're wrong!" she pleaded. "I've been in love with you for years, but I've always been afraid to do anything about it. Not anymore." She pushed into him again, pulling off her top as she kissed him.

Lanrete gently pushed her back to arm's length again and sighed heavily. "I don't want this," Lanrete said. "I'm sorry. I'm in love with someone else."

Jessica froze, her eyes beginning to water as she looked down at the ground. She slowly pulled her shirt back on and moved out of the room in a daze, never looking back at Lanrete as she exited his quarters.

Gefrey in orbit around Werthae, Huzien home system

The HSS *Gefrey*, capital ship of the Fifth Huzien Imperial Fleet, was in orbit around the gas giant Werthae, the largest planet in the Huzien home system.

Lanrete hesitated at the door to the fleet admiral's quarters. Letting out a slow breath, he chimed it. The door slid open to reveal Jenle Frema, her hazel eyes widening slightly even as she forced her face to remain passive.

"Which kind of visit is this?" she asked.

Lanrete moved into the room and kissed her, taking her into his arms as she instructed the door to close. She grinned wide at him as he began to kiss her neck. Her uniform came off quickly as Lanrete followed in kind, the two stumbling to her bedroom.

Lanrete caught sight of her perky, athletically toned breasts, moving to kiss them as she moaned in anticipation. Jenle pulled Lanrete on top of her as they made their way into the bed, and she began to stroke his member.

Lanrete let the anticipation build. They kissed before Lanrete entered her with a deep stroke. Jenle wrapped her arms around Lanrete, pulling him close as he built up a rhythm, one that allowed the two to make love long into the night.

The next morning, Lanrete lay next to Jenle, watching her silently. She began to stir, her eyes opening and going to his.

She smiled, turning over to face him as a necklace fell onto the bed from her chest. She glanced down at it in confusion, her eyes suddenly going wide. She looked back at Lanrete and sat up, picking up the necklace and turning it over in her hands. "Is this . . ."

"Will you be my *eifi*?" Lanrete asked.

Jenle's face lit up as a tear rolled down her cheek. "Of course!" She leaned forward and wrapped Lanrete in a hug. "I can't tell you how long I've waited for this day."

"I know. I'm sorry I kept you waiting."

Jenle pushed Lanrete back and moved atop him, pulling the necklace over her head and letting it fall. Lanrete smiled, the image of Jenle with the necklace resting on her chest filling him with a sense of peace. She lay on top of him, and Lanrete wrapped her in his arms. The two stayed in that position for a long moment until Jenle eventually pushed herself up and stared down at him.

"I hope this doesn't mean you expect me to adopt the barefoot and pregnant persona. I have a fleet to command."

Lanrete smirked. "Whatever you do to stay comfortable on your ship is none of my concern."

Jenle laughed.

EPILOGUE

S oahc paced the condo he had acquired on Peshkana. He was in a grah tree on the other side of town from the one that housed Tashanira's sister and baby Hesre. He spent much time practicing the new abilities that he had taken some time to understand.

That moment when he had stopped time under the guidance of an awakened Lanrete in the Heart of Corruption had been eye-opening. His whole understanding of how the universe operated had been thrown out of the window and replaced with a new set of unknowns. He felt like an Argent acolyte gaining their first taste of what powers the Enesmic held.

He focused intently on the piece of fruit from which he had taken a few bites at the start of this session. The fruit was a delicacy native to Peshkana. Its appearance was a mix between an apple and a pear in a shade of orange.

He touched the Enesmic and worked through it to grasp hold of the strands of time he had come to recognize pervaded each thing on the Havin plane. The strands differed, some very thin while others were thick. Many of them differed in color. He didn't fully understand what those facts meant, but he saw it as a challenge to figure out.

Utilizing the same technique the awakened Lanrete had taught him, he stopped time for the piece of fruit. Visually, it appeared as if Enesmic energy held the strand taut when time was stopped for it. He again tried to sever the strand, but nothing happened. He couldn't sever it like he had been able to sever the strand of Enesmic energy that powered a cihphistic manifestation.

He theorized what might happen if he could figure that out, but left those to the realm of theory and focused back on the task at hand. Working with the Enesmic, listening intently to the song and communing with it at a level he had never been able to do before, he slowly caused the bite marks in the fruit to disappear.

He felt an overwhelming pressure hit him, as if what he was doing was against the natural order of things. That pressure pushed not only against him but the fruit as well, and he let go of his hold of the strands. The fruit returned to the state it had been in with the bite marks.

Soahc smiled. He could now reverse time, not just slow it down as he had done with Entradis's energy sphere or halt it like the rift.

He had made progress.

Hiesha Nihjar
Seli VII, Tuzen Empire space

A Revfa blade exploded from a man's chest, staining his white cloak with red stitching. He had been sitting in a circle in a dimly lit back alley room with three other individuals clothed in similar garments.

The Chaah around him burst into motion, the terrible howling from the Revfa blade filling the small space. Another Chaah ran into the end of another Revfa blade that severed his head from his body. The two remaining Chaah broke into the weaving of Elhirtha, but the bodies of their fallen comrades were consumed by the blades that killed them, burning away whatever life energy they had attempted to use.

Desrin charged at another of the Chaah, slicing open her stomach and cutting her in half with a heavy downward strike that sliced through the woman like a hot knife through butter. The remaining Chaah attempted to flee but came face to face with Hiesha, who kicked them back to the ground with a ceremonial weapon that had the feel of a Revfa blade but without the critical element that made it alive and truly dangerous to him.

"Traitor!" the Chaah man spat at Hiesha. "You will never find a place among them! They will kill you when your usefulness is done."

"Alinos is the one who betrayed me, who betrayed my cell." Hiesha shook her head. "I don't care what happens to me. I only desire to be there when Alinos breathes his last."

Nestis drove his Revfa blade through the neck of the Chaah, and another terrible howling filled the room. Desrin and Nestis looked to Hiesha, whose skin was crawling at the sound. She felt their hungry gazes on her, their blades seeking to skewer her like they had the other Chaah in the room. The tainted marks in her skin glowed with an otherworldly luminescence that she tried very hard to hide. At that moment, she thought her life forfeit.

Then their eyes relaxed, and they glanced away from her, searching the room. She let out a sigh of relief.

Jenshi Runso
Six Months Later
Hurisew, Thae, Huzien home system

Jenshi stepped from the transport shuttle and pulled his duffle bag close to him, his gaze going up to the sky. He took a deep breath and pushed forward, his mind clear for the first time in a long time.

He had acquired a property near the Dahca Sea on the continent of Hurisew in a small town named Jasa a long time ago. He hadn't been there in years and determined it to be as good a place as any to spend time alone, trying to figure out what was next for him.

The towering space conduit provided an impressive backdrop to the transport hub. It was packed with people, one of the busiest conduits on Thae. Hurisew was known first and foremost for commerce, and it was one of the primary trade hubs on the planet.

"For the Tuzen Empire!" a man yelled from farther in the crowd.

The sound of weaponsfire caused Jenshi to duck down, latent instincts kicking in as he crawled on the ground toward the sound. A large man with a familiar face appeared above him. He was wearing a military uniform and extended a hand to Jenshi.

"Let's get you out of here," the man said.

Jenshi glanced at the rifle in the man's hand as the crowd dispersed in a panic, screaming and running everywhere. Jenshi looked over to see the dead body of a Tuzen man with munsha marks running down his face. Security swarmed on the dead Tuzen, and Jenshi accepted the man's hand. He quickly led him out of the area, Jenshi sticking close to his side as they exited the transport hub.

Jenshi stared at the man curiously for a long moment. "Thank you," Jenshi said. "Do I . . . know you from somewhere?"

The man smiled at Jenshi and nodded. "You saved my life on Neth. My medvak system had failed back in that cave when the planet was being overrun. I didn't get a chance to thank you, but because of you, I'm standing here today."

Jenshi smiled and then glanced back in the direction of the dead Tuzen. "I'm not sure what just happened, but I have the feeling that you just saved a lot of people's lives." He turned back to face the military man. "I'm sorry. I didn't catch your name."

"Larl Iunar."

"Well, Mr. Iunar. I seem to have lost all my friends due to poor life decisions. Would you be willing to take up that mantle?"

Larl smiled at Jenshi. "For the man who saved my life? Happily. Let's go get you a drink."

APPENDIX

CHARACTER ARCHIVE

Name | Species | Character Class (if applicable) | Short description.

FOUNDER'S ELITES

Arnea Henson | Human | Former aeroponics gardener of the *Foundra Ascension* and wife of Marcus Henson. Leaves with Marcus when he retires from the Founder's Elites.

Artinre | Uri-Huzien Hybrid | Wopan | Killed in ambush protecting Tuzen delegation in Alliance City.

Kera Oghenthen | Huzien | Archlight | Part of the Elites during the formation of the Huzien Alliance.

Ameen | Huzien | Secnic | Part of the Elites during the formation of the Huzien Alliance.

Asfeyra Mau Bertuferi | Uri-Huzien hybrid | Wopan | Founding member of the Founder's Elite, participated in mission on Guymulagi.

Aurari Netzcha, lieutenant (also known as Auri) | Huzien | Losrim | Administrative coordinator of the *Foundra Ascension* and personal assistant to Founder Lanrete.

Bevi Jegkirn | Huzien | Sentinel | Founder's Elite killed by Uriel when he attacked the armory on the *Foundra Ascension*.

Carrus Weswer | Huzien | Sentinel | Protects the Tuzen delegation in Alliance City during an assassination attempt.

Cenxra Mau Gehreyati | Uri | Wopan | Founder's Elite killed when trying to return Entradis to his cell on the *Foundra Ascension*.

Davis Kartwall | Huzien | Ciedalif | Dies in the events of the Star Harvester.

Dera'Liv Elax Ashfalen | Das'Vin | Yu'shae of Serah'Elax Rez Ashfalen. Joins Serah'Elax on the *Foundra Ascension*.

Dexter Pinsten, Sentinel commander (code name: Lifetime) | Huzien-Human hybrid | Sentinel | Member of the Founder's Elite. Chief intelligence officer of the *Foundra Ascension*.

Erbubuc Tamn | Ken'Tar | Nistiff | Nistiff monk who rescued Marcus on Tenquin and later becomes a member of the Founder's Elite.

Jefre Mau Neighheart | Uri | Wopan | Cannot stop terrorists from warning allies of Founder's Elite presence on the Star Harvester.

Jenshi Runso, colonel (code name: Unbreakable) | Huzien | Cidelif | Member of the Founder's Elite. Chief medical officer of the *Foundra Ascension*.

Jessica Olic, major (code name: Phoenix) | Huzien | Redalam-Wopan | Member of the Founder's Elite. Lead combat instructor of the *Foundra Ascension*. Immortal.

Kera Oghenthen | Huzien | Archlight | Saves Lanrete's life on the Star Harvester.

Lanrete, Founder (code name: Paragon) | Huzien | Redalam and combat Cihphist | One of the Founders of the Huzien Empire, ultimate leader of the Huzien military, and leader of the Founder's Elite. Commanding officer of the *Foundra Ascension*. Etan Rachnie council member. Immortal.

Macaf Yeqir | Human | Archlight | Founder's Elite killed by Uriel when he attacked the armory on the *Foundra Ascension*.

Marcus Henson, major (code name: Tempest) | Human | Archlight | Former member of the Founder's Elite. Close friend of Lanrete.

Nebu Ferhar | Huzien | Ciedalif | Founding member of the Founder's Elite, participated in mission on Guymulagi.

Neven Kenk, captain (code name: Prodigy) | Human | Secnic | Member of the Founder's Elite. Chief engineer of the *Foundra Ascension*.

Qwen Ointas | Huzien | Sentinel | Founding member of the Founder's Elite, participated in mission on Guymulagi.

Serah'Elax Rez Ashfalen, avatar | Das'Vin | Scion of Ashna | Zealous warrior in service to the Ashna Maidens who lost her second mother and sister twin in a pirate raid on Firyia as a young child. After defeating Sephan and saving the Ashna Maidens, becomes an envoy to the Huzien Alliance and joins the Founder's Elites.

Tashanira Yen Unvesal, major (code name: Banshee) | Uri | Wopan | Member of the Founder's Elite. Combat instructor of the *Foundra Ascension*.

Taylor Zeen | Huzien | Secnic | Founding member of the Founder's Elite, participated in mission on Guymulagi.

Uriel Kervid | Huzien | Redalam and combat Cihphist | The First Elite. Created the Founder's Elite in partnership with Lanrete. Adopted son of Lanrete. Immortal.

Urt Nevgambe | Huzien | Ciedalif | Doctor who Uriel sees when he can't sleep, member of Founder's Elite. Eventually killed by Entradis.

Xer Yuino | Huzien | Archlight | Founding member of the Founder's Elite, participated in the mission on Guymulagi.

Yuvan Nolli, captain (code name: Lancer) | Tuzen | Secnic | Deceased member of the Founder's Elite and former husband of Zun Shan.

Zun Shan, captain (code name: Nexus) | Huzien-Human hybrid | Secnic-Cihphist | Member of the Founder's Elite. Chief science officer of the *Foundra Ascension*. Former chief assistant of research & development to Ecnics in the MinSci. Killed by Entradis.

SHAN ESTATE TRUST

Bevhar | Huzien | Nurse for the Shan Estate Trust. Collects Neven's sperm sample at the request of Lansa.

Deferl Hecnin, colonel | Huzien | Losrim | Captain of the *Castrin* and retired colonel from the Huzien military.

Hesre Yen Kenk | Uri-human hybrid | Child of Tashanira Yen Unvesal and Neven Kenk.

Lansa Shan | Huzien | Mother of Zun Shan.

Lasicov Virtok | Vempiir | Personal assistant to Neven.

Muytef | Human | Head chef of the *Castrin*.

Rex Gefret | Huzien | Attorney for Shan Estate Trust. Executes the will of Zun Shan.

HUZIEN GOVERNMENT

Cislot, Founder | Huzien | Cihphist | One of the Founders of the Huzien Empire and ultimate leader of the Huzien government. Executive chancellor of the Huzien Alliance. Immortal.

Hass Lier | Huzien | General of intelligence during the formation of the Huzien Alliance. Fails to provide adequate safety protecting the Tuzen royals and resigns shortly after the formation of the alliance.

Huiara Mau Gehreyati | Uri | Prior personal assistant to Cislot. Born and raised on Thae. Current govnus of Huza.

Marcias Yonvi, restendi | Huzien | Elected head of government for the Huzien Empire.

HUZIEN MILITARY

Andrex Dominu, general of intelligence | Human | Sentinel | Oversees command of all Huzien Empire covert intelligence.

Jenle Frema, fleet admiral (Lady Luck aka LL) | Das'Vin-Huzien hybrid | Losrim | Fleet admiral of the 5th Huzien Imperial Fleet in command of the capital ship HSS *Gefreh*, which fought in the battle of Tar'Ki system.

Hucara Juk Gin, general of the mobile infantry | Uri-Huzien hybrid | Losrim | Commands the 103rd Huzien Mobile Infantry, which is rebuilt after being mostly destroyed at the battle of Neth and is reassigned to the 5th Huzien Imperial Fleet.

Larl Iunar | Huzien | Losrim | Soldier rescued by Jenshi on Neth during the Rift War. Saves Jenshi's life during a terrorist attack on Thae.

Lucien Entret, admiral general of the imperial fleets | Huzien | Losrim | Oversees the imperial fleets of the Huzien military.

Ranmor Wesla, supreme general | Huzien | Losrim | Oversees the day-to-day operation of the Huzien military.

Retyu Dewerter, fleet admiral | Huzien | Losrim | Historical fleet admiral who was in charge of the 3rd Huzien Imperial Fleet. Killed by Lanrete due to attack on Uriel.

Richardre Vean, lieutenant | Uri-Huzien Hybrid | Losrim | Commanded the military company tasked with protecting Pree, earning the favor and attention of Lanrete during the Rift War. He is assigned to the 103rd Huzien Mobile Infantry and enters into the Archlight program.

Uyam Ikol, fleet admiral | Huzien | Losrim | Fleet admiral of the 3rd Huzien Imperial Fleet. Commanded the capital ship HSS *Lukim*, lost in the battle of Neth during the Rift War. Had an affair with Hucara Juk Gin.

MINSCI (MINISTRY OF SCIENCE)

Aru Ghaian, feshra | Huzien | Secnic | High-ranking scientist in the Min-Sci and creator of the Nisic line of reactors. Chief engineer of the *Foundra Conscient*. Immortal.

Augamentres, feshra | Huzien | Secnic | She created the technology that powers the vast oceanic cities across Thae and personally designed Trutara. She was the lead Feshra on the creation of the Zun Gate. Immortal.

Charlene Yentu | Huzien | Secnic | Project lead of BRAS power frame at the MinSci. Prior mentor to Neven.

Ecnics, Founder | Huzien | Secnic-Cihphist | One of the Founders of the Huzien Empire and leader of the MinSci. Etan Rachnie council member. Immortal.

Kaloni Setla, Feshra | Human | Secnic-Cihphist | Head of the Department of Cihphist Technology. Etan Rachnie council member. Provides Soahc with the Jehu to go into the Enesmic plane to rescue Brime.

Kechu Fen | Huzien | Chief architect for the synaptic systems intelligence (SSI) project at the MinSci. Creator of the SSIs Lahl and Ellipse. Best friend of Neven Kenk.

Phenste Wahkin, feshra | Human | Secnic | Head of the Department of Advanced Computing & SI Research at the MinSci.

Remi Etwa, Feshra | Huzien | Secnic | Head of the Department of Weapons Development at the MinSci. Next in line to be chief assistant of research & development.

Triny Hazce | Huzien | Secretary to Ecnics.

TUZEN EMPIRE

Anima, empress (Ageless Empress) | Tuzen | Liajhem | Empress of the Tuzen Empire and founder of the Liajhem, an order of assassins and Cihphist hunters.

Enara (Ageless Princess) | Tuzen | Ageless Princess of the Tuzen Empire. Had a child with Uriel.

Ories Turbus | Tuzen | Wopan | Most trusted advisor to Tirivus.

Tirivus, emperor (Ageless Emperor) | Tuzen | Wopan-Cihphist | Emperor of the Tuzen Empire and executive chancellor of the Huzien Alliance. Immortal.

ALLIANCE GOVERNMENTS

Adjunct Primus | Omiciri | Governing official of the Omiciri who comes to the Huzien Empire seeking help.

A'Amaria Schen | Hauxem | Cihphist | Also known as Seshat, the Information Broker. Ex-wife of Lanrete. Influential Hauxem leader. Sexually assaults Neven and leaves a psychic imprint on him. Immortal.

Bur'Jexti Kefer Homun, heir'luia | Das'Vin | Oversees the physical and emotional well-being of the Das'Vin species. Offers assistance to Dera'Liv to bring her and Serah'Elax back to Das'Vin space.

Feyura Mau Gehreyati | Uri | Cihphist | Tribe mother of the Mauveh tribe. Former uterga to Soahc. Is called the Mother of Immortals. Immortal.

Gafgen Meutrol, high master | Vempiir | Cihphist | High Master of the Vempiir dominion and head of coven Meutrol. Immortal.

Hexa'Gevhre Quen Orecha, heir'apthai | Das'Vin | Diplomatic leader of the Das'Vin Republic and executive chancellor of the Huzien Alliance.

Lumira Yen Unvesal, matron mother | Uri | Matron mother of the Yenta tribe who becomes a Tribe mother. Mother of Tashanira Yen Unvesal.

Mel'kaka Hurn | Ken'Tar | Leader of the Ken'Tar people and executive chancellor of the Huzien Alliance.

Vanether Meutrol, rakeguard | Vempiir | Cihphist | Woman who Neven visits on Piro to get information about restoring a *ha'ishi*. Member of the Vempiir government as part of the Rakeguardian Consensus.

Yugalen Meutrol, arch lord | Vempiir | Cihphist | Commanded the Vempiir forces that stood against Sagren in the battle of Tar'Ki system and lost her life. Daughter of Vanether Meutrol.

ETAN RACHNIE (CIHPHIST SCHOOL AND HOME OF THE ARGENTS)

Brime Wewta (Mistress of the Enesmic) | Human | Cihphist-Argent | Wife to Soahc who gets transported to Enesmic plane during the Rift War. Becomes a powerful Cihphist and equal to Soahc in ability after being instructed by the Rel Ach'Kel. Immortal.

Desrin, Shaper | Human | Argent Chaah hunter | Legendary Chaah hunter of the 9th degree. Partner to Nestis. Immortal.

Merbi Teral, headmaster | Human | Cihphist | Handles day-to-day administrative responsibilities of Etan Rachnie. Etan Rachnie council member.

Migund Harvey, Shaper | Human | Argent | Powerful telepath who helped Bresha with counseling sessions.

Narmo Swela, First Argent | Vempiir | Cihphist-Argent | Responsible for the Argent system at Etan Rachnie.

Nestis, Shaper | Huzien | Argent Chaah hunter | Legendary Chaah hunter of the 8th degree. Partner to Desrin. Immortal.

Noez Aeel, Argent general | Huzien | Combat Cihphist | New Argent general who replaced Ristolte Aris. Etan Rachnie Council member.

Ristolte Aris III, Argent general | Huzien | Combat Cihphist | Previously responsible for the military branch of the Argents. Former Etan Rachnie council member. Former mobile infantry elite. Killed while assisting Soahc in rescuing Brime from the Enesmic plane.

Soahc (Destroyer of Worlds) | Human | Cihphist-Argent | Founder of Etan Rachnie and legendary Cihphist who destroyed the original Ginea, the ancient home planet of the Humans. Reunited Humans and led them to join the Huzien Empire while becoming a trusted friend of Lanrete. Etan Rachnie council member. Immortal.

Vades, formerly Bresha Vecen, Shaper | Human | Cihphist-Argent | Argent shaper previously possessed by Sephan. Immortal.

CHAAH

Alinos Yui | Human | Chaah Cihphist | Leader of the Chaah cell on Tenquin who escapes after sacrificing his comrades.

Hiesha Nihjar | Huzien | Chaah Cihphist | Chaah member who faces off against Marcus, Erb, and the Chaah hunters on Tenquin. Wife to Orech, who is spared by Desrin and Nestis. Currently prisoner at Etan Rachnie.

Orech Nihjar | Huzien | Chaah Cihphist | Deceased Chaah member. Former wife to Hiesha. Sacrificed by Alinos to fuel Elhirtha.

Yuemon | Human | Chaah Cihphist | Former apprentice of Soahc. Founder of the Chaah. Immortal.

Adinah Kenk | Human | Industry-renowned robotics engineer and mother of Neven Kenk.

Anhara | Uri | Maid of Lanrete's estate on the outskirts of Huza.

Arlea | Huzien | Ninth *eifi* of Lanrete. Responsible for the drastic shift in Lanrete's personality that led to the person he is today. Died almost forty thousand years ago.

Entradis | Huzien | Cihphist | Traitor of the Huzien Empire and wanted criminal responsible for the deaths of thousands, including Zun Shan and Yuvan Nolli. Mentally unstable. Immortal.

Envero Olic | Huzien | Father of Jessica Olic. Farmer in the Setna Isles. Hates the Huzien Empire.

Erisya Yetrewna | Huzien-Das'Vin hybrid | Wife of Cislot. A lawyer who enjoys fine art and the opera. Introduced to Cislot by Hexa'Gevhre Quen Orecha, the Das'Vin *heir'apthai*.

Heenara Rai Fedni | Uri | Former *eifi* of Lanrete. Died over two thousand years ago.

Jasha Olic | Huzien | Mother of Jessica Olic and wife of Envero Olic. Farmer in the Setna Isles.

Michael Kenk | Human | Robotics engineer and father of Neven Kenk.

Nalle Libl, CEO | Huzien | Chief executive officer of eshLucient Corporation and biological daughter of Founder Lanrete. Immortal.

Nesal'Velexi Ashfalen Rez | Das'Vin | Deceased *wo'shae* of Serah'Elax, killed in pirate raid on Firyia.

Ovah'Hal Velexi Rez | Das'Vin | Deceased *uma'shae* of Serah'Elax Rez Ashfalen and *yu'shae* of Nesal'Velexi Ashfalen Rez, who was killed on Firyia in a pirate raid.

Telanre | Uri | Uri psychologist that Tashanira talks about when trapped on the shuttle with Neven.

Tetenira Yen Unvesal | Uri | Sister of Tashanira Yen Unvesal, welcomes her back home on Peshkana.

Uerser Mau Tenju | Uri | Galaxy-renowned artist and creator of many priceless pieces of art in Ecnics's personal collection featuring Jun'Serentan women.

Zefa Meutrol | Vempiir | Secnic | Granddaughter of Gafgen Meutrol. Posed as a potential mate to Neven by Gafgen in an attempt to bring him into the Meutrol line.

Zeh'Jer Uina Dester, Feshra | Das'Vin | Renowned Das'Vin in the field of psychotherapy and biology. Neven gives them the cure for restoring a *ha'ishi*.

OUTER RIM PIRATES

Bevherk Hechet | Tuzen | Space pirate | Historical leader of Het Wrast Aht. Worked with Lanrete to maintain peace between Het Wrast Aht and the Huzien Empire.

SYSTEM INTELLIGENCES/SYNTHETIC LIFE-FORMS

Asha | SI | Advanced systems intelligence created by Zun Shan. Primary SI core matrix resides on the *Foundra Ascension*.

Cathid | Synthetic Life-form | Synthetic life-form created by Ecnics after an encounter with the Ascended.

Ellipse | Synthetic Life-form | Originally a prototype synaptic systems intelligence created by Kechu Fan with Neven as her host. Evolves with Neven to become a true synthetic life-form.

Lahl | SSI | Prototype synaptic systems intelligence created by Kechu Fan. Host is Kechu Fan.

ENESMIC BEINGS

Augrashumen (the Valorous) | Rel Ach'Kel | Mysterious being that rescues Brime in the Enesmic Wilds and trains her on the Enesmic plane. Closely watches the happenings on the Havin plane involving Eshgren. Immortal.

Cirfuletanas (the Empyrean Betrayer) | Eshgren | First to betray the Rel Ach'Kel and the first Eshgren. Immortal.

Cresala | Ceshra | Cihphist | Overlord of Sagren that defeated the Argent battle party and captured Bresha Vecen during the Rift War. Immortal.

Eheriequyturjin (the Abettor) | Eshgren | Cihphist | One of the Betrayers. The Eshgren who faces Soahc on the Enesmic plane in the Enesmic Wilds before Soahc is saved by Augrashumen the Valorous. Immortal.

Grilmuqshen (the Exemplar) | Rel Ach'Kel | Mysterious being on the Rel Ach'Kel Council. Fuses essence with Tashanira Yen Unvesal to protect her after attack by Eshgren. Immortal.

Aersheju (the Inciter) | Eshgren | Fuses its life essence with Tashanira's baby on Enesmic plane. Immortal.

Hashalem | Ceshra | Cihphist | Former overlord of Sagren who led the attack on Tar'Ki during the Rift War. Immortal.

Hiweretpor (the Perspicuous) | Rel Ach'Kel | Mysterious being on the Rel Ach'Kel Council. Immortal.

Nufresha | Ceshra | Cihphist | Overlord of Sagren that fled from Soahc's wrath on Pree, leaving her forces to get wiped out during the Rift War. Captured by Soahc and Brime. Immortal.

Sagren (the Fallen Commander) | Eshgren | Cihphist | One of the Betrayers and leader of the force that attempted to wipe out life on the Havin plane during the Rift War. Killed by Soahc and Lanrete in a covert assault on Sagren's stronghold world. Immortal.

Sephan (the Deceiver) | Eshgren | Cihphist | One of the Betrayers. Possesses the body of Bresha Vecen to gain access to the Havin plane during the Rift War. Once Sagren dies, launches a plan to infiltrate the Ashna Maidens. Defeated and sent back to the Enesmic plane by Serah'Elax and Brime. Immortal.

Vesgrilana (the Sagacious) | Rel Ach'Kel | Mysterious being that is particularly interested in Soahc. Leads the Rel Ach'Kel Council. Immortal.

GLOSSARY OF TERMS

CHARACTER CLASSES

Archlight - Archlights are towering beacons on the battlefield and centers of support for their fellow combatants. Through intense genetic modification and physical enhancement, Archlights become beasts of men who can withstand intense situations that seem impossible for even the most hardened veteran soldier. With their massive signature armor, incredibly immense shields, and powerful lance rifles, they stand at the forefront of combat on every battlefield.

Argent - Argents are masters of the cihphistic arts who undergo intense training learning the secrets of the Enesmic. Argent initiates are inducted into the Order of the Argents only after completing extensive trials. The Argent title carries with it not just power but a strict code upheld by the order. Argents can be seen wearing the traditional vestments of the order and wielding immense power. Involved in all facets of galactic affairs, Argents serve in positions ranging from diplomats to strike team members and are a force to be reckoned with.

Cidelif - Cidelifs are combat doctors. They work on the battlefield, offering support through frontline triage and amplifier-enhanced Cihphist ability. Utilizing various medical techniques, Cidelifs can quickly stabilize dying soldiers and get them back to the frontlines. Unlike traditional medics, Cidelifs are fully qualified doctors.

Cihphist - Cihphists are wielders of intense power, ranging from telepathy and telekinesis to kineticism and metaphysicism. In some cases, Cihphists can manipulate Enesmic energy to not only enhance their native abilities but also shape the world around them. Through intense study and training, Cihphists become masters of various schools of focus, with the most elite mastering them all.

Combat Cihphist - Combat Cihphists are the most recognizable on the battlefield, with unique military uniforms that signify their status and rank. They employ a technique that allows for their Huzien blade to hover in midair and act independently of their actions. Through intense physical, mental, and Cihphist training, Combat Cihphists are the epitome of the Huzien military, with exceptional individuals becoming elites who are, in essence, walking forces of destruction.

Liajhem - The Liajhem are a sect of elite and covert assassins who master the art of killing Cihphists. They are attuned to the Enesmic in a way that allows them to hunt Cihphists like bloodhounds, and they have mastered techniques that enable them to inhibit a Cihphist's ability to wield the Enesmic. With their signature daggers and ability to defeat cihphistic defensive manifestations, they can quickly massacre even the most powerful of Cihphists before they have time to react.

Losrim - Losrim are combat specialists. They excel with all forms of mobile combat weaponry and are the core of the Huzien military. Losrim appear decked out in the standard-issue military uniforms of the Huzien Empire. They adhere to a strict code of honor and employ methodical precision with years of intense training that morphs them into efficient killing machines.

Redalam - Redalams are masters of the Huzien blade. They train extensively, learning the many different forms and techniques necessary to be labeled a Redalam. Redalams can be identified by their signature blades, uniquely customized to each individual and family, which they wear strapped to their hips. All Redalam blades are named by their wielder.

Secnic - Secnics are masters of technology. They are seen wielding a variety of experimental and advanced technologies in original, inventive ways. From experimental gravity control harnesses, where the Secnic can manipulate the gravity around them, to sophisticated power armors that the Secnic wields as either a second skin or a massive frame. The one thing that remains consistent with Secnics is their affinity for weaponized technologies of an advanced or experimental nature.

Sentinel - Sentinels are the silent hands of the Huzien Empire. They live in the shadows and exist everywhere, from the most battle-worn battlefield to the capitals of rival nations. Through intense training, honing both the mind and body while utilizing the most advanced technology in the Twin Galaxies, Sentinels strike fear into enemies of the empire. A good Sentinel will never be noticed. With their staple personal cloaking technology, astonishing Cihphist ability, and specially designed silent sniper rifles, they are the model assassins.

Wopan - Wopans are martial artist gun masters. On the battlefield, they display a mastery of gun arts utilizing their token machine-gun pistols in brilliant displays of acrobatics and hand-to-hand combat. Through intense training, Wopans develop deadly skills in close-quarters combat. You will rarely find Wopans alone; they usually work alongside other units to deal with forces that could potentially overwhelm them.

Das'Vin - From the planet Desc'Ri. Due to there being no separate genders, Das'Vin have characteristics that would be viewed as both male and female in other species. They have *ga'hei* marks, which are distinct elevated marks that vary in pattern and are unique from individual to individual. They exist all over the body of each Das'Vin and vary in color, ranging from light pink to dark brown.

Eeriteen – From the planet Ashnali. A matriarchal society in the Outer Rim. Corded tubular bones cover their bodies, and they have thick tubular appendages that function as additional limbs that complement their arms and legs. The Ashna Maiden order grew out of an extremist sect in their species, who zealously worshiped the goddess Ashna. Constant war with pirate bands led to the sect claiming dominance and establishing the order as it exists today.

Human - Originally from the planet Ginea, they now reside on New Ginea, a terraformed moon that orbits Thae. Soahc destroyed their home world, Ginea, during their civil war. The war scattered Humans across the Twin Galaxies, ultimately leading to their induction into the Huzien Empire. They have the appearance of Huziens except without esha marks and with smaller builds.

Hauxem – From the planet A'Ahaula. Member species of the Huzien Alliance. Hauxem have a diminutive build and are often mistaken for teenagers. They have intricate patterns on their heads that take the place of hair in most other species.

Huzien - From the planet Thae. They have esha marks, and their shape and size vary depending on the person. Esha marks usually start at the temples and go down the length of the body to the outer thighs of both legs, continuing to the feet. The marks vary in color from light brown to black. The esha marks can bulge slightly when the person is irritated. Due to the high gravity on Thae, Huziens have developed above-average strength compared to most species.

Jun'Serentan - From the planet Spir'Terta. Their skin has a tightly corded muscular appearance, and they come off as very smooth and bonelike. They have intricate patterns in their foreheads that are distinct from person to person. They have no hair but instead have different design patterns on their scalp that complement their forehead patterns. They also have ribbed flesh in some regions of their body, such as their necks, underarms, inner thighs, genitals, and butt.

Ken'Tar - From the planet Tar'Ki. Their most distinguishing feature is two sets of arms for a total of four. Their first set of arms is where they would typically be on most species. Their second set of arms starts right below their main pair and forward, more on their abdomen, so as not to overlap with their main pair when at rest. It is very rare to see an obese or out-of-shape Ken'Tar, as it takes very little physical activity to stimulate muscle building, and their metabolisms are unique in that they adjust dynamically to the individual's food intake. Because of their hulking builds, Ken'Tar are exceptionally strong, far outmatching Huziens and Vempiir. They also stand head and shoulders above the other species, with their average height above seven feet. Ken'Tar have fur that covers every part of their body. The thickness of the fur for Ken'Tar varies slightly from family to family, but generally, all Ken'Tar are short-haired.

Ku'Ven - From the planet Venta. They are tall and lanky with striped, azure-colored skin. They have elongated ears with intricate ear canals and hair on the top of their heads. They have hair that can grow very long, and many females in their society have hair that can stretch to five or six feet in length. It is traditionally worn as braided and is naturally curly.

Lux'Ameni - From the planet Lux'ian. They are squat creatures of small stature. Their bodies are rigid, with large eyes on the sides of their head that they can move independently. They are similar to walking lizards but have large flat tails that they use for balance with large three-toed feet. Their mouths are large, and they have long tongues that can extend to the length of their bodies.

Tuzen - Originally from the planet Thae, now residing on New Thae. They have munsha marks, and their shape and size vary depending on the person. Munsha marks start at the center of the forehead and at the back of the head. From there, they go down the length of the body, both in the front of the person and in the back to the inner thighs of both legs, where they continue down to the feet. Although Tuzens have been away from Thae for over 80,000 years, they still retain some of the above-average genetic strength that the Huziens benefit from. However, New Thae does not have the same high gravity level as Thae.

Uri - From the planet Peshkana. They have fur that covers most of their body. Certain parts aren't covered, such as the soles of their feet and hands, stomachs, and genitals. Fur thickness varies depending on the origin region. Uri have distinct oral fangs when compared with other species in the galaxy, except the Vempiir. They also have a tail that can range in size from long to very short and ears reminiscent of cats in many sizes and shapes.

Uri have heightened agility and reflexes that exceed most other species. Their culture is one of community and integration with nature. They are a sexually liberal species with a common multi-partner culture. Due to being colonized by the Huziens, they experience prejudice in Huzien society and are often viewed as an inferior species. The tribes in Uri society, in order of importance and influence, are the Mauveh, Uhabi, Yenta, Ijakei, Tohsah, Lonlue, Heisrano, Avetri, Gavana, Jukazi, Quapo, Zopaku, Ovapu, Raitin, Kaxtuar, Nijhun, and Swihen. Each tribe has a unique fur pattern, the most notable being platinum fur with champagne hair for the Mauveh, yellow-gold fur with golden blond hair for the Uhabi, and tiger-striped fur with black hair for the Yenta.

Vempiir - From the planet Piro. They have very sharp teeth with exceptionally long canines. Due to their purifying of the gene pool via genocide many millennia ago, very few physically imperfect members of Vempiir society exist today. A moderately high gravity on their native planet has led to their species having strength on par with Huziens.

CORPORATIONS

eshLucient – Conglomerate. Headquartered on Zen. Capital goods, industrial goods, electronics, software, investing, energy, communications, healthcare, real estate, services, technology, and bio-engineering. The majority shareholder is Lanrete. It is currently managed by his immortal daughter, Nalle Libl.

Encro Motive - Technology. Headquartered on Thae. Automotive, shuttles, and starships.

HighStar Cruise Lines - Hospitality. Headquartered on Arcadia II. Hospitality, travel, and tourism.

Ganrele Retril Corporation - Conglomerate. Headquartered on New Ginea. Capital goods, industrial goods, consumer goods, clothing, and services.

Kekid Group - Real estate. Headquartered on Thae. Construction and property investments.

Somift Technologies - Technology. Headquartered on Thae. IT services, technology, software, and electronics.

Accelerated Cognitive Processing (ACP) – Utilizing a dedicated artificial brain, a synthetic life-form can accelerate the speed at which they process the world around them, making it seem like the physical world has stopped.

Aurtivus superweapon – The primary part of the planet cracking weapon technology built into capital ships of the Huzien Imperial Fleet. A tunneling beam establishes a clear pathway to the molten core of a planet, at which point the Aurtivus superweapon is activated in the form of pulses that magnify the energy threshold within the planet, creating an unsustainable reaction that forces the energy to explode outward, destroying the planet. Named for Feshra Aurtivus, a renowned Feshra in the field of weapons development.

Automated Trauma Management System (ATMS) – Specialized trauma unit equipped on emergency trauma tables within shuttles and ships that don't have full medical facilities. Can repair severe to moderate injuries and provide lifesaving care.

BRAS power frame - Biomechanical recon assault support frame built by Neven at the MinSci. Utilized in the battle of Neth by Neven.

Echaic cannon - A large ship-grade cannon with a nesmonic core generator. It releases a high-yield projectile capable of quickly eating away energy shields and can blast holes through even the toughest armor. It is the primary weapon of capital ships and dreadnoughts. Due to its nesmonic core generator, the pull on the ship's reactor is minimal. It can function with the absence of a ship reactor for a short duration, requiring only a brief burst of power from the ship-based reactor to kick-start a depleted nesmonic core.

Feponic cannon - Secnic weapon technology that fires powerful, energized balls of plasma.

Ghostnet – A type of mobi channel connection off official channels that utilizes underground Gnet relay networks for data transfer and communications. Utilized heavily by hackers and criminals for illegal activities.

Gravimetric thrusters - Specially designed microthrusters that manipulate gravity to create thrust.

Gravity Control Harness (GCA) – Specialized armor created by Neven Kenk based on research by Zun Shan that combines gravity manipulation technology with Wopan kinetics to create a high mobility suit ideal for a skilled Wopan. Is the basis for the Vrit suit deployed into the military.

Holodisplay - A holographic display screen that is projected by a micro-base station. These micro-base stations can be built into desks, rooms, and even clothing or skin. The size of the screen is determined by the type of micro-base station utilized.

Hologrid - A type of advanced holodisplay built into an entire room or area. This allows full-scale holographic representations of people or objects to appear projected anywhere within the hologrid.

Hypress basin - A high-powered faucet that opens into a long shallow bowl, the housing normally hidden from view and only appearing when approached. The bowl is designed to break the water evenly, which glides away without splattering back on the user. The faucet also allows for a multitude of different modes, including dispensing filtered drinkable water.

Liphojam - A medical device used in the place of needles or syringes. It carries a payload of nanites that are transferred through the skin and that can be outfitted with various forms of medicine. The nanites can intelligently apply the medicine where needed most and utilize the body's resources to rebuild tissue.

Power core - Advanced microfusion cells that provide personal power sources. Power cores are utilized in devices ranging from weapons to power armors to power frames. Power cores have a smaller footprint than reactors and are more versatile. Power cores include (in order from lowest yield to highest yield) the Cuden, Eshre, Eshre II, Gefreg, Eshre III, Sefnev, Vengrin, and Sefnev II.

Meglift - An advanced form of elevator that functions on a string of powerful magnets. Employing frictionless technology, the meglift can exist in a vacuum and rapidly cover superstructures in seconds, propelling the inhabitants up hundreds of floors safely in no time. Meglifts employ inertial dampeners and move both vertically and horizontally.

Mobi device - A small device that can range in design from an implant to a pin-sized computer. It is usually connected via a retinally implanted display within the user's eye (called a micro-display), where it projects information. It can also wirelessly interface with compatible devices for more intensive tasks. It is capable of interfacing with global and galactic communications systems via relay networks and acts as an individual's single most important personal device. The key feature of mobi devices is the neural interface that comes with the micro-display. This allows users to send mental commands to their mobi to perform actions.

Nanitically enforced glass - A highly durable composite glass utilized in starship construction. A layer of nanites exists within the glass that can rapidly repair damage and eliminate cracks.

Nanoplexi - A highly durable composite metal used in the construction of starships, power armors, power frames, and a host of other technologies and constructs.

Nesmonic core generator - An advanced power core that serves as an independent power source for most starships' primary weapons systems.

Omnfridge dispenser counter - A large counter with an intricate food storage and preparation system inside. Controlled by mobi synchronization, the system allows for the preparation of a myriad amount of food types. Most items are created in-house by a complex 3D printing system that can develop foods from organic raw materials.

Plexicarbonite - A very strong material used in the construction of Huzien blades and support structures.

Reactors - These devices employ advanced hyperfusion technology that allows for a sustainable energy source utilized on both planets and vessels. Reactors include (in order from lowest yield to highest yield) the Feng, Hurion, Vashra, Gunion, Nies I, Nies II, Ouma, and Nisic.

Skin resolver - A special grenade that disintegrates organic material in a short radius. It passes through inorganic material harmlessly and is the ideal form of explosive for space pirates.

Suplight drive - A type of advanced faster-than-light propulsion system that allows for intergalactic travel. The Herv suplight drive is a small drive used by shuttles for travel between planets within solar systems. The Vush suplight drive is a starship-grade drive that allows for travel between solar systems. This is the most common suplight drive. The Tria suplight drive is for larger starships and megaships. This allows for faster travel between solar systems and is more advanced than the Vush suplight drive. There are other experimental suplight drives that are not in mass production.

Systems intelligence - A system that can take a problem and create a solution without interaction with a biological being. It can generate code and applications for the purpose of solving the problem. It can also spin up and tear down platforms and network resources independently and install and configure the applications on said systems. It can also improve itself with time and develop a personality if permitted.

Vencom rinse chamber (VRC) - A type of chemical that has the composition of water but that displaces dirt and other foreign materials from the skin and leaves thoroughly cleaned skin behind. It has the added benefit of detoxifying the skin. Most Vencom rinse chambers have a secondary mode that blows powerful streams of warm air around the user to dry and remove any remaining Vencom rinse quickly. It is so effective that users rarely need towels to dry off completely.

Yuvan System - Enesmic-resistant shielding that defeats crushing forces applied to the target.

MISCELLANEOUS

Anavarin - The "Heaven" of the Vempiir, established by major religion. When a Vempiir is killed, they must wait at the gates of Anavarin before they are allowed entry into paradise. If vengeance is obtained for them, they are permitted entry. Otherwise, they wait until the end of time.

Ashna Maidens - Holy female warriors with a strict code of honor. Not aligned to any particular empire or alliance, the Ashna Maidens are seen as a police state that operates on the Outer Rim of the Twin Galaxies. All Ashna Maidens take a vow of celibacy in service to their goddess Ashna.

Ashna Council - Fifty women in the Ashna Maidens who oversee the day-to-day operations of the order. They report to the Ashna Mothers but are also responsible for appointing new Ashna Mothers.

Ashna Mothers - Ruling council of five women seen as the embodiment of Ashna, the ultimate leaders of the Ashna Maidens. Ascended former high priestesses of Ashna.

Betrayer - An Eshgren. A fallen Rel Ach'Kel.

A'Aceph - Hauxem familial units, where all virile males are free to mate with all virile females without restraint or restriction.

A'Ayuwri'Aret - A highly technical Hauxem dish usually served in high-class restaurants.

Bau - A variation of the Enesmic assassin with larger scimitar-like blades and stronger appendages designed for more frontline combat.

Chaah - An organization of rogue Argents that plot against the Argents, attacking them openly. Made up of Argent rejects who failed or refused to adhere to the Argent code.

Cihphism - The art of bending Enesmic energy to one's will. Has four major schools of mastery: telepathy, telekinesis, kineticism, and metaphysicism.

Das'Vin drone carrier - Robotic vessel that houses the drones utilized in a Das'Vin drone division. It has advanced construction systems that build new drones to replenish reserves. It is an uncrewed vessel.

Das'Vin high command ship - Command ship of a Das'Vin drone division. Contains Das'Vin personnel.

Das'Vin swarm command ship - Drone coordination starships responsible for controlling the drone carriers. Contains Das'Vin personnel.

Darbol Alliance - A competing alliance of different races that borders Huzien Alliance space.

Divinebreath - The name of the Redalam blade utilized by Lanrete. Depicts a wind design on the blade.

Empyrean Betrayer - The first Eshgren. The first to betray the Rel Ach'Kel.

Enesmic assassins - Beings of pure death. They live for only one purpose: to kill from the shadows without mercy. Their bodies are hard to see even when they make themselves visible, and they can hide from sight. They have long, narrow appendages concealing all types of brutal weapons with which they are exceptionally skilled. Their bodies are cloaked in deep shrouds of tattered, ethereal cloth.

Enesmic beings - Beings not native to the Havin plane that originate from the Enesmic plane. Include the Rel Ach'Kel, Eshgren, Ceshra, and Vahne. Eshgren and Ceshra have black blood, whereas Vahne and other lesser Enesmic beings have silver blood.

Enesmic energy - An elemental force that exists throughout the Twin Galaxies that can be manipulated via Cihphism.

Enesmic rift - A large gateway to the Enesmic plane created by Sagren. The result of continued expansion of the Enesmic tear under Sagren's manipulation. Allows for the passage of powerful Enesmic beings into the Havin plane.

Enesmic tear - A small gateway to the Enesmic plane. Allows for increased flow of Enesmic energy into the Havin plane. Also allows for the passage of weak Enesmic beings into the Havin plane.

Gafi'opiyu - A snakelike creature that attacks with four large scythe like appendages. It has a large body that it can use to rise like a human on its back. It can move incredibly fast and has a long, narrow, blade-like mouth. Radiates an aura of terror that creates irrational fear in the minds of those who haven't shielded their minds.

Gi'A'Fan Collective - The Collective is made up of a mesh of species that have been forcefully merged into it, a combination of alien genetics leading to something that looks more like a monster than a sentient being. They are a greatly feared species across the Twin Galaxies.

Guymulagi – Splinter cell of the pirate band Het Wrast Aht that hides out in Huzien Empire space.

Global docking center (GDC) - The central docking hub of a planet or colony that allows for the embarkment and disembarkment of ships to and from a planet or colony. Coordinates all ship activity on the planet to ensure smooth operation of extraplanetary travel.

Grah trees – Large skyscraper-sized trees that the Uri turn into living structures without killing or significantly altering the tree

Het Wrast Aht - Largest and most influential pirate band in the Outer Rim.

Huzien Intelligence Network (HIN) - A top-secret communications channel that also serves as an information network for confidential resources and unit deployments. This channel is maintained and operated by the Huzien Intelligence Agency and is not an Alliance resource.

Immortals - Beings who do not age. They can be killed by normal means but will not age past their biological prime. They also have heightened regenerative abilities.

Lefon blast - Raw energy summoned from the Enesmic plane that is then funneled at the target in a powerful beam attack.

Streamsong - The name of the Redalam blade gifted to Neven by Lanrete. Depicts a flowing river design on the blade.

Suhnret - It has the appearance of a giant wolf and feeds off the life essence of other beings. They grow in size and power from picking the life essence off their prey with their horrid maws. They can feed off Cihphism and are greatly feared by Cihphists.

Systems defense contingent (SDC) - A group of ships designated to patrol and protect a specific planetary system. Usually part of a more extensive fleet responsible for safeguarding a sector of space.

Unquenchable - The name of the Redalam blade utilized by Jessica Olic. Depicts a flame design on the blade.

Alliance City – Floating superstructure above the continent of Cirame on New Ginea. The place where the Huzien Alliance was formed.

Ceiling City of Okren – The location where the Huzien Empire gifted the world of New Thae to the Humans to be their new home and where they were inducted into the Huzien Empire.

Desc'Ri - Home world of the Das'Vin Republic.

Enesmic plane - A plane of existence that exists outside the Havin or "normal" plane. This plane is the source of Enesmic energy that flows within the Havins' plane of existence. Home to Enesmic beings.

Etan Rachnie - Special Cihphist school created by Soahc. It also serves as the base camp and recruitment center for the Argents.

Eirphoda System – Ken'Tar home system and connecting point for the Zun Gate.

Exfan – City Neven relocates to on Ruekae, a sprawling technologically advanced metropolis with a mesh of different alien species from across the Twin Galaxies.

Ginea - Original home world of the Humans. Soahc destroyed it.

Haula - Home world of the Hauxem Exchange.

Kaswif - Colony that the Founder's Elite fled to after the destruction of Pree.

Maandreo - Closest galaxy to the Twin Galaxies, Aru sets out there to establish a portal back to the Twin Galaxies.

New Ginea - New home world of the Humans and capital of the Huzien Alliance. Orbits Thae as one of its moons. Gifted to the Humans by the Huziens after an agreement between the Founders and Soahc.

New Thae – Home world of the Tuzen Empire.

Neth - Large planetary colony that was overrun by Sagren's forces. The 3rd Fleet was destroyed while protecting this planet from Sagren's fleet.

Nex'Rav'Ni Corridor – A section of space with unnatural gravity wells and other unique properties that restrict suplight speeds. The properties also limit the size of ships that can enter into the corridor.

Peshkana - Motherworld of the Uri people. A forest world under the control of the Huzien Empire.

Piro - Home world of the Vempiir Dominion.

Pree - A small planetary outpost near the borders of Alliance space. Home of the observation outpost destroyed by Sagren.

Reath - Planet owned by Soahc. Location of Etan Rachnie.

Raifac – Continent on New Ginea.

Ruekae – Independent planet and hub for scientific achievement in the Twin Galaxies. Home of the Shan Estate Trust's top space station resort.

Septna Engineering Bay - MinSci engineering lab where Neven helped design the BRAS power frame.

Sigmaphus - A massive black hole deep in Huzien space, *Zatcal* is in orbit around it.

Tar'Ki – Home world of the Ken'Tar Republic.

Tenquin – Recently terraformed world where the first mission of the Founder's Elites takes place. This later becomes a colony where the current Founder's Elites crash-land from the *Empress Star* failed hijacking.

Thae - Home world of the Huzien Empire and former home world of the Tuzen people.

Therus – Former moon of Thae that is terraformed and turned into New Ginea. Gifted as the new home of the Human Republic.

Traet University - Renowned university with many programs but most notable for its science and engineering curriculums.

Trustinum University - Renowned medical university with premed, biotechnology, and other biology-focused programs.

Twin Galaxies - Home to the Huzien Alliance, Darbol Alliance, and a host of other galactic empires, the Twin Galaxies are the result of two colliding galactic bodies. It is also referred to as the Havin plane and is officially called the Twin Galaxies of Oaphen Asracka.

Un'Nee – A city on the Das'Vin home world of Desc'Ri. It is a beautiful beachfront place known for being a primary vacation destination across the Huzien Alliance.

Zatcal – Maximum security prison locked in orbit around Sigmaphus, a massive black hole deep in Huzien space. Brutal prison for the most notorious criminals in the Huzien Empire. The place where Lanrete threatens to send Jenshi after the attack on Neven.

Zen - Planet owned by Lanrete.

HUZIEN WORDS

Burra - Dad. Father.

Burush - Son.

Cith – Huzien and Tuzen profanity typically used to insult a woman. When used for a man, it is meant to insult their masculinity.

Cusshin - Derogatory term for a half-Huzien individual, usually used when the other half is Human.

EetUra - Declaration of enthusiasm. Used by members of the Huzien fleet as a statement of enthusiasm.

Eifi - Wife, female life partner.

Feshra - Master of technology. It is used for those who are recognized as masters of a technological craft or who are great engineers. It is a formal designation in the Ministry of Science, which is bestowed by Ecnics and carries great prestige, influence, and power.

Hahva - Great teacher.

Larush - Daughter.

Lurra - Mom.

Lurratha - Mother. Formal version of Mom.

Nusba - Husband, male life partner.

Obrehen - Blood brother. It describes someone who is not related by blood but holds a bond as significant as family.

Reka - Racial slur for a Tuzen, used as an insult.

Restendi - Head of government. Elected president of the Huzien Empire.

Tedr - Evil.

Vusg - Huzien and Tuzen profanity. It means to have sex with someone. It also means to ruin or damage something.

DAS'VIN WORDS

As'crefa - Command council. A group responsible for the deployment of the Das'Vin military.

Dru'sha - Life partner. Used to describe the mates or life partners of the Das'Vin.

Em'fa - Half-breed. An individual who is half Das'Vin.

Fra'sha - Whore. With a severed *ha'ishi* at the death of one's *dru'sha*, the Das'Vin can become a *fra'sha*, who freely engages in sexual acts with other *fra'sha* or non-Das'Vin. No *ha'ishi* will be formed, nor will any mental connection be made.

Ha'ishi - A deep mental connection shared between two *dru'sha* that allows the exchange of feelings and emotions. Depending on the Cihphist sensitivity level of the two *dru'sha*, thoughts and messages can also be exchanged.

Hala'a - Term used to describe Das'Vin children.

Heir'apthai - An elected member of the Heir'Klaxem who is the diplomatic leader of the Das'Vin Republic. Holds the Huzien Alliance designation of executive chancellor.

Heir'Klaxem – Governing council of the Das'Vin people. It is made up of the heir'apthai, heir'nezu, and heir'luia. Collectively influence and set the direction for the Das'Vin Republic. Act independently but consult each other when necessary.

Heir'luia - An elected member of the Heir'Klaxem who oversees the physical and emotional well-being of the Das'Vin species.

Heir'nezu - An elected member of the Heir'Klaxem who oversees the scientific and academic progress of the Das'Vin species.

Ma'eh - Evil.

Nuy'zer – Das'Vin outsider. A Das'Vin not raised in Das'Vin society who hasn't been socialized into Das'Vin culture, principles, and values.

Uma'shae - Title for the biological non-birth mother of a Das'Vin.

Wo'shae - Sister twin. The title is shared by two Das'Vin *hala'a* who were born during the same dual pregnancy.

Woth're - Sisters. Comrades. A term used to relate a Das'Vin to another Das'Vin.

Yu'shae - Title for birth mother of a Das'Vin.

HAUXEM WORDS

A'acuy - The peak of a Hauxem female's fertility cycle, when their pheromones are strongest, and they can entice potential males to impregnate them.

A'akugentai'a – Hauxem profanity. It means to have sex with (someone). It also means to ruin or damage (something).

A'asentup'akugen'avi – Phrase that combines *a'akugentai'a* with "get off me."

KEN'TAR WORDS

Acete'tesen - Primary male mate.

Crece'cesen - Primary female mate.

Haa'eag - Evil.

Te'cesen - Ken'Tar offspring, children.

URI WORDS

Uda – Spouse, partner.

TUZEN WORDS

Okam – My heart, a term of endearment.